FOUR
ROADS
CROSS

FOUR ROADS CROSS

■ ■ ■

Max Gladstone

TOR

A TOM DOHERTY ASSOCIATES BOOK

NEW YORK

FOUR ROADS CROSS

Copyright © 2016 by Max Gladstone

A Tor Book
Published by Tom Doherty Associates, LLC
175 Fifth Avenue
New York, NY 10010

www.tor-forge.com

Tor® is a registered trademark of Tom Doherty Associates, LLC.

The Library of Congress Cataloging-in-Publication Data is available upon request.

ISBN 978-0-7653-7942-9 (hardcover)
ISBN 978-1-4668-6841-0 (e-book)

Our books may be purchased in bulk for promotional, educational, or business use. Please contact your local bookseller or the Macmillan Corporate and Premium Sales Department at 1-800-221-7945, extension 5442, or by e-mail at MacmillanSpecialMarkets@macmillan.com.

First Edition: July 2016

Printed in the United States of America

0 9 8 7 6 5 4 3 2 1

FOUR ROADS CROSS

1

Tara Abernathy's first job as in-house counsel for the Church of Kos was to hide a body.

A Blacksuit led her down a winding stair to a windowless stone room, empty save for a sturdy table, a counter, a sink, and Alexander Denovo's corpse.

Her old teacher and tormentor looked much as she'd last seen him—at least, physically. Even in death, his lips kept their self-satisfied smirk. The eyes had lost their triumphant gleam, though, the conqueror peering from behind the bumpkin professor's. He wore off-the-rack approximations of his usual wardrobe: tweed jacket with elbow patches, red suspenders, brown shoes. Of course they hadn't let him keep his own clothes in jail. A Craftsman's jacket might hide anything.

He was dead.

"Did you kill him?" she asked the Blacksuit. "Did Justice?"

The burnished silver statue answered: *No.* Familiarity bred neither contempt for nor comfort with Blacksuit voices, which did not carry through the air so much as manifest in the mind, built from screams, skewed cello notes, and breaking glass. *He died in his cell, of a heart attack.*

Blacksuits did not lie, at least not in their official capacity as representatives of Justice. Nor did they murder. They preferred to execute.

Tara walked a slow circle around the body. The signs were right. They would be, no matter Denovo's true cause of death. No one who went to the trouble of breaking into the cell where the Blacksuits held the man, killing him, and escaping without detection would leave signs he'd perished of anything but natural causes.

"He's a Craftsman," Tara said, to remind herself as much as the Suit. "He murdered gods. He bound the wills of hundreds to his service.

He almost destroyed this city. Hells, he almost became a god himself. He wouldn't die like this."

Nonetheless.

"I won't bring him back for you," she said.

We did not expect you to. Quite the opposite, in fact.

"You want me to make sure he stays dead."

The Blacksuit nodded.

Tara cracked her neck, then her knuckles. "All right. Let's get
started."

The problem was simple, insofar as the necromantic logic of the
Craft was concerned. A hundred fifty years before, as the first Deathless Kings formed a society free of divine meddling—and, inciden-
tally, of mortality—they'd faced a practical concern: How does one
discourage antisocial behavior among formerly human beings for
whom life imprisonment is a brief inconvenience, if not an undefined
term, and the death penalty a slap on the wrist? How do you keep a
necromancer bound to the world by thousands of debts from climbing back out of her grave?

The answers ranged from grotesque to merely inhuman, but all
shared a theoretical foundation: you don't let the dead go free.

Tara set her purse on the counter and produced from within a retort, a bit of silver chalk, three gas burners, several large pieces of
glassware, and two silver bracelets. She shucked her jacket, rolled up
her sleeves, donned the bracelets, and struck them against each other.
They sparked, and slick black oil rolled from them to cover her hands.
The glyphs machine-tooled into her forearms glowed silver against
her dark skin. She drew her work knife from the glyph above her
heart, and its moon-lightning blade cast queer light into the corners
of the stone room.

Denovo lay before her.

She took a deeper breath than she cared to admit she needed, and
touched the cold dry skin of his temple.

"Hi there," the corpse said.

Ms. Abernathy?

"It's all right," Tara told the Blacksuit. She forced her heart back
to a slow and proper rhythm. "He's dead, but there's still power inside his body. That power can"—she groped for terms the Blacksuit

would understand—"push on my memories of him, like organ keys. The gloves keep most of it out, but he was strong. I'll be fine." She made her knife sharp, took hold of his collar, and carved off his clothes.

"Fine," the corpse said in a wry voice. "Will you be fine, Tara, really? Fine, in this benighted city, slaving for a mad goddess and an equivocating god not fit to kiss a Craftsman's boot?"

Answering a phantom's taunt was bad form, but she was not being graded here. "Kos Everburning is a good God. He stayed out of the Wars. He's needed an in-house Craftswoman for a long time. And Seril isn't mad anymore."

Ms. Abernathy?

"You can wait outside," she told the Blacksuit, "if you'd rather. This will take a while, and you'll make me nervous if you just stand there."

The statue flowed out the door and shut it after, leaving her alone with the body.

She removed his shoes one at a time, and cut his trousers off. He lay nude on the slab, paunchy and pale.

"Such service," the corpse said. "I should come here more often."

"You're an asshole," she told him, without rancor. What rancor could there be in a statement of fact? She donned a surgical mask and returned to the table with a glass jar, a rubber tube, and a silver needle. The needle she slid into his arm, and the glass jar began to draw his blood—eight pints. Fortunately, the jar, like her purse, was larger than it looked from outside. "You always were."

"I helped you, Tara, as I helped all my students. I made you part of something bigger: a community dedicated to the pursuit of knowledge, the advancement of Craft, the salvation and elevation of the race."

"You stole minds. You tried to break me, and when I fought free you tried to destroy my career." The exsanguination vessel worked fast; his skin tightened as his veins collapsed. "When that didn't work, you followed me to Alt Coulumb, and now you're dead and I'm not." She pressed the skin taut below his collarbone's V, sliced a straight line down to his groin, and peeled back his chest. Slabs of muscle and fat glistened, and she cut into these until she bared the bone. "I guess that settles the question of whose methods work better."

Spectral familiar laughter answered her. "Please. You had two gods, Elayne Kevarian, and a host of gargoyles and Blacksuits on your side. You didn't beat me so much as outnumber me. But you can't outnumber what's coming."

She pressed her lips together, and flensed his legs. Silver glyphlines sparked around tibia and femur; his patella sported a star with six, no, seven, no, six points. As she cleaned his bones, she carved through Craftwork sigils, hidden mechanisms and machines. In his left thigh she found a bullet wrapped with scar tissue.

"I wanted to kill Alt Coulumb's god and take his place," he said. "It was a long shot, but if I'd won, imagine the rewards."

"I'd rather not." Corpse meat squelched beneath her gloved hands. Blood did not stick to her shadowy gloves.

"But now—do you have any idea of the weakness of your position? Your moon goddess Seril has returned, in secret of course, since half the city still hates her. They've hated her for decades, since she abandoned them to fight in the Wars and died. That she's back, concealed, changes nothing. Kos will defend her to the death—so she's a weak spot, pure leverage for your enemies to exploit. Hundreds of Craftsmen find the very existence of a godly city in the New World an affront. You've given them an opening. When they learn Seril's back, girl, they will come for you. They're not as smart as me, nor half so ambitious. They won't pussyfoot like I did. They will kill your gods, and your friends. They'll carve them to pieces. They will occupy this city and remake it into a gleaming citadel of Craft and commerce. No more Criers—newspapers on every corner and zombies in the market. You'll weep if you live to see it. You'll wish you'd never clawed your way out of that fleaspeck town where Elayne found you."

She scooped out his organs, one at a time, weighed them piece by piece, and burned them to ash.

"You have my job for the moment, sure. Enjoy it while it lasts."

"This wasn't your job," she said. Meathooks of Craft raised and turned the body. She tore off his back in a single sheet.

"I was the Cardinal's advisor for forty years."

"And you used him to kill his own God."

"If you don't use people, they use you. The whole world's chains, Tara—Gerhardt said it, and the God Wars proved him right. When I worked with the church, I made sure I wrapped a chain firmly around its neck. You've fused one around yours and handed them the dangling end. You can't command these people from within—and command's the only way you'll beat what's coming."

The slab lay empty save for the bones. To a laywoman all skeletons looked more or less alike. Experts could read differences: healed fractures, specific ratios of limb length to torso. Tara had never seen Alexander Denovo's bones before. She would not have recognized him had she not carved him apart with her own hands.

"This city will stand," she said.

"What city? It's a mess of gargoyles and priests, Craftsmen and common folk, gods hidden and revealed. When trouble comes, they'll tear out one another's throats. You can't stop them. Either you'll be chained to them—one piece of a breaking machine—or you'll be alone, a girl naked against a flood. They won't trust you. They won't follow you. They won't work with you unless you kneel to them, and if you kneel, they lose anyway."

"You're lying." She made her knife thick and sharp and heavy, a cleaver built of light.

"I'm in your head. I'm your worst memories of me, your greatest fears. And the greatest fear of all—the one that still makes you sweat at two in the morning when the world's quiet—is that I was right all along. That I was right, and you are—"

Her blade parted skull from spine.

The voice stopped.

"Come back," she told the Blacksuit. "I'm ready."

She nestled the skull in a lead-lined box filled with packing immaterial and followed the Blacksuit to the lowest levels of the Temple of Justice's evidence locker, past impounded drugs and weapons and grails and tools and artifacts too strange to describe with a single word. She placed the skull box beside his personal effects and warded them thrice with shadow and silver to prevent Craft from leaking in or out. When she closed the door, the light above clicked from red to green.

She woke that night, on her bed in her coffin-sized bedroom, to moonlight through the window. A goddess sang.

Tara's heart beat fast. She lay in her own sweat and waited for dawn.

The day after Tara moved into her new office, once she unpacked her books, installed the nightmare telegraph, set up the astrolabe, and routed out the spy in the lobby, she laid a piece of cream-white paper on her desk and wrote, in large ruby letters at the top: "In Case the Survival of the Moon Goddess Seril or the Presence of Her Gargoyles in Alt Coulumb Should Become Public Knowledge Before She Regains Sufficient Power to Defend Herself."

This did not leave much room on the paper. Fortunately or, rather, *unfortunately,* she did not know what to write next.

She stared at the paper. She clutched the pen barrel between her teeth. She threw a tennis ball against the wall and caught it until her neighboring tenant asked her to stop. That consumed roughly two hours, during which no further words appeared on the paper. She walked Alt Coulumb's streets. She immersed herself in its libraries. She consulted the stars and the scholars of Craft, though in the latter case she kept the details of her query general. She spoke with gibbering horrors from beyond the edges of time, and erected elaborate palaces of possibility, networked and interlaced contingencies, none of which satisfied.

After all this, she returned the paper to her desk and wrote, in small letters beneath the overlong heading: "We are probably screwed."

Then she burned the paper, because it was a stupid document to leave lying around, even in an office secured by the finest geases and traps she, a graduate of the Hidden Schools, could Craft.

Tara scattered the ashes in Alt Coulumb's harbor on three separate days. Then she devoted herself to Establishing a Sufficient Worshipper Base for Seril, and to the other, more public duties of the in-house counsel for Alt Coulumb's other, more public God—and in this manner she passed a nervous year, until Gabby Jones spoiled everything.

2

Stone wings shook Alt Coulumb's nights, and godsilver shone from its shadows.

Gavriel Jones fled through garbage juice puddles down a narrow alley, panting tainted humid air. Dirty water stained the cuffs of her slacks and the hem of her long coat; behind, she heard the muggers' running feet.

They did not shout after her. No breath was wasted now. She ran and they pursued.

Dumb, dumb, dumb, was the mantra her mind made from the rhythm of her run. She'd broken the oldest rules of city life. Don't walk through the Hot Town alone after midnight. Don't mix white wine with red meat, look both ways before you cross, never step on cracks. And always, always give them your purse when they ask.

She ran deeper into the Hot Town, beneath high shuttered windows and blank brick walls scarred by age and claw. She cried out, her voice already ragged. A window slammed.

Above, a full moon watched the chase. Ahead, the alley opened onto a broad, empty street. Beneath the sour-sweet stink of rot, she smelled spiced lamb. Someone was selling skewers on the corner. They might help her.

She glanced back. Two men. Three had approached her when she ducked into the alley for a cigarette. Where was the third?

She slammed into a wall of meat. Thick arms pulled her against a coat that smelled of tobacco spit and sweat. She kneed him in the groin; he pulled his crotch out of reach, hissed, threw her. Gabby slammed to the ground and splashed in a scummy puddle.

She kicked at his knee, hard but too low: the steel toe of her boot slammed into his shin but didn't break his kneecap. He fell onto her, hands tangled in her clothes, her hair. She hit his nose with the crown of her head, heard a crunch. He was too far gone on whatever dust propelled him to feel pain. He bled onto her face; she jerked her head aside and pressed her lips closed, don't get any in your mouth don't get any in your *mouth*—

The others caught up.

Strong hands tore the purse from her, and she felt her soul go with it. They tossed her life between them. The boot came next, its first hit almost delicate, a concertmistress drawing a fresh-strung bow across clean strings. Still hurt, though. She doubled around the leather, and gasped for air that didn't reach her lungs.

His second kick broke her rib. She hadn't broken a bone in a long time, and the snap surprised her. Bile welled in the back of her throat.

She pulled her hands free, clawed, found skin, drew more blood. The boot came again.

Still, up there, the moon watched.

Gabby lived in a godly city, but she had no faith herself.

Nor did she have faith now. She had need.

So she prayed as she had been taught by women in Hot Town and the Westerlings, who woke one day with echoes in their mind, words they'd heard cave mouths speak in dreams.

Mother, help me. Mother, know me. Mother, hold and harbor me.

Her nails tore her palms.

Hear my words, my cry of faith. Take my blood, proof of my need.

The last word was broken by another kick. They tried to stomp on her hand; she pulled it back with the speed of terror. She caught one man's leg by the ankle and tugged. He fell, scrabbled free of her, rose cursing. A blade flashed in his hand.

The moon blinked out, and Gabby heard the beat of mighty wings.

A shadow fell from the sky to strike the alley stones so hard Gabby felt the impact in her lungs and in her broken rib. She screamed from the pain. Her scream fell on silence.

The three who held and hit her stopped.

They turned to face the thing the goddess sent.

Stone Men, some called them as a curse, but this was no man. Back to the streetlights at the alley's mouth, face to the moon, she was silhouette and silver at once, broad and strong, blunt faced as a tiger, long toothed and sickle clawed with gem eyes green and glistening. Peaked wings capped the mountain range of her shoulders. A circlet gleamed upon her brow.

"Run," the gargoyle said.

The man with the knife obeyed, though not the way the gargoyle meant. He ran forward and stabbed low. The gargoyle let the blade hit her. It drew sparks from her granite skin.

She struck him with the back of her hand, as if shooing a fly, and he flew into a wall. Gabby heard several loud cracks. He lay limp and twisted as a tossed banana peel.

The other two tried to run.

The gargoyle's wings flared. She moved like a cloud across the moon to cut off their retreat. Claws flashed, caught throats, and lifted with the gentleness of strength. The men had seemed enormous as they chased Gabby and hit her; they were kittens in the gargoyle's hands. Gabby pressed herself up off the ground, and for all the pain in her side she felt a moment's compassion. Who were these men? What brought them here?

The gargoyle drew the muggers close to her mouth. Gabby heard her voice clear as snapping stone.

"You have done wrong," the gargoyle said. "I set the Lady's mark on you."

She tightened her grip, just until the blood flowed. The man on the left screamed; the man on the right did not. Where her claws bit their necks, they left tracks of silver light. She let the men fall, and they hit the ground hard and heavy. She knelt between them. "Your friend needs a doctor. Bring him to Consecration and they will care for him, and you. The Lady watches all. We will know if you fail yourself again."

She touched each one on his upper arm. To the gargoyle it seemed no more consequential than a touch: a tightening of thumb and forefinger as if plucking a flower petal. The sound of breaking bone was loud and clean, and no less sickening for that.

They both screamed, this time, and after—rolling on the pavement filth, cradling their arms.

The gargoyle stood. "Bear him with the arms you still have whole. The Lady is merciful, and I am her servant." She delivered the last sentence flat, which hinted what she might have done to them if not for the Lady's mercy and her own obedience. "Go."

They went, limping, lurching, bearing their broken friend between them. His head lolled from side to side. Silver glimmered from the wounds on their necks.

And, too, from scars on the alley walls. Not every mark there glowed—only the deep clean grooves that ran from rooftops to paving stones, crosshatch furrows merging to elegant long lines, flanked here by a diacritical mark and there by a claw's flourish.

Poetry burned on the brick.

The gargoyle approached. Her steps resounded through the paving stones. She bent and extended a heavy clawed hand. Gabby's fingers fit inside the gargoyle's palm, and she remembered a childhood fall into the surf back out west, how her mother's hand swallowed hers as she helped her stand. The gargoyle steadied Gabby as she rose. At full height, Gabby's forehead was level with the gargoyle's carved collarbone. The gargoyle was naked, though that word was wrong. Things naked were exposed: the naked truth in the morning news, the naked body under a surgeon's lights, the naked blossom before the frost. The gargoyle was bare as the ocean's skin or a mountainside.

Gabby looked into the green stone eyes. "Thank you," she said, and prayed too, addressing the will that sent the being before her: *Thank you.* "The stories are true, then. You're back."

"I know you," the gargoyle replied. "Gavriel Jones. You are a journalist. I have heard you sing."

She felt an answer, too, from that distant will, a feeling rather than a voice: a full moon over the lake of her soul, the breath of the mother her mother had been before she took to drink. "You know who I am and saved me anyway."

"I am Aev," she said, "and because I am, I was offered a choice. I thought to let you pay for your presumption. But that is not why we were made."

"I know." The pain in her chest had nothing to do with the broken rib. She turned away from the mass of Aev. "You want my loyalty, I guess. A promise I won't report this. That I'll protect and serve you, like a serial hero's sidekick."

Aev did not answer.

"Say something, dammit." Gabby's hands shook. She drew a pack of cigarettes from her inside pocket, lit one. Her fingers slipped on the lighter's cheap toothed wheel. She breathed tar into the pain in her side.

When she'd drawn a quarter of the cigarette to ash, she turned back to find the alley empty. The poems afterglowed down to darkness, like tired fireflies. A shadow crossed the moon. She did not look up.

The light died and the words once more seemed damaged.

She limped from the alley to the street. A wiry-haired man fanned a tin box of coals topped by a grill on which lay skewers of seasoned lamb.

Gabby paid him a few thaums of her soul for a fistful of skewers she ate one at a time as she walked down the well-lit street past porn shop windows and never-shut convenience stores. The air smelled sweeter here, enriched by cigarette smoke and the sharp, broad spices of the lamb. After she ate, even she could barely notice the tremor in her hands. The drumbeat of blood through her body faded.

She tossed the skewers in a trash can and lit a second cigarette, number two of the five she'd allow herself today. Words danced inside her skull. She had promised nothing.

She realized she was humming, a slow, sad melody she'd never heard before that meandered through the C-minor pentatonic scale, some god's or muse's gift. She followed it.

Her watch chimed one. Still time to file for matins, if she kept the patter simple.

3

Tara was buying eggs in the Paupers' Quarter market when she heard the dreaded song.

She lived three blocks over and one north, in a walk-up apartment recommended by the cheap rent as well as by its proximity to the Court of Craft and the market itself, Alt Coulumb's best source of fresh produce. Now, just past dawn, the market boiled with porters and delivery trucks and human beings. Shoppers milled under awnings of heavy patterned cloth down mazed alleys between lettuce walls and melon pyramids.

As she shouldered through the crowd, she worried over her student loans and her to-do list. The Iskari Defense Ministry wanted stronger guarantees of divine support from the Church of Kos, which they wouldn't get, since a weaker version of those same guarantees had almost killed Kos Himself last year. The Iskari threatened a breach of contract suit, ridiculous—Kos performed his obligations flawlessly. But she had to prove that, which meant another deep trawl of church archives and another late night.

Which wouldn't have felt like such a chore if Tara still billed by the hour. These days, less sleep only meant less sleep. She'd sold herself on the benefits of public service: be more than just another hired sword. Devote your life to building worlds rather than tearing them down. The nobility of the position seemed less clear when you were making just enough to trigger your student loans but not enough to pay them back.

Life would feel simpler after breakfast.

But when she reached the stall where Matthew Adorne sold eggs, she found it untended. The eggs remained, stacked in bamboo cartons and arranged from small to large and light to dark, but Adorne himself was gone. Tara would have been less surprised to find Kos the Everburning's inner sanctum untended and his Eternal Flame at ebb than she was to see Adorne's stand empty.

Nor was his the only one.

Around her, customers grumbled in long lines. The elders of the market had left assistants to mind their booths. Capistano's boy scrambled behind the butcher's counter, panicked, doing his father's work and his at once. He chopped, he collected coins with bits of soul wound up inside, he shouted at an irate customer carrying a purse three sizes too large. The blond young women who sold fresh vegetables next to Adorne, the stand Tara never visited because their father assumed she was foreign and talked to her loud and slow as if she were the only dark-skinned woman in Alt Coulumb, they darted from task to task, the youngest fumbling change and dropping onions and getting in the others' way like a summer associate given actual work.

Adorne had no assistant. His children were too good for the trade, he said. School for them. So the stall was empty.

She wasn't tall enough to peer over the crowd, and here in Alt Coulumb she couldn't fly. A wooden crate lay abandoned by the girls' stall. Tara climbed the crate and, teetering, scanned the market.

At the crowd's edge she saw Adorne's broad shoulders, and tall, gaunt Capistano like an ill-made scarecrow. Other stall-keepers, too, watched—no, listened. Crier's orange flashed on the dais.

Adorne remained in place as Tara fought toward him. Not that this was unusual: the man was so big he needed more cause to move than other people. The world was something that happened to black-bearded Matthew Adorne, and when it was done happening, he remained.

But no one else had moved either.

"What's happened?" Tara asked Adorne. Even on tiptoe, she could barely see the Crier, a middle-aged, round-faced woman wearing an orange jacket and a brown hat, an orange press pass protruding from the band. Tara's words climbed the mounds of Adorne's arms and the swells of his shoulders until they reached his ears, which twitched. He peered down at her through layers of cheek and beard—raised one tree-branch finger to his lips.

"Encore's coming."

Which shut Tara up fast. Criers sang the dawn song once for free, and a second time only if the first yielded sufficient tips. An encore meant big news.

The Crier was an alto with good carry, little vibrato, strong belt. One thing Tara had to say for the archaic process of Alt Coulumbite news delivery: in the last year she'd become a much better music critic.

Still, by now a newspaper would have given her a headline reason for the fuss.

The song of Gavriel Jones, the Crier sang.
Tells of a New Presence in our Skies.

Oh, Tara thought.

Hot Town nights burn silver
And Stone Men soar in the sky
Pray to the moon, dreams say
And they'll spread their wings to fly.
A tale's but a tale 'til it's seen
And rumors do tend to spin
I saw them myself in the Hot Town last night
Though telling, I know I sin.

Tara listened with half an ear to the rest of the verse and watched the crowd. Heads shook. Lips turned down. Arms crossed. Matthew Adorne tapped his thick fingers against his thicker biceps.

Seril's children were playing vigilante. A Crier had seen them.

The song rolled on, to tell of gargoyles returned to Alt Coulumb not to raid, as they had many times since their Lady died in the God Wars, but to remain and rebuild the cult of their slain goddess, Seril of the moon, whom Alt Coulumb's people called traitor, murderer, thief.

Tara knew better: Seril never died. Her children were not traitors. They were soldiers, killers sometimes in self-defense and extremity, but never murderers or thieves. To the Crier's credit, she claimed none of these things, but neither did she correct popular misconceptions.

The city knew.

How would they respond?

There was no Craft to read minds without breaking them, no magic to hear another's thoughts without consent. Consciousness was a strange small structure, fragile as a rabbit's spine, and it broke if gripped too tightly. But there were more prosaic tricks to reading men and women—and the Hidden Schools that taught Tara to raise the dead and send them shambling to do her bidding, to stop her enemies' hearts and whisper through their nightmares, to fly and call lightning and steal a likely witness's face, to summon demons and execute contracts and bill in tenths of an hour, also taught her such prosaic tricks to complement true sorcery.

The crowd teetered between fear and rage. They whispered: the sound of rain, and of thunder far away.

"Bad," Matthew Adorne said in as soft a voice as he could make his. "Stone Men in the city. You help the priests, don't you?"

Tara didn't remember the last time she heard Matthew Adorne ask a question.

"I do," Tara said.

"They should do something."

"I'll ask."

"Could be one of yours," he said, knowing enough to say "Craftsman" but not wanting, Tara thought, to admit that a woman he knew, a faithful customer, no less, belonged to that suspect class. "Scheming. Bringing dead things back."

"I don't think so."

"The Blacksuits will get them," Adorne said. "And Justice, too."

"Maybe," she said. "Excuse me, Matt. I have work."

So much for breakfast.

4

One does not need an expensive Hidden Schools degree to know the first step in crisis management: get ahead of the story. If that's impossible, at least draw even with it. Tara, who had an expensive Hidden Schools degree, hunted Gavriel Jones.

The Crier's Guild was more hive than office. Stringers, singers, and reporters buzzed like orange bees from desk to desk, alighting coffee mugs in hand to bother others working, or pollinate them with news.

"Late report by nightmare telegraph, lower trading on Shining Empire indices—"

"You hear the Suits busted Johnny Goodnight down by the docks, taking in a shipment?"

"No shit?"

"—Haven't found a second source for this yet, but Walkers looks set to knock down those PQ slums for her new shopping center—"

"Still missing your bets for the ullamal bracket, Grindel's about to close the door—"

"—Loan me a cigarette?"

"Do you really want it back?"

They didn't let people back here, exactly, but Tara wasn't people. She forced her papers into the receptionist's face—I'm Ms. Abernathy, Craftswoman to the Church of Kos Everburning, we're working on a case and want to check our facts, without pause for breath. Then she held the receptionist's gaze for the ten seconds needed for the word "Craftswoman" to suggest shambling corpses and disemboweled gods. Not that most gods had bowels.

Useful mental image, anyway.

The young man grew paler and directed her to Jones: third desk from the back, on the left, one row in.

They'd thrown desks like these out of the Hidden Schools in Tara's first year, chromed edges and fake wood tops that didn't take the masquerade seriously, green metal frames, rattling drawers and sharp corners. Thrown them, she remembered, straight into the Crack in the World. If you have a hole in reality, why not chuck your garbage there? At the time they'd also thrown out a number of ratty office chairs like the one in which Gavriel Jones herself reclined, one muddy shoe propped on the desk. The Crier held a pencil in her mouth and a plainsong page inverted in her hand. She straightened the foot that propped her, then relaxed it again, rocking her chair back and forth. Her free hand beat syncopation on her thigh. A cigarette smoldered in the ashtray on her desk. Tara frowned at the ashtray and the smoke. She might work for Kos, but that didn't mean she had to approve of the weird worship the fire god demanded.

Or maybe the Crier was just an addict.

"Ms. Jones."

Jones's hand paused. She stopped rocking and plucked the gnawed pencil from her teeth. "Ms. Abernathy. I took bets on when you would show up."

"What was the spread?"

"You hit the sweet spot."

"I'm getting predictable in my old age."

"I won't pull the story," Jones said.

"Too predictable."

"At least you're not getting old. Not like the rest of us, anyway." Jones pointed to the paper-strewn desktop. "Step into my office."

Tara shifted a stack of blank staff paper and leaned against the desk. "You're starting trouble."

"We keep people informed. Safety's the church's job. And the Blacksuits'."

"You didn't see the Paupers' Quarter market this morning when they sang your feature."

"I can imagine, if it's anything like the rubbernecking we had up north in the CBD." She grinned. "Good tips today."

"People are angry."

"They have a right to be. Maybe you're an operational atheist, but most folks don't have the luxury. We've had problems with gargoyles before. If they're back, if their Lady is, that's news." Jones had a way of looking up at Tara and seeming to look—not down, never down, but straight across, like a pin through Tara's eyeball. "We deserve to know how, and why, the city's changed beneath us."

"Who are your sources?"

One of Jones's lower front teeth had been broken off and capped with silver. "Do you really think I'd answer that question? If people are worshipping Seril, a church rep is the last person I'd tell."

"I don't need specifics," Tara said.

"I met a girl in a bar who spun me a tale. She worked delivery, and some hoods jumped her and stole her satchel. Way the contract was written up, she was liable for everything inside. Small satchel, but you know Craftfolk. Whatever was in there, it was expensive—the debt would break her down to indentured zombiehood. She knew a story going around: if you're in trouble, shed your blood, say a prayer. Someone will come help. Someone did."

"What kind of bar was this?"

That silver-capped tooth flashed again.

"So you write this on the strength of a pair of pretty blue eyes—"

"Gray." She slid her hands into her pockets. "Her eyes were gray. And that's the last detail you get from me. But it got me asking around. Did you listen to the song?"

"I prefer to get my news straight from the source."

"I did legwork, Ms. Abernathy. I have a folder of interviews you'll never see unless a Blacksuit brings me something stiffer than a polite request. Women in the PQ started dreaming a year ago: a cave, the prayer, the blood. And before you scoff, I tried it myself. I got in trouble, bled, prayed. A gargoyle came." Her voice lost all diffidence.

"You saw them."

"Yes."

"So you know they're not a danger."

"Can I get that on the record?"

Tara didn't blink. "Based on your own research, all they've done is help people. They saved you, and in return you've thrown them into the spotlight, in front of people who fear and hate them."

Jones stood—so they could look at each other face-to-face, Tara thought at first. But then the reporter turned round and leaned back against her desk by Tara's side, arms crossed. They stared out together over the newsroom and its orange human-shaped bees. Typewriter keys rattled and carriage returns sang. Upstairs, a soprano practiced runs. "You don't know me, Ms. Abernathy."

"Not well, Ms. Jones."

"I came up in the *Times*, in Dresediel Lex, before I moved east." Tara said nothing.

"The Skittersill Rising was my first big story. I saw the protest go wrong. I saw gods and Craftsmen strangle one another over a city as people died under them. I know better than to trust either side, much less both at once. Priests and wizards break people when it suits you. Hells, you break them by accident. A gargoyle saved me last night. They're doing good work. But the city deserves the truth."

"It's not ready for this truth."

"I've heard that before, and it stinks. Truth's the only weapon folks like me—not Craftsmen or priests or Blacksuits, just payday drunks—have against folks like you. Trust me, it's flimsy enough. You'll be fine."

"I'm on your side."

"You think so. I don't have the luxury of trust." She turned to Tara. "Unless you'd care to tell me why a Craftswoman working for the Church of Kos would take such an interest in crushing reports of the gargoyles' return?"

"If the gargoyles are back," she said, choosing her words carefully, "they might raise new issues for the church. That makes them my responsibility."

Jones looked down at the floor. "The dreams started about a year ago, after Kos died and rose again. There were gargoyles in the city when Kos died, too. Maybe they never left. It sounds like more than the gargoyles came back."

Tara built walls of indifference around her panic. "That's an . . . audacious theory."

"And you began to work for the church at about the same time. You sorted out Kos's resurrection, saved the city. Maybe when you brought him back, you brought something else, too. Or someone."

Tara unclenched her hand. Murdering members of the press was generally frowned upon in polite society. "Do your editors know you make a habit of baseless accusations?"

"Don't treat us like children, Ms. Abernathy—not you, not Lord Kos, not the priests or the gargoyles or the Goddess Herself. If the world's changed, the people deserve to know."

Time's one jewel with many facets. Tara leaned against the desk. A year ago she stood in a graveyard beneath a starry sky, and the people of her hometown approached her with pitchforks and knives and torches and murder in mind, all because she'd tried to show them the world was bigger than they thought.

Admittedly, there might have been a way to show them that didn't involve zombies.

"People don't like a changing world," she said. "Change hurts."

"Can I quote you on that?"

She left Gavriel Jones at her desk, alone among the bees.

5

Every city has forsaken places: dilapidated waterfront warehouses, midtown alleys where towers close out the sky, metropolitan outskirts where real estate's cheap and factories sprawl like bachelors in ill-tended houses, secure in the knowledge their smoke won't trouble the delicate nostrils of the great and the good.

Alt Coulumb's hardest harshest parts lay to its west and north, between the Paupers' Quarter and the glass towers of the ill-named Central Business District—a broken-down region called the Ash, where last-century developments left to crumble during the Wars never quite recovered, their land rights tied up in demoniacal battles. Twenty-story stone structures rose above narrow streets, small compared to the modern glass and steel needles north and east, but strong.

Growing up in the country, Tara had assumed that once you built a building you were done—not the farmhouses and barns and silos back in Edgemont, of course; those always needed work, the structure's whole life a long slow deliquescence back to dust, but surely their weakness came from poor materials and construction methods that at best nodded toward modernity. But a friend of hers at the Hidden Schools studied architecture and laughed at Tara's naiveté. When Tara took offense, she explained: skyscrapers need more care than barns. Complicated systems require work to preserve their complexity. A barn has no air-conditioning to break; free the elementals that chill a tower and the human beings within will boil in their own sweat. The more intricate the dance, the more disastrous the stumble.

The abandoned towers in the Ash were simple things, built of mortar, stone, and arches, like Old World cathedrals. If Alt Coulumb fell tomorrow, they'd still stand in five hundred years. Their insides rotted, though. Façades broke. Shards of plate glass jutted from windowsills.

Tara approached on foot by daylight through the Hot Town. Kids loitered at alley mouths, hands in the pockets of loose sweatshirts, hoods drawn up in spite of the heat. Sidewalk sweepers stared at her, as did women smoking outside bars with dirty signs. Girls played double dodge on a cracked blacktop.

But when she reached the Ash, she was alone. Not even beggars lingered in these shadows.

The tallest tower lacked a top, and though black birds circled it, none landed.

Tara closed her eyes.

Outside her skull, it was almost noon; inside, cobweb cords shone moonlight against the black. This was the Craftswoman's world, of bonds and obligations. She saw no traps, no new Craft in place. She opened her eyes again and approached the topless tower.

Sunlight streamed through broken windows. Jagged glass cast bright sharp shadows on the ruins within. Tara looked up, and up, and up, to the first intact structural vault seven stories overhead. The intervening floors had collapsed, and the wreckage of offices and apartments piled twenty feet tall in the tower's center: splintered rotted wood, chunks of drywall, stone and ceramic, toilet bowls and countertops and tarnished office nameplates.

And of course she still couldn't fly here, damn the jealous gods.

A few decades' abandonment hadn't weathered the walls enough to climb, even if she had equipment. She'd scaled the Tower of Art at the Hidden Schools, upside down a thousand feet in air, but she'd had spotters then, and what was falling to a woman who could fly? She considered, and rejected, prayer.

There had to be an entrance somewhere, she told herself, though she knew it wasn't true.

On her third circuit of the floor, she found, behind a pile of rubble, a hole in the wall—and beyond that hole a steep and narrow stair. Maybe they hired cathedral architects for this building. Old habits died hard.

She climbed for a long time in silence and the dark. A fat spider landed on her shoulder, skittered down her jacket sleeve, and brushed the back of her hand with feathery legs; she cupped it in her fingers and returned it to its wall and webs. The spider's poison tickled through her veins, a pleasant tension like an electric shock or the way the throat seized after chewing betel nut. A rat king lived in the tower walls, but it knew better than to send its rat knights against a Craftswoman. They knelt as she passed.

Twenty minutes later she reached the top.

Daylight blinded her after the long climb. She stepped out into shadowless noon. Clutching fingers of the spire's unfinished dome curved above her. Blocks of fallen stone littered the roof. Iron arches swooped at odd angles overhead, stamped with runes and ornaments of weather-beaten enamel.

She turned a slow circle, saw no one, heard only wind. She slid her hands into her pockets and approached the root of one arch. It was not anchored in the stone, but beneath it, through a gap in the masonry, as if the arch had been designed to tilt or spin. She recognized the runes' style, though she couldn't read them. And the enameled ornaments, one for each of the many interlocking arches—

"It's an orrery," she said. "An orrery in your script."

"Well spotted," a stone voice replied.

She turned from the arch. Aev stood barely a body's length away, head and shoulders and wings taller than Tara. Her silver circlet's sheen had nothing to do with the sun. Tara had not heard her approach. She wasn't meant to. "I knew you lived here. I didn't realize it was your place, technically."

"It isn't," Aev said. "Not anymore. When Our Lady fell in the God Wars, much was stolen from her, including this building."

"I thought temples weren't your style."

"We are temples in ourselves. But the world was changing then, even here. We thought to change with it." She reached overhead— far overhead—and scraped a flake of rust from the iron. "Even your heathen astronomy admits that the rock-which-circles-as-the-moon is the closest of any celestial body to our world. We thought to cultivate Our Lady's glory through awe and understanding."

"And then the God Wars came."

Aev nodded. "Your once human Craftsmen, who style themselves masters of the universe, have slim regard for awe or wonder, for

anything they cannot buy and sell. So deadly are they, even hope be-
comes a tool in their grip."

"I'm not here to have that argument," Tara said.

"Our temple would have been glorious. At night the people of Alt
Coulumb would climb here to learn the turnings of the world."

"Where are the others?"

Aev raised her hand. The gargoyles emerged soundlessly from
behind and inside blocks of stone, unfolding wings and limbs—
worshippers who were also weapons, children of a dwindled goddess.
Thirty or so, last survivors of a host winnowed by the war to which
their Lady led them. Strong, swift, mostly immortal. Tara did not want
to fear them. She didn't, much.

Still, preserving her nonchalance took effort.

The Blacksuits could stand still for hours at a time. Golems spun
down to hibernation. Only the faintest margin separated a skeletal
Craftswoman in meditation from a corpse. But the gargoyles, Seril's
children, they were not active things feigning immobility. They were
stone.

"I don't see Shale," she said.

"He remains uncomfortable around you. Even you must admit,
he has his reasons."

"I stole his face for a good cause," Tara said. "And he tried to kill
me later, and then I saved you all from Professor Denovo. I think we're
even."

" 'Even' is a human concept," Aev said. "Stone bears the marks of
all that's done to it, until new marks erase those that came before."

"And vigilante justice—was that carved into you, too?"

"I see you heard the news."

"I damn well heard the news. How long have you been doing
this?"

"Our Lady sent her first dreams soon after our return to the city.
A simple offer of exchange, to rebuild her worship."

"And your Lady—" Tara heard herself say the capital letter, which
she didn't like but couldn't help. She'd carried their goddess inside herself, however briefly. "Your Lady controls Justice now. She has a police
force at her disposal, and She still thought this terror-in-the-shadows
routine was a good idea?"

Aev's laugh reminded Tara of a tiger's chuff, and she became uncomfortably conscious of the other woman's teeth. "Justice may belong to Our Lady, but when She serves as Justice, She is bound by rules, manpower, schedules. Your old master Denovo wrought too well."

Tara's jaw tightened at the word "master," but this wasn't the time to argue that point. "So Seril uses you to answer prayers."

"Seril is weak. For forty years the people of this city have thought Her more demon than goddess. Her cult has faded. Those who hold Her rites—rocks into the sea at moon-death, the burning of flowers and the toasting of the moon—do not know the meaning of their deeds. So we give them miracles to inspire faith. Lord Kos and His church preserve the city, but Seril and we who are Her children work in darkness, in the hours of need."

"Some people wouldn't like the idea of a goddess growing in the slums, feeding off desperate people's blood."

"We have stopped muggings, murders, and rapes. If there is harm in that, I do not see it. You have lived in this city for a year—in the Paupers' Quarter, though its more gentrified districts—and it took you this long to learn of our efforts. Is that not a sign we have done needed work? Helped people otherwise invisible to you?"

Gravelly murmurs of assent rose from the gargoyles. Wind pierced Tara's jacket and chilled the sweat of her long climb.

"Seril's not strong enough to go public," she said.

"Our Lady is stronger than She was a year ago, as She would not have been if we listened to you and kept still. Some believe, now—which is more success than your efforts have yielded."

"I've spent a year chasing leads and hunting your old allies, most of whom are dead, and that's beside the point. It sounds like you waited all of ten minutes before you started playing Robin-o-Dale. You didn't even tell me."

"Why would we tell you, if we knew you would disagree with our methods?"

"I am your Craftswoman, dammit. It's my job to keep you safe."

"Perhaps you would have known of our affairs," Aev said, "if you spoke with the Lady once in a while."

Moonlight, and cool silver, and a laugh like the sea. Tara shut the goddess out, and stared into her own reflection in Aev's gemstone eyes.

"You're lucky they still think Seril's dead. I want a promise from all of you: no missions tonight. And I need you, Aev, at a council meeting soon as it's dark enough for you to fly."

"We will not abandon our responsibilities."

"This is for your own good. And Seril's."

Aev paced. Her claws swept broad arcs through the air. Tara did not speak their language enough to follow her, but she recognized some of the curses.

"No!"

The stone voice did not belong to Aev. The gargoyle lady spun, shocked.

A gray blur struck the roof and tumbled, tearing long grooves in the stone with its landing's force. Crouched, snarling, a new form faced Tara: slender and elegant compared to the hulking statues behind him, majestically finished, limbs lean and muscles polished, but no less stone, and furious.

Tara did not let him see her flinch. "Shale," she said. "I'm glad you were listening. I need your pledge, with the others', not to interfere."

"I will not promise. And neither should they." Aev reached for Shale, to cuff him or pull him back, but he spun away and leapt, with a single beat of broad-spread wings, to perch on the broken orrery arch, glaring down. "We are teaching the people of Alt Coulumb. They've come to believe—in the Paupers' Quarter, in the markets. They pray to our Lady. They look to the skies. You'd have us give that up—the only progress we've made in a year. You ask us to turn our backs on the few faithful our Lady has. To break their trust. I refuse."

"Get down," Aev snapped.

"I fly where I wish and speak what I choose."

"We asked Tara for her help. We should listen to her," Aev said, "even when her counsel is hard to bear."

"It's just for one night," Tara said.

Shale's wings snapped out, shedding whorls of dust. He seemed immense atop the jagged iron spar. "For one night, and the next, and the next after that. We've crouched and cringed through a year of nights and nights, and if we cease our small evangelism, with each passing day the faith we've built will break, and faith once broken's three times harder to reforge. I will not betray the people who call on us for aid. Will you, Mother?" He scowled at Aev. "Will any of you?" His gaze swept the rooftop gathering. Stone forms did not shuffle feet, but still Tara sensed uncertainty in shifting wings and clenching claws.

Aev made a sound in her chest that Tara heard as distant thunder. "I will swear," she said, fierce and final. "We all will swear. We will not show ourselves. We will let prayers pass unanswered, for our Lady's safety."

Tara felt the promise bite between them. Not so binding as a contract, since no consideration had passed, but the promise was a handle nevertheless for curses and retribution should Aev betray her word. Good enough.

"You swear for the Lady's sake," Shale said, "yet, swearing, you turn from Her service, and from our people—you turn from the overlooked, from the fearful. Don't abandon them!"

"And I will swear," said another gargoyle, whose name Tara did not know. "And I." And others, all of them, an assent in grinding chorus. Tara gathered their promises into a sheaf, and tied the sheaf through a binding glyph on her forearm. That hurt worse than the spider's poison, but it was for a good cause.

"Broken," Shale said, and another word, which must have been a curse in Stone. "Surrender."

"Shale," Aev said. "You must swear with us."

"You cannot force me," Shale said. "Only the Lady may command."

He leapt off the tower. Wings folded, he needled toward the city streets—then with a whip crack he flared and glided up, and off, through Alt Coulumb's towers.

Tara gathered her Craft into a net to snare him, hooks to catch and draw him back. Shadow rolled over her, and she cast out her arm.

But a massive claw closed around her wrist, and Aev's body blocked her view of Shale's retreat. Tara's lightning spent itself against the gargoyle's stone hide.

"I can stop him," Tara said. She pulled against Aev's grip, but the gargoyle's hand did not move. "Get out of my way." Growls rose from the other statues, obscured behind the grand curve of Aev's wings.

"His choice is free," Aev replied. "We will not let you bind him."

"He'll spoil everything."

"We are not bound save by our own will, and the Lady's." Again Aev made that thunder sound. Her claw tightened—slightly—around Tara's wrist, enough to make Tara feel her bones. "Even Shale. One child, alone, cannot cause too much trouble."

"Want to bet?"

"Police the city more tonight. He will have no prayers to answer."

"That's not enough."

"It must be."

She remembered a dead man's voice: *you have fused a chain around your neck.*

Tara's wrist hurt.

"Fine," she snapped, and let her shadows part and her glyphwork fade, let mortal weakness reassert its claim to the meat she wore. Her skin felt like skin again, rather than a shell. The world seemed less malleable.

Aev let her go. "I am sorry."

"Come to the meeting tonight," she said. "I'll see myself out." She turned from the gargoyles and their unfinished heaven into darkness.

Somewhere a goddess laughed. Tara didn't listen.

6

Catherine Elle and Raz Pelham sat in a dirty white golem truck in a parking lot across the street from a two-story building that was trying very hard to be nondescript.

She peered through a narrow gap in the curtains over the windows. "For smugglers and slavers, they're not so good at this."

"These guys just make the dreamglass," Raz said. "The trafficking's Maura's job."

"Still. Our den of villainy's first floor is a sleepy little pizza place with a guy reading at the counter. One cook. They're barely trying. I doubt they even have pizza. They'd get the biggest shock of their lives if I walked in and ordered a slice."

"You wouldn't."

"Watch me."

"In or out of costume?"

"It's not a costume."

"I'm not up on the preferred nomenclature. What am I supposed to call your creepy addictive hive mind symbiont?"

"It's less addictive now," she said. "And it works by grace of Goddess. Goddesses aren't creepy, by definition."

"How many goddesses have you met?"

"Shut up."

"We have a few back home in Dhisthra might change your mind is all I'm saying."

"The one I do know's more than enough for me. Maybe too much."

"Fair enough." He returned his attention to his book. "The goddesses I'm talking about might find you tasty, anyway."

Her badge chilled. She reached beneath her shirt collar and touched the icon of Justice hanging there. Moonsilver flowed over her mind like a high wave on a north shore beach, and receded, leaving the world darker until it dried. She listened to the hum of distant voices. "Pursuit team just checked in," she said, interpreting for his benefit. "Maura Varg's in transit with the funds. You identify her, we go in, take them all at once."

"I know the plan."

For a few minutes, neither of them spoke. Raz turned pages.

"Speaking of creepy," she said.

"What?"

"Every few seconds I realize I'm the only one here who's breathing."

"Lifer sentiment doesn't become you, Cat. Watch out or I'll report you to the Association for the Advancement of Undead Peoples."

"Stuff it."

He raised one eyebrow and grinned, baring the tips of fangs.

Cat checked the window again. A driverless carriage rolled to the curb and a woman stepped out: tall and weathered, with a thick neck and a sailor's broad gait, as if she expected the land to betray her at any moment. She wore canvas slacks, leather boots, a shirt patched and repaired with sailcloth, and bore a curved blade through the red sash around her midsection. The only part of the ensemble that did not fit the pirate queen image was the immaculate brown leather briefcase, which cost, Cat ventured, around six hundred thaums. She wondered if the case's ornaments were gold, decided they were, and ratcheted the value up to an even thousand.

"She's not even trying to make this hard," she said. "That's Varg?" She slid forward on the seat so Raz could check out the window. His body didn't heat the surrounding air; the long, lean muscles of his flank pressed cold against her back.

He peeked through the shade. He hissed as light struck him— dropped the curtain and rolled back into his seat, digging the heels of his hands into his eyelids. "Godsdamn. Why don't you people do business at night like normal?"

"Is that her?"

"Yeah. That's Maura."

Cat returned to the window. "Looks like a tough customer. How did you two meet, again?"

"Business, way back. She tried to kill me once; I ate her partner."

"Really?"

"I was young, and we were both sailing for someone I'd rather forget. She was only a privateer in those days. She's always been vicious, but I never thought she'd stoop to the indenture trade."

"We'll stop that."

"You'd better. There are people in her hold."

Maura Varg entered the shop and traded salutes with the man behind the register. He released something he was holding beneath the counter—tension in his shoulder and biceps was right for a blade, though maybe a shocklance or blasting rod or crossbow—stepped out front, walked past Varg, and flipped the OPEN sign in the window to CLOSED.

Varg drummed her fingers on the briefcase. Not a woman who liked waiting, Cat thought. Not a woman who liked much of anything on land. Such prejudice tended to go with the piratical territory.

The cashier took a skeleton key from his pocket, slid it into a crack in the drywall, and turned. A door opened where a door hadn't been seconds before.

One could quibble with mystery plays on many points. Cat's fellow Suits scorned them for a host of small inaccuracies: steel doesn't break that way, no one holds a crossbow like that, how did they reload so fast, no officer in their right mind would go into that house alone. Small details of procedure and weaponry didn't bother Cat much, but the plays got hidden doors wrong every single time. The young bride in "Reynardine" opens the secret passage to find a luxurious staircase, warning inscription in gold on the arch above, rich, plush, and above all clean.

Real hidden passages, now, were by definition places people didn't look, where you never had to entertain company. You entered them only when you needed something from the space beyond, and you didn't linger. Real hidden passages, in Cat's experience, looked more like disused dry-goods cellars.

So she wasn't surprised when the new door opened onto a shabby stairwell made from warped unfinished wood. Black smears marred the plaster wall.

Maura Varg jutted her chin out and up by way of a nod, and climbed the hidden stairs. The cashier closed the door behind her, removed and pocketed the key, and patted the drywall where the door had been.

Cat clutched her badge again and spoke through it to Blacksuits in and out of uniform. "Varg is upstairs. The key's in the cashier's left apron pocket."

Roger, they responded, and though Cat knew the voice, and used it herself sometimes, still she shivered. It was the voice of wireglass things in nightmares, which never lived and so could never die. A year ago, the voice was simply terrifying, which hadn't bothered her. These days there was a song beneath the scream, a face to the silver. A goddess was part of her workday now. That was harder to accept. *Awaiting your signal.*

"It's time," she told Raz.

He took his hands from his face. His cheeks were wet with blood tears. "Give them hells."

She cracked the door and slipped out into the damp, oppressive heat of early afternoon in summer. Alt Coulumb's founders in their infinite wisdom built their city on a marsh—that was one reason, said the city's oldest myths, their land came so cheap. Rivers still ran beneath the pavement and underground, but pave a swamp and you're left with a paved swamp. Two steps out into the sun, and she sweated through her shirt. The city smelled of stone and fish and flesh and thick nose-burning spices. Not every restaurant on this street was a smuggling front, Cat thought. Probably.

She slid a pack of cigarettes from her jacket pocket and tapped them against her palm, spun the box, tapped them again. Fewer people smoked than used to, here in the fire-god's city. Cat herself never started—reaction to her dad, a shrink would probably say, if she went to one. But stepping out for a cigarette was a good cover.

She faked a cough, pressed her fist against the badge through her shirt. The badge's corners bit her skin. Okay, she told them. Let's go.

Silver shadows rose from the surrounding rooftops, and leapt. Soundlessly they flew and soundless fell. Cat remembered a cruise she'd taken once to see whales. When the leviathan breached, the spray rose twice the height of her boat's mast, and sunlight rainbowed through.

The Blacksuits—not quite black anymore, though the name

stuck—landed lighter on the restaurant roof than the spray had on the ship's deck. Cat barely heard them, and her ears were sharper than most humans'. Three Suits geckoed down the building's walls, spread-eagled above windows, slick silver skin adhering to the brick.

Metal flashed from the alley behind the restaurant.

That was her cue.

She looked both ways, crossed the street, stepped into the pizza place. The bell above the door jangled. The walls looked as dirty from inside as they had through the window. A devotional calendar hung on the wall. Two months had passed since the last page was turned.

"Hey," she said, letting her accent thicken to its old richness. A girl can leave Slaughter's Fell, but the fell never quite leaves her. "Gimme two slices of pepperoni and a cup of coffee to go."

Apron looked up from the book he was reading behind the cash register. In the rear, the cook—Cat's uptown-bred coworkers liked to say, "Where they find these guys I'll never know," but Cat did know, when she was a kid back in the fell she knew ten guys and their fathers who all looked like this, fake tan, gym, and dank cologne, bad hair-cuts and bad tattoos and not enough sense to leave a business that grew more dangerous as it grew richer—the cook, call him Sideburns, who Cat figured might actually be able to make a grilled cheese sand-wich if you presented him with bread, cheese, butter, a frying pan, a burning stove, and a map, Sideburns whom no one had hired for his culinary acumen approached with a slow, dangerous gait. He wore heavy rings on his right hand and didn't look sweaty so much as bronzed. In a different age, guys like Sideburns would have followed guys like Apron as they in turn followed purple-robed emperors to glory.

So much for history.

"Oven's broken," Apron said.

She tapped her cigarettes. "Just a slice? Don't need it hot, just my buddy's hungry, you know. And coffee."

"No coffee," Apron said. "No slices. Go to Farrell's down the road. And there's no smoking here."

The restaurant was very quiet. Cat, who knew how to listen, heard a soft metallic click. A drop of sweat rolled down Sideburns's jaw.

"Look, man, I'm in a hurry, are you sure you don't have—"

"Listen." Apron slammed shut his book and loomed over the counter. "We don't have nothing. Take a hike."

"Sure," she said. Raised her hands. Apron wore a sharp expressive scent, which Cat could have identified if she wore her Suit. The Suit knew more than she did. Operating plainclothes, she always felt as if someone had chopped off her extra arm. "I don't want trouble."

"This ain't trouble," he said. She wished he had not sounded almost human there. It made the next bit harder. "So long as you get—"

She struck him in the neck with her cigarette packet. An alchemical switch snapped within the paper, metal prongs struck him, lightning flashed. He slumped twitching onto the counter. Sideburns rushed forward, but Cat heard a poured-water sound and when she looked up she saw Sideburns struggling against a quicksilver-skinned woman who held him in a sleeper hold, pinching off the blood flow to his brain. Sideburns was smarter, or better trained, than Cat gave him credit: when he couldn't pull the Suit's arm down, he thrust his hips into her. When that didn't work, he tried to claw her face. Fingernails skidded over silver. Thumbs found eye sockets and gouged, but the Suit didn't notice. Score another point for mind-bonding—some responses you couldn't train out of human bodies, no matter how damage-resistant they might be, but the Suit knew better than to let its host get scared.

Cat caught Apron by the collar, dragged him up onto the counter, pulled the key from his pocket, and ran to the wall. The door opened, and revealed the stairs.

Behind her, in his last flailing seconds of consciousness, Sideburns made his smartest move. He couldn't break the Suit's grip, couldn't save himself, but he could kick over the kitchen rack. It fell, struck the sink, rained bowls and platters and tongs and boxes onto tile.

From up the stairs she heard a voice. "Stevie?"

Two Suits had followed the first through the rear window. They ran past her now, a blur of silver and steel, rapid footsteps. Upstairs she heard a crossbow twang, a scream. Moonlight called her, the hungry pit at the back of her mind yawning deep as voices issued from it in ecstatic chorus—

Breaching window—

Blast rods at the door—

Go go go—
Kitchen secure—
She has a rod—

A fist the size of a carriage struck the ceiling over Cat's head. Roof timbers strained, cracks spiderwebbed across plaster, dust fell. She knew the layout of the dealers' second-floor apartment: large kitchen in back where they packed the product, living room–turned–guard post in front, sitting room in between, locked bedroom door. Targets swarming, five in the kitchen lit red in her mind's vision, four in the front, two in the middle, and one asleep or tripping in the bedroom. Maura Varg stood in the sitting room, smoking blast rod in her hand, charge expelled. Varg's skin flushed as systems inside her spun up, gave her strength and speed. She struck the locked door with the palm of her hand so hard its wood split up the center—

Cat swore. The Suit in the kitchen was busy, binding Apron and Sideburns amid the mess of fallen pots and pans.

If Cat donned her Suit, she could be outside in a second, bursting through the plate glass window to the street. Instead she ran out the front door, turned the corner so tight her shoes slipped on concrete and she almost fell, caught herself on the ground with one hand—

Glass shattered above as Maura Varg dove out the bedroom window, shard-misted, forearms crossed to shield her face, farther than a running jump should have taken her, and arced headfirst toward the pavement.

Cat sprinted across the street toward her, arms pistoning. If she could catch Varg before she came upright—

A cry from her left, and too late she heard the triple-beat of a horse at gallop. *Should have closed the street*—she looked left and saw wide black equine eyes and rearing hooves and a rider's moon-shaped face beneath an absurd tricornered hat as the hooves came down. She dodged through molasses, the horse eighteen hands at least and plunging, and she knew what those hooves could do to human flesh—

She fell into the silver void, into the ice-melt lake that waited at her brain stem's root, and leapt clear of the hooves, which could not hurt her anymore, because she wasn't human anymore exactly.

Nor was she, exactly, Cat.

But she didn't want to hurt the horse.

Hooves fell, slow as a ballerina's lofted leg descending. Somewhere a butterfly's wing beat. On North Shore, a wave rolled onto the beach and did not roll back.

She stood in the road, a statue of fluid silver. Behind her, other Blacksuits secured the apartment safe house, which she saw in flashes: dreamglass piled on the kitchen counter, broken bones and windows, captives splayed on the floor. Safe. In front of her, Maura Varg fled into an alley. Cat followed her. She closed with Varg, not fast enough—the woman's glyphwork must be pushing her to the edge of sanity, to outrun a Suit. Alley shadows fell slick on Cat's skin, and far below the world she heard the sunken moon's song.

A carriage pulled up at the far end of the alley, door open. She saw it, and through silver the other Suits saw it, too, and Justice activated plainclothes officers nearby for pursuit. Varg would make the carriage before Cat could catch her. Normal horses couldn't outrun a Blacksuit, but not all horses were normal.

A black, burning blur fell on Varg from the rooftops. She struck pavement and then the alley wall, skidded, found her feet in a tussle with a smoking human figure. Not a Blacksuit—and really burning, skin licked by flame, charcoal flakes falling as he moved. Fangs flashed bone white within the fire.

Raz.

Varg jumped on him. He hit her three times; the fourth time she caught his wrist. Glyphs shone noon bright on her arms. She spun him around and caught his neck in the crook of her arm. Her blade steadied against his throat.

Cat stopped.

They stood opposed in the alley.

"That's right," Varg said. "Don't move."

Varg backed toward the carriage. Cat took two steps forward.

Raz's fires died, leaving scales of char like a snake's dried skin about to shed.

"I'll kill him."

Cat had seen Raz survive a broken neck. But she didn't know his limits, and did not want to test them now.

Seize her, the silver sang. Hold her. Bring her to Justice.

She forced the Suit aside, and fell from heaven's gates. Silver seeped away and she was only Cat again.

The knife pressed into his skin.

She held out her hand—pink, weak, shaking with aftershocks of ecstasy. Varg could break her now, if she wanted. "Let him go. You can't run."

"I can run forever," Maura Varg said.

Her glyphs guttered like 3:00 A.M. coals.

Raz smiled, though maybe he was just gritting his teeth.

Then he hit Varg hard in the face with the back of his head.

Varg's nose shattered. Her knife tore into his neck. He fell, limp. Varg staggered, and in that second Cat leapt on her, threw her into the wall, hit her in the face, the jaw, doubled her over her knee. Varg crumpled and lay still, though breathing.

Cat ran to Raz.

Blood poured down his collar, a red scarf over his bleach-white shirt. His hand rose, trembling, to his neck, but could not reach.

She knelt beside him, took his wrist, felt the direction he wanted it to go, and pressed his hand against his wound. His teeth were white and sharp.

She shed her jacket, unbuttoned her shirt cuff, and pushed it up. Scars marked on her forearm, paired pinpricks, long gashes, faded, yes, but there was only so much a year could heal. If she was younger, they might have healed completely.

She raised her wrist to his mouth. His nostrils flared. There was a need in her—gods, such a need—hunger for the fullness she'd abandoned a year ago, but she found herself here anyway, in the alley, so weak.

His fangs bared.

She shivered in anticipation.

He pressed his lips together, shook his head.

She slumped beside him. "You really." She was breathing hard, and not from the run. "You really should let me know what can kill you."

"I'm." His first try was wet and windy at once. He spit blood onto the pavement. "I'm not exactly sure. Extended sunlight, probably. Decapitation. It's not like there's a manual. And only dumb kids go around trying to off themselves."

"Yeah?"

"It's an existentialist thing."

"Never did trust philosophy." A pause, in which she failed again to find her breath. "You didn't know you'd survive that?"

"I've had my throat slit before. I don't experiment, but other people always seem happy to oblige."

"Pirate."

"Cop."

She shrugged. "Thanks."

"Hells. Now we have her, you have an excuse to take her ship. That's the real prize. Rescue the people she's smuggling, save the day. And I needed to work on my tan."

She punched him in the arm. He winced.

Inside her, the pit still yawned, and beneath that pit, another, deeper.

7

The goddess addressed Cat in the shower, in her mother's voice.

Catherine, why do you turn from me?

Oh, I don't know if I turn from you as such, she replied as she shampooed. We have a close working relationship.

You live inside my body, yet we don't talk like I do with my children.

I barely had my life figured out working with Justice. Then you came along.

You visited back alley bloodsucker dens for the thrill of being drunk. Does that constitute having your life figured out?

I didn't say I had it figured well. Just figured. She soaped down, rinsed off, turned into the shower spray. I was raised to think you were dead, and a traitor. Your children were my childhood ghosts.

That isn't my fault.

She shut off the water, reached blind for her towel, and rubbed herself dry.

I can help you. We can be closer than the structure of Justice allows. You are a priestess. You have made a vow. You could perform miracles.

Miracles aren't my job.

The voice did not answer. Somewhere beneath her feet, the moon smiled.

She had a fresh change of clothes in her locker, and as she put it on she convinced herself she felt clean.

She was halfway through the paperwork on the morning's raid when a duty officer—Cramden, she thought, beneath the Suit—came to tell her Tara Abernathy was looking for her. "Send her back," Cat said, and watched him go, smooth and assured, rippling silver.

She hadn't made progress on the paperwork when the door opened again. She looked up from the form, exasperated. "How do you spell 'ceiling'?"

Tara wrote the glyphs in air with her fingertip and shut the door behind her. "Long day?"

"Two long days," she said, "and it's only one thirty. It'll be four long days before I'm done."

"I need you at a meeting tonight."

"Can't. I have an operation. And this." She fanned the forms.

"Paperwork," Tara said, skeptical. She paced the confines of Cat's office, and "confines" was the right word: a cubbyhole of the Temple of Justice intended for solitary monastics meditating on their Lady. A bas-relief of a robed woman occupied one wall, its eyes notched out with a clean chisel strike. What light there was shafted through high slit windows; there had been more direct sun before they built the bank next door. "Why do you need after-action reports? Justice is in your head."

"Paperwork makes us more than just another gang. In the year since Seril came back, it's grown more important than ever. She has opinions—Justice didn't."

"Justice claimed she didn't. Study her arrest record and you'll see patterns emerge. Not nice patterns, either."

"At least she was fair."

"She arrested me for treason. You'll excuse me if I don't share your estimation of her impartiality."

"Slow down, college girl. You broke a lot of laws, even if you stopped bad people from doing worse."

"You, and your Blacksuits, almost got us all killed. Or enslaved."

"You hypnotized me and sent me into a vampire's sickroom, knowing I'd shove my arm in his mouth. I'm only here at all because he has more self-control than either of us."

"You—" Tara's voice went sharp and hot, and she wheeled on Cat with one hand raised. But she stopped herself, and closed her mouth, and sat at last in the chair across from Cat's desk. "You were telling me about the paperwork."

Cat assembled the sheets into a pile. "Seril's bound by the same rules as Justice—but she's conscious, and her perspective warps things.

We've stepped up the plainclothes officer program as a result. Used to be intelligence gathering only, moles and vice, but now it's expanded to a double role, intelligence and oversight. The guys with families don't like it—if they show their faces, they're exposed to revenge and old-fashioned blackmail. Those of us who don't have as much to lose, step up." She dropped the papers into a wire tray. "So, much as I miss our pleasant chats, I'll pass on the meeting."

"The gargoyles are exposed," Tara said.

"I heard. You talked to Gabby Jones down at the guild?"

"She won't pull the story. She's right not to. It is the truth, even if it's the wrong truth." Tara scraped one fingernail down her chair's leather armrest. "We need to regulate the damage, which means keeping Seril and Aev's people under wraps. I got most of them to promise to cut out the vigilantism, but Shale won't, and Aev won't let me stop him. So Alt Coulumb has to be the safest city in the world, starting tonight."

"I'm beginning to get the impression this isn't just about me coming to your meeting," Cat said.

"You have a lot of Blacksuits booked for an operation tonight. Cancel the op. Put them on the street instead."

"No."

"This is a big deal, Cat. We need the city safe tonight."

"This morning Raz helped us catch an indenture-trader in a drug bust. That gives us grounds to seize and search her ship, to save those people. If we don't take them tonight, her crew has standing orders to sail out of reach. You want that on your conscience?"

Cat wasn't good at reading people, but even she could see the *yes* in the set of Tara's shoulders, in the angle of her head and the tension at the corners of her mouth. And even she could see the woman recoil from that yes. "No," she said.

"I'm sorry."

"It's the right thing to do," Tara told Cat, and herself.

Neither of them spoke for a while.

"Tara," she said at last, "is it normal to hear gods in your head?"

"I'm not a person of faith," Tara replied. "Sort of the opposite."

"You know how these things work, though."

"From the outside. But no, it's not usual."

"Seril talks to me, sometimes."

"The gods." Tara steepled her fingers, and in that gesture she recalled Ms. Kevarian, Tara's teacher, mentor—and Denovo, too, the monster whose student Tara had been. "They aren't part of time and space like we are. They're second-order effects of humanity. We feel them. When we pray, or take the field against them, we . . . bind them into time. But they don't do small talk. In general, only saints can hear their voices."

"So I'm talking to myself."

"I doubt it. We've changed. Take you, for example: you were a bit rudderless a year ago."

"Hey," she said, but didn't mean it.

"And now you're tied to a being who's nothing but direction. Maybe that makes the difference. And Seril's a smaller god, not spread between as many worshippers. So each one means more to her. Or maybe she thinks you're a saint." Tara shrugged. "I kill gods and guard them, and raise them from the dead when they die. I don't pray."

"But you're hearing voices, too," Cat said.

Tara drummed her fingers on the arm of her chair. The wall clock ticked. She nodded, once.

"At least I'm not going mad alone."

Tara stood. "Meeting's at seven, at the Temple of Kos. Can you come? Please?"

"We sail at eight."

"It won't take long."

"Why do you want me? This whole thing's above my pay grade."

"We saved the city," Tara said. "We're responsible for it now."

"I wish someone had told me before I decided to save it."

Tara laughed without sound. Then she shook Cat's hand and left.

8

The Paupers' Quarter market closed at one, and afterward, as ever in time of crisis, Matt Adorne and the other market elders met for lunch at Cadfael's Bar and Grill.

"It's a travesty," whitebeard Corbin Rafferty raged, punctuating his tirade with a long swig of dark beer. "We sacrifice to God and we pay dues to Justice. And in return they let godsdamn Stone Men," his voice shaking, "Stone Men haunt our streets. Bloodthirsty." He stuffed his mouth with burger, bit down hard, and gnashed. "We have to do something."

"They don't sound bloodthirsty." Matt lowered his own voice in hope Corbin would match him. Why shout? The rooftop was empty as usual; hells, the whole place was empty this early in the day, with all the office drones at the paper shifting they called work. Every man and woman gathered around the table, Matt and Ray Capistano and Ray's boy and Sandy Sforza and her girl and Corbin and his three daughters, had put in a fuller day than the suited kids who'd taken to renting Quarter rooms in the last few years, the alchemists' assistants and junior accountants, payroll associates and lesser Craftsmen and other sacrificial lambs of the Central Business District, could conceive. A market man's life was hard: rise at three thirty, truck out hours before sunup to meet the farmers and load the wagons. Two hundred pounds of eggs weighed as much as two hundred pounds of anything. Truck back into town in time to meet restaurant buyers and then stand a solid seven hours offering goods for sale. Some men worked harder, sure. Once the construction boys and dockhands clocked out at sunset, dust-caked and sweaty, they'd have earned their beers, but in the meantime Matt and his comrades were emperors of the roof.

And empresses, Sandy would add.

But Corbin raged on. "You don't know from Stone Men, Matt. My dad fought 'em when they went mad back in the Wars. Lost an arm. They'll snap you in half if you blink wrong. And you heard the gods-damn Crier." Corbin washed down his burger with more beer. His daughters sat beside him, tight, silent. Claire, the oldest at seventeen, carved her chicken into squares and speared the squares with her fork; for her, food was a battle you fought so you could fight other battles later. Ellen, middle child, ate quickly and carefully as a bird, and kept her head down; Hannah, youngest, faked the same attitude, the same downturn, but when her father wasn't looking, her gaze slipped up and left to rest on Ray's son's mouth. Matt wondered often about their lives—Rafferty was a man for drinks and a bar fight in time of need, not one you trusted with your home address. "They're fouling our rooftops. Chasing through our alleys. Flouting laws."

"And since when have you," Sandy said as she grabbed a chicken wing, "given a dog's cock for laws flouted or otherwise, Corbin Rafferty? I've heard you say at this very table"—knocking with her fingers on the wood—"that it's this city's laws that ruin us."

"Once I say a thing, you'll stalk me with it to my grave, Sforza."

"And stab you through the heart with it to make sure you're dead, and good riddance to the world." She laughed; Rafferty's girls didn't, and Rafferty himself laughed too loud.

"If we are to sacrifice at all," he said, "we should be repaid. Monsters on our own rooftops, and the lot of you don't mind?"

"Likely just tall tales," Matt said. "Crier says they've been here a year. I never seen one."

"But Matthew," and that was Ray, leaning back on two legs of his chair, balanced as perfectly as the log cabin of chicken bones on his plate. No one could leave so pleasant a mess as Ray. "Of course you haven't seen them. They come to those who need help, and when was the last time you needed any?"

Matt drank. "Don't see the problem," he said, after. "Even if they are here. So long as they help people."

"Maybe someone doesn't want help," Corbin said. "Maybe what helps you, hurts me." He tossed a wing bone down as if casting thunderbolts upon a sinner. "If the Stone Men are back, Lord Kos ought to shatter them. We need Blacksuits on every roof."

Ray snatched a celery stalk and knifed its hollow full of blue cheese. "You haven't been to church often this year, have you, Corbin? Plenty of sermons about coming to terms with old enemies."

"You mean they're going soft."

"I mean none of us knows the whole story. Stone Men don't touch my business. Why should I worry about them?"

"A man ought to own his city."

"In a single question," Ray said, "I can prove incontrovertibly the Stone Men are no cause of concern for folk like us, who keep our beaks down: Have we ever seen these creatures?"

Matt followed Ray's gaze around the table: Ray's son, face buried in his second burger, shrugged and shook his head and chewed. Sandy Sforza drank her beer and shook her head as well. Sandy's daughter Lil was staring at Ray's boy's barbecue sauce–streaked face with a sickened expression entirely unlike Hannah's, but when she realized the others were watching her, she said, "No." The gazes slid to Matt, who grunted no, as did Corbin.

"There you go," Ray said. "If they're in the city or not, what's it matter to us?"

Slow jowly nods around the table. Corbin cracked his knuckles, frowning.

"We've seen," an unsteady voice began, then stopped. Matt looked over in time to see Claire Rafferty draw her hand back from Ellen's shoulder. Ellen's pale cheeks colored red, and she returned her gaze to at her plate, as if she'd never spoken.

"Girls," Corbin said in the voice he adopted while trying to sound nice, or at least less angry. It rarely worked. "What have you seen?"

"Nothing," Claire answered, cold. "Father."

"Don't lie to me."

"Ellen's telling stories," Hannah said.

"I'm not." The second time Ellen spoke, she sounded less hesitant. Still, she spoke into her plate, afraid, Matt thought, to face the table, and especially her father, who watched her with an expression darkened by the beers he'd drunk. "You saw him, too. You both did."

Claire took Ellen's wrist.

"Girls." Corbin's tone changed, and they turned toward him like iron filings when a magnet drew close. "Let Ellen talk."

Ellen paled, and Matthew wondered not for the first time, and not for the first time stopped himself from wondering, what life was like inside the Rafferty house.

"Tell me," Rafferty repeated.

"There's a prayer," Ellen said. "We all know it. We all dreamed it. And I used it." Rafferty leaned toward his daughter, his brows knit tight, the blade of his jaw unsheathed. "I didn't ask for anything," she said. "I never would have, but I was scared for you."

"Ellen." Claire's voice, sharp, a shutoff. "This isn't the time."

"Two months back you weren't home, hadn't been since the day before. The second night we decided, all of us, that we should look."

Sandy laughed, and Ellen fell silent. The glare Corbin shot Sandy was vicious, though not so vicious as the one with which she answered him. Corbin turned back to his daughter. "Go on."

"We started early and went to the addresses on your matchbooks. No one had seen you. We got lost. The streets kept turning around." Which meant they'd been in the Pleasure Quarter, Matt thought, though Ellen wouldn't say as much: the Pleasure Quarter, where the city's shattered-glass grid tangled to a briar patch of nameless avenues—the paths of long-dead cows codified by concrete. Playground, the market boys called it, the kids without stall or family who carried and carted for tips: walk in flush with soul, walk out empty save for memories of red light that dulls tears and washes flaws from skin. Matt imagined three Rafferty girls wandering through that maze at night. A sphinx smile darted across Hannah's lips.

But Ellen was still talking: "I said we should try the prayer, ask for help. Hannah and Claire didn't want to. It was my idea."

Thankful eye flicks from sister to sister, which Matt recognized only because the Adorne household of his boyhood communicated in the same code, five siblings united against the Old Man.

"You prayed," Matt said, because Corbin would have said worse.

Ellen looked up from her plate. "I cut myself, bled, and prayed. Then the statue came."

Left and right down the table, all sat in their own silence: sisters scared, Corbin in rage-tinted wonder, Ray eager, Sandy skeptical, Lil awed either by the story or the equally fantastical occasion of the Rafferty girls speaking. Ellen sounded drunk on memory. "He looked like the stories say, with eyes like jewels and wings of stone. He gathered us up. His arms were thin, but he was strong. Not like a person. Strong like an arch." Those last words broke the spell she had cast upon herself, and her fear returned. She glanced to her father, and back down. "He flew us home. Fast, over the rooftops, and high. They can fly, even here, so they must be right with God, mustn't they? He said if you weren't back by morning we should get the Blacksuits. He said if we were ever in danger, we should call him again. He looked worried for us. Then he left. You came back"—this to her father—"when we were all asleep. You were sick the next day. That's all."

"Is this true?" Corbin asked. The other two girls had sat very still through the telling.

"It's true," Claire said at last.

"But—" Hannah started. Claire looked at her but didn't speak. She stopped.

"It's true," Claire repeated.

"And you all say they're not a problem. They've been under my roof. They've touched my girls."

"Sounds like they did you a favor."

"What they've done, Sforza, is beside the point. What they might do, matters. Stone Men are traitors, butchers. So, my daughters can call them. Let's call them to the square tonight. Let's have it out face-to-face. No more shadows, no more tall tales."

Ray shrugged. "Doubt we'll see anything."

"You call my girls liars." Corbin's voice tightened to breaking.

"It sounds like a story, is all. And even if they call, who's to say the Stone Men come? But I'll watch. The boy can make the morning runs tomorrow."

"Hells, I won't miss this," his son said around a mouthful of burger.

"Then we'll both be tired on deliveries, and so be it when we crash and suffer grievous death."

"You're tempting fate," Sandy said. "This is a damn fool enterprise and I'll not lend it my support."

"But you'll come if we do it." Corbin's teeth were thin and white. "Just to watch, of course."

Matt drank. He realized everyone was looking at him. He crossed his arms and leaned back. "It's their choice."

"Excuse me?"

"The girls," Matt said. "We do this only if your girls want to."

Ellen looked to her father first, then Claire, then nodded. Matt had seen that expression on young soldiers in the Schtumpfeter Museum's God Wars paintings—kids sent to do and die on distant sand. He felt he'd done something wrong, and the tightness around Sandy Sforza's mouth, the sharp lines in her brow, suggested she agreed.

Matt thought he should stop the whole thing then, argue Rafferty into letting his girls alone, convince them all to leave the affairs of Gods and monsters to greater fools who didn't have to work for a living. But he said nothing, and the others planned against the night.

9

Twilight in Alt Coulumb summer is a wrestling match, or a bout of violent sex. Sun and moon share the sky, the west blushes with exertion, the first and most aggressive stars pierce the blue to begin their evening's battle with streetlights and office windows. The night's triumph is inevitable as prophecy, but wet air holds the day's heat, sweaty fingers tangled in solar curls. The heat lasts even as the sky fills with stars.

Some parts of the city only live on such an evening. Far to the east, the Pleasure Quarter offers cosmopolitan seductions to sailors fresh ashore, to foreigners from the Old World, from Iskar or the Gleb or from Dread Koschei's realm in Zur, from the Skeld Archipelago with its small gods and sunken cities, from Southern Kath where skeleton kings command indentured zombie hordes to work plantations in blistering heat. Hot Town's something else again: footraces and drug trade, street music on drums and guitar, food carts selling a hundred variations on fried dough with cinnamon and powdered sugar, cheap carnival rides powered by burly mustachioed men, streetwalkers in private practice. This is where Westerling locals come to sweat and eat and shop and drink and sweat some more, as their parents did and their parents before them down the long centuries before Craftsmen stole fire from the gods and made the world weird. The Hot Town opens storefront windows and unrolls rugs of wares onto sidewalks and streets. Turquoise pendants and silver wirework glitter beside dyed silk scarves and shawls and stalls of pirated books and obscene unlicensed street theater.

So fixed were the people milling about their business of pleasure that they missed the broad-winged shadow that flitted overhead, gray against the darkening blue, as night wrestled day to the ground and kissed him so hard their teeth clicked.

Aev knew the scene below of old, had watched the street fair for centuries since her first kindling within a stone egg perched atop Alt Coulumb's highest tower. The vices did not change so much as the clothes in which the practitioners wrapped themselves. She'd suffered forty years of exile in the Geistwood, hemmed in by trees, robbed of stone and familiar streets, but this was home. What matter if it feared her? What matter if these ants below thought her a harbinger of doom, believed Her Lady dead? Peace came with time and effort, and stone was well suited for both.

Aev flew east and south along the Hot Town strip, skyscrapers to her left, brownstones and tenements to her right. Fountains of ghostlight erupted at irregular intervals from gridded streets. The moon hung slivered in the sky, but growing—gravid with uncertain future.

Ahead of her rose the Temple of Kos in the center of the green: an enormous black needle that burned in the vision of the heart.

Once the God's radiance would have been tempered by moonlit silver chill. But the goddess, returned though She might be, swollen from the echo Aev had sheltered in Geistwood shadows, was small set beside Her lover. He was a city and more, grown fat on foreign trade, while She belonged to Her children alone.

Aev sang in flight.

Wings flower-petal-spread
And teeth and claws the thorns
I grow to seek my Mother's light
Her flesh my flesh, her skin my form—

Doggerel not worthy of inscription, but when moved to sing, one sang.

The moon swelled with her voice. Cold fire danced along the crystal lattice of her nerves, and she heard with heart's ear an answering song.

She flew in widening circles until she reached the temple's peak, at such height the city seemed made from children's toys. The sea spread east past the docks to a horizon silver flashed by moon. She darted across the temple green. Any who looked up would take her for a swallow or a tiny bat. Deprived of context or comparison, they couldn't know her size, or guess her speed.

She landed lightly on the roof, wings flared to brake. The wind of her arrival blew back the hood of the monk who awaited her: a tall thin young man with hollow cheeks and a shaved tonsure, whose cigarette was mostly ash. She knew him: the boy who fell and rose again, born aloft on the fire of his reborn God. "Abelard," she said. He still flinched at the sound of her voice. "You look well."

"Aev." He bowed, with hands pressed together. She'd said "well," but he looked paler than she remembered. He was not often in the sun. He lit a new cigarette from the ashes of the old, and ground the last beneath his boot.

"Those things will kill you."

"Not while God provides." He took a drag. "Besides, it's comforting. Did you have a nice flight?"

She nodded.

"Come on. They're waiting for you."

She furled her wings and let him lead her into her Lady's lover's temple.

10

"This is the simplest way to kill a god," Tara said. She stood at the foot of a long table in a dark room in the upper reaches of the Temple of Kos Everburning. A whiteboard on a pine easel somewhat spoiled the hidden chamber's overall severity. "You find a flaw in his defenses. A deal that cannot be broken. A treasure the god cannot help but defend. Then you hammer it until the god breaks."

Around the table sat the guests she'd spent the day inviting. At its head loomed dark-skinned Cardinal Evangelist Bede, globular beneath his crimson robes and puffing on a pipe, beside Technical Cardinal Nestor, a thin cold man with a thin cold face, elevated to his current post for stability more than genius. Neither of them looked at Aev, who stood, since no chair was large or strong enough to hold her. Abelard sat between the cardinals and the gargoyle, hands twitching in his lap. Across the table, Blacksuit representatives held attention. Catherine Elle uncrossed her legs. To her right sat Commissioner Michaels, a woman in her early fifties, heavy with strength. These would be enough for tonight's purposes.

They watched her.

"You all have heard the news by now: for a year, Seril's children have been offering, let's call them neighborhood watch services, throughout Alt Coulumb. Pray, shed a little blood, and the gargoyles will aid you."

"We should have been told," Michaels said. "We should be working together."

"We would have told you," Aev shot back, "if your people hadn't stoked hatred of Seril for four decades. We have to build love for Our Lady—not for Justice, but for the Goddess in Her own aspect."

Cardinal Evangelist Bede withdrew his pipe. Smoke wreathed his round face. "The church could have supported your mission. Subtly."

"Our Lady is not your Lord. The Church of Kos has done good to redress the evil its priests wrought. But unless you mean to schism—no?—you cannot create worshippers for Seril. We must do that ourselves."

"These are all good points," Tara said. "But they aren't why I called you here. The problem we face tonight is thaumaturgical, not strategic." Stares around the table, ranging from blank to knowing to (in Abelard's case) worried. "Aev's actions did not matter so long as they were secret. Now the gargoyles have revealed themselves, questions will follow. Their answers invite more questions. And at the end of the chain, Alt Coulumb will face a crisis of faith like none we've ever seen."

Nestor tapped a long thin finger on the table. "Our God died last year."

"Briefly," Tara said. "Due to bad actors misusing privileged information. Last year we dealt with a few traitors. I'm worried about a systemic attack. About war."

"Explain."

She opened her mouth, but Bede spoke first. "She's talking," he said, "about a credit crisis."

Confused silence around the table. Gazes shifted back to Tara.

"Kos the Everburning is one of the most stable gods in the world," she said. "Alt Coulumb didn't fight in the Wars, so it wasn't razed; its confirmed neutrality back then indicates it will stay neutral in future conflicts. As a result, this city is one of the few places gods and Craftsmen coexist. Kos capitalized on his position. Your God's credit rating is impeccable—even his death and rebirth didn't shake it, though Cardinal Evangelist Bede and I had to do some rapid footwork to ensure that. Kosite debt is a storehouse of value around the world. Gods and Concerns and Deathless Kings on six continents buy church bonds, which brings the city a regular flow of liquid souls. Kos has leveraged himself well, thanks to the work of the Cardinal Evangelist and his team."

Bede dipped his pipe in gracious acknowledgment.

"But Kos's position depends on the market's faith in his stability. How many souls does he possess? What are his liabilities? How risky is his behavior? For forty years the answers to these questions have been clear. But suppose the math changed. Suppose, say, Kos Everburning was found to have immense undisclosed liabilities."

"Craftsmen wouldn't have the same faith in him," Abelard said, clearly uncomfortable with the use of "faith" in this context.

"And if that happens, Kos's risk of default rises. Firms holding church stock will claim we lied to them. Our creditors might argue that, given the undisclosed risks, we sold them debt under false pretenses—so we owe them more soulstuff. A lot more. Which, of course, makes our debt even riskier to hold. And the spiral continues. Craft firms gather, smelling blood. The world's trust in Kos collapses, while his need for the funds guaranteed by that trust balloons." She brought her hands together. "Which is only the first problem."

"That sounds bad enough," Cat said.

Bede nodded, and took up the thread from Tara. "It is, for us. But the trouble cascades. Because Kosite debt's been safe for decades, thaumaturgical markets use it as a baseline. Whole economies in the Vinelands between Dhisthra and the Shining Empire depend on church bonds. If our bond prices collapse, many thaumaturgical instruments will become impossible to value—and uncertainty in high-energy magic is, to put it mildly, not good."

"Not good?"

"Imagine demons pouring out of rifts in reality the size of continents. Cities compressed to one-dimensional points. For starters."

"Which means," Tara said into the silence, "the Craftwork world can't afford to let Kos's value collapse. If they lose confidence in him and in the priesthood, they'll attack. Rather than allowing him to die, they'll kill him and rebuild him to save themselves. Skyspires encroaching on Coulumbite airspace, dragons in the heavens, demons creeping out of downtown shadows. They have to save the world, you see."

She let the silence stretch. They sat in the center of the God's power, in a great and prosperous city, and she had to make them feel uncertain. She thought she'd succeeded.

Hooray.

"But all this," Abelard said, "happens only if Kos has undisclosed liabilities. Which he doesn't."

Bede's chair creaked.

"Not by your standards," Tara replied. "But Seril complicates things."

"Complicates doesn't sound good. I don't like complicates."

"Even though they don't share explicit contractual bonds, Kos and Seril are linked by, let's call it sentiment. Kos died last year because he tried to support Seril in her exile. To a Craftsman, that looks like an under-the-table guarantee that Kos will bail Seril out if she's in trouble. And this is a goddess who makes trouble for herself—remember, she ran off to the Wars and left Him."

Aev growled. "She fell in combat; She stood alone against murderous hordes."

"Which sounds great in a poem," Tara said, "but to a banker the important word is 'fell.' Seril takes big risks, and they don't always work out. Let's say an Alphan Securities banker wants to analyze Kos. She learns that Kos protects Seril—who tends to find Herself in sticky, fatal situations. Seril lacks assets or income. Her power's tied up in the gargoyles and in Justice, neither of which is liquid. To our banker, Seril looks like a massive undisclosed liability—Kos has given tacit backing to a volatile, costly entity. Now that people know the gargoyles are back, they're already wondering if Seril's come, too. When she's found, and she will be, we'll see our first test of the tacit guarantee. Someone will try to kill you and your people." She nodded to Aev. "If Kos defends you, an attack on him will follow soon after, through the courts."

"We do not need Kos to defend us," Aev said.

"You might. This isn't a battlefield. Your enemies won't announce themselves. They don't want a fight. They want you to die."

Nestor leaned forward in his chair. "Why are we just hearing this now?"

"You," Cardinal Bede said, "are hearing it because the time has come for you to share the uncertainty Ms. Abernathy, Aev, and I have shared for the last year."

The gargoyle nodded. "Why do you think we have kept such a low profile?"

"This is your idea of a low profile?" Nestor asked.

Aev's growl caused the easel to rattle against the stone floor.

"We don't have time for recrimination," Tara said. "We need to work together."

The Technical Cardinal frowned. "What options do we have?"

She remembered that burned paper, but she said, "At Cardinal Bede's direction, your priests have spent the last year preaching groundwork for Seril's return, which gives Her more faith to draw upon. That's good. And Aev and her people have built themselves a solid mystery cult from scant resources, based on dreams and aid in dark alleys. Much as I wish they'd taken fewer risks, they've built the foundation for a Serilite movement in Alt Coulumb. It would have worked if we had more time."

Stone wings twitched in the dark room.

"In addition to encyclical support, I have diversified our Lord," Bede said, "using commodities investment to reduce his exposure to a sudden collapse in our creditworthiness. That protects us in the short term, ensuring Lord Kos will not walk weaponless to battle, if it comes to that. Meanwhile, Ms. Abernathy has pursued options for protecting Seril Herself."

Tara recognized her cue. "Seril's lack of liquidity is Her main weakness. By attacking the gargoyles, a Craftswoman can hurt Her directly. I've spent the last year tracking Seril's treaties with old gods, without much luck. Other than Kos, most of Her partners died in the Wars, and their debts to Seril were written off in the necromantic process." That dead end had taken eight months of work. "My next step's to seek property Seril lost in the God Wars. This is a long shot: the Wars were hectic, and many Craftsmen immediately used power they seized from one god to kill another. But we might find something useful. Meanwhile, we have to ensure news of Seril's survival breaks under conditions we control. Aev's people have promised not to answer prayers. I've called for double Blacksuit patrols in the Paupers' Quarter during the next few nights. In the meantime, bring any ideas, concerns, fears, or prophecies to me first." She looked around the table. "Some of you have to run. I'm sure there are more questions. I'll stay to answer those. I know the news sounds bad. But we can win this. We will."

Nods, with determination in various shades of grim.

She'd convinced no one. But they pretended they believed her, that everything would work out for the best.

Tara hadn't expected more. She didn't quite believe herself, either.

Abelard excused himself; Aev followed. So did Cat. That left Tara, the Commissioner, and the Cardinals—and then the hard questions came.

11

Cat closed the conference chamber door, guillotining Cardinal Bede's rambling many-subclaused question before His Eminence reached a verb. The door she'd chosen led to a stone landing and a stair winding down and up. The hem of a rust-red robe disappeared around the stair's descending turn. "Abelard," she called, but he didn't stop, and she found herself alone on the landing. Or so she thought.

A stone rumble from the shadows brought her hand halfway to her badge before she recognized the voice. "I do not think he wishes company," Aev said.

"Do you guys have lurking contests or something?"

Aev stepped forward. Light chiseled her planes and angles from the black. "Why?"

"If so, you'd take the ribbon."

Aev gestured to her bare stone torso. "Where would I pin a ribbon?"

Cat looked away. "I haven't seen Abelard in a while, is all. Guess he has better things to do than talk. Tend the boilers, power the city, keep us from freezing in our beds or roasting in our towers. At least it's a distraction."

"Ms. Abernathy's claims concern you."

"It's all so far above my pay grade." Cat pointed down through the floor. "Thought we could work it out together, Abelard and me, but he hasn't been himself these last few months. Then again, I don't suppose any of us has been herself." She frowned. "Themselves? Themself?"

"It's easier to say in Stone."

Of course. What else would be easier in Stone? Poetry? Wrath? Prayer? "Why do you have your own language anyway?" Cat asked instead. "There's only like thirty of you, and you were built—made—"

"Shaped, we say, or carved. And we were not always so few. We were made of Alt Coulumb, not born of it, so the Lady gave us our own tongue. You could speak it too, if you opened your heart to Her."

"Not likely," she said, but Aev didn't rise to the bait. "How many of you were there?"

"Two hundred fifty-six, as of the eighth carving. Some fell in the Wars, and after. Some perished in exile. There is a grove in the Geistwood where many stand who gave up hope of seeing home again. They set aside the quickness of their body and sank their roots into living stone. They will not move for a turning of the world."

"Gods."

"We who hoped endured, and returned to aid a city that fears us. But now our very existence has placed our charge at risk."

"Your charge. You mean, us."

"Yes."

Cat had grown up hearing stories of Stone Men. You weren't supposed to call them that now, but cradle tales and bedtime stories cut into bone. Unnatural creatures, her grandfather said. Smoke tinted her memories of the man, scarred and weather-cracked and half blind, his voice heavy with faithful decades of cigarette ash. He told her stories of Seril's death, of her children's mad grief, of talons and blood. And today she stood, grown, in a cramped stairwell, before their leader.

Aev was beautiful—not like art was beautiful, which was fine by Cat since she lacked taste for art, but beautiful like a thing made for a purpose. Her talons were sharp, her teeth were long. How many had she killed in the Wars?

"You waited here for me," Cat said. "Why?"

"You saved us all. When we returned, we almost died at Denovo's hands, at the hands of Justice whom he warped against us. You resisted. You broke the chains that bound your soul, and stopped him. But you have avoided us in the months since."

"You're intimidating."

"We scare criminals and fools. We pose you no danger."

"I—look. I'm a straightforward gal. Tara's the one for all the"—she waved her hand in a vague circle between them. "You know, scheming and plotting. I like things I can see and punch. Kos powers Alt Coulumb, and priests tend his machines. Fine. The Blacksuits work with Justice—and Seril, now—to help people. You guys, I don't know how you fit."

"Neither do we."

Cat held a smart reply ready on her tongue, but it slithered down her throat instead to nestle cold and prickly in her chest. "What do you mean?"

"We had a place here once," she said, "but our home has changed. Now we skulk in shadows, for our presence endangers those our Lady shaped us to protect. We are servants denied service. Even the little we do, it seems, is too much. We were not made to be secret ministers. If we hide forever, what difference remains between us and the frozen ones who wait in the Geistwood grove?"

Cat looked into Aev's eyes and saw herself distorted looking back. "You have any plans for the next few hours?"

The huge head cocked to one side, and the fanged mouth compressed to a thin smile. "I intended to lurk."

"Want to come for a ride?"

12

Alt Coulumb's docks lost none of their savor at night. In the handbook of the Palatine Perfumers' Guild, the recipe goes like this: Mash a global civilization of some four billion human beings and another, say, half handful billion others into a fine paste. Pound that mash against a mile of coastline and let dry in the sun, then steep the resulting extract in fish oil and engine grease. Salt heavily with sweat and spray. Zest the ambition of a thousand tradesmen and -women and small-business owners, from the rug-crouched silver seller to the mustachioed and gaptoothed iconmonger and the clutch of tattooed young women who sold dreamdust at the docks for the Farwright Syndicate. Add three-quarters of this zest raw, then gently blowtorch the remainder to lend that brutal sour edge of hope betrayed, since some ships never come in even for those who wait daily by the docks 'til long past dusk. Round out the odor with a long list of prosaic cargo: saffron, sandalwood, and cinnamon, paper, steel, demon-haunted manufactured goods, long planks of magisterium and sheafs of synthetic dragonscale (inferior in all respects to the real thing, save only for the practical point that the synthetic variety need not be harvested from a dragon), bananas by the crate and oranges by the tube and soybeans by the ton, green bottle after green bottle of wine, and of course the flat nothing-scent of the airtight vessels made from the processed bones of eons-dead monsters in which alchemists stored their toxic earths and strange silvers. Garnish—lightly—with what the Palatine Perfumer's Guild's contributing writers describe, in a rare and generous bout of euphemism, as "effluvia."

The handbook includes a sidebar note indicating that, like most such purely descriptive recipes, the journeyman should regard this as a test of his own nasal and artistic fortitude, as well as his extraction skills. Sales, if any, will be small.

Cat gnawed the last meat from a skewer as she climbed the gang-plank from the docks to the *Kel's Bounty*. "Law on deck!" the bos'n called, and she sketched a salute to the array of not-quite-savory characters that turned to her. By day the *Bounty* was a ship like any other, mortal-crewed with sailors from throughout the known world, with a slight bias to Archipelagese. The night crew hailed from a wider range of ports of call.

Raz appeared at the upper deck's rail. "What kept you?"

"Meetings," she said.

He leapt over the rail, somersaulted, and landed light-footed on the boards. His eyes were true red in the moonlight, not the burned scab color they seemed in daytime shadows. "Anything important?"

"Probably," she said, "but it'll keep. Glad to see you aren't on fire anymore."

He wiggled his fingers. Thin scars crisscrossed his palm, tracks left by sunlight. The regrown skin was even darker than the rest of him. "There's a reason I tan. Course now I'll have to even out, or I'll get blotchy."

"Some leech you are. Isn't your guys' thing more a sort of deathly pallor? I knew girls on the club circuit who went through my salary in white pancake makeup every month."

"Dumb. Scenesters imitating form over function. Shoreland suckers in the Old World, the ones with castles, drew lines from skin to status—if you were pale, it meant you could afford people to do things for you in the day. The paler you are, the faster you burn, so if you're really pale it shows you're not scared of the peasants-with-pitchforks routine. Which is all well and good until you forget to adjust your clocks for daylight savings time, some traveler you wanted to put the moves on pulls off the window blinds at dawn, and you go up like dryer lint."

"Daylight what?"

"It's an Old World thing. Are you ready to sail?"

Her pocket watch was ticking. "Yes. Everyone's aboard?"

"Hold's packed with your creepy friends."

"Again with the creepy." She waved at the crew scuttling, skittering, and lurching around the *Kel's Bounty* deck. "What do you call these?"

"Sailors," he said, and turned from her and raised his hand. "Cast off!"

In the rigging, a woman with the legs and abdomen of a spider shouted, "Aye!"

They made good time out of port—the *Bounty*'s wind walker filled their sail with a steady breeze, and Raz took the helm. "Promise to cover for me with the pilots' guild. I don't want to end up on their bad side."

"As far as the port authority is concerned, none of this is happening."

"They don't like to be reminded some of us have been sailing this harbor since before they were born." He spun the wheel, called for depth, adjusted again. Sighted on something she couldn't see with his spyglass, collapsed it, let it dangle from his neck.

The ship swayed, and Cat almost fell, but caught herself with a lunge for the rail. "You have the edge of experience?"

"This spyglass of mine's older than most pilots on the river." He touched the symbols stamped into the bronze. "A relic of my vital days. Locals sail the harbor more often. If there's a new wreck I don't know about, if the sandbanks have shifted, if you put in port chains or kraken mines, we're in trouble."

"Trouble?"

"Can you swim?"

"In my own body, yes. If I put the Suit on, I sink."

"I'll try not to wreck us, then."

"You weren't doing that already?"

Fangs glinted in the moonlight as he grinned.

Despite Cat's misgivings about the skeleton crew, they seemed at least as competent as the mortal variety. Raz's sailors were not linked like the Blacksuits were through Justice, but they'd worked together long enough to even out the difference. A hand of bone tossed a coil of rope to the chitinous claw of a mantis-thing, who scrambled up the mast so lightly its needle-tipped feet left no tracks on the wood. The spider-woman called depth, a skeleton whose bones were half-replaced with metal checked the charts, and a raven cawed from the crow's nest.

"The *Dream* is moored," Raz said once they cleared the harbor, "just leeward of the cape. You can see her lanterns from here." There were no lights on the *Bounty*'s deck—most of the crew could see by moon and stars as if by daylight—so Cat's eyes were well-adjusted to the dark. He pointed to three small bright flickers near the ocean's face, like candle flames or stars. "That's not good," he said. "Plan was, run silent until we're alongside. We've snuffed the running lights—which, in case you ever try this on your own—"

"Without our civilian contractor?"

"Running without lights is stupid, and dangerous. Never, ever do it unless you can see at least as well at night as you can during the day, and want to sneak up on someone, and are a pirate."

"What's the problem?"

"They're past the city's no-fly zone. You see that line there, where the water's less shiny?"

"Yes."

"They'll have scouts in the sky, and any sky watch worth its salt can see in the dark. There goes our element of surprise. We can probably still catch them—but then this goes from a sneak-and-board to high-seas battle against professionals."

"Isn't that your area of expertise?"

"Part of lasting long enough to develop that expertise," he said, "has been deploying it as seldom as possible. I have people who can take out their recon if we make it to the open ocean, but we're inside the zone. Your Suits can fly, right?"

In theory. In practice, flight involved more collaboration with the Goddess than anyone on the force had managed so far. "We're not trained for aerial combat. Most officers don't even know how to make the Suit grow wings."

"No time to try like the present," he said.

"I have a better idea."

She did not exactly pray. She wasn't talking to a god—or goddess, for that matter. Just sending a message.

Keep telling yourself that.

Her own thought. Probably. Either way, she ignored it.

Waves lapped the *Bounty*'s sides, and the deck rolled gently beneath them. In the distance, wind whistled over sharp rocks.

"I'm waiting," Raz said.

He looked up as the whistle approached.

Aev fell from heaven in a granite blur and flared her wings to arrest herself one foot above the deck. She landed with a soft tick of talons on wood, but her weight still set the ship rocking.

"Can I help?" she asked.

Raz swore in a language Cat did not recognize, and removed his cap. "I think you can, at that."

13

Matt half-hoped their plan, concocted over drinks at lunch—their scheme, to be honest—would end as so many others did, in a third (or fourth) round of beers and someone's finally remembering they all had shops to open come morning. Public displays of civic fervor were no fit pastimes for small business owners. Leave adventures to kids dumb as they'd once been, a new crop of which the Quarter sprouted every year and ate faster.

But Corbin Rafferty did not calm. The idea stuck in his mind like a fishhook in the lip, and he would not stop wriggling long enough to let others pry it out. He took to the street, and Matt followed.

Determination straightened Corbin's weaving path. He visited taprooms and tea shops whose owners he knew, and regaled them with his plan. He met customers on sidewalks and outside construction sites and playing ball on public courts, and in each venue he proclaimed: I'll bring the Stone Men for you all to see. Come to the market tonight at nine. The message took them as far as Hot Town before Matt noticed the Crier following them, a bow-shouldered man in guild orange. He dropped into a convenience store, waited for the Crier to pass, then stepped out behind him.

"You want something."

The Crier spun and stumbled and caught himself on cracked pavement. He had to look a long way up to meet Matt's eyes. "Just a story."

"You have the story already."

"One witness is nice; twenty would be better. If your friend—or his daughter—calls the Stone Men, and they come, that's news."

"Maybe they won't show."

"That's news, too."

"Come tonight, then," he said. "Stop following us."

Matt didn't wait for the Crier's answer—walked past him, instead, to join Rafferty, who was haranguing a demolition guy, regular customer of Matt's, a big round man who bought a dozen eggs every other morning. Every day Matt expected to learn the demo guy's heart had burst. Maybe he didn't eat all the eggs himself.

Rafferty burned out around four in the afternoon beside a bratwurst stand—sat down on a dirty bench and leaned over his knees, head bobbing. Carriage wheels rattled over uneven cobblestones. Matt set a hand on Rafferty's back, but the man didn't react. Matt didn't worry. Rafferty's flare-ups came and went like heavy traffic down a poorly paved street, leaving torn ground and deep holes behind.

After a while Rafferty looked up, staring through his stringy hair. "You're still here."

"Maybe you shouldn't do this, Corbin."

"I have to show them."

"Ellen didn't sound happy about it. She sounded scared."

Rafferty's head jerked around. All weakness left him. He looked like he did before he threw a punch. "What are you saying?"

"Nothing. Come on, Corbin. Let's get you home."

He half-carried Rafferty to his street, in spite of the stares of stroller-pushing moms and dads, and jeering kids on stoops who should have been in school. The man insisted on walking the last half block to his building and letting himself inside. Matt watched, then went home himself, found Donna working over a ledger she'd brought from the office. The kids were still at school. He hugged her from behind and thought about Rafferty's wife and the ruin the man had made of himself in the three years since her loss.

"You smell of beer," Donna said, but she kissed him back anyway, then shoved him off. "Shower. Sleep."

He lost the rest of the day to fitful dreams of stone teeth and nails, and the tension in the Rafferty girls, like they were still pools about to freeze. He tried to open his mouth, but he had no mouth. He woke at sunset, scoured sober, with a bad taste on his tongue like a small furry thing had died there.

When he reached the market, he had to push through a crowd—unfamiliar folks for the most part, strangers called by strangers called by friends—to the clearing at the center, a bare twenty-foot circle around a ghostlight lantern that underlit the crowd's faces green, made them seem ghoulish. The brownstones around the market square stared down on them all, silhouettes in their windows. Uptown nobs watching the little people's show. The rent here had been too high for normal folks for years. Maybe these posh types had already sent rats to the Blacksuits—pardon me, there's a disturbance in the market square, perhaps you could come inquire.

Rafferty and his daughters stood in the circle's center, the girls on the dais where Criers sang their news, Rafferty pacing before them. He wore a red coat and walked with the swagger stick he sometimes carried. Uncombed hair fountained from his scalp.

The others stood around the inner edge of the circle, uncomfortable. "I thought you'd keep him out of trouble," Sandy said when Matt reached her.

"I did," he said, knowing he hadn't.

A Crier stood across the circle from Matt and Sandy—a woman wearing a narrow-brimmed hat and a long coat, watching.

Rafferty began without preamble. "We all heard the news. Stone Men are snouting into our business, breaking our laws, preaching false gods." Uncertain nods. "And the Blacksuits do nothing. They make like nothing's happened. I will show you the truth. My daughters have seen the Stone Men. My Ellen will call them. The Stone Men will come, and we'll all see. Blacksuits can't ignore that."

"What," someone called from the crowd, "if they don't come?"

"Then the Criers are lying, and my girl is. But she's not." Ellen tensed so much at that she might have been a mannequin. How had Corbin brought them here? Wheedling? Promising? Shouting? He didn't hit them, Matt thought. Hoped.

"We can't let him do this," Sandy said. "With the girls."

"The girls said yes."

"That was bullshit at lunch, Matt, and it still is. They're terrified. They can't say no to him. You saw it. I thought you'd talk him down this afternoon."

"I didn't hear you try."

"He doesn't listen to me."

"Nothing for it now."

"Nothing but to hope this works," she said. "With so many people watching, he can't back down if it doesn't."

Rafferty paced around the lantern, casting shadows.

"Well, then," he told Ellen. "Go on. Pray."

14

Tara slipped into the boiler room of the Church of Kos and landed soundless in shadows. Enormous metal tanks, basins, and pipes swelled in angry twilight to fill the vast chamber. Gauges ticked up. Valves opened and closed. Hydraulic fluid surged through pipes. Steam hissed. Far away, a great gear wound and wound. She smelled copper and concrete and burned air, which did not bother her. She felt the presence of a god, which did.

"Abelard?"

She heard footsteps behind a huge compression tank and moved toward them. The red and the rhythm and the smell reminded her of walking through a giant heart, and the impression was not far from truth. These boilers and generators and coils translated Kos Everburning's heat into the power on which his people relied. She understood the dynamics of their faith, but its machines were alien to her. Growing up in the country, a girl awed by tales of the urban horrors her grandparents fled to live as tillers of soil, she'd known no device more complex than farm equipment. When she ran away from home to seek those horrors herself, she found teachers who preferred sorcery to mechanism. Generators and pipes remained strange to her. In a way, she was trespassing now more than she had the year before, when she walked on the flesh of the dead god himself.

He hadn't been dead, of course. Which was part of their current problem.

Rounding the tank, she saw more pipes, more valves, more pulleys and belts and shifting gears, oil-slick surfaces none of which had the decency to keep still and let her find the man she sought.

She peered beneath the physical world. All this metal was quite simple on the level of Craftwork: tricks to convert energy from one form or vector to another. To her gaze the machines pulsed in heartbeat time, and there, in a nook ten feet off the ground, nestled between a wall and a steam tank, was a man's spinning soul.

"There you are."

"Can anyone hide from you?" His voice echoed.

"Not like that," she said. A ladder led up to his nook, concealed behind a bundle of thin pipes. The rungs were warm. "Kos could hide you if you asked; He couldn't do the same for me, because of my glyphs."

"No hide-and-go-seek for necromancers."

"Oh, we play. We hide in bargains and loopholes and fine print." Tara crested the ladder and pulled herself into the niche between tank and wall. Abelard sat within, legs curled against his chest, arms crossed on his knees. Beneath him lay a thin pallet, and across from him a small altar. Tara tested the floor for dust, and sat. "You sleep here?"

"Sometimes," he said. "How do you sleep?"

"Well," she replied. "On my back."

"I mean, you see things with your eyes closed."

"So do you. Light filters through the lids, creates patterns, that warm pink edge to darkness. You can't turn off your skin, can't close your ears, but you sleep fine."

"Not these days," he said.

"Why did you leave the meeting?"

"Did I miss much?"

Here in the half-lit dark, she felt like she could say anything. "Same story as ever. Don't like the news? Question the bearer."

"I'm sorry."

"It could be worse. Sometimes clients play dumb—they go to you for expertise, then argue with your conclusions. Back in Edgemont I hung out my shingle and dealt small-time magic, before Ms. K found me. You know what phrase I learned to hate more than any other? *How bad can it be?*" She leaned her head against the cool rock. Hair bunched and coiled against her skull. "You should have stayed. You could have helped them understand."

"Cardinal Bede knows more about bond markets than anyone else in the church; Cardinal Nestor's a wise Technician. I'm . . . me."

"You kept your God alive when everyone gave him up for dead. You kept faith when there was no chance your faith would be rewarded. Those old men don't know what that was like. What you did. What you almost lost."

"I died, Tara. Let's not put too fine a point on it."

"I was getting to that," she said. "Let me build up a rhythm."

He tapped cigarette ash onto the tray atop his little altar. "The Council of Cardinals wanted to canonize me. There was a whisper campaign around the solstice."

"Saint Abelard. You'd fit right in with the gaunt-faced fossils in the murals."

"The Cardinals are afraid—they think I'll undermine them by going directly to God. And I fear them, too. Cardinal Gustave was a pillar of strength, and he betrayed us all. Do you think he could have done that without help?"

The metal heart throbbed around them.

"If it's any consolation," she said, "conspiracies don't tend to be the massive webs you'd imagine from mystery plays and adventure novels. More often you have a few people willing to do bad things to get results, and a few more who look the other way while everything stays quiet. That's what happened to me back at the Hidden Schools. Professor Denovo had been binding wills, stealing minds, for years. But he was famous, and his lab produced groundbreaking results, so people looked away. They didn't ask. They didn't even whisper. And when my friend Daphne and I started to work with him, we were so excited we didn't realize the danger until it was too late." She waited, and listened to gears.

"What happened?" he asked after a while. His voice sounded flat and small.

"She broke. Wrung out from the inside. They sent her home co-matose. The shock freed me. I destroyed Denovo's lab in revenge, and got myself graduated with extreme prejudice, and Ms. K found me, and you know the rest." She envied the priests their smoke, some-times. Cigarettes gave you something to do with your heart: you concentrated everything you should be feeling to an ember and let it burn. "Nobody in your church had anything to gain by doubting the official story about Seril. That's all Gustave needed. That's why you're important, why you should be at that table, asking questions Nestor and Bede are too hidebound to ask."

He wasn't looking at her.

"Dammit," she said, "I'm trying to help," and realized when he froze that she'd let too much anger out. "Sorry. It's not like I have some immense fund of experience and wisdom to draw on. I lived on the road longer than I've been a professional Craftswoman. You think the Cardinals distrust you, gods, would you like to borrow my skin for a while? I'm a Craftswoman, and I'm young, and I've ironed the accent out of my voice but they still know I come from yokel country. I can do things they can't, and that's all I have over them: their crazy atavistic fear of people who can raise the dead and carve their names into the moon. So they listen to me. But I need help. I can't do this alone."

The words burst from her like rust water from a tap, rough and fast and without warning. They left a bitter taste in her mouth.

Abelard whispered something she couldn't hear over the noise of the boiler room and her own heartbeat.

"What?"

"I'm sorry. I hadn't thought. This is hard for you, and you're a long way from home."

"That's not what you said."

He stared at the tip of his cigarette. Then he turned to her. The darkness made his face a mask, and she remembered those mosaic saints twisted by the tortures that earned their place in heaven. "I said, I don't think I trust God anymore."

She waited.

"I carried Him inside me for three days and didn't notice, even when He worked miracles through me."

"Kos hid himself. And he was only half-conscious, or less, the whole time. Mostly dead, and scared for the shreds of life that remained to him."

"Did He have so little faith as to doubt He could turn to me in His need? Did He fear I would refuse Him? Gustave fell from pride—he did not hear the Lord's will. Did Kos doubt my faith?"

"No."

"You don't know that."

"Ask him, then. He's your god."

"Would He tell me the truth?" Abelard raised his hand, and flames surrounded it. Tara flinched from the sudden light and heat.

"How long have you been able to do that?"

Abelard waved away the fire. "He's given me gifts. I don't know if the truth is one of them."

"Trust him," she said. "He's not that bad, as gods go. And he needs your help. So do I."

"When you came to Alt Coulumb, I had years of novitiate left, decades to grow in faith before anyone asked me to make big decisions."

"And by all rights I should be a junior associate somewhere, making bank, not sleeping, paying down my student loans, following orders like a golem all day. That's not how it worked out. I don't mind, except when I look at my account balance. But we're here together. We can do this."

"Maybe."

"Abelard, you did the right thing under pressure. You will again."

"I wish I had your confidence."

"I wish I had your student loans."

"I don't have student loans."

"Right."

Either he didn't get the joke, or didn't think it was funny. He sat beside her, limp. She wished she could reach inside his skin, snatch him from whatever mental cavern he'd chosen to hide within, and pull him free. "Look. We both stumbled into weird spaces in our careers. People need things from us we're not sure we can give. Doubt's healthy. But we can't let it cripple us."

"Why not?"

The question took her aback. She'd never considered letting herself fail before—the struggle's difficulty always seemed proof of its value. "If we do, they win: the Cardinals who wonder why you're at the table, or I am. The little gnome in your skull who says you shouldn't be here, and when you try and fail it laughs and says, 'See? You never should have tried at all.' "

"He's in your head too?"

"Inside everyone's, I think."

"You don't let on."

"Mine's loud enough I got deaf to the little bastard a while ago."

She looked down at her hands, and over at his, and before she could think better of it she laid her left on his right. Abelard was skin and gristle and bone. Not fit for roasting, Ma would have said. "The church will need a saint before this is over. It'll need you. And I might, too." Gods and demons, but that last felt hard to say—like peeling a hangnail into blood. What diagnosis would a headshrinker make of a woman who found admitting weakness less terrifying than necromantic war?

His hand stayed limp under hers. "I'll try," he said, and smiled weakly.

She hoped her disappointment didn't show. "Good."

She'd reached the ladder down before he spoke again. "We can win this, can't we?"

"Sure," she said, covering the lie.

15

Cat dove from the *Bounty* in the dark.

She never liked swimming. She liked it less in the ocean, and even less at night, but duty and preference were rare bedfellows. Not even bedfellows, she thought as the black water closed over her. They'd had one bitter night when duty and honor were on a break and preference was too drunk to remember she hated duty's smirk and the way he treated waiters.

How could you not like swimming? was one of those questions fellow gym rats asked, with a precious emphasis on the last word. So calming, so rhythmic. Good for your back and blood pressure. Cat didn't like calm, and she distrusted rhythm. More to the point, the Suit sank, an after-effect of its connection to the gargoyles and their goddess: she wasn't made of stone, but the Suit convinced the world she was. Dive Suited and you'd tumble to the seafloor, which admittedly helped when the time came to dredge Alt Coulumb's harbor.

So if you were a Blacksuit and knew how to swim (which Cat did, because, dammit, instinctive hatred for an activity was just the world's way of challenging you to master it), you sometimes ended up doing things like this: swimming un-Suited, read weak, read human, leading a team toward an anchored ship after dark, with—how deep was the water here, a few hundred feet?—anyway *too much* water underneath you, and Lord Kos alone knew what monsters below, star kraken and bloodwhales and saltwater crocs. She surfaced, gulping air.

The ship's swelling sides blocked out the stars. Moonlight glinted off the black paint that named her *Demon's Dream*. Cat turned onto her back to watch the bowsprit figure pass overhead: crystal carved into a woman's shape. The rest of Cat's team followed her, dark V's against dark water.

The ship rocked as she slipped along its starboard side. Waves lapped barnacled boards. Anchor chain links rasped. She stopped near the chain, touched the wet hull, and triggered her climbing bracelets. Her hands burned as if she'd rubbed them hard against rubber, and when she touched the hull, her fingers stuck. She pulled herself out of the water and triggered her anklets; her toes clung to slick planks. Her team followed, smooth and slow. Their wetsuits wept themselves dry as they climbed.

Strange to feel safer clinging by magic to a pirate ship's hull than swimming out of sight beneath.

She paused below the railing, counted footfalls, and timed the operation.

Ten sailors on deck, two more than Raz expected. Varg's delay might well make her XO paranoid. Others would be asleep, many on deck on such a warm night. Good thing Raz's team had done this before.

She heard creaking sheets an instant before the watch called: "Sail approaching off the port bow!" Raz ran dark, not invisible.

Boots drumrolled on deck: eight pairs, she thought, approached the port rail. Even the two that remained starboard turned to watch. Sergeant Lee, beside her, pointed up. She shook her head and waited for the signal.

"*Kel's Bounty*," came Raz's voice, very near. "Raz Pelham here, bearing a message from Captain Varg."

"She's late."

"Problems landward. I have a letter from her, sealed. Permission to come aboard?"

"Why run up on us dark like that?"

"You want the coast guard to see us both? Then I'll light my lanterns."

"Send the letter over."

Come on, she thought, give the cue. You've made your distraction; we can take it from here.

"Varg told me to deliver it in person."

"She have anything else to say?"

"Just that."

"You won't set foot on this ship. Send the message over, if message you have."

"Get your first mate down here so I can talk this out with him."

Rustling on deck—sleeping sailors rising. Shit. They'd hoped to take the *Dream* without alarm, in case they had Craftsmen or other emergency precautions. Wake too many of the deck crew and there'd be no way to distract them all. Stop this now.

She triggered the Suit. Ice slammed through her veins, and a silverblack hand seized her heart. In a single pull she vaulted the rail, landed soundless on deck, choked out the first sentry in two heartbeats and the second sentry in two more. The rest of her team landed with a rainfall patter, and six Blacksuits stood aboard the *Dream*, unnoticed—at least, that was the plan.

"Blacksuits!" someone cried.

A man stood on the quarterdeck, pipe in hand, beside a canvas chair. She'd counted boots and hadn't counted him, because he wasn't walking. Stupid. Justice's conclusions rushed back into her along the quicksilver link: Raz's reluctance to give the signal, trying to attract the lookout's—the first mate's—attention. She didn't swear, but wanted to.

Didn't freeze, either. Cat sprinted to the stairs, leapt up, vaulted over, struck the man with the pipe so hard he spun first, then fell. She caught him before he hit the deck, not gently.

Too late, too late; her team charged the men at the port rail—five on eight, trivial for Blacksuits, but the sailors asleep on the forecastle were waking. They rolled to their feet and drew weapons whose edges wept with a sickening enchanted light.

Lee hit the inquisitive watchman first, and hard—threw him over the railing. He screamed when he fell, which didn't help. *Keep it quiet,* thought all the Suits at once, as they took out the remaining sentries. But by this time the forecastle was awake, and cabin doors burst open, disgorging more of the *Dream*'s armed and angry crew.

Cat dived into battle. The man in the lead, a tall Iskari with thick braids and a curved cutlass, swung; she blocked his blade with her forearm and was not cut, but nevertheless it stung, and numbness took her arm. Not fast enough. She butted him in the face with her forehead, and he fell.

Another blade swept toward her. She dodged, dancing over the Iskari's fallen body, but stumbled into a third sailor, who tried to grab her arm. He couldn't hold her but slowed her down enough that the next cutlass almost caught her in the side. She swung the man who'd grabbed her around into the second sailor. He hit hard and let her go.

She fought through a mess of bodies and swinging blades that spread numbing haze where they cut. Grapnels arced from *Bounty*'s deck to the rails of *Dream*, and Raz's people scuttled across like evil acrobats: skeletons and leeches, a snakeling corkscrewing along steel cable to wreathe a sentry in the cords of its armored body. Where Blacksuits struck, Varg's sailors fell; Raz's people joined the fray, tangling swords with their rib cages, forcing living sailors screaming to the deck. Raz leapt from ship to ship and laid about himself with cutlass and fierce fanged smile, dueling three sailors at once.

On the forecastle, a woman leveled a crossbow at his exposed back.

A year ago, Cat would have been submerged entirely in the Suit, barely conscious, her body a higher power's puppet. No longer. She was herself enough to seize control.

The Suit said no. She was holding down half the forecastle by herself, pinballing from pirate to pirate; she risked letting them regroup, had to trust Raz to evade the shot, or the sailor to miss.

Cat said yes. She forced divinely wrought muscles to obey her, tore free of the scrum, and vaulted into the sailor's line of fire. The quarrel crackled through the air, and Cat caught it in her hand.

Her skin burned even through the Suit. Lightning discharge blanked her. She slammed to deck planks, stunned. Saw Raz turn, shocked—then spin back around as a sword raked his side and blood stained his shirt. Cat, struggling to regain her feet, saw one of the sailors she had been fighting sprint toward the gong at the bow, grab its hammer, and strike.

The gong made no sound.

Nor did anything else. Silence covered the deck.

She tried to rise but could not. An enormous weight pressed her down; her Suit strained and surged, and with tremendous effort she forced herself to stand, every movement trembling at the max-rep edge of her enhanced strength. The gong's silence pealed through her. Raz sunk to one knee. Blacksuits and sailors and skeletons alike lay prone.

The captain's cabin opened, and a figure of knives and wheels emerged. Clawed feet cut into deck wood, and the lenses within its eyes slipped from point to point of focus. Scalpels unfolded from its fingers, and springs turned wheels within the hollow of its chest.

Golem, Cat thought, though she had never seen a golem like this before—a mouthless work of art, moving delicately despite this weight that pressed upon them all. Maybe it was immune, or so strong it did not feel the pressure. It approached Raz and bent over him. Scalpels clicked into place. Its head turned sideways, considering how best to cut. Internal mechanisms ticked through the artificial quiet, as if she held a watch to her ear. The ships' lanterns glinted off its blades as they slid, so gently, along Raz's jaw.

Then Aev fell out of the sky on top of it.

Knives blunted and thin metal limbs snapped beneath a ton of high-velocity gargoyle. Gears and springs and shattered glass flew out in all directions. The deck stove in beneath her feet. Lightning danced from broken planks, and the strange weight that bound Cat to the wood vanished. She rose, as did the other Blacksuits; Raz and the crew of *Bounty* and *Dream* took longer to recover.

The golem's skull rolled from its shattered body. Aev looked down at it, quizzical, then crushed it to dust with her heel. A shadow rose screaming from the metal husk, and faded on the wind.

What took you so long? Cat asked.

Aev pointed up with one clawed finger. Cat looked, saw nothing, then heard a whisper of wind. A huge bat-winged creature fell to splash between the two ships. It lay faceup in the water, twitching in its swoon.

"Busy," Aev said.

They secured the ship in minutes. *Dream's* remaining crew surrendered; Blacksuits moved through their ranks, taking names and faces for prosecution. Raz's crew spidered up the rigging to prepare the *Dream* for sailing into port.

"Do you feel useful now?" she asked Aev after the worst was done.

"I enjoyed this," the gargoyle replied. "But what was our purpose here? Helping pirates take a merchant ship?"

"Follow me," Cat said, and led her down below.

The gargoyle could not use the ladder—too heavy—so she jumped into the hold, splintering more timber when she landed. The ship rocked, and Cat steadied herself on the wall. Belowdecks the *Dream* smelled foul, animal stink mixed with tar and pine. She worked fore past wine barrels and bales of cloth and crates marked for Iskar and the Schwarzwald. A black wall closed off the forward hold; the wall had a single door without handle or visible lock save for a shimmering Craft circle.

"We've suspected Varg of zombie trading for a while, but without proof we had no excuse to search the ship." They'd taken an amulet from Varg's coat that afternoon, and she drew it from her belt pouch now. "But she reached out to a dreamglass supplier in Alt Coulumb this time, and dreamglass is illegal in the city, so." The seven-pointed star on the amulet's face matched the symbol at the Craft circle's center; she applied the one to the other, twisted, and the door creaked open. Chill wind fogged her breath. "Here you go."

Aev entered the cold, dark room. Cat could barely see the hold's contents over the swell of her wings and back, which was just as well; it wasn't a good sight. "They're shipping bodies."

"Those people are still alive, just suspended." Frost crisped and blued the bodies' skin. Looking at them tightened cords in Cat's chest. She slid past Aev into the hold and touched a sleeping woman's shoulder. The flesh was softer than if she were frozen. A hundred, perhaps, lay on racks. When Cat drew back her hand, it was chilled beyond her blood's power to warm.

"Who would let this happen?"

"Let doesn't have much to do with it," she said. "They're indentured, people who've mortgaged themselves away, suspended their own wills while the body works to repay their debt. It's cheaper than raising a corpse, if you believe that. Dead stuff decays, you know. These people live without any choice but to do what their contract holder tells them, until the indenture's done."

"Slaves," Aev said.

"Zombies. Craftwork isn't supposed to let people become property, but there are ways to treat the one like the other if you're a sick kind of clever, and no one catches you. Which is why people like Varg deal dreamglass: every price is a negotiation, and nothing skews negotiations like addiction. You hook people, then raise the loan rates until indenture's their only option. And if they don't have the resources to hire a good Craftswoman, the indenture deal can be pretty bad."

"This is allowed?"

"Not in our city," she said. She didn't say, *but we can only stop it when we find it* or *but who knows how people make the fortunes they invest with us* or *but you won't find one port in the world this business doesn't pass through.* Aev's claws tightened on the doorjamb, leaving deep grooves in the wood. "Come on. Let's get up top."

Raz met her on deck with a blanket for her shoulders. She accepted it with a nod and stood shivering by the wheel for reasons that had nothing to do with the night air.

"More down there than we thought," Cat said. "I bet Tara can wake them."

"We'll figure something out," he said. And then: "That was a brave dumb thing you did, catching the bolt for me."

"I saved your life. Maybe."

"I'm not exactly alive. And the golem could have killed us all if not for Aev."

"And I brought her along. So, you're welcome."

"You should have let her take the shot, I mean, instead of letting the sailor reach the gong."

"The Suit agreed with you, for what it's worth."

If he understood, he didn't acknowledge it.

Aev joined them, and faced homeward toward the horizon candelabra of Alt Coulumb. Her lips peeled back to bare teeth, but no sound escaped her throat.

"Something wrong?"

"The city," she said. "I am too late."

"What do you mean?" Cat asked. But before Aev could answer, the moon opened.

16

Ellen did not pray at first. She stood shadowed by lamplight, before her father and the market square crowd. Her left hand closed white-knuckled around her right. She looked back at her sisters; Hannah turned away. Claire did not, but Ellen avoided her older sister's gaze as if there was fire in it.

Matt read that fire: if Ellen had not spoken at lunch, she would not be here now.

Whispers rippled from the clearing to the crowd's edge and back. The Crier took notes.

By Matt's side Sandy stood silent, tense. What should he do now, with all these people watching and Rafferty pacing, his high color deepening to purple?

"Ellen," Rafferty repeated, in a tone of voice Matt could tell he thought was kind. "Pray. If you've told the truth." Which even Matt could tell was not a choice between two roads so much as the choice between a devil and a cliff.

Ellen's head bobbed. The first time she tried to speak no words came out, but on the second they emerged: *"Mother, hear me—"* the prayer the Criers sang this morning, its words made eager by her fear.

She watched her father while she spoke, as if the man was a crumbling wall that might collapse on her at any moment. She cut her finger with a knife from her belt. Blood welled to fall on stone.

No noise dared intrude. People must have breathed, hells, Matt must have breathed himself, but he only heard the splash.

A loud whip crack split the night, and he jumped. A hundred eyes darted skyward at once, toward the stars and moon. No winged shape passed overhead, no shadow rose from the rooftops. Shifting wind had snapped the flag on the market's flagpole. Matt laughed nervously, and others joined him.

Sandy held herself tense as a watch spring. The Rafferty girls did not laugh, either. Hannah and Claire watched Ellen, and Ellen stared at their father, and Corbin Rafferty was silent and still and grim.

He raked the circled crowd with his regard. The blotched colors of his face merged and deepened. "Don't you laugh at my girl. She said she saw the Stone Man. She said it came, and it came." He swung back to Ellen. "Go on. Call it. Now."

She gave no answer. Whatever she willed against him when she drew her knife, whatever doom she hoped to call down from the skies, it had not fallen.

"She made the whole thing up," a man shouted outside the circle. Matt didn't recognize the voice, or else he would have made the owner regret speaking. "She's cocked, Rafferty."

"You call my girl a liar?" Corbin's voice low and dangerous now, as Matt had seen him crouch in bar fights. "Pray, Ellen."

She lowered her head. Rafferty clutched his stick in a strangler's grip.

Before he could do anything, Sandy spoke. "Corbin, she's telling the truth."

"Of course she is."

The Crier kept writing. Matt wanted to break the woman's pencil.

Sandy looked like she'd just torn off a bandage over a burn. "Look, I heard the same voice as Ellen, in my dreams. Most women in the Quarter have. But do you think this works like Craft, you just wave your hands and make things happen? The Stone Men didn't come for a prayer, they came because your girls needed them. It's wrong to draw them out like this."

"The Stone Men don't get to come into my family whenever they think it's right. They don't own our city."

He roared that last, and Ellen flinched.

"You think," Sandy said, "maybe they're cutting in on your business?"

"What the hells is that supposed to mean?"

"You scared Ellen might call the Stone Men down on you someday?"

Rafferty stopped as if someone had nailed his feet to the ground. Only his head turned toward Sandy. "What did you say?"

"I said it's disgraceful the way you treat those girls, shout them scared of their own damn shadows." She stepped into the open space, toward him. "I say you're scared they might call the Stone Men on you. I say stop this now and let these people go home."

"I did this for us."

"You do everything for you, Corbin. Let it go."

Corbin Rafferty's eyes went wide as an angry horse's, and showed as much white, and he grew very still. Folk at the crowd's edge turned away.

Rafferty's shoulders slumped.

Sandy relaxed, too. But the girls did not, and neither did Matt, because he'd seen Corbin Rafferty drunk, had seen him fight, and knew his tell: that moment of slack before he moved snake-quick with a bottle or a nearby chair. Or with that cane, which he swung up and around, toward Sandy—

But the cane never fell, because Matt ran forward and grabbed Rafferty's arm. Rafferty twisted fast and vicious, pulled free, and struck Matt in the side of the head. He stumbled back, ears ringing and wetness on his temple and his cheek. Matt smelled Corbin's whiskey, saw his white teeth flash as the cane came down; he put his hand in its way, but the cane knocked down his arm, then struck the side of his head. Matt barreled forward. His shoulder took Rafferty in the stomach but the man squirmed like a hooked eel and Matt couldn't hold him. The audience roared and Sandy joined the fray and somewhere a large beast or a small man snarled, and Ellen's prayer rolled on like a river, or else that was the blood throbbing in his, Matt's, ears.

There came a crash and a splintering sound, followed by a hush.

Even the Crier's pencil stopped scratching.

Matt forced himself to his feet.

The top half of Rafferty's stick lay broken on the ground. The man himself had drawn back, hunched around his center, clutching the remnants of the cane. Sandy wasn't bleeding. The girls were safe.

A Stone Man confronted Corbin Rafferty.

He did not resemble the monsters of Matt's imagination or his father's stories. The Stone Man was thinner than Matt expected, carved with lean muscle like a runner or dancer. His face was narrow and short muzzled with a bird's quizzical expression, and his wings were slender and long. Maybe their kind came in as many shapes as people.

"Shale!" Ellen sounded happy for the first time in the years Matt had known her.

Rafferty recoiled. One crooked accusing finger stabbed toward the statue. "There! You see. They sneak around our city, taking what's ours!"

The gargoyle's—Shale's—expression didn't change like a normal person's. It shifted, like windblown sand. "We take nothing," he said. "We help."

"We don't need your help."

"If someone asks," the gargoyle said, gentle as a footfall in an empty church, "should I refuse?"

Rafferty spun from the gargoyle, to Matt, to Sandy, to Ellen. Whatever he sought from them he didn't find, because he revolved on Shale again, still holding the broken cane.

Then he ran toward the gargoyle and stabbed his chest with the splintered end of his stick. Matt tensed, waiting for claws to wet with blood.

The gargoyle took Rafferty by the shoulders.

The moon came out.

Before, the moon had been a slender curve. No longer. An orb hung overhead, and there was a face within it Matt recognized from a distant past that never was, and since it never was, never passed. Shadows failed. Silver flame quickened within paving stones.

Alt Coulumb lived. There was a Lady in it, and She knew them.

Matt was not a religious man—he sacrificed on time and paid little heed to the rest—but this, he thought, must be how the faithful felt: seen all at once in timeless light.

There was no source to this light, but Corbin Rafferty stood at its center, transfixed, reflected on himself in that moonlit time.

The moon closed.

Corbin's knees buckled and he fell.

Clocks started again, and hearts. Blood wept from the wound on Matt's face.

Matt thought the gargoyle was as shocked as anyone, and awed, though he covered it fast. "Blacksuits are coming," he said to them all but mostly to Ellen. "This is their place. I must go."

He left in a wave of wings. Sandy limped to Matt and touched the skin around his wound; her fingers stung. The girls watched, quiet, still, as Corbin Rafferty wept.

The gargoyle was right. Soon the Blacksuits came.

And the Crier wrote the whole thing down.

17

Tara collapsed on her walk home.

She'd been turning the Seril problem over in her mind—gods and goddesses, faith and credit, debt and repayment and Abelard's despair and the gargoyles atop their ruined tower. Swirled round with sharp-toothed dilemmas, she marched past the shadow people who drifted down the sidewalk toward home or gym or bar. A beggar held out a cup and she tossed him a coin with a few thaums of soul inside. Might as well be kind while she could afford it. Soon none of them might have the luxury of generosity.

The man thanked her with a wave of a soot-caked hand as she swept past. Strings of curses ran together inside her skull. Streetlights cast bright puddles on the pavement.

Brighter than usual, in fact, and of a different color too, as of molten silver. Far off, a giant struck a mountain with a hammer in heartbeat time. She stumbled. Eyes closed, she searched the lightning-lit world of Craft for the source of her sudden weakness, but saw nothing—and beneath the nothing, a tide. Her knees buckled, and she fell beyond herself into a sea of churning light whose waves sang a chord no choir could have matched. And she saw—

The market square, unfamiliar faces. Matthew Adorne, bleeding. The fierce man from the produce stall wept beneath a moon that was also a face she knew—mother and tiger at once. And Shale stood before them both, Shale overshadowed by his Goddess, Shale the clawed vector for a Lady who refused to hide.

Something soft struck her whole body at once, as if she'd fallen onto a featherbed from a height.

Rough fingers touched her cheek. Her vision focused and refocused until it carved the beggar from the moonlight haze. The lines of his face mapped a territory of confusion and concern. "Miss?"

"I'm fine," she said, and realized she was lying on the sidewalk, staring up at the moon. When she tried to stand, the world spun sideways.

"You fell." His breath smelled harsh and there was liquor in it.

She took quick inventory: skirt and stocking torn by impact, jacket dusted with road, a scrape on her cheek. Unsteady sitting, and more unsteady rising. Her soul, that was the problem: her soul ebbed out, a few hundred thaums gone, like leaves into a fire. "Did you feel that?"

"What?"

"Nothing. Thank you." She pushed a few more thaums into his hand, but he forced them back.

"You need help."

"Which way to Market Square?"

"Left at Bleeker," he said, "but the stalls are closed."

She could not run, but after she killed the pain receptors in her ankle, she forced herself to a brisk walk.

By the time she reached the market, there was little left to see— only a crowd around the Crier's dais, and there, interviewing a young dark-skinned couple whose body language screamed "traumatized onlookers," Gavriel Jones.

"Excuse me," Tara said to the couple, politely as she could manage, then grabbed Jones's trench coat and pulled her aside. "We need a moment."

"Ms. Abernathy. Care to comment on tonight's events?"

"What did you do?"

"I don't *do*." Jones raised her hands. She still held her notebook. "I came for a color piece, reactions to this morning's story. Are you okay?"

"Let me see that." She tried to grab the notebook, but Jones hid it behind her back.

"You'll hear everything in the dawn edition."

"Give me a preview. Please."

"Another gargoyle in the open, and a genuine miracle. I've never seen a better prompt for poetry."

"Don't sing this," she said. "It's not what it looks like."

Jones looked at Tara as if she'd grown a second head.

"You don't know the full story."

"Are you implying, on the record, that there is a full story for me to know?"

"Do not test me, Jones. I might bring you back to life just to kill you again."

"You use that line on all the girls?" Jones straightened her coat and stuck her pencil behind her ear. "We have gargoyles on the roof-tops and a goddess in our sky. A goddess who's supposed to be dead. What right do I have to keep this secret?"

"There's more at risk than you know."

"Fill me in."

"I can't."

"Typical Craftswoman," she said. "Force a few dead gods to dance for you, all of a sudden you think you know what's best for everyone. No trust in people."

Trust, the moon whispered in her ear.

"Don't give me that," Tara said. "You say you care about people, but you don't help. You just watch them fall and write about it."

"That's my job. I saw a fight, I saw a gargoyle, I saw a miracle. You want me to help? Where were you? Where were the Blacksuits?"

"You choose what to watch." She reined her voice before it rose to a shout. "You choose what to say."

"And you choose what to show me. You know exactly what's going on here. You've known since the beginning. When the church hides, I go digging. And this is the second time you've tried to shut down my story." The couple whose interview Tara interrupted shifted behind Jones, on the verge of leaving. Jones held a hand up to Tara and turned back to them with an easy smile. "Just a sec, sorry." The couple didn't seem happy, but they didn't leave either. "We're done, Ms. Abernathy. Unless you have something you want to tell me."

Tara had summoned dead things to walk, ridden lightning; she knew the seventy-seven names of Professor Halcyon. There were ways to deal with this damn Crier, full of smug certainty. She could seize Jones's mind. Wouldn't be that hard—tell a story to bring the woman in, lower her defenses so Tara's Craft could take hold. She'd done it before.

As it had been done to her.

So easy.

Tara cursed the teachers who gave her options that were always easy, but never right.

"Report the gargoyles," she said. "Hold off on the rest, the miracle, and I'll give you an exclusive like you won't believe."

"When?"

"Two days," she said. "Sooner, I hope. I need to make arrangements."

Jones's face betrayed little. "Deal. But this better be big."

"Trust me."

18

Tara did not look at the moon while she stormed the three blocks to her apartment. The moon didn't seem to care. She slammed her front door open with a Crafty glance, and mailbox ditto. Bad form, she reprimanded herself as she marched upstairs, flipping from envelope to envelope. Ms. Kevarian would be disappointed. The weak-willed gratified themselves with needless displays of power. The shadows that stalked Tara, the deep drums her footfalls became, the tarnish that spread from her touch on the banister—these seemed impressive but were at heart only a child's tantrum strained through sorcery.

She allowed herself the tantrum's comfort. Ms. Kevarian wasn't here.

You shouldn't be either, chattered the contemptible voice in the back of her head. You should have stayed with her.

And left Alt Coulumb to weather this storm on its own? No. She'd chosen this path. She'd walk it. She just had to get hold of herself.

The mail did not reassure. This week's *Thaumaturgist*. An advertisement from a continuing education course. A sealed letter with an Edgemont postmark she'd not open yet. And, at the bottom, a utilitarian envelope from the Hidden Schools, containing a student loan bill.

"Fuck." She leaned against her apartment door, 403. Her heart was racing for reasons that had nothing to do with the stairs. She stopped it entirely, and stopped breathing too. Her limbs chilled and she heard small sounds—carriages on the road outside, mice skittering over floorboards, a drunk man's laughter from the first floor, and beneath all these the bass fiddle note of the revolving world.

Okay. She started her heart again, breathed. Physical form had this to recommend it: your lungs let you know when they were happy.

She fished her keys from her purse, but when she reached for the latch, it popped open of its own accord. Still leaning against a suddenly open door, she lurched to catch herself on the doorjamb. Envelopes fell, and the *Thaumaturgist* flew like a drunken bird, flapping and spinning to land open to a two-page spread about the lure of shadow banking.

She knelt to retrieve her fallen mail.

Then she noticed that her apartment was not dark.

Nor were the lights on.

She closed the *Thaumaturgist*, set it on the table by the door along with the bills and letters, and took a deep breath. Then she looked up.

"I don't believe you."

"You do, though," the goddess said. "On some level." She stood by the counter of Tara's kitchen-living-dining room, holding a knife. She looked precisely like Tara, only she glowed, and her jacket wasn't torn. "I made you a snack." She pointed to a bowl.

"Carrots."

"Simple, I grant, but you wouldn't believe how hard it is to *do* things with matter. Given how vigorously you people invent fables about machines that fly and boxes that talk, you'd expect opening a refrigerator door or picking up a kitchen knife to be easier. Every activity on this plane involves so many counterbalancing forces and microscopic, hells, quantum interactions; I would have made you cookies but I never can remember how the proteins denature. Besides, you should eat healthier."

"You pull that stunt, then lecture me on my life choices?"

"The man was hurting his friends. He would have hurt his children next. In many ways he has already. He was scared, and alone, and do you think Shale breaking his arm would have helped?"

"So you broke his mind instead."

"I offered him perspective. You people get so closed up inside those little brains. Their structure changes in response to thought, you know, like your muscles respond to use. The used parts bulk up. Bad training develops uneven strength; it takes time and painful work to balance unbalanced muscles."

"Or a shortcut that deprives someone of all agency."

"Trust me, this guy needed help. I did no permanent damage, just gave him short-term access to better cognitive machinery, superior theory of mind. What he does with the memory of that is up to him. Have a carrot."

Tara grabbed the bowl from the counter. She'd had a late, fried dinner, and her stomach was growling. The carrot crunched. She didn't remember having carrots in her fridge, but she thought better of raising the point. "You could have asked before you used my soul to save his."

The divine light dimmed, which Tara chose to read as embarrassment. "Here." The goddess held out one hand, and a spark took shape. "Repayment with interest. I wish I could offer you more, but I'm close to the wire as it is."

"What about Justice? Not to mention that fat chunk of soulstuff Kos gave you last year?"

"You know the difference between an asset and an income stream. As for Justice—she's strong. Since I joined with her, it's been a challenge to remain myself. I hear her in the back of my mind, like a heresy. Some nights I really do believe all that punishment-fit-the-crime stuff. Her jackboots march through my dreams." She shivered. "You know what that's like, not being sole master of your mind, always afraid this thing you hate will rear back up inside you and make you dance."

Tara grabbed the spark from the goddess's hand. Soulstuff sang through her blood, and the world bloomed with missing colors. "I want your word you won't steal from me again, or borrow without my permission. Your binding pledge."

"Fine," the goddess said. "My word: I will not take from you again unless you will it. Okay?"

"Deal." The promise settled as a lock between them. "I didn't think you could do that in the first place."

"The rules are looser between a Lady and Her priestess."

"Oh, no."

"Not that you're a good priestess: you don't sacrifice or pray, and you ward your dreams so thick I'm surprised you haven't gone insane. Humans need to dream, you know. It's how the mind breathes. But you have fought on my behalf. You let me live inside your heart.

I must admit, this is a new one on me: I've never had a Craftswoman priestess before."

"I'm not a priestess."

"You just don't like the sound of the word. Priestess." She savored the sibilants. "How else could I talk to you like this?"

"You're smaller than most gods. Makes it easier for you to assume human forms and speak human speech."

"I couldn't talk this way with most priests, back in the day—I've been inside your skull. That, plus being, as you say, smaller, spread among fewer minds, it does help. It's like we have a bond."

"That's deeply creepy," Tara said. "And you've changed the subject. You've exposed us."

"What's the alternative? I can't lean on Kos forever. I need my own operation. I spent most of his gift sending dreams, answering prayers. When the Criers' story hit the streets, my new followers began to doubt: maybe it's just the gargoyles, maybe there's no goddess after all. I had to show myself. It was a calculated risk, and it paid dividends. I have power to share now. People are remembering. I'm sorry I had to take from you to make it happen."

Tara ate another carrot.

"Have you ever loved someone?" the goddess asked.

She set down the bowl.

"You don't know what it's like to be down here when he's up there. With so few faithful left, I live at your speed. I think the way you think. Even"—she gestured at her body, Tara's body—"reduced like this, my mind's wider than those meat brains of yours, but I should be deeper, bigger, the way he is. Thinking in this register feels like talking after a helium hit. I sound ridiculous to myself. Imagine being so close to your other half, and still so far below. Can you blame me for wanting more?"

"If it hurts the city? Yes."

The moon-Tara crossed her arms and waited.

"Fine," Tara said. "You want to be public, we can do that. You have an interview with a Crier tomorrow night."

"What?"

"A woman named Gavriel Jones." She felt very tired. She took that feeling, crushed it in a vise made of will, and tossed it into the corner of her mental attic with all her other weaknesses. "We jump the news cycle, come clean. Tell the people of Dresediel Lex you're here for them. You're back, to heal forty years of wounds."

"You want me to preach through the news."

"Maybe that's not how things worked back when you were starting out."

"When I was starting out," she said, "there were still—what's the Kathic name for those big furry things with the tusks?"

"Mammoths," Tara said. "The Crier wants a story. Give her yours. After what you did tonight, our only option is to go public as fast as possible."

"Thank you," the goddess said.

"It's nothing."

"It isn't, though. Craftswomen don't believe in gifts."

"Some of us do."

Seril could look awfully patient when she wanted. In the pits of those shining eyes, Tara saw herself as her mother might have seen her, complete in all her flaws.

"I do need help," Tara admitted at last.

The goddess, to her credit, did not laugh.

"I need your archive. Your old records."

"I don't have anything like that."

"Impossible."

Seril shrugged. "I was never the bookish type. I lived in shadow and claw and moonlight. My children were poets and mystics and warriors, not accountants."

"You must have left some scripture, some trail."

"Why would I need scripture? My children are living sermons."

"In case you ever wanted to prove your claim to what you own."

"If I have a thing, it is mine. What does a claim matter?"

"Gods," Tara said.

"Clearly."

"You can't possibly be this dense."

"Excuse me?"

Tara's apartment wasn't large. She squeezed between her stained red couch and the bookcase. From the top shelf she took a slender black notebook and tossed it onto a skull-embroidered end pillow. "That's the notebook I used to jot down my first experiments with Craft. Take it, if you can."

The goddess raised one eyebrow.

The room darkened and spun. Shadows danced. The walls shook, and dust rained down.

Dust ceased to rain and shadows stilled and light returned. The notebook had not moved.

"What exactly are you trying to prove?" Seril asked.

"That book's mine. I wrote every word myself. My name's inked on the inside cover in my own blood, and worked in glyphs I created back when I thought I'd invented a game of catching stars and stealing souls. No one can take that book from me unless I let them, and even then there's a limit to how much they can do with it. This book here," she pulled a thick red-and-black tome labeled "Contracts" from the shelf, "this bears my name, but only in pen, and my first name, too, and lots of people share it. Besides, there are a few thousand copies of this edition. You could lift it without much effort. And this," she returned the textbook and selected a dog-eared Cawleigh paperback from the lowest shelf, "I got this for two thaums from a secondhand dealer dockside. You could beat me half to death with this if you wanted."

"I'm considering it."

"The more proof you have something's yours, the more you control it. That's not even Craftwork, it's basic Applied Theology. I can't believe you don't know this stuff."

"How do your cells do what they do, Tara? How do the impulses that bounce around that magnificent magic-addled hunk of ganglia atop your spine work together to be a person? What laws do they obey? Can you describe them to me?"

"You used to be bigger than Justice. I want to learn what happened to all that power." She realized, then, that Seril had grown very still. "I'm sorry. I didn't mean—"

"It's fine."

Tara squeezed back around to the couch and sat, hands interlaced, not looking at the goddess for a while. When she trusted herself to continue, she said, "I got carried away."

"It's fine, I said. Do you mind if I sit down?"

"No."

She did, beside Tara. "There was a war, you know."

"Oh yes."

"Some days 'was' seems the wrong word, given how long the Wars lasted and how they shape us still. Everything Kos is, comes from his neutrality back then. His priests are brokers to the world—so he's bound by your rules. Not so badly as the poor neutered godlings of Dresediel Lex, or for Spider's sake the Iktomi, but still bound by treaties and contracts and worse. But I—you have to understand, back in the Wars it seemed your kind would break the world before the century's end. Your power grew each passing year, and your claws pierced deeper."

"We're better now. More sustainable."

"An argument for another time," she said. "I fell in the battle that made the Crack in the World."

"I've seen it," Tara said.

"Grass grew there once."

"Not anymore."

"We fought. You people have such grand names for yourselves, don't you? The King in Red. The Lady of Sorrows."

Look what we were fighting, Tara almost replied, but this wasn't the time.

"Belladonna Albrecht trapped me in the Badlands, but I escaped her. The King in Red caught me in the sky, and choked me, and drew his burning knives and began to carve. It hurt. It hurt so much that I spent all I was—almost all—to stop him, to fight that pain. And the more I fought, the more he cut."

Tara had read textbooks about this strategy. Hearing Seril say it felt different.

"My next memories are dragged out and slow," she said. "Rage and exile, moonlit dances beneath tall trees. I might have stayed there forever, a shadow of a shadow forgotten by history, until your people ground the world to dust. But Kos found me, and my children saved me. As did you. And here I am. That's what happened."

Tara's throat was tight, but she had to speak, and so she did, choosing each word with slow care. "The King in Red stole from you. If you died, what he took would be his by right of salvage—but you didn't die, so his title isn't clear. He holds parts of you that weren't remade into Justice. If we get them back, and this is a big if, we can restore your former strength. Kos's debtors won't be able to use you against him. But the King in Red is a powerful Craftsman. Alone, I couldn't beat him in a hundred years. Proof would give me leverage. That's why I need documentary evidence."

"I wish I could help you," she said. "Documents are Kos's style. Fires must be monitored, tended. The engineers came to him, or he to them, because they are of a kind. I am different. Stone is stone, the moon the moon. Each is its own temple."

"Oh," Tara said. And then, in a different tone of voice: "Oh." She stood and turned a slow circle, staring around her as if her room's walls had fallen down at once. "Of course." She clapped her hands and laughed—a deep, long wizard's guffaw. "I have to—excuse me."

And without another word, she ran out of the room, leaving behind a puzzled goddess and a half-eaten bowl of carrots.

19

Abelard finished his third watch vigil in the Sanctum of Kos Everburning. He knelt before the glistening brass-and-chrome altar, said the final words—*until ash and dust kindle once more to flame*—amended his final *amen*, and felt the grace of God ebb. Lord Kos was kind, and Lord Kos was gentle, and Lord Kos was a fire that consumed. And though Lord Kos had flowed through Abelard tonight, had burned in His disciple's heart, a space lingered between them.

Kos understood, was the mad piece of it all. The Everburning Lord knew Abelard's hidden pain and would let Abelard confront that pain on his own time. Which comprehension displayed such depth of trust Abelard staggered to conceive it, for Kos had been betrayed by His own priests before.

The altar flame twisted, casting golden light on the carved beasts and heroes that lined the sanctum walls—and the bas-reliefs, long stored and now returned, of the gargoyles and their Lady.

Abelard dusted off his knees, bowed his head in thanks, and walked to the window, tapping out a fresh pack of cigarettes. He tore the pack open, fished a cigarette from within, and rolled it between his fingers, contemplating the tobacco. Outside, below, beyond the green circle of the Holy Precinct, lay Alt Coulumb: street corner constellations, drifting smoke.

God's curiosity and concern licked the edges of Abelard's mind even as fire licked the cigarette tip.

Cardinal Evangelist Bede awaited Abelard in the vestry. The big man filled much of the narrow space, and his pipe smoke filled the rest. He'd been examining a relic case when Abelard entered, and did not turn from the case at first.

Abelard bowed. "Cardinal Evangelist. Glory to the Flame."

Bede waved one hand in a vague circle. "And let all that's ash burn once more. Was your vigil enlightening?"

Abelard removed the sacred stole from around his neck, passed it through the smoke of the incense smoldering atop the room's small shrine, and folded the velvet in quarters before draping it over a hook. He removed, also, the flame medallion, a larger version of the one he wore beneath his robes. "I am ever at the Lord's service."

"That bad, eh?"

"No!" But the Evangelist was grinning. "I pray at my Lord's pleasure." He removed a cloth from the altar cabinet and began to polish the medallion, which phrase, he remembered with a quirk of the mouth as involuntary as it was unpriestly, had taken quite a different meaning when he and the fellows of his novitiate hit puberty. One hundred circles spiraling out from the center, clockwise and counterclockwise, each side, while reciting the Prayer of the Burn. The cloths themselves, once sooted, would be burned, and the ashes distributed to the poor. They had healing powers. After six years of vigils, and two of Technical Novitiate, Abelard could have recited the Prayer of the Burn with full colophon in reverse and played two hands of contract bridge at the same time.

—*The world, o monks, is burning*—

Religion, he reminded himself, was more than miracles. The word's root meant to bind—binding man to concept through ceremony, and man to man through ceremony as well. "Man" being gender neutral in this case, of course, though he imagined trying to make that argument to Tara and amended his thought to "person." Not that "person" scanned as well, but perhaps that was a commentary on the thought, or the language, or the culture that framed the language that framed the thought, or the relationship between thought and culture and language because what was culture but the product of thoughts framed by language framed by—

Abelard, Cardinal Gustave had said in their first confession after he joined the Technical Novitiate, in that grated, shadowed booth with the wooden bench that creaked when you sat upon it wrong, Abelard, faith is a business of the mind and heart, but it must be a business of the body, too, because God is in the body as He is in the world. That is why we build, and study what we have built. Things and deeds matter more than words.

Then again, that attitude hadn't worked out well for Cardinal Gustave.

—*The world, o monks, is burning*—

"Very quiet over there, Brother Abelard."

"Contemplation of the divine demands silence, Your Grace. Only in silence may we hear the hiss of leaking gaskets of faith, or the flapping of the fan belts of human flourishing."

"Quoting Tooms to a Cardinal? Bold."

Abelard's cigarette slipped. "I'm sorry, Your Grace, I didn't mean—"

But Bede was laughing, still before the relic case. "Abelard, do you think being called 'bold' is an admonishment?"

"It sounded like one, Your Grace."

"I remember your preparations for Novitiate, evaluating the different arms of the church. I was so glad to hear from Gustave that you were called to Tech. When we spoke about evangelism, I thought, here is a man of deep and sensitive faith. Too sensitive for the harsh world. Machines and scholarship and prayer seemed more your métier than Craftwork and deals with demonic powers. And now look at you. Friends with Craftswomen. Quick with a comeback. I seldom misjudge a man to this degree."

Abelard finished polishing the medallion and returned it to its case. Soot stained the cloth he'd used, but not enough for holiness yet; he stored the cloth as well. "Cardinal, are you here for a reason?"

"I go nowhere without a reason, preferably several. I like to ponder the relics. These aren't our greatest wonders, the treasures of the church vaults. But it is right and good to preserve and contemplate markers of the priests and saints whose tales will be told when I am dust. Do you have a favorite?"

"St. Hilliard's Grease," Abelard said without hesitation.

"Why?"

"It's the only lubricant on the shelf. Our saints leave behind an awful lot of wrenches and calipers and slide rules which, you know, they're great for building and tightening and plotting and planning, but the priesthood tends, I think, to forget that once you build a system you have to keep it running. For every St. Raymond who invents the ball-socket valve, for each St. Veek's golemetric engine, there's a Sister Miriel who spends her life running around making broken things work. St. Hilliard realized the great engines of her time were falling apart too soon, and by meditating on the seeds of flame and St. Vilchard's Oil devised—you know all this already."

"Storytelling is a proclamation of faith," the Cardinal said. "Continue."

But while Abelard's words still resounded in the caverns of his mind, it took him a stammering few seconds—with the Cardinal looking on, so patient—to find the thread again. "Her grease worked well with the machines of her time, and is still used today in systems for which we cannot rely on alchemical synthetics. St. Winnick's Wrench is rusty, we've improved welding technology since St. Alban's day so her torch is—well, not useless, but outclassed. But St. Hilliard's Grease has a shelf life of centuries. I could take that pot down to the boiler room tonight and do good work with it."

"Whereupon Sister Reliquarian would have you promptly immolated."

Abelard flicked ash from his cigarette into a black-and-gold ashtray inscribed with the Fire of God. "I don't mean I would, just that it's possible, and I respect that. Lots of people do good necessary work that's overlooked because they didn't happen to build something huge, or convert a continent of barbarians which probably never existed anyway."

The Cardinal nodded knowingly. "Ah, the Good St. Vanturok. Though it does say something about the church of his day that they were willing to trust a man who rowed into the ocean on a coracle and rowed back ten years later claiming he'd discovered a new continent."

"What's your favorite relic?" Abelard asked, realizing belatedly that he should have made some effort to find this out before launching into an oblique condemnation of half the contents of the case.

"Despite its rust," the Cardinal said, "I've always been partial to St. Winnick's Wrench. For similar reasons to your affection for St. Hilliard, in fact: it's an old tool, not adjustable, iron-made rather than stainless steel, and so rusty despite Sister Reliquarian's efforts that I doubt you could use it to adjust a bolt without flaking away half the thing's substance. But it reminds me that we must do the best with what we have. If we are to believe those Ebon Sea philosophers who claim there is such a thing as an ideal wrench, a wrench of which all other wrenches are made in imitation, then the wrenches we hold are no more like that ideal wrench than we are like the ideal being in whose pattern we are formed. Yet such are the tools we must use, and such are the men we must be." He touched three fingers to three points around his heart—a triangle pointing up. "My thoughts tend this way when I find myself mourning the state of the world and the weakness its inhabitants, ourselves included."

"Your Grace," Abelard said when he was relatively certain the Cardinal was not engaged in a drawn-out dramatic pause. "Earlier you said you go nowhere without a reason, preferably several. I don't think you came here at this hour to contemplate relics."

The Cardinal surged to his feet, robes billowing around his body like a red tide. "Abelard," he said. "Walk with me."

The Cardinal led him from the vestry past a row of chapels where priests and monks crouched praying, to a lift that ran the tower's height. It opened on the sixty-first floor, the Evangelate Offices, and Abelard blinked. Walls of smooth dark stone were the norm in the Temple of Kos Everburning; they did not insulate well, but cheap heating bills were one of the many benefits of working for a God of Fire. The Evangelate, however, looked like a Craftsman's office suite: tall windows of clear glass instead of stained, with blond wood everywhere, smoked glass office walls at the perimeter and low gray-walled cubicles within.

"I haven't been up here in a long time," Abelard said. "You remodeled."

"We have appearances to maintain," the Cardinal replied. "We deal with many beings, Craftsmen not least among them, who find such surroundings preferable to black stone and stoked flames." As he led the way through the cubicles, Abelard noted a few lamps flickering. He was tall enough to peer over the cube walls; behind one he saw a young tonsured man bent over a table of figures, and a short-haired woman beside him, their heads and shoulders identically slumped.

He followed Bede into his office, which was the kind of office a man like Cardinal Evangelist Bede should have: large and spare save for a few awards on the wall and a small ornate devotional altar that gleamed from frequent use. A monthly calendar on Bede's desk displayed woodcuts of bulldogs.

"Are you sure this gives the right impression?" Abelard said. "Your partners are dealing with a church, I mean, not a bank."

"But the church serves as a bank," Bede replied. "We lend and guarantee and underwrite. A Concern halfway around the globe might borrow from Lord Kos knowing nothing of his doctrine other than that He has power He is willing to lend, for reasonable rates."

Abelard pointed to the altar. "May I?"

"Be my guest."

He lit a stick of incense and recited a quick prayer. Bede's voice rumbled beneath his own. When Abelard turned from the altar, the Cardinal's head was lowered. "You're worried," Abelard said.

"Of course," the Cardinal replied. "It is one thing to recognize a danger and quite another to face it." He unlocked the top drawer of his desk and withdrew a thick black folder, which he opened, then turned so Abelard could read. "By showing you this I am, let's say stretching, a thousand confidentiality agreements. I bind you to silence by your faith in God and your loyalty to the church."

"I accept your charge," Abelard said automatically. He stuck his cigarette behind his ear and ran a finger down the margin of the first page. Frowned. Turned to the second, and the third. Hesitated over a pie chart, then a bar graph, then back to the pie chart. Fanned the remaining 150 or so pages. "What is this?"

"St. Hilliard's Grease," Bede said. He sounded tired.

"I don't understand. I'm pretty sure you made up most of the words here."

"We had to. There weren't words for what we were doing when we started doing it." Bede unlocked the larger, second drawer of his desk. Abelard craned his neck and saw within a library of similar black folders. "This isn't everything, of course. There are piles and piles in the church archives. I know you Technical types don't enjoy thinking of our work this way—or of our God this way either—but we don't have the luxury of siloed faith tonight."

Abelard returned to the pie chart. "Does this mean what I think?"

"The yellow slice is what we'd call organic worship—that's to say, souls available as a result of confirmed faith in Kos, priests and Alt Coulumb's secular citizenry combined. The green slice represents missionary work, which produces a real, if variable, return on investment. Sometimes you get lucky and find fertile, troubled territory—we've had good success in the Northern Gleb since the struggle there began—but you can't count on missionaries. You're just as likely to lose your investment. And sometimes, God forbid, you suffer a disaster like the Southern Kathic expedition."

"Those two slices are less than half the pie. What's this big blue piece?"

"Transactional work," Bede said. "My role. The reason this office looks the way it does. The reason, if you pay attention, you'll catch Technical Cardinal Nestor giving me the side-eye at council meetings. This income relies on our partners' faith we'll remain stable and make good on future obligations. And the red element down here, the quarter slice, that represents specific promises to perform—cities that rely on Kos for power, our contracts with the Iskari Defense Ministry, that sort of thing."

"This is way too simple. I've seen these contracts in person. They're huge, complex. A breakdown like this—"

"My boy, believe me, I do not mean to elide the complexity of our work. You've seen the circulatory system firsthand, an honor I have not received. This merely indicates where the blood comes from, and where it goes. Some in this church overlook the importance of the Evangelate's work, because it bears so little connection to their naive sense of a church's role. But if our deals collapse, which they will if our partners lose faith, Kos will suffer effects comparable to those of a body deprived of half its blood." The Cardinal closed the folder, returned it to his desk, and locked the desk. He sat. He laced his fingers together and watched Abelard over the lacing. "I hoped you could talk to God for me."

Ash dripped from Abelard's cigarette onto his robe. He brushed the ash away and stamped out the cinder, leaving a gray smear on the carpet. "Sorry," he said.

"Overdue for a wash."

He knelt and tried to scrape the ash out of the fibers of the rug. "You don't have some spot treater? I mean, sorry, but it does stain."

"You have an interesting way of ignoring questions."

He stopped scraping, and stood instead, hands in pockets, weight shifting from foot to foot. Smoke drifted from his cigarette. "You want me to convince Lord Kos not to support Seril if She needs Him."

"That's the most elegant solution, as our partners learn of the goddess's return. I will assure them she stands alone—aside from her involvement in Justice. Her obligations are not our Lord's. She is a separate entity. There may, naturally, be tests of that position, as Ms. Abernathy said this evening." The fingers de-laced. "Seril is not strong enough to stand on her own—or to refuse His aid if He offers it. We need to convince Him to leave her to defend herself. I'd go to Him, but since Gustave's treachery He has been more reserved with the Council of Cardinals than ever."

"Can you blame him?"

"This is not a question of blame. It is a question of what is, and what must be." The incense on the altar burned low. Bede replaced it. "I know how this looks. You distrust me, as does my Lord. I do not relish being held in such low esteem by a bright young priest and by the Master I serve, but these are strange times and I forgive you both. But, Abelard, this is the only way I know to save us."

"Tara's research—"

"Is a long shot. You know this, as does she. We cannot rely on her success. Not every hard decision is an evil plot."

Abelard took a long, slow drag on his cigarette. God was in the smoke, and God was in his heart, and God was in the blood that burned through his veins and the air into which he exhaled, and others too, all through the city, a constant heartbeat. To live was to be loved was to burn.

—*the world, o monks*—

He remembered how cold he had been without that fire.

"I'll talk to Him," he said. "But I can't guarantee He'll listen."

"I ask no more," the Cardinal Evangelist replied.

20

Aev chased Shale over rooftops and down dark alleys and from skyscraper to skyscraper. The whelp was small and weak, but fast—a flash of stone in motion behind a pinnacle, a glint of emerald from an antenna. He changed to human shape once and almost lost her in a crowd in the Pleasure Quarter, until she spotted him slinking down a peep show alley without regard for the fleshlings gyrating meatily in the red-lit windows. She swooped to cut him off at the alley's end, but he must have seen her—his stone ripped free of flesh again and in three seconds he'd reached the rooftops. In four he was gone, leaving in his wake a shocked dope peddler and a number of fleshlings who'd ceased, however briefly, those meaty gyrations.

"I didn't do anything wrong," he roared back at her in Stone, over the rattle of the elevated train down which he ran, leaping from car to car. Within the cars, screams and shouts—panic at heavy footfalls on metal roofs. "They needed help. The Lady willed me to go. I don't see why you're so mad about this."

That brought her up short. In surprise she almost let an overhead pylon strike her in the face. "You don't see why I'm so mad about this. You don't see why I'm so mad?" She spotted him two blocks back, climbing a skyscraper. She leapt off the train, wings spread, but by the time she brought herself around he'd vanished again. She flew forty stories up a jewel-faceted tower and perched at its peak, steadying herself against one of the needlelike protrusions Tara called nightmare antennas. Terrors clawed at Aev as she held it, like a kitten testing its claws. Not for the first time Aev wondered what exactly had broken inside Tara Abernathy's mind that let her judge her way of life normal.

Where, in the streets below, in the alleys and dead ends, in the shop windows and blacktop street ball playgrounds, where was her wayward son?

She remembered her debates with the Lady about carving him. We're strong, Aev had said, almost too strong, and fierce. Perhaps we need a young one who's fast, who can move unseen in shadows, a king of infiltrators and sneaks, a messenger no door will bar.

Should have made him clubfoot and slow, and ironed out that infuriating spark of personal initiative.

(Not really, but some days she wished.)

There. Two skyscrapers over, by a tower with a starburst logo and the legend GRIMWALD HOLDINGS—Shale was a winged black slice against garish ghostlit colors. She launched herself into space, mouth wide to drink the moon.

He hid in shadows, so she searched every shadow. He flew and she flew faster. He reared and she doubled back. No crowd could conceal him, no bolt-hole was deep enough to hide.

But he was fast. She'd carved well, with the Lady in her hands.

And he must have known this would happen, that midway through the chase her rage would unclench and leave her simply running, flying, as she had done centuries ago when Alt Coulumb was a small town and she its sole guardian. He must have known, because when she cornered him on a low roof between two skyscrapers near Uhlan and Brakenridge—when she slammed into him and they tumbled together on gravel, spinning, tearing gouges in tar paper, a ball of claws and teeth, and she ended the tumble on top, legs pinning his wings to the roof—he bared his throat to her and said, with an imp's smile she never could harden herself against, "Good chase, Mother."

She sat back on her haunches astride him. "You don't even understand"—that last word even more a growl than usual in Stone—"why I'm angry."

"Can you get off me?"

She bared teeth.

"It's hard to talk this way, is all."

One wingbeat drew her to her feet. He stood more slowly, exaggerating submission. She'd seen him kip up from worse falls. "Your stunt risked the Lady's life."

He picked gravel out of his ears and brushed more from the hollow between his neck and collarbone. Across the street, a billboard man with improbably orange skin blew smoke rings into the night. The rings, swelling, faded to air. "Let's not do this here."

He flew slowly, painted greens and oranges and browns by billboards and streetlights. She followed. A late-night worker gaped from a high window at them both, and Shale waved. Aev landed after him, on an observation deck beneath a towering nightmare antenna. The city lay below, river flowing down to bay and blackly glittering ocean. Out there, Captain Pelham's crew guided the captured *Dream* and its foul cargo to port.

"I've seen the view before, Shale."

"But it's no less beautiful for your knowing it," he said. "They pay to come up here these days, the humans I mean. In the forty years since we left the rooftops, they've learned to love them." He patted coin-op binoculars mounted at the observation deck's edge. "Five-year-olds press their faces to this lens and stare out to the edge of the world."

"Wearing skin has fogged your mind."

"The Lady made me to walk among them, with your hands. Will you blame me for that?"

"I blame you for your meathead stunt tonight."

"I know those girls. Their father's a broken man—all the anger inside his skull has left a calculus of hate. We want followers for our Lady. Do we serve Her by deserting her people?"

"You did not intervene in the market to serve Her."

"She asked me to go there."

"You petitioned Her! You wheedled and convinced because you didn't want to let that girl down. You had to be the hero. And now we all might die because of your pride."

"As if I'm the only one."

"What are you saying?"

"You saved the reporter."

Aev walked to the high railing, vaulted over, and let herself fall.

She grabbed the roof's edge and jerked to a halt above the windows; her talons scarred the concrete, leaving grooves that caught moon- and city-light.

"Mother?" Shale asked from behind her.

She said nothing.

He lowered himself over the edge and hung beside her in the calm of the wind.

"I have risked us all," he said after a while.

"No," she said. "And yes. You're right. Last night I tried to let her suffer. I thought: this reporter tempts fate and tests Seril. Let her save herself. I made myself watch her suffering, because I owed that much at least. But in the end I only hurt the ones who hurt her. I am angry at you because I am angry at myself, and I am angry at myself because I cannot fault my actions—or yours, though they send us teetering across a narrow bridge."

"I was proud," he said. "And I did not want to disappoint her."

The ledge crumbled beneath Aev's grip. Concrete dust rained down sixty stories. She caught a chunk large enough to cause damage when it reached ground level, crushed it to sand, and let the sand drift. "Humans would not find this calming," she said.

"Fear is different for each being that fears."

"And stone fears change," she said. "Change for us is a permanent unmaking. But our Lady is of the moon, and change is Hers: new life from death, waxing from waning. She waxes now, and we tremble. This may be blasphemy, but it is also right, for though She is Herself, we are still stone." With her free hand she indicated Kos's black tower. "Great Kos stands alone and strong. He has power, and privilege by virtue of his power. But His power comes, as ever, from mortal fuel—and so mortal strictures bind him. We are free, and poor, and dangerous—to our enemies, but also to ourselves. In my anger and fear, I might have hurt you. I am sorry."

Shale did not answer.

Aev heard a scraping sound, and smelled the sharp tang of spent lightning.

She looked down. A cold blue blade jutted from a window beneath them. She watched it slice a circle in the glass. A human head emerged from the hole, black curls bobbing. Then the head disappeared, only to pop back through the glass facing up. Tara Abernathy looked frustrated. Then again, she often did, at least when Aev saw her. "Aev! Didn't expect to find you here."

"Ms. Abernathy. Good evening."

Beside her, Shale tensed.

"Shale," she said. "I'm sure Ms. Abernathy means well."

"Her good intentions rarely come with deeds to match."

"Cut off a guy's face once," Tara said, "and he'll remember for the rest of his life."

"It left an impression."

"And you've thrown us all into the fire tonight. We're even, maybe. I hoped we could start fresh."

"What do you want?"

"Poetry lessons."

21

"I need a drink," Cat said once Raz's sailors moored *Dream* and *Bounty* both and reefed the sails and jagged the mainmast and scuppered the jibjaw or whatever it was they'd been up to while she packed *Dream*'s crew into Blacksuit wagons. "And before you get clever, I don't mean the kind where I'm the beverage. Care to chaperone?"

Raz signed a few forms and handed them to his ship's clerk. "You want me to come along and make sure you have no fun? Happy to oblige."

"More like play designated hitter."

"Is that a sports thing?"

"It's like a designated driver, only if I'm too drunk to hit someone, you do it."

"Sounds fun," he said. "My Alt Coulumb nightlife's a half century out of date, and the last time I chose a bar in this city I ended up brainwashed. You know a place?"

She bared her teeth at him, though hers were somewhat less pointy. "I can think of a few."

Tara stood beside Shale on the skyscraper's roof. Aev had left them— flitted off to brood on the abyss. They watched the horizon and the water, neither wanting to speak first.

Shale gave up the contest. "You can't fly."

"I can," she said. "Just not in Alt Coulumb, thanks to your ever-so-progressive local interdict."

"The skies belong to the Lady," Shale said. "It would be a perversion for you to fly through them."

"That's what counts as perversion for a gargoyle? You must have a boring sex life."

"Reproduction works differently for us."

"I bet."

Shale shifted uncomfortably. "Our poetry can only be read from the air. How will you read it if you cannot fly?"

"I was hoping you'd carry me."

"You trust me to do that?"

"No," she said, with more nonchalance than she felt. "But I figure dropping me would cause more trouble than it's worth. And after all you've done tonight, you owe me."

A calculating silence ensued.

"I have apologized for the face thing," she said. "Every time I've seen you. Except for this afternoon, when you were on too high a dudgeon for me to get a word in edgewise."

"You've seen me maybe three times in the last year."

"I thought you needed space to heal."

"After you cut off my face."

She rolled her eyes. "There's not even a scar."

"Where should I hold you?"

Tara had not given much thought to that question. "Around the waist, probably."

"Very well." He grabbed her about the waist and jumped off the building.

Psychiatrists and headshrinkers from realm to realm associate dreams of flight with sex for a reason. The thematic and mechanical differences are obvious—fewer bodily fluids tend to be involved in flight if all goes well, and the typical flight's also short on funny faces. But there's a breathless novelty to the first touch of both that experience tends to mellow. A flightless being's first takeoff introduces her to a new dimension; the twentieth time her case team boards a dragon gondola to some mid-Kathic city that barely rates a dot on the map, the rush fades. Spend enough time away from skies or sheets, though, and the novelty returns.

It had been a long while since Tara last flew.

At first the sensations blurred together: rush of wind, lurch in stomach, pull of gravity, talons pressed against her ribs, terror of the monkey brain realizing its body has jumped from an impossibly tall tree toward a branch it can never, ever catch—

And then the quaking of her obliques, because she hadn't thought through the consequences of her entire weight resting against Shale's hands. The gargoyle's claws pressed into her diaphragm. Far below, streetlights bounced and circled, and streets wove together. "This isn't comfortable," she wheezed. "Maybe if I were to lie on your back?"

"It wouldn't be steady. There are wings there."

"Hm." She puzzled through the issue as well as she could while hanging doubled over from a gargoyle's claws.

"How did you find me?" Shale asked.

She'd hoped he wouldn't ponder that particular detail. "I left a tracking glyph under your skin last year."

He dropped her.

She screamed at first, no denying that. Best get the scream over with and turn one's attention to the inciting issue, to wit: falling. Not quite enough altitude for the soul-parachute trick, too far from neighboring buildings for magnetism to help. She spun as she fell, which made things harder, the world by turns sky and walls and rapidly approaching road and walls and sky again—she spread her limbs, twisted to counter the spin and control her horizon line—she could lasso the buildings, or else Shale, if she could get a bead on him when she spun skyward again—

She hit stone far too soon, which was an unpleasant surprise, but she wasn't dead, which she found more agreeable. The stone she'd struck was moving, and warm to the touch. When her senses righted themselves, she realized she lay on Shale's back. His wings beat three, four times—the ripple of his shoulder blades' muscle reminded her of lying on an inflatable raft in surf on her spring break trip to the Fangs back in school—and they rose again. She swore in five languages, then started to slip; panicked, she caught his hold of his wing, which veered them abruptly left until she let go. At last she locked her arms around his neck, and her knees at his flanks. He was taller than her, which helped. His wings pressed against her sides on the updraft, but not tight enough to hurt.

"Jerk," she said.

"Witch."

"Fair." She laughed. They spiraled higher into the night.

Matt and Sandy Sforza almost came to blows over the question of who would host the Rafferty girls. Neither wanted to let them go home alone. Sandy thought they'd be more comfortable with a woman, but the room Sandy and Lil shared was barely large enough for the pair of them, let alone three guests. Matt's place was closer to the edge of town, and his boys could share a room, though Simon would complain.

All of which would have meant nothing if the Rafferty girls didn't want to go with Matt, but when he asked, Claire said yes. She'd tended to Ellen and Hannah after their father collapsed, after the Stone Man left, after the Blacksuits came.

Sandy gave them a lift in her wagon; she still lived, and parked, near the market, though the last decade's rising rent had forced her and Lil to carry their lives on their backs snail-like from apartment to apartment until they bought their present coffin. Matt did not know if she stayed for the commute, or for her pride. Sandy's people had lived near the market since they first came from Telomere; so had Matt's, but he'd got in too many fights over the old ways with his old man back when his old man was the type to fight with fists to care much for history. Bruises and swelling obscured the ways things had "always" been.

Matt's father claimed the way things had *always* been went back to the Old Empire, to legions marching in conquest for their blood-cult masters. As far as Matt was concerned, that *always* ended when the Adornes shipped out from the Old World. Some people in Alt Coulumb had an *always* of equal age—the families who'd lived here since first light—but growing up, Matt realized that in spite of the stories his dad spun, his *always* was just the way the world had worked in the twenty years from the day he became a man to the day the city outpaced him. Old Adorne couldn't understand that the Paupers' Quarter near the market had become a place where uptown nobs and smart-dressed folk like Ms. Abernathy lived for the cheap rent and what realtors described as the "charming street scene." Dad once said anyone in a suit who walked west of Sixteenth deserved what was coming to them.

Matt himself was nearing the end of his *always*. The city his sons knew, he didn't. Maybe that was why you had kids these days, when you didn't need them to work the farm: so you could learn from them how to live in peace after your always ended.

He sat next to Claire and across from Ellen and Hannah in the back of Sandy's cart. Ellen had fallen asleep on Hannah's shoulder, and Hannah herself slept against a flour sack, and Claire stared behind them into traffic, cross-legged and awake. She rocked with the rhythm of the wheels. Sandy's left front shock needed work. Ray's second cousin was a mechanic, did his novitiate with the church before he decided he liked marriage more than metal, and found Mike. Maybe Matt could talk to Ray, ask him to have his cousin give Sandy's shocks a look some night. While Sandy slept, of course, because he doubted she could pay and he knew she wouldn't take charity.

Matt let his thoughts run because he had no idea what to say to Claire, and because the silence had wormed between his lips and down his throat into his stomach where it rolled with each rattle of Sandy's left front wheel.

Matt had never spoken with the girls alone, though he'd worked beside them for years. He knew their father well enough, but the man was a colleague and his daughters were his business.

But the man had hit Matt with a stick, and Sandy, when he wasn't any drunker than he had been before in Matt's presence and (gods) even at Matt's urging. The medic had shined a light in Corbin Rafferty's eyes, numbed the cut on his scalp and stitched it closed, and the whole time Rafferty hadn't moved.

"I don't know what happened," Matt said. "I've never seen your dad act like that before."

"I have," Claire said.

"I mean, I've seen him drunk."

"That's not drunk," she said. "It's what happens when he's sobering. He hits whatever's near. Breaks furniture."

"He hits you?"

"He hasn't," she said. "Yet. We keep away. Lock ourselves in our rooms."

"You don't need to say anything you don't want to."

"And you don't need to hear anything you don't want to," she said. "You never have before."

He thought about blindness, and said nothing.

"Thank you for offering us a place to stay," Claire continued. "Ellen will be grateful."

He wasn't sure how to take that, so he left it.

The doom that came to Chez Walsh looked like Cat in leather and denim, with Raz in tow. Raz still wore his whites; Cat had stopped by the temple to change, and left him waiting under the gaze of a goddess who was no longer blind. Cat didn't go out often these days, but she still kept clothes in her locker.

"Promising," Raz said when she led him down the Pleasure Quarter alley. Puddles of gray water reflected buzzing rooftop ghostlights and brightly colored billboards bearing images of smiling men, one of whom—a toothpaste ad—had been aftermarket modified with a spray-paint ball gag and the tagger's circle-trumpet glyph.

"You'll like this place. I used to come here all the time." And it felt so good to be back—good and shudderingly transgressive. She'd left this life and these alleys behind, left the joy of fang in vein. But tonight she had fought pirates, saved a hundred people from misery, polished off a protracted operation. Triumph flushed her. She was done running from herself—time to celebrate how far she'd come from the addled addict of a year before.

Raz stepped over a fishnet-stockinged someone enjoying a chemical sleep in the lee of a metal trash bin. The someone had bandages up and down their arm. "Folks don't clean up after themselves in this part of town?"

"She's fine," Cat said.

"The bandages, I mean. Impolite not to close your people up."

"They're a fashion statement." Bass pounded beyond the unmarked ironbound door. THE RATS! screamed a chalk sign on the wall beside the door, sharp-edged balloon letters flanked by lightning bolts. The chalk bore the same circle-trumpet glyph, which Cat bet belonged to a new artist on the block.

"Ravings of madmen?"

Cat shook her head. "That's the band. They're great, actually. We're in luck."

The door opened. Bass flooded the alley. The sleeping someone tossed. Two young men staggered out, arms wrapped around each other; the lighter-skinned one had fangs. The bouncer pushed a larger, angrier guy out after them. He recovered his footing and ran back toward the bar, but the bouncer's gloved fist clipped him on the jaw and he fell, hit the wall, and slid down to join the crumpled someone, who drew away into a fetal position by reflex.

The bouncer filled the door: a broad-shouldered woman with angular muscles and short spiked orange hair. Cat remembered her from the bad old days. "Hi, Candy," she said, and thumbed left at Raz. "I brought a friend."

"I don't think she's convinced," Raz said, and flashed the woman a smile with a little tooth.

The bouncer opened for them like a second layer of door. Cat tipped her as they entered the pulsing dark, the dancing strobes, the surging mass of sweat and flesh and black lace where she'd spent too many years of nights.

It felt like coming home, to a home smaller and shabbier than remembered but still homey. Pool tables in front, unoccupied, beside the bar. Stage on the back wall, cage fronted in case of zealotry, dance floor ringed by private booths. The smoke of a hundred cigarettes congregated in the ceiling. "I missed this place," she said. She'd taught herself to dread Walsh's bar while getting sober, but here it was, a refuge where she'd passed hard times. She loved it, though she didn't trust the way she loved it, like an echo of an unheard noise.

"Good music," Raz said, bobbing his head almost in time with the beat.

"Ms. Elle!" A voice from the bar, round and big. She turned and with unechoed joy saw double-chinned Walsh, a year grayer but his paunch and big arms and pockmarked face unchanged. He raised one arm above a row of patrons bent over their personal drugs. "Come here."

"Walsh." She slapped him a high five over the rounded back of a man with a lizard's head. "How's the life?"

"Fat and happy. Didn't expect you to take my advice when you were last here. It's been a while."

"And a while again," she said.

"Haven't seen you before, sailor."

Raz's hands were deep inside his pockets. "Nice place you have here."

"What's tonight's poison?" Walsh asked. "Some choice kids on the floor today, if either of you are looking for a fang."

"Whiskey for me." She held up thumb and finger to gauge the amount. "I'm on a diet."

"Sailor?"

"Same," Raz said.

"Don't need to keep up appearances." Walsh pointed to the dance floor. "The booths are cheap, and the crowd's willing."

"Whiskey, thank you."

Walsh passed the drinks with a skeptical expression; Cat paid before Raz could try. "What have I missed?" Cat asked.

"Same scene: changes and never changes. You remember Brad?"

"Pale kid with the needle teeth, yeah. In from the boondocks."

"Let himself go a few months back."

"No shit."

"Full out with the claws and everything. Candy took him down, with help. Almost had to call the Suits, but everyone's okay, except for Brad." He stabbed his sternum with the tip of his middle finger and made a face. "Shanda moved back down to Alt Selene, her grand-kids need some help down there. The Strings broke up, got back to-gether, broke up again. It's life."

"Or something like it," she said, completing their old phrase. "It's good to see you again, Walsh."

"Same here, kid. Get out on the floor!"

Raz had taken his whiskey and looked, not tense exactly, but distant.

"I'll play some pool first," Cat said.

Walsh kept rein on his surprise. "Get on, then. Take table two."

They wormed through the crowd to the empty table. "I can't play with you," Raz said.

"Don't be so sure." She racked the balls, rolled them back and forth on green felt, switched two solids and stripes.

"I'm stronger. My heart doesn't beat, and I don't have to breathe. It wouldn't be fair."

The cues were still horrible and gnarled. She ground blue chalk against the tip, and inhaled, smelling sweat and blood in a good way. Familiar, long-absent scents of stale beer and cloves tickled up her nose and back down her throat. Her tongue woke wet in her mouth, and she felt an anticipatory thrill, like a man had turned a key in her spine to tighten her nerves like piano wire. Tuning her.

Somewhere in that thrashing crowd was a fang to make her feel the way she used to want.

She leaned her hip into the table, sighted on the cue ball, and sank two solids on the break.

22

From the air, Alt Coulumb made no sense. Taking the city part by part, you could mislead yourself into believing it obeyed a higher logic: the Business District to the north had gridded streets and avenues, but fanning around the clockface that order broke to jags, as if the Sacred Precinct was a rock thrown through a window and the rest of the city the window's shards. "Cow paths," she said as they flew south toward the university.

"I don't understand."

"We didn't have many trees back home, but I climbed the ones we did have. This looks like cow paths from overhead."

"You did not grow up in a city?"

Tara caught her breath as Shale's wings spread to mount an updraft. "No."

"Where?"

"You wouldn't know it."

He said nothing.

"Edgemont," she relented at last. "Little place at the eastern edge of the Badlands. Farm country. Lots of corn. Very flat."

"Near Lark's Ridge?"

"Twenty miles northeast," she said automatically, then: "Wait, how do you know Lark's Ridge?"

"We passed through on the way to the wars. There was not much ridge to speak of."

"Yeah, well, we didn't have much mont to edge on either—just enough for the quarry." The city wheeled below, the Business District clocking around to three and six and nine and back to midnight or noon. "Lark's Ridge in the God Wars. Weird. What was it like back then?" That would have been forty years ago, around the time Tara's mom's folks fled the siege of Alt Selene west to Edgemont.

"Small." His deep voice cut through the buffeting wind. Stars hung overhead—more stars the farther they rose, but still too few for Tara's comfort. Cities of the Craft were more careful about light pollution. "Wooden. We were not comfortable there. They had a high temple to their earth goddess, with a clock tower. Aev tried to perch on the tower, but its wood was weak, and she broke through." He chuffed a laugh.

"I know that church! They rebuilt the roof. They said it was God Wars damage but not—that was you?"

Shale leveled out to glide over the university. Postage-stamp quadrangles lined by fake battlements interrupted the crumpled streets. "If you ever tell Aev I told that story, I will deny it."

"Your secret's safe with me. Do we really have to be this high to see your poems?"

"The oldest ones," he said. "Can you read our glyphs?"

"Almost. I've only had a year to work on Stone, and human vocal cords aren't shaped right for the phonemes. I might need your help."

"It is difficult to translate poetry."

"I just need the meaning."

"Just the meaning?" He turned to look at her over his shoulder, which made them tangle into a roll. She screamed a little—understandable given the circumstances, dammit—and clutched his sides with her knees like he was a horse in full gallop. Her grip on his neck tightened enough to crush a human trachea. Good thing Shale didn't have one.

"Don't do that!"

"Meaning," he said, righting their course, "comes from rhyme and rhythm and form. You can't just fill a page with words that have the same definition as the original. True translation requires understanding the associations and contexts of the source language, then shifting all that into the target tongue. The greater the poet, the harder the translation. And Stone's not even—how would you render a second-voice bass tonal shift rhyme in Kathic?"

"Come again?"

He demonstrated: two syllables with the same tenor voicing, but the first she felt as a steady rumble in Shale's skin, while in the second the rumble started faster but slowed. "The first word renders in Kathic as *turtle*. The second is a second-person-plural pronoun addressing a subgroup of a collective."

"This is awfully technical."

"Poetry is glory to the Goddess."

"That doesn't explain the jargon."

"We had," Shale said after a long, silent swoop, "a lot of time in exile. I thought perhaps if we could, ah, publish our songs, maybe we could draw others toward the Lady. I subscribed to journals by mail. Submitted poems. Received rejection letters. There are advantages to being able to pass for human. Did you just giggle?"

"No." She pushed from her mind the image of Shale, dressed in stitched-together rabbit furs or whatever he wore for clothing in human form out in the countryside—hells, had he even worn clothing?—arriving at some log-cabin town's post office with a sub-scription card for *Poetry Fancier's Quarterly*. "So, these poems you've recorded in Stone—they describe the Goddess. They're an authoritative representation of her."

"Strange phrasing."

"I'm translating," she said. "From my language to yours."

Miles west, at the airport, a great glittering beast ascended into the night, tail sweeping a swath through clouds. Its blackness blended with the space between the stars.

"Yes," he replied.

"Which returns us to my question: Do we have to be this high to see the poems? I've seen them before, in alleys, from street level."

"Codas," he said. "Fragmentary midcentury additions of the min-imalist school. Many of what you thought complete works were can-tos of longer poems designed to be read overhead in moonlight at a particular angle."

"If we're meant to be viewing works in alleys from overhead," Tara said, "we're still too high. I can't see any building walls from here."

"You see nothing for which you are not prepared to look."

Below her, the city turned silver all at once.

An instant before, they'd flown above an Alt Coulumb dark and jeweled as ever. Then, as if they crossed an invisible threshold, the streets transformed to rivers of silver-blue light. From ground level the effect would be too subtle to notice, since light would never strike the right angle for more than a thumb-size piece of pavement. A drunk might see a patch of glory in an alley shadow and mistake it for a streetlight reflection. This was more. The city was built around luminous words.

"Cow paths," she said.

"Some," Shale acknowledged. "But how do the cows know which paths to walk? They followed tracks we carved."

"It's beautiful."

"Yes."

"What does it mean?"

"That," he replied, "is harder."

Cat won three games and Raz two. "Superior strength. Hah." She sank another ball, missed her third follow-up shot, passed to him; he dropped three, then scratched. "What's with the whiskey, anyway?"

"I'm in the man's bar. Passengers on my boat pay for the privilege. Shouldn't I pay him for his floor space?"

She knocked back her own, and tasted fire and smoke. Then she bent to the table and lined up angles in her head. "We're paying for the table. And you're in demand here. Plenty of people would be happy to give you a drink. Not on the dance floor—that's the only rule. Don't want the place to get slippery."

"That's how you think I work? Canvassing a room of people I don't know for a taste—"

"I don't judge. You do what you need to live."

"I don't need that."

"You have to drink sometime."

"It's personal."

"You can tell me."

"I don't like to talk about it."

The angles settled in the green felt's reflection behind her eyes. Her heart did beat, so she slowed it, and she did breathe, so she waited for the pause after exhalation. The crack of the balls reminded her pleasantly of breaking someone else's bone.

They finished the game in silence, relating through force and spheres that disappeared into velvet pockets. The band rocked. Four of the booth curtains had been drawn when she came in, and seven were now. She'd seen the seventh curtain close as Raz lined up a shot on the eight ball: two women, one older than Cat, the other younger and rounder, both hungry, and she couldn't tell which had the teeth. She hadn't expected to be so aware of the curtains. She liked this place. She liked Walsh. She liked the music. She liked the damn booths and the damn red leather upholstery in them and the stupid paintings of naked women who didn't look how naked women looked and were all twined round with rose vines and thorns. He missed the eight. She didn't.

"We saved lives tonight," she said. "We fought and won. Dance with me."

"Fine," he said, though it hadn't been a question.

He offered her his whiskey, and she took it, swallowed it, set down the glass. Grabbed his hand, smoother than any sailors' she'd felt. No hemp rope could burn his skin. He followed her with a look on his face like she was a chess problem or a tricky knot he wanted to untie. The whiskey felt good. Girls to the left of them, boys to the right of them, and she pulled him into the valley of the dance.

Music was a way to lose yourself, music good and loud with a pulse you could follow, a double beat that vined through your ears and mouth into veins and spread shoots, leaves, flowers. Drink-sweat and too much perfume and leather and slick vinyl and hair pressed close to her. She smoothed her skirt against her hips and danced. Somewhere a singer sang. There were flowers in her arms and her stomach and deeper. She raised her arms like wings.

And he danced with her. It happened unsteady and slow as new spring, but he did dance. His eyes, which he'd held half-closed since entering the bar, opened, and she saw the whites around his ruby-stained brown irises. By the second song he forgot himself and smiled.

She forgot herself and moved toward him.

There was bass and there was guitar and there were drums and a piano only it wasn't a piano exactly but some strange machine that worked with spinning cylinders of glass crackling Craft, and bodies pressed them close, and she danced with the crowd and they with her and he with them and then they were together, and the crowd held fangs and blood that called for them and the fangs were white and dark blood flushed faces red and there was so much wanting in this room, wanting to vanish, to be drawn under another's power into a mouth—

She danced with him, and he with her, wound tight as clocks were wound in Iskar, so tight his skin might sing. She touched him. She pulled him toward her. He followed. She kissed him. He kissed her back. Her lip slid between his teeth, and the teeth touched her, and she pressed her lip against them and her skin parted and there was a sharp sharp stab of joy—

that all went wrong at once.

He pulled back.

She stumbled into him. Beauty raged in her vein. There was nothing she could not be, there was no mold into which she could not be poured, the draw had been so strong and rich, and at its withdrawal she clutched for him, seeing too late his sudden horror at her himself, at what they were—at what they were about to—at what they, at what *she*, had—

He staggered into the moshing crowd, knocked into a blond-dreadlocked man, who shoulder-checked Raz back, and Raz, eyes wide and wet like marble library lions' eyes in rain, moshed the blond-dreadlocked man harder than he'd ever been moshed before, sent him tumbling airborne into a pair of shirtless bodybuilders who fell like pool balls run from a single shot, two left side four right far corner six right side *thunk thunk thunk*, until only blond dreads was left standing, spinning, laughing a wild *woo* with hands raised in horn-sign as the fallen rose and piled on him in turn.

Raz looked uncomprehending at them, at her, and left.

She ran after him.

He snaked through the crowd. She never could have caught him but for Candy at the door, who blocked him in while she admitted two new customers—so Cat, ignoring Walsh's waved good-bye, reached the alley before Raz left it.

"Raz!"

He didn't turn.

"Don't run from me."

He stopped. "Then what? Do you want me to stay?"

"Did it look like I was pushing you away?"

"It looked." He moved toward her so fast he didn't seem to cross the intervening space. So damn quick with blood in him—how long did he *go*, anyway, without feeding? How long could he? And how would the hunger of a single taste after deprivation feel? She knew. She was all need, a single exposed nerve. Her clothes rasped her skin. Her skirt's hem was tight as a knife. He was close, though not close like he'd been when they danced, not close enough she could touch him without his letting her. "It looked," he said, softer now, "like you were out of control."

"You responded. We kissed, dammit—"

"Don't pretend that's all. I tasted you. I could break that building in half if I wanted. I could fly." She'd never heard such disgust in his voice before.

"I wanted it. So did you."

"I can't believe we're having this conversation. I thought you wanted to fix—"

"To fix myself? To fix what's fucked-up about me?"

"I didn't mean that," he said, too fast.

"I see the way you look at me, like I messed up somewhere. You're always in control, you never put a foot wrong. You never jump a ship before the signal comes. You never take a risk that's not worth it. Unlike me. To all the hells with that. I know how the change works. I know you had to want to be what you are."

"I wanted not to die," he said. "Okay? I wanted to survive. And since then I've maintained. I've managed. All this"—he waved in a big circle—"these booths and blood and just taking from one another all the damn time. So when some kid loses control and gets a stake through the heart, it's a piece of gossip to you people. It's my life."

"Is that what this is about? Brad?"

"You have a problem. You admitted you have a problem."

"I've been working on it for a year."

"Great. A year."

"Fuck you, a year's a long time for someone who can die. And I'm tangled, but I know enough to tell the difference between something I need and someone I want. I was wrong, fine. I'm not fucking perfect. But you're the one who keeps pulling back."

He dropped his hands. "You want me to be the monster here, fine. I can do that. I've had plenty of practice."

And he walked away.

The someone in fishnets by the trash heap had curled against the former bouncee. He passed her a cigarette. The someone took a drag and passed it back.

Cat swore in a growling grinding language not meant for human throats. Then she turned and ran.

23

Tara could not take notes on Shale's surging back, and as the moon arced through the sky, the angle from which the road sigils were visible changed too. The night ran long and late with flight and rest. They landed on an ivied university battlement at 1:00 A.M. and Shale brooded northward as Tara scratched lines in her black notebook.

"Lady of the skies?"

"Lady of the skies," he confirmed.

"All the skies?"

"She could not be Lady of all the skies. Each sky has its own Lady. But she is Lady of all skies over us."

"I always thought that was weird. I mean, if we have three women of different faiths in the same army and they look up, they're looking into the same sky."

"Same space," Shale said. "Different sky."

"And this is her oldest epithet."

He nodded.

She heard whispers from the tower to her left, and a scrape of lockpick over tumblers and teeth, and drunken laughter not quite stifled. She doubted students were supposed to climb up here—schools probably had to make rules about this sort of thing when students couldn't fly—but explanations would be awkward. She hurried her notes. Shale's religious signeurage did not quite mesh with modern ownership models, but she could bridge the gap. She'd learned how in the Hidden Schools, back when she wasn't doing the same thing these kids were: breaking into places she shouldn't be, and climbing towers not made for climbing.

"Are you done?"

"Done enough." She capped her pen and slipped pen and notebook into her purse. Behind them the lockpick raked again, and a latch clicked open. "Let's go." She grabbed Shale. His wings spread, squeezing her ribs, and he lunged out over the city. Drunken students screamed as a half-seen shape swept above them through the dark.

"You were angry this morning," she said as they gained altitude. She'd hesitated on this conversation's edge all night, unwilling to bring up a subject fraught for them both. But they had worked well enough, and she did not want to leave the wound unstitched.

"I still am."

"I told the truth. We're weak. Exposed. We need to be careful."

"We were made to guard this city. It is hard to hide and serve. You ask us to deny what we are. And your use of 'we,' there—you aid us, but you are not us. You are more at home in our own city than we are. You do not have to hide."

"I suppose not," she said, remembering.

Tara's mom had first warned her to keep hidden. Tara had brought her a fallen star, crackling in her hand. The sky hung thunder-dark overhead, but not so dark as Ma Abernathy's face. Tara's mother never hit her, like most Edgemont parents hit their children. Tara had never squirmed on her village schoolroom seat from switch marks. Nor had Ma Abernathy honed a scalpel of guilt like the mothers of her classmates at the Hidden Schools. Concern was her tool.

Tara'd run out into the rain, age ten, beneath a tornado-dark sky. She heard whispers on the wind and singing in the stars, and talked back, sang up, calling to the voices until the storm came, all spinning noise and fire, a solstice festival in the sky. She chased the voices into the fields, through sheets of rain, through broken whipping cornstalks, clothes plastered to her skin, hair a tangle of heavy rings. Then the thunder spoke, and a star fell. She caught it in her hand and brought it home.

Her mother met her on the cornfield's edge in the thrashing rain, as wet through as she. Her father had run into the fields after Tara and hadn't yet fought his way out. Tara held the star. It danced as it burned. She didn't know her mother's story then, didn't know about Alt Selene and the siege from which Ma's people fled, didn't know that to her mother the fire Tara held was a weed with roots in the guts of their history. Tara only knew that the light sang, and made her blood sing too.

Let it go, her mother said. Let it go and don't pick it up again.

Tara closed her hands and the fire entered her. Water steamed from her skin and she felt herself burned dry. She fell into her mother, and looking up saw only fear. She was sick for a week afterward, and her parents waited until she got better to talk to her about the future, about small towns and discovery, about hiding. About being anyone but who she was.

"I will ask a question of my own," Shale said.

Tara waited.

"Aev stopped you from binding me at the tower this morning. Yet with your glyph, you could have found me yourself, or cursed me from afar, without her knowledge. Why didn't you?"

"Because Aev didn't want me to," she said. "And because it's so easy for me to catch people, to force them. Too easy for me to think it's right. But I'm still not certain I made the right decision. You've brought us to a dangerous pass."

They flew for a while in silence.

"I have enough," she said when she did. "Let me down."

"Where do you live?"

She shouldn't tell him, but she told. They swept above the Paupers' Quarter market and north, where narrow brownstones flanked narrow tree-lined streets. He landed on her building's roof. Her arms felt loose in their sockets. When she rolled them, her shoulders popped. "That makes up for skipping the gym today. Lady of Skies and Earth. I need to visit the sanctum tomorrow, do a records search."

"What did you learn?"

"Why you can fly and I can't."

"I don't understand."

"I don't want to go into detail in case I'm wrong." She thumbed her notebook open and added a line to the glyphs she'd drawn there. "I'll need you later. You're right about translation. I can report your claims, but your testimony will help. The court's not built for gods."

"I noticed." Shale let his wings furl and his arms fall and his face droop. She did not know what a sigh would look like coming from a creature without lungs, but she thought it might look a great deal like that. "If I can help, tell me and I will." He had more to say, so she waited. "I did the right thing tonight, but I understand Aev's anger. I was not selfless in my work. I wanted to help those girls, to justify their love of me. I asked the Lady if I could aid them, and She said yes."

Tara looked up from the book. "She said yes for her own reasons."

"Not entirely," he said. "You'll find me when you need me, I suppose. You always can."

He took two steps toward the roof's edge. She wanted to reach for him but her hands were full; she snapped the book closed, let the pen fall, and caught him by the wrist as he was about to fly. "Shale." His weight almost pulled them both over. His talons tore silvery grooves in the brick as he steadied himself. "Hold still."

He did.

For this she did not need the knife. Glyphs on her hands and wrists gathered starlight. Shadow wet her fingertips. She touched his forehead, which was smooth and cold. A horse-skin twitch rippled through him—his body remembered the last time she'd touched him like this, and what she had done after. Her nails peeling back his face.

"Trust me," she said.

He did.

She painted shadows across his forehead, down cheek, beneath chin, up again, and over. Crystal lines pulsed beneath her shade: the patterns of his being. Between her and those lines lay an ugly angular mark. Its edges had spread in the last year as his soul shifted to incorporate the scar. She dipped her fingers through his skin, too fast for him to react, and caught the scar as if catching an eyelash against the white of an eye. She lifted the scar free, and let him go.

He stared at the brand of light she held.

"This is the tracking glyph. I'm not sorry I did it—if not for this, Kos would be dead and so would you. But I understand why you're angry." The next bit was hard to say. "I had to depend on myself for a long time. I got used to being right, or thinking I was, because if I doubted myself I'd break. And rightness always felt like this all-or-nothing thing. It's much easier to think everything I've done is justified than that I've done wrong things for right reasons. I don't regret what I did. But I apologize for it." She tore the glyph in half. It disintegrated, and the sparks swirled back up her fingers and through her skin.

"I understand," he said.

"How can I find you if I need you?"

"Go to a rooftop at night. Speak my name. I will come."

He spread his wings. Their wind made her blink, and when she recovered he was a curve of arched and moonlit stone, rising.

Okay, she told the moon. I have to admit, that was pretty cool.

She had documents to read, contracts to hunt, records to trace. But those could wait for morning, and she'd best catch what rest she could before time started running fast. She went below, and after a while she slept, with a goddess's laughter in her dreams.

Donna was waiting when Matt came home. The boys were in bed and, speaking of miracles, asleep. Donna hugged him. "I heard." She didn't say from whom. She looked at his bandage, not underneath it, and pressed her temple hard to his, opposite the wound. She smelled of sage.

Before he could reply, she slipped from his arms and turned to the Rafferty girls, offering drinks, blankets, taking their threadbare coats. The teakettle cried from the kitchen and she swept back bearing a tray of mugs of chamomile and honey with a drop of whiskey in each. Ellen and Hannah accepted. Claire refused the tea, asked for water instead. Sandy Sforza waited by the front door, out of the way. Matt got her a beer. She drank half as Donna woke Peter and hustled him to his brother's room—the oldest gives the most, Donna said when Peter groaned. The girls would have Peter's bright green room, with its narrow bed and a low bookshelf that bore only textbooks and a heavy rubber sphere for ullamal. The bed slept one; Donna made Hannah a pallet on the floor with good blankets and a stiff pillow. Claire took the couch.

"You're okay," Sandy said. Matt didn't know if it was a question, but he answered yes anyway. "I can't stomach the rest of this." She passed the beer back, gave him an open half hug to spare her ribs where Corbin had hit them.

Donna waited until they were in bed, lit by one candle and the city outside their window, to let her mask slip and the worry show. She rolled against Matt beneath their thin sheet, draped her arm across his belly, and squinted at his bandage. "He did that with a cane?"

"He was out of his head. When Sandy stepped in, he went for her. I don't want to talk about it."

"The boys will tell everyone," she said. "You haven't fought in a long time."

"Haven't had to. How was work?"

"The usual," she said. "Sums and more sums, and sums for dessert. Will the girls stay with us long?"

His back hurt. Not because of the fight; his back had been hurting lately, was all. "I know quarters are tight."

"They can stay as long as they need," Donna said. "I wanted to know if you saw them going back to their father." She said the last word as if she doubted it applied.

"He's worse than I knew." Which was a lie. He'd just not seen how bad. Drank with him plenty, and worked beside him, beside the girls, for years both before and after the mother left. He rolled the sheets off him onto Donna so he lay bare to the darkness of their closed room. "I love you," he said, and kissed her.

"Of course you do," she said. He got out of bed. She didn't ask why. If she'd asked, he would have said he needed a glass of water. That would not have been a lie, but it would not have been the complete truth. He did not know what he needed.

He tied the belt of his robe and opened the door to the living room slowly so the sound of the latch did not wake Claire. He padded past the couch. She curled strangely on the cushions under her sheet, her head propped against the armrest so if her eyes were open she could see the front door, and Matt's. But her eyes were closed, and she was still.

He poured a glass of water he didn't want to drink. By habit he went back to the living room to sit, then saw Claire beneath the blanket, and turned back toward the kitchen. "You don't have to go," Claire said. Her voice was low, but she wasn't whispering. She sounded as flat now as she had in Sandy's wagon. "This is your house. You can sit."

"This might be my house," he said, "but it's your room for now."

She shifted on the couch.

"I'm sorry," he said. "I knew he was an angry man."

She sat up, keeping the blankets tight to her neck like a barber's smock. "He's sick."

"I knew he drank. Looked like he kept the business together okay. That was all."

"I kept the business together," she said. "And took care of him when he came home. Made sure the girls were out of the way when he got angry." Girls, she said, as if she wasn't one. Maybe she wasn't. Maybe she hadn't had room to be.

The front door, he noticed, was ajar, as was the door to Peter's room where the girls were sleeping. He swore. Water sloshed onto his hand; he set the glass down and reached for his shoes. "What's happened?"

"Nothing," she said. "Ellen's gone to the roof to talk to the moon. She does that sometimes. Listen."

He did. Donna had left the kitchen window cracked to let the apartment breathe. Outside, wind slipped between fire escape bars and kicked cans down the street. Above its whistle he heard singing.

He started to say, she'll wake the neighbors, or, people are trying to sleep. "She's good."

"Yes," Claire said. "I thought she made it all up at first: the moon and the prayers. I had the same dreams, but that's all I thought they were. She was lonely. I thought she was cracked—she couldn't handle him, she couldn't toughen like me or hide like Hannah. But she sings to the moon, and maybe the moon sings back. What do you make of that?"

"I don't know," Matt said.

"Mr. Adorne," she said. "When will you go to work tomorrow morning?"

"I leave at half past three."

"If there's room in your cart, we can take deliveries together." He did not answer at first. "Please," she said. "I don't know how long they'll hold Corbin. We have stock to sell. I can pay for cart space if it's at a premium."

"I don't—we have plenty," he said. "You should rest a day or two."

"Ellen sings. Hannah runs. I work."

"I'll wake you," he said, "at quarter 'til."

"You won't have to."

He washed the glass and left it on the drying rack and walked back across the carpet to his room. "Good night, Claire."

"Good night, Mr. Adorne."

Donna wrapped herself around him when he lay beside her. The room was hot and so was her skin, but he needed her heat, and let her hold him when most nights he would have nudged her off. He stared up into the darkness, thinking about his boys and listening to the soft wordless song through his open window.

Cat hit the rooftops running. There was a black hot pit of rage inside her, and if she ran fast enough she could leave it behind. In the Pleasure Quarter you could run for blocks from roof to roof before you hit a street broad enough to make you jump. She wasn't alone up here. On nights like this, roofs were balconies for drinkers and dreamdust drifters. She ran past cots where hungry dreamers twitched and rolled, adjusting phototropically to her desire.

Oh there was a litany of curses inside her skull.

Oh she'd needed him.

Oh she was coursing on the cold fluid pleasant numbness that fang sent through her and oh she was hungry for more—

But that wasn't the source of her anger, or her loss, and he both was and wasn't the one she hated.

She grabbed the badge at her neck and let the Suit pour silver over and through her. But though it made her strong, though it made her fast, it didn't feel the way it had back when Justice was a cold clear mind without an I inside, the working out of brutal math. Now the ice joined her to something else. She felt the others in the back of her mind, but she was still herself, still Cat.

Faster, though, and stronger. She leapt from roof to roof, and the drunks and dreamdust trippers, the tripmasters and cots and clouds of smoke, the railings and roads all blurred. She leapt over alley after alley, ignoring the bloodrush.

Fine, she thought up to the immense cold silver web. Fine, she screamed at the moon. You want me to let you in. Take me, then. I've worked and worked, and here I am back where I started. My room's a cot and a dresser and a mess. You want worship? Take it all. Take everything I have. Drag me back to where I was before: at least in you I had a space where I was gone. Peel me out of me.

She reached the broad ring road at the Quarter's edge. She couldn't jump that distance. She gathered herself and spread wings from her back and flew.

At the apex of her arc she realized she was falling.

Her wings slipped on the wind. She tumbled, mouth open beneath the silver mask, screaming through the sky to land and skid on a roof. The force of her fall blinked off the world. When she came back to herself, she hurt. She lay, human again, in torn clothes at the end of a furrow her fall had plowed through gravel. Gasping. Salt tears wet her face. She hadn't cried in a while.

She became aware, later, of a shape crouching over her, massive and stone. Aev settled beside her.

Cat lay still, not knowing whether she was dreaming.

"I'm here," Aev said, soft as an avalanche.

"I fell."

Her touch on Cat's arm was firm and light. She used the pads of her fingers, not her talons. "It's hard to fly," she said. "But you can learn."

On the Alt Coulumb docks, in the hold of a ship, a hundred bodies waited, and other minds waited within.

24

No pig wants to start the morning trussed.

This one woke on its back in a forest clearing. Nearby, past screening shrubs and evergreens, large wagons rolled down a highway. The pig did not know *highway* or *wagons*, but it knew the sound. Rough, heavy cord bound its trotters. It squirmed and surged and wriggled. The coils on its left foreleg began to slip.

A knife flashed in the cold, too bright for pain. The pain came later. Then—nothing.

Two women stood in the clearing. The pig bled on bare earth. The blood from its opened throat traced drunken spider trails along the soil toward a circle of burned pine needles around the corpse. When the blood reached the circle's edge, it pooled as if it had run against glass.

The younger woman sheathed her work knife. Her hands were clean. She pondered the blood patterns within the circle.

"Camlaan First Credit and HBSE are on board, Ms. Ramp," she said after a long silence of mental calculation. "Shipping arrangements have been settled." She pushed back her hood. The face revealed was smooth, and smiling. "Looks like we're ready."

The second woman said, "Well done, Ms. Mains." She reviewed the blood herself. "Competently read. Though your knots are loose. He almost slipped free."

"Thank you, ma'am. I'll review my knot work today."

When the older woman withdrew from the circle she brushed the fingers of her gloves together as if rubbing off a stain, though she had not crossed the circle herself or approached the blood. "Onward, then."

Ms. Mains removed her work robe and packed it inside a valise that was larger inside than out. She made sharp folds and dangerous corners. "Alt Coulumb, ma'am?"

"In haste. The church needs time to ponder our proposal." She produced a coin from her sleeve, examined its head and tail, and closed it in her fist.

"It's so nice to take country walks," said Ms. Mains brightly as she lifted the valise. "I think someday I'll move out here. Get a nice house. Settle down. Raise chickens in the backyard. Even pigs." She drew her fist to her mouth as if to catch the laugh that escaped. "After I retire from the firm, of course."

The older woman opened her fingers. The coin was not there. "Leave all this? You'd be bored blind in a week."

Ms. Mains considered asking which "this" she meant. It occurred to her, not for the first time, that Madeline Ramp did not quite live in the same world she, Ms. Mains, occupied. For Ms. Mains, the sky was pale blue some pansies fade to, and beyond the clearing's edge brown earth rolled southeast through pine forests to a low brook that might contain a few trout. For Ms. Ramp, there was a dead pig in the center of the clearing, some quantity of useless information in front of her, and behind her, the road to work.

Ms. Ramp turned to go, then turned back to the pig and moved her finger in a sharp cutting motion. Skin peeled from its belly and invisible knives carved out a square of flesh eight inches on a side and an inch thick, muscle marbled with fat. Ms. Ramp muttered beneath her breath and the flesh shrank, dried, colored. The sky deepened (Daphne Mains thought) to the violet of a pansy's core. Ramp spread her fingers, and the flesh sectioned into narrow strips. The scent of seared meat filled the clearing. When she was done, still gloved, she plucked a piece of bacon from the air and ate it. Grease glistened on her gloved fingertips. "Would you like some, Ms. Mains?"

"I ate at the airport, ma'am."

"Not even a light snack?"

"No, thank you."

"Your loss," she said, and left the clearing, crunching. Ms. Mains followed with the valise.

As they left, the spider-tracery of blood clotted. The first flies landed to drink, and died. Later, crows landed to gnaw the spoiling flesh.

They died, too.

Tara was three coffees into the morning by the time she reached the Alt Coulumb docks and the *Dream* moored there under Blacksuit guard.

Cat met her on the pier. She looked, charitably, horrible: Tara associated the kind of circles under her eyes with fistfights more than restless sleep, and her skin was worryingly pale. But she clutched her coffee firmly, and her expression seemed set. Tara decided to keep this professional. She and Cat could be combative enough under the best circumstances.

"Late night?" Cat said, when she was close enough.

Oh, fine. "Looks like I'm not the only one."

Cat pointed with her coffee toward the *Dream*. "The operation was a success." Which wasn't the whole story, to judge from her tone of voice, but it was a start. "I think by right of salvage this belongs to me. What do people do with boats, anyway?"

"Sail them," Tara said, climbing the gangplank. "And it's not yours. You found it occupied. If you took it, you're engaged either in piracy or law enforcement."

"Bit of both, in this case. Law enforcement with pirates."

"Is there more coffee?"

"I don't know if I'd call it coffee exactly," Cat said. "More like coffee-adjacent."

"Adjacent is fine. I didn't sleep until after two." She'd promised herself bed after Shale left, but the silver poems lingered in her mind. And then, being too tired for cause-and-effect thoughts like "I have to get up in the morning," she'd read her mother's letter, or tried, and when that didn't work she read her student loan statement again, and then her balance book, and decided that if she ate instant noodles for the next month maybe she could pay down the principle. She had planned to sail straight for the church archives this morning but ran aground instead on the message Cat left with her office doorman. "What can I do for you?" Four Blacksuits stood on the ship's deck, immobile and faceless as unfinished statues.

Cat led her into the hold; once she saw the refrigeration wards, she understood. "Indentures. Zombie traders. They docked here?"

"Not their idea," she said. "Raz knew that the captain, Varg, was involved in the trade, but she never docked with us, just anchored out of port and ferried in. We caught her in a dreamglass deal in the city, which gave us grounds to search and seize the ship."

"Clever." Tara tugged the door open. Icy air vented into the hold. Row upon row of bodies lay in the cold dark, clad in rough canvas, immobile. Men and women from the Gleb, by the look of it. Tara's shiver had nothing to do with the temperature. "Gods."

Cat propped the door open and followed Tara inside. Her coffee started to steam again. "I hoped you could wake them up. We tried dragging one out of the freezer but he started . . ." She shook her head. "It looked like a seizure. We put him back."

Tara paced the hold. Bodies lay four deep on either side. "What do you normally do when you catch a zombie trader?"

"They don't pass through here often, since Kos forbids indefinite indentures and debt slavery. Most of the time indentures just wake up when they're brought in. It's traumatic, but I've never seen anything like this. I figured you could help. If not, we can hire someone, but I know Craftsmen aren't wild about property seizures."

Tara frowned. "They're not property. That's the problem. The Craft depends on freedom of contract: people can trade away whatever they want, except their ability to agree to trades. But they can offer labor as collateral."

"That's the same thing."

"Not technically," she said. "But practice is the problem." She searched the room. There were many ways to cool a space: elementals were the most common, but none lived here. This ship's owners must have used unshielded Craft to suck heat from this space to power something else. But what?

There. A line of pulsing red was worked into the timbers of the hold. Tara wiped frost from the bulkhead. There, carved with exact knifework, lay nesting geometries of Craft. She cut a piece of canvas from an indenture's trousers and continued around the hold, wiping away the frost. By the time she completed the circle, she shuddered with lost heat and had to return to the hold and rub her hands until feeling needled back into her fingertips.

A Blacksuit brought Cat a form to sign, and she did. "I don't understand how you can let this happen," Cat said. "It's disgusting."

"I agree. This is part of the reason the Craft's uncomfortable with addiction and games, even stories. Prices are a negotiation. If you control desire—if you make people want something—you can do strange stuff to them. That's before we get into newfangled treachery, like balloon payments and variable interest rates. Most forced indentures wouldn't hold up in court, but few victims have access to Craftsmen."

"So why haven't they woken up?"

"Because that room technically isn't part of Alt Coulumb. It's Kavekanese territory; the whole place is a chapel to one of their idols."

Cat frowned. "To a fake god? Can they do that?"

"Sure. Kos is bound to recognize the Kavekanese pantheon, otherwise he wouldn't be able to do business with Concerns based in Kavekana, which is most of them. So he can't overrule the circle."

"And why can't we drag them out?"

"Without the permission of the person who holds the indenture, dragging them out means you're trying to void their contract. Which Kos is bound to enforce in this case, because of the good faith clauses in his treaty. When you pull them out, Kos fights himself. Like one of those finger traps."

"Can you fix it?"

She shook her head. "This is why I studied necromancy. Dead things behave predictably. Transactional work would give a dragon a headache. Their Craftswoman has tied this declaration of territory to a powerful, open-sourced binding ward. If that ward had a weakness in it, a million Craftswomen would have found it by now. We can fight her on the particulars of the case, by asserting primacy—basically, refusing to recognize the Kavekanese claim to their territory. In Crafty terms, it's like sticking your fingers in your ears and shouting really loud to keep the other person from persuading you; it's not good form, but it works temporarily. For that I'd need Kos's backing, though, which he can't give, because of the treaty. It's a neat trap."

"But Kos isn't the only God we have available." The top button of Cat's shirt was open; she reached beneath and fished out an ivory pendant Tara knew too well.

She did a little math in her head. Removed the black book from her purse, consulted her notes from yesterday's flight. Lady of Sky and Stone, okay, and the moon had tidal influence. "Cat, that's a really good idea."

"You don't have to sound so surprised."

"As Justice, she's pledged to support Kos; as Seril, she's independent. And since the Blacksuit is a repurposed temple contract, you're technically her priestess. You said you seized this boat—"

"Ship."

"Ship, you seized it with other Blacksuits?"

"And with Raz." She made a face when she said his name.

"Something wrong?"

"Don't start."

"Fine," she said. Cold bodies lay behind the closed door. "So, you and Raz. Anyone else?"

"Aev."

"Good. We can claim Seril, rather than Kos, seized the boat. Ship. Seril died—at least, we all thought she did—before they started building idols on Kavekana, so she's never signed a full-faith-and-credit agreement with them. That should work."

"So Seril gets the ship."

"In a way, the timing's perfect. Yesterday I would have said no, because this would tip off the world that Seril was still alive. But we're announcing her survival in an interview tonight. I can set up the triggers in advance. When we're ready, you and Raz sign the paper and wake these people up, giving us more evidence Seril's separate from Kos—because if she was not, we couldn't break this circle." She rifled through her purse. Vials, vials, astrolabe, sextant, compass, paring knife, rabbit's foot, black bag, silver nails, more vials. "Shit. Do you have any cinnabar?"

"I'll send someone," Cat said.

"We need the good stuff. There's a guy on Twenty-third and Vine—"

"I'll send someone."

"And I'll get to work."

25

Matt woke at quarter to three as usual, and found Claire sleeping. He lit the stove with his morning prayers, made coffee, and pondered eggs. The coffee smell woke her, and she entered the kitchen wearing Donna's robe belted tight around her waist and closed up to her throat. Couch cushions left a deep crease down her cheek.

"Coffee?" she asked before he could offer. Her voice was a crackle of dead leaves. He poured from the percolator and she drank as if racing to reach the bottom. "Thank you," she said when she finished, and he poured more. The coffee filled in the cracks of her voice.

"Do you like eggs?"

"Every way but boiled."

He'd planned to take a few hard-boiled from the bowl in the refrigerator, but she was a guest. "Cheese?"

"Yes." She poured herself more coffee. Emptied the percolator halfway through the cup. "I'm sorry. I didn't ask if you wanted—"

"I'll make more." He was not whispering, but he talked low. "I don't have company in the mornings."

"I'll do the coffee. You make eggs."

He grated a handful of sharp cheese, heated oil, cracked the eggs into a bowl, did his best to ignore Claire moving through the kitchen. Her footsteps weren't Donna's, and he hadn't realized how unused he was to anyone else's presence here. "Coffee's in the cabinet upper left of the sink." Outside the sky was still black, and streetlights burned. Scramble, scramble.

"You buy it ground?" As if he'd confessed to killing children.

"The store grinds it for the percolator."

She kept quiet, leaving him space to ponder the wrongness of his opinion. She dumped grounds into the sink, which made him wince— they didn't have a disposal. He remembered yesterday's sharp-edged conversation and compared it to whatever was happening this morning, so early that Donna still called it night. There was dew on the window. The eggs set; he tossed in cheese, and didn't correct her about the grounds in the sink.

She watched the coffee as if it were the spring's first flower opening from a bud. Snapped off the burner, poured fast. When he drank, the flavor opened and kept opening into the back of his throat.

"Good eggs," she said around a mouthful.

"What did you do to the coffee?"

"If you overboil it, there's too much acid," she said. "The taste's weaker than it should be but that's what you get using ground beans. I added cinnamon, but it's not the same." She shoveled the remaining eggs into her mouth, swallowed hard, then added coffee. "Good, though."

"You'll have to show me."

"It's easy."

Dishes in the sink. He grabbed his jacket. By the time he returned, he found she'd washed the dishes, racked them to dry, and scooped the grounds out of the sink.

He stabled the wagon in a garage three blocks over. The morning's chill fingers ignored his jacket, shirt, and skin, shoved right into him to grab handfuls of viscera. Claire kept her chin down. Theirs was the first cart to leave the garage; the golem plodded forward on four legs. They descended the garage ramp to the street and picked up speed as they drove west through drifting mist beneath a sky still hung with stars.

"I'll take the leads," Claire said when they cleared the quarter's edge. "You can sleep."

The offer confused Matt. He had not considered letting someone else drive his cart, because he never had someone else to do so. Navigating the morning with this girl beside him made his whole routine, the road and the cart and the mist, seem strange. "I can't sleep once I'm awake," he said. That sounded like a riddle told by those head-shaved kids who studied with the Shining Empire sages down on Bleeker, so he tried again. "I mean, I don't nap."

"I'm the same," she said. "I asked because it's boring to sit here with nothing to do."

The golem trudged through the muck of unswept streets.

"You've worked golems before?"

"We have one."

"We'll switch off. No sense just one of us being bored."

She accepted the leads. Her hand wasn't so steady as Matt's. She took corners harder and stopped faster, and hummed tunelessly as she drove, notes crushed and skewed and not at all like her sister's song. But she watched the road. Donna always made fun of Matt for his caution with the leads. Came from the business: eggs were strong, but he didn't like to jostle them. A carton broken was a carton lost.

"You drive often?"

She let the wheels roll the question under and golem feet trample it. When he thought it crushed to death, she spoke. "I drive most days. Dad doesn't tend to wake this early. When he's sick, I go. When he isn't, I pretend I'm sleeping."

When she said "sick," he heard hung over, and remembered Corbin's foul look in the stalls of a morning. "It's good of you to take care of him."

"I take care of the girls."

He almost asked what she meant by that, by not including herself with her sisters, but he had an idea. "It's not fair that you have to do so much."

"How's your head?"

He didn't understand the question. She touched her own left temple; he mimicked her, and felt the bandage there and the scab beneath. It was a dull ache.

City gave ground to country as grudgingly as the night surrendered to dawn. Trees replaced sidewalks, grasses invaded the gaps between buildings. The sky crushed houses down to soil. They made good time thanks to Claire's driving. Fields opened, with dirt roads winding into them, and they followed those roads, collecting from her suppliers and his. "Didn't know you had a girl," Cummings said when Matt picked up his eggs.

"I don't," Matt said. "Just doing a favor for—" A friend? Was Rafferty a friend? Was he doing this for him? "Just doing a favor."

Cummings came from people who didn't talk much and spoke mostly with their faces: brows raised, lips pursed, cheeks hollowed, breath drawn through the nose. He spit into the dirt. "Mighty fine. Mrs. Cummings made more coffee. You want some?"

"Could use some, thank you, Samuel."

Cummings brought two mugs. "Bring 'em back tomorrow is all."

"Thank you," he said, and she said to him when he brought the mugs to her. The coffee wasn't as good as Claire's, but it passed.

26

The runner from the Church of Kos found Tara an hour and a half later. She'd mainlined two more cups of coffee-adjacent liquid to stop the glyphs from squirming beneath her knife as she carved them. The cinnabar was the good stuff after all. Once Tara was in motion, she found the chill invigorating.

Occasionally as she worked she added up the fees she would have billed for this job in private practice—like humming, only with regret instead of music. She could be off with Ms. Kevarian in the Archipelago, jetting from case to case rather than miring herself in local politics. Certainly she'd have made more progress on her debt. But then who would have been left to help these people? Or deal with Gavriel Jones?

Or to swear a blue streak when she opened the sealed scroll the runner brought her and read: representatives from Grossman and Mime arrived to meet with Cardinals, come at earliest convenience?

Cat spun around and dropped into a fighting crouch when Tara stormed onto the deck. "What the hells is going on?" She had to sprint to catch Tara.

"I'm done downstairs," she said, and tossed Cat a scroll. "Get Raz's signature; this will wake them when the time's right. Meanwhile, make sure no one goes inside, and if anyone does, don't let them touch anything. I have to leave."

"What is it?"

"I'll explain later." She ran down the gangplank to the docks, past the Blacksuit cordon into a haze of spice and silk and shouted sales pitches. A kid tried to pick her pocket but she caught her wrist and let her go. Past the market, she raised one hand and swore to pass the time until a cab arrived.

Abelard met her at the sanctum doors. He paced outside the front steps, leaving little holes in the gravel when he turned. Just like old times.

"Bede's meeting the Craftswomen now," he said. "They arrived an hour ago. Took a red-eye from Dresediel Lex, they said. Two of them. I didn't get their cards. They just showed up and demanded to speak with the Cardinals. The senior's a woman named Ramp."

He led her through the forechamber with its stained glass and pointed arches and vaulted columns and kneeling faithful. No amount of people gathered here could possibly make the place feel full, but the pews were packed, and even side shrines occupied. Abelard led her at a jog down a hall so narrow it seemed more like a fissure in rock than a space built for humans. "Madeline Ramp?"

"That's the one." They stopped in front of a lift. Abelard pushed the UP button, and as they waited, asked, "You know her?"

There were many ways to answer that question. "She's a demonic transactional specialist. She was coauthor on a paper I read back at school. Very high-level stuff."

"What was the subject?"

"Strategic modeling in distributed action networks."

"What does that mean?"

"It'd take more than an elevator ride to explain." The doors dinged and rolled open. "What matters is the name of the first coauthor."

Abelard followed her into the lift. "Denovo."

A demon in suspenders with a slim, collected smile. The skeleton on the slab. "Alexander Denovo."

"She's here for revenge."

"There are many stories about Madeline Ramp," Tara said, "but revenge isn't her style. Denovo worked with lots of people. She's a Craftswoman, a successful academic, a partner at a top-level firm. There are lots of reasons someone might hire her."

"Denovo could get to people, though. Influence them."

"He was subtle, and strong, but I doubt he could have bound someone and left her high-functioning enough to operate as a partner in a named firm. He was a renowned scholar for decades. The fact someone worked with him doesn't make that person automatically horrible. It just means she could stand being in the same room with him long enough to agree on a paper topic."

"That's enough to make her suspect in my book," Abelard said.

They reached the sixtieth floor and the doors rolled back. Up here the priesthood's architects had abandoned stone and stained glass for pale wood and wall-to-wall carpet—practical. It was easier to set up sympathetic tricks with stone. To listen through wood, a Craftswoman needed a splinter from the same tree. Not a perfect ward, but every little bit helped.

The conference room at the hall's end had its blinds drawn. Tara checked her own reflection in the glass, straightened jacket, adjusted cuffs, smoothed skirt. Decent armor for a meeting, coupled with her high confidence after solving the indenture problem. She could deal with Madeline Ramp.

She opened the door and stepped inside.

And stopped on the threshold. Abelard bumped into her, which was fortunate. If not for him she might have remained frozen forever.

Cardinal Bede sat at the conference table smoking, and Cardinal Nestor beside him. At the far end of the room stood Madeline Ramp: round faced and smooth as a lizard in a lavender suit. She wore thin leather gloves—at least, Tara thought they were gloves. "Ms. Abernathy!" Ramp said. "Pleasure to meet you. I've heard so much about you from my colleagues. I'm glad to see they didn't undersell. I was just explaining our position to your clients."

Tara was not looking at Ramp. The Craftswoman might have turned into an eel for all she cared. Tara had last seen woman beside her—pale hair, full mouth, pockmark on the left cheek—being carted comatose from the Hidden Schools. She was awake now: dressed and sharp, and smiling. "Hello, Tara."

"Daphne," she said. The name fit out Tara's mouth, which was a feat. She walked, wooden, to the desk and sat. "I didn't expect to see you here." Which was a dumb thing to say, but she had not prepared any one-liners for the occasion.

"You already know each other," Ms. Ramp said. "Wonderful! Then we can get right to business. Ms. Abernathy, I'm here on behalf of a consortium of Grossman and Mime clients—" A folded piece of paper lay on the table before her, and with a flick of a gloved finger she floated it to Tara. Tara could have guessed most of the names. Take every bank and private equity fund mentioned more than once a year in the *Thaumaturgist*, cross out those run by gods or their representatives, and that was the list, less a few exceptions. Alphan, HBSE, First and Major, a double handful of Concerns representing net deposits of a few hundred million souls. Church shareholders and creditors.

No surprises, but that didn't make reading the list any easier.

"—To investigate allegations Kos Everburning has substantial offbook liabilities. I know you've heard the same reports I have, and I want to stress that we hope to resolve this situation in a straightforward, mutually agreeable fashion. We're not interested in posturing, and the last, and I do mean *last*, thing my clients want is for this to affect their bottom lines."

Ramp's eyes were flat as the gold circles that sometimes flashed inside a cat's. And beside her sat Daphne Mains: former classmate, fellow victim, the woman whose breaking had forced Tara to confront the blight Professor Denovo made of her life, the woman Tara thought dead in every way that mattered.

Focus, dammit.

"I'm happy to hear," Tara said, "your clients are concerned about proper bookkeeping and the risks of disguised liability." Especially since most of them had their own dump heaps for underperforming assets, she did not say. "But Kos Everburning's dealings are all aboveboard."

"As I told Ms. Ramp," Bede said.

"I wish I could leave it at that." Ramp's wide smile showed too many teeth. "But what are we to make of reports Kos is backing a fledgling goddess?"

Abelard sat down beside Tara, stiffly. The question had been directed at Bede and Nestor, but if Tara let the Cardinals speak there was too much risk they would lie, or try something clever. Madeline Ramp would eat their clever alive. "I've heard the same reports," Tara said. "And I understand why they give your clients pause." Don't look at Daphne. Watch her boss, and keep your voice level. Were Ramp's teeth filed to points? "There is another goddess operating in Alt Coulumb, by mutual agreement with the Church of Kos. Their relationship is based on nonoverlapping magisteria. A few onetime grants of soulstuff have changed hands, but no formal dependency exists. Your clients can rest assured her presence does not alter Kos's risk profile."

"Gargoyles on rooftops, and moonlight in alleys," Ramp said. "I'm not the only one in this room who's drawn the obvious conclusion. Seril, or a new entity assuming her portfolio, is at work. The old moon goddess and Kos were lovers, if I understand correctly. That's a lot closer than nonoverlapping magisteria."

"The two entities aren't necessarily the same," Tara said. "And even if they were, there's no dependency. Kos and Seril ruled together before her death, but their operations were distinct, as should be obvious from Seril's participation and death in the Wars, and Kos's neutrality. If she's back—or another entity has assumed her mythological role—that entity would have the same relationship to Kos. Again, hardly an undisclosed risk."

These words were courtesies, outlines of attack and defense, salutes and overtures, acknowledgments of strength and weakness outlining one direction their battle might run in court. Ramp leaned back, at tremendous ease. "Tara, my clients are afraid Seril—let's just call her that—affects Kos's ability to fulfill his obligations. If she's running around without any formal limits, who knows what she might do? She was vicious, in the Wars." Ramp's shoulders twitched, a mock shiver. "If someone like that's in the picture, my clients face a lot more risk than was disclosed to them when they acquired substantial stakes in Kos, especially when we take into account Kos's near death last year. Now—" Tara was about to respond, but Ramp raised one glove, fingers spread—the leather was diamond-patterned like alligator hide and grooved where the lines of her palm would have been. Ramp had, Tara saw, a very long life line. "I know, and won't insult you by claiming otherwise, that my clients supported Kos's resurrection. We accepted your argument that his death did not reflect underlying thaumaturgical issues, especially after Alexander Denovo's insider trading came to light. But if Seril's back, she's a liability. And if she is a liability, my clients deserve to know, so they can manage their exposure. That only stands to reason."

Abelard, beside Tara, sat statue stiff. He'd almost smoked his cigarette to the filter. Ash dripped onto his robe.

That was the trap: Ramp, plain speaker, chaining fact to simple fact and every link biting into their collective throat.

"You can check our books," Tara said.

"It's the implicit guarantee of support that concerns us, not the quality of your records."

"There is no implicit guarantee."

"I wish I could believe that." She displayed her empty hands: a gesture evolved by tool-using apes back in the mists of time to show they bore no weapons. It didn't work well for a Craftswoman, whose weapons were invisible. "Unless you show me a binding document forbidding mutual support, my clients will not accept the absence of such a guarantee. We move a lot of power through Kos's church. We're not here to play the bad guys, Tara. We just want to protect ourselves."

"What's the point of a superfluous document?" she asked. "Kos has issued the party in question two start-up grants of soulstuff while she develops her own operation. Plenty of gods offer short-term dispensations of grace. He hasn't guaranteed loans for this party, or offered regular assistance, as a review of our books will show." She did not say: and if he has, you can't prove otherwise. Nor did she say: and I hope he's listening. "I'm sorry you came all this way for nothing."

Ms. Ramp had a wide smile. "Not for nothing."

Tara risked a quick blink to survey the conference room with a Craftswoman's eyes. Standard darkness and lightning lines, distorted by the warmth of Kos's presence within his temple. Ramp was many armed and wetly glistening; beside her, shadow-wrapped clockwork wireframe, sat Daphne.

Daphne's hand lay palm up on her lap. Lines of spiderweb silk glimmered there: letters. LUNCH?

She almost laughed, but managed to keep her composure. Daphne watched Ramp, and Tara, and the Cardinals and Abelard, with the determination of the perfect young associate.

"I," Ms. Ramp said, "will review Kos's recent records myself this afternoon. I hope what I find confirms your story, and sets my clients at ease."

"Of course," Tara replied, to both.

27

Captain Maura Varg drummed a syncopated rhythm on the interview room table in the Temple of Justice. A column of light drifted through the high window.

Cat sat across from her, with Lee to the left, composed and silent. "We're here whenever you're ready to talk, Maura."

"Don't like the beat?" Varg accelerated, drumrolled. "Keeping a different pattern with each hand's the hard part. And I want a Craftsman in the room before I talk to you."

"Stop drumming."

She did, leaned back in her chair, and planted her boots on the table.

"Boots down."

Varg returned her feet to the floor. "I could do jumping jacks."

"Cut the shit."

"Bring me a Craftsman."

"What possible out do you think you have in this situation?"

"I know my rights."

"We caught you in a dreamglass factory. You ran, resisted arrest, assaulted a civilian."

"Civilian? You mean Raz?" She laughed. "Tackled me first. I grabbed him in self-defense."

"You cut his throat. I don't think those wings will fly you far."

"He pushed into the knife. Which he wouldn't have done if he thought there was a chance it would harm him."

"Not necessarily true."

"You know him better than I do? After what, Officer Elle, a few weeks all told on portside visits?" She shook her head. "He's a mystery to you. You suckered me in here, fine. You seized my ship. You want to play the do-gooder by strangling legitimate commerce, that's your damage. But you got what you got on false grounds, and I'll drag you and Justice into court to prove it."

"False grounds? You brought enough soul into that house to buy a full dreamglass shipment."

"An agent hired me to make a trade. She told me where to go and when to get there and what to do once I was there. I'd just realized what was happening—I was about to leave before you jumped in."

"You set your briefcase on the table and picked up theirs."

"They looked similar. Either way, this stinks. I do business in Alt Coulumb. If I was buying dreamglass, why would I buy from a local supplier? I can just weigh anchor and sail somewhere it's legal. You set me up, and I want a Craftsman."

"You'll get one, don't worry," Cat said. "And when you do, I'll see you go down for a kidnapper, a smuggler, and a slaver."

"All that just 'cause I cut the guy you want to ride."

Cat stood. "What did you say?"

"He's dropped by Alt Coulumb more in the last year than in the forty previous, but I didn't expect he'd go through all that trouble for someone like you. He didn't used to care for girls with habits. Maybe he's slipping. They do, you know, when they're long in the tooth."

Cat had grown in the last year. There was a time, not long past, when she would have leaned across the table and broken Varg's jaw. When she wouldn't have stopped with the jaw.

Time was past. That was good, she told herself.

Still felt like hells that all she could do was say, "Fuck you," and walk away.

"I don't know how you stand it here," Daphne said to Tara as they walked down the stone paths of the Sacred Precinct, full from a Business District lunch for which Daphne'd paid. Which was only rational: Daphne was the one making a firm salary.

This wasn't how Tara envisioned their reunion. They'd talked over lunch—salad, lobster ravioli in a butter sauce, a glass of wine for each—but the conversation stayed light. New books read. Old friends, roommates, rivals moved on to positions of influence. Val worked with Halcyon Vega at Varkath Nebuchadnezzar, which seemed an odd choice since everyone expected she'd go straight into necromancy. No surprise to anyone Chris Li talked his way into a Judicial clerkship, though both had their doubts about how a Xivai beach bum born and bred would adapt to a year in Trälheim. Tara lost herself so deep in the conversation she could almost ignore the ticking clock in the back of her mind, counting the time she should have been at work. By the time the check came, they had broken through the shell of their shared history to find the silence beneath.

So Tara led them to the Sacred Precinct, to stone-edged gravel paths. Around them, monks and priests strolled in hooded silence. Two old nuns laughed across the grass. A bearded man counted rosary beads on a bench.

"Daffy," Tara said, changing the subject, and Daphne chuckled at the nickname. "What's the last thing you remember from the Schools?"

"I don't know." She kicked the gravel hard enough to leave a trench; small rocks bounced off the toe of her shoe. Mess up the leather doing that, Tara thought. Daphne's family had enough nice things she'd never learned to care for them. "It's all muddled. My last clear memory's junior year spring break. My junior year, not yours, when we went to the Fangs."

"That's clear for you? Blood and hells. I lost a day in that mess."

"You, me, Julian, Chris, Val, Mike Ngabe. Playing soccer on the beach. You got mad at Mike for something—"

"I fell," she said. "He laughed at me."

"So you built an affinity between the ball and his sunglasses. Broke his nose."

"I didn't think it would hit him that hard. And I was drunk."

"After that it's muddy." She picked up two rocks and juggled them as they walked: a trick, she'd told Tara many times before, of throwing the second when the first began its descent. Tara never mastered the timing of the fall. "I remember working in Professor Denovo's lab. Really tremendous fascinating stuff, vivisecting gods, experimental faith dynamics." Tara remembered that tone of voice: the drunkenness of discovery. The rocks Daphne juggled were small; Tara could not hear their impact on her skin. "He liked my work. I remember his smile." Tara clenched her jaw to keep herself from saying something stupid. "And I remember cutting things open, peeling flesh like a kid opening a birthday present. Working ten hours at a stretch hunting a slice of new knowledge. Draining myself so far I didn't feel I was moving so much as being moved, like a puppet with a hand inside me. I remember grays. I remember lots of gray, toward the end. Not recognizing my face in the mirror. Waking up in bed in a strange body." She caught both the rocks and squeezed. Glyphs sparked on her fingers, and a fine dust rained onto the gravel.

"Daphne, I'm sorry."

She opened her hand. Dust coated her palm, surrounding a small sculpture of a sparrow with wings stretched. Its tiny head revolved. Wings flapped, but the sparrow could not fly.

"It's the local gods," Tara said. "They don't let things fly that they don't own."

She held out her palm and Daphne passed her the bird. Tiny talons pricked her skin; it chirped. "I didn't see what was happening to you until too late," Tara said. "He was in my head, too. When you collapsed, when they took you home, that shocked me sober. I snapped out of his control. I got revenge, or tried. I burned his lab. They kicked me out. I thought you were gone."

"I woke up a year ago, in my house, with a headache. I spent weeks in the garden watching flowers. It took a long time to piece myself together. The chance of getting a job was low, but then Ramp came with an offer from Grossman and Mime. They were interested in everyone who worked with Professor Denovo. A lot of our friends ended up there. Ramp is a tough boss, but she has a sense of humor and enjoys her work, which is more than I could say for many Craftswomen."

"It doesn't bother you that she used to work with Denovo?"

"He was a good teacher," she said. "A hard driver, but you'd have to be to get as far as him."

"He sapped your soul. He bound us to serve him. Our minds pointed where he wanted them to point."

Something clicked closed behind Daphne's face. "What did he do that everyone you've ever worked with hasn't? People bind each other. That's all the Craft is."

"You went home in a coma."

"I chose to work hard. If my body couldn't handle it—"

"That's what I'm saying, Daphne. You didn't choose."

"Fine," she said. "I don't want to talk about this anymore."

Tara wanted to take her shoulders and shake her, but she didn't. The bird flapped its wings and sang frustration. "You're happy where you are?"

"Are you?"

"Of course. I'm helping my friends. I'm protecting my city."

"Seriously, Tara?" She pointed up. The Sanctum of Kos towered overhead, huge and black, buttressed and bubbled with lifts and turrets and bay windows. "Working for a god? It's cool you have so much authority, but don't you see this is a dead-end gig?"

"Alt Coulumb's an important place, and I'm working for the biggest game in town. Doesn't seem dead end to me."

"You can't even fly here. Working in-house at a church, hells, they'll never pay you half what you're worth. What kind of career prospects do you have? Will you take holy orders or something?"

"I don't plan to."

"There you go. I mean, I'm sure you think you can do good work here. But did you really leave Kelethres, Albrecht, and Ao for this?"

"I saw what my life at the firm would have been. Traveling from city to city without knowing any of them, having clients and colleagues and puppets instead of people. Alt Coulumb's more than a convention hotel, a handful of boardrooms, and the nice restaurants the firm will pay for. I have friends here. They need me."

"Friends," she said, "don't command gods, or raise the dead, or drink the light of shadows or hunt nightmares or make deals in blood or anything you trained for. I know what you went through to reach the Hidden Schools. Years of wandering the desert working shit jobs, learning whatever hedge magic you could from sun-blind witches and confidence tricksters, all to pass the entrance exams. And once you made it, you worked harder than any of us. Why throw it all away?"

"Because it was rotten. Our teacher was hurting you. Hurting us."

"That's not right and that's not even what I mean." Her voice rose, and her arms too. Glyphs on her skin glowed and gravel whirled beneath her feet. "You're so—" But Daphne didn't say what Tara was. She let her arms fall. The gravel stilled, leaving spiral grooves centered on Daphne's scuffed shoes. "Damn, I'm sorry. You ran. You were better than all of us, every single one of us, and you ran. I know the in-house rates gods pay, and I know the rent in Alt Coulumb, and the thought of you of all people sitting in a coffin-size studio stressing whether you can pay down your loans this month—it sickens me. If half the stories I heard about what you did last year during Kos's resurrection are true, you could have written your ticket at Keleth-res Albrecht or any other firm. I can't believe you see your future here, protecting god-botherers from their own dumb mistakes."

"You want to offer me a job."

"I want to help my boss. But I asked her, and if you're looking, we could make room. Not in this matter, of course."

"I'm not looking for work," she said. "I know what you're trying to do. And it's sweet, Daffy. Tempting, even. I wouldn't have under-stood what I'm saying now either, a year ago. I don't blame you for being who you are, and wanting the things you want. You're a master of the universe. Congratulations. I thought I wanted that, too. Turns out I didn't."

"The schools' collections department doesn't care what you want."

"There are trade-offs, sure. I won't deny that every few days I want to grab the Council of Cardinals by the neck and shake them until their heads do the bobble doll thing. But I'm doing good work."

"That's a god-botherer's line."

"The Wars are over," she said. "It's not us versus them. There's room to work in the middle." She held out her hand. *A little help here?*

Silver flowed through her mind and down her arm. The bird sculp-ture hopped twice more, and on the third hop, flew.

"Nice," Daphne said. "But it proves nothing. Gods took away your wings. Of course they can give them back and call it a miracle." But her smile was a younger woman's smile, a smile like the one Tara re-membered.

"I was trying to be symbolic," Tara said. "Hells. I know you want to help me. Thanks. Same goes for you. If you're ever looking for a change—"

"If I want to crash my career into a mountainside, I'll give you a call."

"Deal. I have to get back to work, but there's a place over by Seventeenth with great frozen lemonade—good for a pickup before an afternoon of doc review."

"Thanks," Daphne said. "It's good to see you, Tara."

They walked back through the garden. The stone bird flew widening circles overhead.

28

Five hours of archival research later, Tara hung in the astral void above a living god.

Kos Everburning, like all his divine ilk, did not quite exist in the usual, physical sense of the term—but human minds weren't good at comprehending n-dimensional noosphere entities, half-network and half-standing wave, propagating in all directions at once through time. They *could*, of course. Tara had worked out the theory from first principles back at the Hidden Schools, the derivation of divine anatomy from raw data being a particular favorite of problem-set-dependent TAs. But nightmare matrices did the math for you these days, if you didn't mind shifting some particularly difficult problems to universes where they happened to be easier. Then, back-convert the mess to three spatial dimensions with a fixed arrow of time—and, since everyone who's going to deal with this particular simulation will be a Craftswoman well versed in anatomy and forensics, add a filter to present the data analogically in terms of corpses. Just don't go too far, since a simulation this detailed is a new cave chamber inside the old philosopher's cavern, and if you're not careful you might tunnel into another chamber already occupied by capital-letter Things.

Even convenient fictions can delve too greedily and too deep.

Tara's head ached, and she was in desperate need of a second lemonade. She'd started after lunch with a deep dive into the Court of Craft across town, where carts guided by rat brain brought her volume after volume of notes and ledgers. Claims there matched her notes from last night's survey, but she needed more, and so returned to the sanctum to pace above Kos Everburning's body.

The diagnostic Craft she used had been built to display Alt Coulumb's God in cross section through time: a three-dimensional flip-book showing a naked continent-size man whose limbs hung limp in a dark sea, whose face shone too bright to look upon. It was meant to deal with well-structured archive data.

It wasn't made to model the living operations of the God.

She watched him—watched Him, the capital letter inserting itself slyly despite her insistence that adulation of a client was counterproductive.

She heard Him breathe.

His heart beat and blood surged in His veins. She'd thought to walk on His skin, to take inventory from up close as she had when He was dead, but the closer she drew the harder it was to keep her heart from matching time with His, to keep His heat from suffusing her.

Even at this distance—a mile up in notional space, far enough away that she could see His edges—Kos distorted the surrounding world. So much so, in fact, that she almost didn't notice when the simulation tore.

A ripping sound filled the synthetic dark as great wounds gaped in the fabric of unreality.

Multifaceted eyes stared through diamond slits, and spider legs clawed the void. She called on her Craft, forged chains of light to stitch the cut universe back together.

When she was relatively certain she wouldn't die in the next few minutes, she searched for the problem's source.

She didn't have to search long. She recognized the scream.

Abelard had taken shape in the nightmare half a mile beneath her, spinning over the Body, arms pinwheeling in a futile attempt to steady himself. The glowing tip of his cigarette trailed circles around him.

She stopped his spin with a thought and a slight tweak of the dream's parameters.

"You shouldn't be here," she said.

"How you get used to that, I will never know." He brushed stray hairs back into his tonsure, and straightened his skewed robes. "Um. I seem to be upside down."

"Gravity's relative to your body here. Your modesty's safe. You really should go." She righted him with a twist of her forefinger.

"I hoped we could talk," he said when he recovered.

The stitches with which she sealed in the sky surged as the Things beyond adjusted their attack. "This isn't a good time."

"What are you doing, anyway?"

"Looking for evidence," she said. A stitch gave way, and a tendril of shadow wormed into the dark. She shredded it. "I wanted to see how Kos owns the sky."

He pointed up. "What are those?"

"Demons. Don't worry about it."

"Sounds like I should."

Vines of light wound about the wound, and sharp darkness tore her bindings from within. "I'm running a lot of poorly structured data through the system. Too much of that and the nightmare snarls. Demons are like us, really—but their worlds work on different logic than ours. Points of divergence let them cross over without a summoning contract, without limits. You have to work hard to make one of those in physical space, but analytical engines aren't continuous. If I break the simulation, they can get in."

"That sounds bad."

She swooped toward the body, and brought him with her. "Annoying, mostly, here in n-space. If they breach, we pull out, shut the simulation down, start again. So long as we don't bring them back to the supposedly real world with us."

"Is that possible?"

"I'm warded, so they can't crawl into me—not without a fight. You, though—"

There came a massive pulse against the curvature of nothing. Her stitches distended and the wound opened like a mouth, only instead of teeth it was full of eyes.

"Hold on a second," she said. "I'm almost done." Great tubes sprouted from the god's body, vessels bearing His power, His blood out into the world. The city formed around them, like the impression of a body beneath a rubber sheet.

"Tara," Abelard said, afraid. Great hands tore the folded newspaper of the dream down the center. Logical consistency stretched like taffy. She hurt, and ignored the pain. Kos's power blushed through the ghost-glass city's sky. Drawing closer, she saw the blush was in fact a candyfloss haze of hooks wrestling with a Great Unseen.

Demon thorns pulled the edges of the world-wound wide. Beyond spread a noonday kaleidoscope of blunt angles and teeth, a story in which she had no part, which would consume her and her world alike. Four bridge-wide stitches remained, and fractal blights wilted their edges. One gave a sound like a bass string breaking. Three left. Two, soon.

"Tara!"

But that Great Unseen, the mystery against which Kos struggled to own the sky—she recognized it. Drew close to the hooks. Squinted. And saw a series of numbers in the tangle of each hook, and glyphs: *Kos Everburning v. Red King Consolidated.*

The last stitch broke with a bone-shivering A-sharp. The whole sky split at once. Arms that were tongues that were spears flew down.

But Tara and Abelard were not there anymore, and then the world was not, either.

Orbs of Tara throbbed flutterstep beneath wingskin as if rocked in pleasure. Eyes, she opened them. Air, she breathed it, and the dust it held. Ears, she heard with them the silence of a large paper-filled room, and the panting of a terrified monk. Skin, with curves of the stuff she felt the grain of a stone floor under her. She should install a bed in the archives someday.

Oh, and she had blood too, and a mind, and emotions not yet fully understood, one of them a distant cousin of compassion. Abelard. She sat up. Mountains of leather-bound codices and racks of scrolls swayed like willows blown in the storm of her unsettled mind. He sat cross-legged across the silver bowl at the archive center from her. He held his cut finger in one hand. The singed coppery smell of burned blood rose from within the bowl.

She stood, though her legs seemed unfamiliar devices. Leaning against her thighs, she orbited the bowl. "You okay?"

He stopped praying. "I thought it would be easier when He was alive."

She pulled him to his feet, though her own balance wasn't perfect and she almost toppled them both into a case of scrolls. "He's more complicated alive than dead." Back in this world they agreed was real, she could ditch the capital letter. "You cut your finger yourself?"

"Pierced it. With a needle."

She winced.

"Don't worry, I burned the needle first."

"Use alcohol next time."

"Are those things—"

"The demons?"

"Will they be there the next time you go into the dream?"

"No. I shut it down completely. That notional world doesn't exist until I need it again. Why did you come looking for me?"

"I need your advice," he said. "About God."

As they walked through paper mountains toward the lift, he told her about his conversation with the Cardinal. She pressed the button and waited as motors surged behind closed doors. "You want to know if I think you should do it."

"The Cardinal's right. Lord Kos might listen to me. But isn't it hubris to give a God advice?"

"You're asking the wrong person," she said, "when it comes to avoiding hubris. My teachers thought gods were a quaint affectation." She remembered the goddess in her room, wearing her face. Remembered, too, Daphne's flightless bird. "If the outside world thinks Kos will come to Seril's rescue whenever she's in trouble, that's bad for both of them. Debts falling due, margin calls, flights of wicked angels in the skies, spiritual armageddon."

"So you think I should do it."

"From a Craftswoman's perspective, sure. But no Craftswoman would be caught dead kneeling to a god." *It sickens me,* Daphne'd said. Was Tara a Craftswoman anymore? She had her glyphs. She had her power. What else was there? "You have to weigh the options yourself. But the Cardinal's right about the danger."

The lift arrived, bearing a trio of maintenance monks headed down. One of them, a large woman, worked the beads of her rosary until the lift reached the twelfth floor, and the trio left together. Abelard did not speak until they reached ground level and stepped into an empty hall. "I know you'll do the right thing," Tara said, "whatever that is. You might as well stop fretting. You're not binding yourself to a contract, or incurring debt."

"You're more confident than I am."

"That's what friends are for."

"Thank you for last night," he said, "for the encouragement. I was selfish when we talked. I didn't realize how hard this is for you."

There was a cold breeze in the narrow hall. "What do you mean?"

"You're out here on your own. I have the church, and Kos. Cat has her force. You should have a firm, Craftswomen and Craftsmen at your side. But you don't. It's just you, and you're not even from here. You're so good at what you do that it's easy for me to think you don't need anything or anyone. But that's not true. Whatever you were doing in the library, it was dangerous."

"Not for me."

"What if your wards didn't work as well as you hoped? What if the demons were stronger?"

"It was a calculated risk. My calculations skewed when you dropped in, that's all."

"I'm not questioning your abilities."

"That sure sounds like what you're doing." A door opened and closed. Footsteps trickled over the nave's stone floor. A men's choir sang. The sound seemed to come from everywhere at once. Tara couldn't make out the words, but the harmony was close and smooth. She made herself smile. "I can do this," she said. "I just need to be smarter than everyone else. So what else is new?"

"Cat and I are here for you. You've spent the last year working and sleeping, outside of one poker night that didn't go well. If you wanted to, you know, have a beer, or anything—well, I'm here. That's all I wanted to say."

Her watch chimed. "I have to go."

"See you later," he told her retreating back.

29

Daphne met Ms. Ramp on the roof of the Alt Coulumb Arms a half hour before sundown, on schedule. Ramp was eating pistachios from a bag. They cracked in midair in front of her, and the nutmeat floated to her mouth. The shells crisped to ash and rained as a fine powder to the roof.

"How did you find your meeting with our dear Ms. Abernathy?" Ramp said.

Daphne sighed, and set her briefcase on the gravel. "Went about as well as you expected. I don't get it. The Tara I knew would never be satisfied with these conditions." The brass latches popped and the briefcase clamshelled open, whereupon she opened it a second time, space unfolding from within until a three-meter pallet heaped with fabric and rope lay before them. "You think they got to her? Religious experience triggers an endorphin rush, which leads to dependency. Gods push inside your head. Like distributed Craftwork, but for everything at once."

"Possible." Ramp knelt, gathered striped fabric in both hands, and dragged it back over the gravel. "But you can't assume mind control every time someone's goals differ from your own."

"She wanted to get out of her hick town. She wanted to be somebody."

"And she's ended up in Alt Coulumb, which is hardly a hick town. She is a person of local importance. I bet she even thinks she's doing the right thing, in that wonderfully abstract language young people use, as if there were a 'right thing' independent of context, interest, or timing." She fluffed the fabric. A cloud of packing dust cracked from its taut surface. Daphne connected a hydrogen tank, and the balloon inflated. "If you build a roof without walls, it will fall. Build walls before foundation, and they will collapse. Lay a foundation without digging out the soil, it will crumble. Does that mean it is wrong to build roof or walls or foundation? Not at all. Whenever we build, we must dirty our hands first."

The balloon bellied up, straining against the ground lines Daphne tied. In the gilded afternoon, its white-and-red curve seemed obscenely medical. Daphne pondered the exact source of her fear of that shape. A memory bubbled from deep nightmare: her hand sawing silverskin from a knob of flesh. But the hand wasn't hers at all. The flesh, though—and somewhere, in the dark, she heard a man's laughter. Her knees went slack. She slumped against the balloon, which bobbed and swung.

"Daphne. Come back to me."

"I don't," she said. "I can't." The ghosts of laughter wouldn't fade.

Cool gloved fingers touched Daphne's temple through the layer of sweat. Daphne felt a small blade enter the side of her neck and twist, and she heard a dubious hum. The seesaw pitching of the world resolved, and colors lost their bite. "There," Ramp said, and drew the blade away. A drop of blood dried on her gloved fingertip. "I'm sorry if meeting Tara was too much for you."

Daphne forced her back straight and unclenched her hands from the ropes. Synthetic fibers had left crisscross tracks on her palms. "It's fine. I feel." There were words somewhere to match her feeling. She touched her neck. The wound was gone. "I feel bad for her. She's fallen so far."

Madeline Ramp examined the blood on her glove as it dried, as if she could read the remnant stain like tea leaves. "Daphne," she said in the same soft voice, "Ms. Abernathy won't join our cause just because we ask her to. If her loyalty's misplaced, we will have to fight her—break her down and bring her into the fold. Do you think you can do that? If not, you can sit this one out. You've done so much."

At those words, the ground under Daphne gaped. She could fall back into purposeless void—into pondering the milk-swirled depths of teacups as women in pale dresses moved around her and whispered: *Don't take the tea, you'll upset her.* A mother wept somewhere, a mother who might have been hers.

All that smeared memory of tea and milk and hospital gowns had ended with five words: *I have work for you.*

"I can do this," she said.

"Good." Ramp vaulted into the basket and extended her hand to Daphne. "Come, then. Let's dirty our hands."

She cut the anchor lines, and the balloon rose over Alt Coulumb.

Tara found Gavriel Jones in the plaza before the Crier's Guild entrance, on the southeast corner of Providence and Flame. Guild spires cut the scudding clouds above the gathered audience: nobles and merchants and bankers mixed with cabdrivers and off-duty construction workers in dusty coveralls. Hot dog and pretzel carts did brisk trade at the square's edge.

Alt Coulumb's people had come for the news.

"Crowded," Tara grumbled after she shoved past stevedores and stockbrokers to reach Jones by the stage. "I thought we had a deal."

"We do," Jones said. "But rumor travels faster than truth. People hear what's said between the lines. I hope your exclusive's worth the delay."

A hush capped the crowd's murmur, as if a conductor had given signal. The Guild's front doors opened and two lines of velvet-robed choristers emerged in step. At the square's edge a man argued with a hot dog seller, and traffic clanked and clattered as usual, but the silence by the stage was so deep Tara could hear each singer's footfalls. Onstage, they curved into a shallow U. A singer in darker robes stepped forth, raised her hand. Tara heard a pitch but saw no pipe.

That morning's song had been a stripped-down version of the Paupers' Quarter fight, sans goddess: incantation more than melody, like the call-and-response hymns from Edgemont services. The simple line emphasized the words, which were the point.

At least, Tara had thought they were.

But words were not the point of the Criers' song that night. Tara heard a theme stated in the bass and restated, discordant, by other voices, describing the Paupers' Quarter gathering. The music swelled, shards of melody grating against one other, when Shale arrived. And then, the piece trembled on the verge of decoherence—she was not musician enough to give what happened its proper name. Harmonic fragments locked into a new, shining tone, a strange expanded inside-out chord, a brilliance. She caught her breath to keep from weeping.

Exhaustion, she told herself. Heightened emotions from two days' hard work.

She knew she was lying.

No single word betrayed Seril or broke Jones's promise. But Shale—although four decades of suspicion had primed the crowd to call him a monster—brought them glory through this music.

The choir held the chord, shifting like the light a full moon cast through diamond. Then came the dying fall, a restatement of the initial themes to summarize the night's events.

Tara's eyes were hot. Entirely due to the intensity with which she'd watched the stage. Of course.

The song ended. The audience stood rigid as if a current ran through them.

Applause came in torrents.

Tara turned to Jones. The journalist had her hat cocked back, her chin up, her hands in the pockets of her overcoat. The corners of her mouth turned up.

"Between the lines." Tara had to shout to be heard through the cheers.

Jones shrugged. Every line on her face said, satisfied. "I've waited a long time for something to fit that music."

"You wrote that?"

"A year back. Finally had cause to use it."

"That was"—she searched for the right word—"more generous than I expected."

"You keep trying to cast me as a villain, Tara." Jones looked like a wine connoisseur after a fine sip of a joyful vintage, holding the sensation's ghost in her mouth and mind as it faded. "I'm not. Our goals are different, that's all."

"Come on," Tara said. She checked her watch. Fifteen minutes gone. She wasn't sure whether she was surprised the song was so long, or so short. Clock time didn't map to music. "I have a friend who wants to meet you."

Claire stocked the stall and kept it herself all day, without father or sisters, complaint or apparent fatigue. She even smiled when she thought Matt wasn't looking, though not more than once or twice an hour and never more curve than the blade of a paring knife. The produce moved. She kept the books and collected soulstuff for the family shrine. Sandy dropped by after the fiercest wave of customers passed to talk with Claire. Claire answered her politely—not that Matt was eavesdropping, only they were close enough he could hear her tone of voice.

Sandy visited his stall next. "You well?" Capistano'd come by too and asked the same question, but when Matt answered yes, the other man did one of those nods you could do only if you had a neck as long as his, where the whole head moved independent of the body like a spring-spined toy doll, and left. Sandy stayed. "And the girls?"

"Them, too."

"I came over here to tell you off for letting Claire come to work," she said. "But I won't."

"Wouldn't stay behind. Strong kid."

She gave him a sideways expression he couldn't read.

"You should get your shocks fixed, on your truck. Ray's cousin knows a guy."

"You said that last night."

"I did." Though he didn't remember. "Thanks, Sandy."

He took Claire to Cadfael's that afternoon. They ate in a silence that seemed deeper than the silence of the morning mist and country roads. She ate little, and though she looked at his beer when the waitress brought him one, she ordered tea.

"I'll go see Father tonight," she said. "Sandy says they took him to Branch Staffords. He's still asleep."

"Good of her to look into that," he said. "I'll go with you, if you want company."

She chewed each bite of chicken breast ten times before she swallowed. "I do. Thank you."

They took the cart back to the garage near Matt's apartment and walked home. A light sea breeze cleared the air of smoke and damp. Hannah and Ellen and Donna weren't home. Donna had left a note: she'd taken the girls with her to work.

"They won't be home 'til late," he said. "We could pick them up before we head over."

"No," Claire said. "They don't need to come with us."

So as the sun fell faster, they rode the trolley southeast to Branch Staffords Hospital, three blocks of red brick cubes with tall curtained windows. As they descended to the curb Matt saw a ripple in the top-floor curtains and looked up into a face staring down: dark eyes and an open mouth. Claire led him across the street. An orderly in the first building directed them to a second, who directed them to a building back behind the parking lot. Crossing the parking lot, Matt watched his feet. He did not want to see the dark eyes and the open mouth again.

"Are you okay?" Claire said.

Fine is what he meant to say, but what he did was, "My mother passed here, three years ago. That was her room." Third floor from the top, second from the left, north wing. "We expected it, but she didn't go clean."

"I'm sorry." She held her hands in front of her skirt.

The east wing orderlies consulted a book heavier than most scriptures Matt had seen.

"Relation?"

"I'm his daughter," Claire said. "Matt is a friend of the family."

They rode up three floors in a white lift that smelled of alcohol. Matt leaned against the rail to the rear of the lift. Claire touched nothing.

Rafferty lay in a bed. He did not move. "He had a rough night," the nurse said. "He's unconscious, but you can watch him if you want."

"Thank you," Claire replied. "This is all we need."

The man left them in the room together. There were no bags and drips, no tangled wires, and fewer of the foul smells Matt remembered from his last visit.

"I don't need you," Claire said. "Go, if you want. I know the bus route back to your place."

Matt's mother had not known where or who she was when she died. There had been love in the room, but bile and blood, too. It was a bad echo of birth, her eyes dark as the inside of her mouth. She did not understand what was happening. For Matt, the memory was one more weight to carry, and there was no place in him where it could rest easy, this ungainly thing that clunked and rattled but would not break.

"I'll wait," he said.

30

Raz opened the captain's cabin door on Cat's third knock. He paused when he saw her and shook his head as if she'd slapped him. "Who let you on board?"

"Davis," she said.

"Davis."

"Don't blame her. I'm on official business." She raised the scroll Tara gave her. "Salvage agreement for the *Dream*. We need to sign it there."

"Let Davis sign it. She's co-captain."

"She wasn't in command when the salvage took place. We don't want any loopholes."

"Give me a minute to square this lot away," he said, and turned to his crew. Even angry, Raz moved beautifully—perhaps a particular grace emerged from his anger. The crew scattered before him like goats before a lion. *Bounty*'s early evening business took less time to settle than she expected, probably due to the fact that Raz was three, four times faster than most humans. He blurred around the edges.

"Let's go," he said when he was done.

She passed him the scroll, which he skimmed as they walked over. "I don't understand this."

"Tara says if we took the *Dream* under Coulumbite authority, we can't wake up the people in her hold. If we claimed her under a different authority"—with a meaningful nod toward the new-risen moon—"we can wake them, just like that. But since you were involved, you need to sign."

He reread the scroll, examined it front and back. "Okay."

"Any questions?"

"Do whatever you want, and justify it later if you don't like the consequences. Sounds like your kind of plan."

"That was beneath you," she said. *Dream*'s gangplank was down. She climbed first, and he followed her. The cry came: "Captain on deck!" The skeleton who'd given it saluted them with a clatter of finger bone against skull.

Raz returned the salute. "Come on. Let's finish this."

Abelard joined vigil early. Outside the sanctum window, the blued sky deepened to black. Around him, the Sanctum of Kos Everburning beat like a heart. Hydraulic fluid pulsed through pumps. Steam sang down pipes. He lit incense in the Everburning Flame and knelt before the chromed altar with hands outstretched. Firelight glazed the faces of long-dead saints, women and men of faith who'd raised Alt Coulumb from river mouth port to metropolis, who'd shed their blood for God, who'd let the Lord's heat work through them. As a novice, he dreamed of following their path.

Some felt he had.

He had been convenient to God back then, that was all.

But he could earn his place.

His voice framed the prayer. He'd knelt here so often the words seemed to speak themselves. These days he struggled to keep his heart in the ceremony, to feel the ritual as praise rather than a series of rehearsed steps.

Tonight the words formed as they should: *Glory to You, Everburning, Ever-transforming*—and within them he framed his appeal.

We need to talk.

The world around him took fire, and he was lifted.

His body knelt. His voice prayed. It was his context that changed. A cold rush climbed his spine, spread through his limbs, and he stood astride the city. But when he looked down on Alt Coulumb's teeming streets and sidewalks and the wharfs that pulsed with broad-backed men and women strong as sprung steel, he saw them as if he was them, as if he moved through and within them, as if his thoughts were pieces of theirs—

*fuck they want to buy at that price **for** I don't even*
  *gotta hold the knife like **this** so you won't cut*
   *even know where **was** he last night and he comes*
   home all
     *consider **the** alternatives*
    *I don't **mind** if you just want to screw*
     *fillet **of** whitefish six thaums a pound*
     God-*damn Blacksuits make it so*
     a man can't live

Gods, or at least the few with which Abelard was on speaking terms, could use human speech, as a person who lacked sign language could point to a flower or a passing cloud. The bigger the god, the harder that became. Rather than reducing themselves to human syntax, larger deities preferred to elevate humans to theirs. That approach had drawbacks, though. Human beings were good at comprehending things that looked, thought, and spoke at roughly human size, speed, and complexity. A modern god in a modern city, networked through faith and bond to pantheons and Deathless Kings around the planet, was larger, faster, and more complex than monkey-derived man. Divine communions sometimes made as little sense as Cathbart's sermons might to an ape. Some saints went mad from the experience.

Not that Abelard could have expressed such thoughts in that moment, borne on the tide of God, burning in the flame at the heart of His city. Kos Everburning, Lord of Flame, gave His servant knowledge of Himself. Tears streamed down Abelard's face.

Through the awe and wonder, though, he thought: you won't get off the hook that easily.

The city web wriggled and drew back, cold, nonchalant. God had no idea what he could possibly mean.

I'm here to talk about Seril. You know what's happening. Everything Tara's said in council. There's no use playing dumb.

(Lord Kos was great and benevolent and wise. Why feign politeness, as if such an Interlocutor could only hear your surface thoughts?)

The city moved. Far below, in a body that was but one axon of the Mind with which he now conversed, he spoke the second stanza of the Litany for the Coming Burn. Ocean rolled against pier and distant sand, with a sound like the shuffling of enormous feet.

I know you love Seril. I know what you went through to bring Her back.

The world collapsed to a spark, all while he was coiled and compressed until thought's whirlpool became a slow sludge spinning downward toward a drain. Curled inside Abelard's cigarette, Lord Kos had been a flame quivering on the wick of a single soul.

But the more you work for her, the more you set us all at risk. Tara says, and Bede says, if you support her, Craftsmen will use that against you. Break you. Seize control of the city. You might die. Seril has to stand alone, or fail.

If there was a change in the God, he did not feel it. The city's many voices receded, and he heard his own again, praying.

The God wanted to know what he thought. Not Bede. Not Tara. Him.

They know the market, Abelard prayed reluctantly. *They know how the world works, and the Craft. They know the risks. I trust them.*

The flame danced within its wire throne.

But do we trust each other?

"It's strange," Daphne said when the balloon reached its intended altitude. She bent over the basket's edge and looked down upon the tops of skyscrapers and jagged streets, as if a drunken civil engineer had broken a case of matchsticks with a hammer, then dropped the pieces on a map. "The sky's so clear."

"It's dirty," Ramp replied. "Smog and smoke and steam and fumes. Though the god does give them a sustainable power source, at least."

"I don't mean the air," Daphne said. "I mean the sky. No spires. No optera. No airbuses or blimps or platforms. We're all alone. We're all alone!" she shouted out to the north, and "Alone!" to the south, but neither horizon answered. Her words didn't echo. They were too high up for that.

"All in good time," Ramp said. She reclined on the nest of cushions she'd made in the basket, and paged through this week's *Thaumaturgist*. A teacup lifted itself to her lips. "Be patient, and be ready."

31

Glyph-lines burned around the door of the *Dream*'s refrigerated hold. Cat climbed down a rope ladder; Raz dropped in straight-legged, and rolled his shoulders, producing a drum line of pops and cracks. "Do I have to sign in blood?" he asked. "Naked, dancing under a full moon?"

"I wouldn't complain."

He smiled halfway but didn't rise to the joke.

"Ink's fine," she said.

"Do you have a pen? I left mine in my other pants."

She produced a ballpoint from her pocket; the white barrel glowed in the shadows. He reached for it. She did not offer it to him.

"So that's why you wanted to come down here," he said. "Privacy."

"We need to talk."

He spread his arms. "Cat, we each have our own problems. When we're close, those problems get mangled together. Best to back away."

"That's why you spend so much time on the ocean," she said. "Can't back off any farther than that. If you could go to the moon you probably would."

"My job is on the ocean. I like my job. If living there helps me manage, why not? You don't understand what I deal with. You think you do, but you don't."

"Because every time I try to get closer, you push me away. You think you're the only one in the world with a problem? There's nothing wrong with you."

He laughed without humor and jabbed a finger toward his mouth where the fangs were. "Everything is wrong with me. You want to learn how far you should trust desire, spend fifty years trying not to see every passing person as a well-cooked meal. Hells, you don't even have to see—you *smell* them. There's nothing natural about this. I was dying, and I was given a choice. I chose to live. Not live—survive. And even that went sour. Life skews. It's skewed us both."

"Which is why you've spent five decades on a rampage, tearing people's throats out."

"Of course not. I have a condition. I manage it."

"Can you extend me the common fucking courtesy of understanding that I'm trying to manage, too?"

"You don't care about me. You need people like me. I've seen it before. For you I'm a hit, that's all. A fang."

"No." She stepped toward him. "I like you." Say it fast, like tearing off a bandage or a scab. "I want you. Maybe you're afraid of what that means. I know I am. But I've known enough need to tell the difference between that and this. And I've known enough suckers to tell hunger from attraction. If you want to say I'm wrong, fine. But I'm not."

He shook his head. "If things were different, maybe. If I didn't have my problem, if you didn't have yours. But now, I can't trust you."

"You can," she said. "You do. But you're scared. Of me, because I screwed you over last year when I was out of my head. But under that, you're scared of yourself."

"If I lose control, people die."

"We can be careful. And if all else fails, I can kick your ass."

This close to a human being, Cat would have felt the warmth. He could feel hers, she knew. He could hear her heartbeat. He was an inch taller than her, which didn't matter except when they were this close. She reached for him.

He took the pen from her and stepped away. He unspooled the scroll atop a crate of dried papaya and read it through once more as Cat watched—bandage peeled back, scab ripped free, blood flowing, stunned by the speed of his retreat.

He signed on the dotted line. Tara's glyphs' light swelled. The boat did not sway, but the world beneath the boat swayed, and settled into a deeper trough.

Raz wrung the scroll closed and tossed her the pen. She caught it by reflex.

"There," he said. "That's done."

She opened her mouth, unsure what to say.

The echoes of the sunset song stayed with Tara through their cab ride to the Ash, which was all to the good, because Jones was no conversationalist. She watched out the window and made notes in her book.

"You've never been here before?"

"Of course I have," Jones said. "But you see something new each visit."

"Just you wait."

When they reached the broken tower, the sky was the blue of blood seen through skin, and pierced with bright stars. Jones followed Tara through the rubble, stepping where she stepped, touching what she touched. "Nice place."

"A fixer-upper." Tara parted the curtain of creepers that lay across the stairwell opening. "Don't touch the walls. I'll keep back anything that could hurt you. And watch your step."

"Can't you"—Jones wiggled her fingers—"make light?"

"You don't want to see what lives on these walls."

They climbed. Jones did not question the few sharp decisive sounds Tara made, or the occasional flash that ensued when she killed something vicious. Tara reminded herself to speak with the goddess—firmly—about the general unsuitability of temple traps and rat kings and hand-size poisonous spiders to modern temples.

As they neared the twelfth floor, Tara found that she could see. The darkness silvered, less cavelike and closer to the dark of starlit cornfield night, swelling with form, navigable despite obscurity.

"I thought you wouldn't make light. Powers man was not meant to know and so on."

"This light isn't mine," Tara said. "It's the courtesy of our host."

Silver chiseled geometry from the dark. They ascended steep stairs. Ahead, the tunnel ended.

Tara expected the roof of the day before, the broken dome and stone-strewn platform beneath the wrecked orrery. What she found was different.

Solid moonlight completed the broken arches and patched and polished the pitted metal. The roof was clean. In its center rose a granite throne flanked by curving horns claw-carved from the rubble that once littered the platform. The carving lacked mortar: gravity locked each piece in place. The work would have taken a human sculptor months without magic or machines, but Seril's children were their own magic, and their own machines.

Gargoyles awaited them.

They stood in a loose circle around the throne. Wings crested monstrous shoulders. Aev, nearest, looked down at the human arrivals with the same composure Tara'd seen on Abelard's face praying, and mistaken for haughtiness. Shale, at the circle's rear, watched Tara, uneasy, trusting. A year ago Tara couldn't have identified the meaning behind his fangs. She could now—and the other gargoyles' expressions too, the determination on the face of tusk-toothed Gar and the haughtiness of scale-skinned Scree, the nervous twitch in great Grimpen's cheek.

None of which mattered beside the light that occupied the throne.

The goddess wore a cloak of majesty. There were many faces within her face.

Tara stepped out of Jones's way. The Crier emerged into the light. Her pen rested against notebook paper. Ink seeped from its tip.

Tara tried to conceal her satisfaction. She thought she did okay.

Jones lowered the notebook and approached Aev. Tara followed, flanking, in case of ambush or gonzo journalism.

"Ms. Jones," she said, "this is Aev, who leads Seril's children."

"We've met."

"You are in much better health than when last we spoke," Aev said with a wry rumble.

"Is this the part where you give me instructions? Don't offer or accept anything? Don't make any bargains?"

"The Lady is eager to meet you," Aev replied. "Any deals you make with her are yours to keep. She will communicate in your mortal tongue."

"Thanks for that."

"Can I get you anything before we start? Water, coffee? Doughnut?"

Jones blinked. "Water, thanks."

"Water will be found."

Shale walked to the rooftop's edge and dove into space.

"Of course," Jones said. "You don't need water yourself."

"Our few needs are met by moonlight, earth, and rain. He will return."

"Thanks." Jones flipped forward in her notebook until she reached a page not blotted with the ink of her surprise. "Let's go."

Aev ushered her toward the throne.

32

Abelard, fire-flooded, spread through his city, burning in ecstasy of communion, remembered his confession to Tara in the temple boiler room. And Kos remembered it too, because Abelard was part of him as he was part of Abelard.

Yet Abelard was still the man he had been a year before, tumbling into darkness, dead, only to learn the darkness into which he fell was burning. That fire buoyed him up. The Lord caught him, time and again, as Abelard caught Him in turn. They fought for each other.

Cardinal Gustave burned in the Temple of Justice, full of rage and futile hope, hair blown in smoke and hurricane winds. Cardinal Gustave fell. Cardinal Gustave, Abelard's anchor, who held church and faithful in his iron conviction's grip—dead, after betraying his Lord for a reason he thought was right.

Peel off the old man's face like a player's mask, and Abelard saw himself.

I must not become Gustave. I must not believe that I know best how God should be in the world. But Gustave was a wise man, and good. If he could turn from You unsuspecting, what might I do?

What was Gustave's fault? Pride, in thinking himself wiser than his fellow priests, wiser even, at the end, than God? But pride stemmed from a deeper source. If pride was flame, what was fuel?

Fear. Fear Kos would reject him. Fear his iron would rust from within.

In the end, it had.

Where does that leave us? he prayed. What can we do in the face of fear?

What else, came the whispered reply, *but love and trust.*

Were the words his, or did they belong to Kos? What was *he*, anyway, but a piece of this burning web spun from a city's dreams? He joined to Him by faith, by the burning of incense, by prayer, by kneeling before a fire. Where did Abelard end and God begin? They grew from each other.

And in that unity he felt Seril, diminished though present—a chill to match His flame, an equal and an adversary, haughty and swift, fluid and eternal. Kos had burned alone for fifty years, with only cables of contract and debt to bind Him to other gods, bereft of gift and humor, of all that matters in life save duty. The city had been His alone.

She was back, but She was weak.

But, Abelard reminded him, Her return had not broken His obligations—to church and city as well as love.

We need to work together, Abelard prayed. And, though the fear was not gone: I trust You.

The web echoed with that word.

Then the Fire said: *You may have to prove it sooner than you think.*

Cat was still deciding what to say when someone knocked on the door to the refrigerated hold of the *Demon's Dream.*

The knock came from within.

She looked from Raz, to the contract he held, and back to the compartment.

"You told me to sign the thing," Raz said.

"I didn't think it would work that quickly."

The knock repeated, a hammer-blow strike.

"Hold on." She raised her voice. "We're coming." She pressed the amulet to the door, turned, and pulled. The door swung open and a chill wind gusted out.

A woman stood behind the door. Frost painted her skin. She lurched across the threshold. Her knees buckled, and Cat caught her by the arm, felt her flesh still stiff and cold. Kos and Seril. There should be someone here to deal with this. Specialists. Doctors. They should have thought. "You're safe," she said. The woman turned to her from the neck up. "I'm Cat. You're in Alt Coulumb." The woman did not respond. What language did these folks speak? Others approached the door, arms slack at their sides, staring.

Raz tore free a tarp that had been lashed over a loose crate and folded it around the woman, rubbing her shoulders through the cloth. He spoke to her, first in a smooth language heavy with *l*'s and aspiration, and when that produced no response, in a more halting, guttural tongue, then a third with singsong tones Cat could barely classify. No answer.

He tried another seven languages then swore. "That's all I've got." The hold was filling slowly with woken, silent people. Raz turned from the woman to the others. "Anyone here speak Kathic? Talbeg?"

The woman quaked in Cat's arms. Not shivering, or at least not shivers as Cat knew them. Heaving spasms. A seizure?

Cat tried to lay her on her back, but the woman shook her off. Then she looked at and through Cat, and opened her mouth too wide. Her teeth were long and narrow.

"Cat?"

The others from the hold stood before Raz: tall and short, muscled and fat and lean, male and female and those not obviously either. Their mouths hung open.

Cat looked back to the woman she held. Sticky darkness seeped between her teeth, and sharp glass gleamed within, swelling as if it approached down a tunnel much longer than the woman's throat. Reflective tendrils skittered against enamel, caught and cut her lips, tensed—

Cat threw herself to one side as a mirror shard shot from the woman's mouth. Raz hit the deck too—shards burst from all the open mouths, a storm of crystal darts unfolding wings and legs, and unfolding again, like those creased-paper birds kids from the Shining Empire made, that when you undid them formed a bird larger than the one they had been. The people from whom the crystals flew all fell like string-cut marionettes.

The glass that missed Cat struck the bulkhead arrow-deep and quivered there as claws tore gouges in the wood. Sawdust and wood chips and scraps of cloth filled the air, and all around the hold there were these *things*, huge winged bugs, reflective carapaced and slick and growing. Their mouths held fangs and twitching blade lips. They were hungry.

Blood seeped from the corner of Cat's ear, from a cut she hadn't felt.

"Demons."

Cat raised the truncheon from her belt, just in time. The nearest demon-bug flew toward her; she batted the glass insect into a bulkhead. It bounced off a tarp, reversed its legs, shook itself, and launched at her again. The second's relief gave Cat's hand time to reach the Justice medallion at her neck, and the cold perfection of service carried her away.

This time, when she swung the club, the creature shattered to smoking shards. One down, forty-something to go.

She looked up. Raz had pulled the tarp from the fallen woman and thrown it to snare a clutch of demons. Legs and mandibles pierced fabric, but before they could fight free he smashed the tarp against the deck. Glass spines cracked. A bug landed on Raz's scalp and clawed bloody strips away. He screamed. Cat leapt, clubbed the thing off him, and it burst into a shower of sharp dust. Blood streamed down his forehead.

They stood ringed by unconscious former demon-hosts, and twenty-five glass insects, now the size of toddlers and still growing. Spindly limbs merged and thickened. Plates of mirrored chitin sprouted between joints. Ruby eyes grew further facets. Claws lengthened and serrated.

Too many to fight.

Raz bared his fangs.

She didn't know how strong he was. But he could bleed. And they could cut him.

They could cut her, too, even through the Suit. This many, they could tear off her arms like children plucking daisy petals. But she could kill—not all of them, the distributed tactical mind of Justice told her. Skill, speed, and strength went only so far against sheer numbers. But she could take many with her.

She spread her arms in front of Raz. In one hand she held her truncheon. Her other hand's fingers lengthened into claws.

Come on, she told them in the Suit's silver-coated nightmare voice. Maybe demons had bad dreams too. *Show me what you've got.*

They stared at her, opened mandibles, wriggled razor mouthparts.

She tightened her grip on the truncheon.

The demons' wings snapped wide, and as one they flew.

They boiled toward the opening of the hold, still growing. Claws scrabbled against timber, and they were out. She ran after them. With a leap she caught the slowest demon's trailing leg; if she'd touched it barehanded its edges would have laid open her palm, but the Suit let her hold it, let her catch its wing too, both of them spinning above the deck of the *Dream*. The demon's head rotated on its neck; fangs snapped, but she was too close for them to bite deep. Its claws, though, could. They tightened like a diamond-tipped vise. One talon tore a line in her Suit. The fluid flowed free of its claw to mend the gap, but not before its talon plunged beneath, exploring her flesh.

She wrapped her arms around the demon's belly and squeezed. Glass squealed, popped, shattered. The Suit closed her wound. She fell, turning, turning, and slammed into the deck. Glass shards rained onto her, melting as they fell. Above, unfolded demons flew. Their wings rainbowed streetlamp light and beat dragonfly fast, gaining altitude, flying inland.

"Ma'am?"

The skeleton-sailor bent over her, head cocked to one side. Concern. How interesting that she could read the man's, no, woman's, expressions. Maybe you had to learn, once you became a skeleton, how to act so people could tell what you were thinking. Like guiding a puppet.

She remembered this feeling from back before Seril's return, when the Blacksuit was still Black. The fog of assurance, the Suit guiding her reeling mind to detached logic.

She stood. The Suit blunted the pain in her side, kept pressure on the wound, guided blood to proper vessels.

Across the city, Justice called her children. *Under attack. All units.* Suits patrolling backstreets paused midstep and turned skyward, preparing to run. But they couldn't fly.

One hand crested the edge of the hold, then another, and Raz pulled himself onto the deck. Regrown skin closed the cuts in his scalp. He did not need to breathe, so he wasn't breathing heavy. He ran to her, held her, his hand tight enough on her arm she could feel it through the Suit's narcotic haze. "Are you all right?"

She wasn't used to laughing through silver. *You?*

"Fine." He turned to the skeleton. "There are injured people in the hold. Help them."

We have to go. Her mind raced through the matrix of Justice, assembling scenarios, considering data. Scraps: the sleepers woke when Raz signed the contract bringing them into Seril's domain. Demons sought freedom. These were bound, now, by Seril's rules alone—and if she died, they'd be free. Limitless.

"You're hurt."

Not much. She stood. *Come on. The other officers won't be able to stop them in time.*

"We can't either."

You can learn, Aev had told her last night, on that rooftop. Well. No time like the present.

Yes we can, she said.

And, in silence, to the moon: you wanted me to pray, dammit. You wanted me to need you. Here you go. Here I am.

The smooth silver of her back rippled, and bulged, and birthed wings.

When she turned to him, he was looking at her differently.

She held out her hand. *Are you coming?*

33

The goddess condensed to human shape as Jones approached. The moonlight whirl receded behind a surface too slick and shimmering for skin. Gargoyles sang, a chorus whose treble notes flirted with the lowest range of human hearing. Theater? No, Tara saw stone faces fixed with holy effort: rising into prayer, lending the goddess the platform of their minds to help her address this faithless mortal.

So Seril had told the truth: Tara was, in some sense, a priestess.

You've fused the chain around your neck, and handed them the dangling end.

Dammit.

Tara saw traces of her own features in the face Seril assumed: her cheekbones, and a line of jaw more her mother's than her own. Perhaps she saw only what she knew to see. That was often the way with gods.

Part of why she didn't like them. Craft was clear: no wiggle room with ink and blood and starlight. A deal worked, or did not. Rights relinquished could not be willed back. Absolute truth issued from signatures on paper. Subjectivity was for people who couldn't hack it objectively.

She had thought like that when she first came to Alt Coulumb. Still did, most days. But then why had she removed her glyph from Shale?

Jones slowed as she neared the throne, like the Ebon Sea philosopher's arrow that crossed first half the intervening distance, then half that, then half again. She stared into Seril's face.

At the foot of the throne she hesitated, and looked away. Tara saw a bright wet line on Jones's cheek.

Tara knew the feeling. She'd felt that way herself last year when the gargoyles introduced her to their Lady. Cynical analysis: gods prompted this neurochemical reaction as a form of self-defense. Awe each human you encounter. Seduce them with ultimacy. If she examined herself the way the schools taught her, she could see classic signs of subversion—a drastic change of behavior upon exposure to a divine being. Broken by blessing. The libraries of the Hidden Schools held volumes about conversion, indoctrination, torture. She remembered the woodcuts of rats in mazes and babies raised in boxes.

Priestess.

But the scholastic method was a conditioning all its own. Any break in the pattern of thought she'd learned was a moral failing, an intrusion of dark powers to be met with suspicion and fear.

Daphne held the flightless bird in the temple gardens.

We're so alone, she thought. We touch one another too firmly and wound or break, or else we pull away. We tell stories in which we are lone noble heroes, until we stand face-to-face with a goddess and see something older and bigger than each of us because it *is* each of us, our souls touching, the subtle interaction at a distance of minds with minds, when we reach the edge of loneliness and teeter uncertain at the brink.

Or else, old teachers' voices whispered, you kneel because you lack the strength to stand.

Jones asked the Goddess a question Tara could not hear.

But she heard the answer: "Yes."

The night before, when had Cat crouched on the roof's edge, Aev told her: first we invite the wind into our wings. Without the wind, we cannot fly.

It sounded stupid. Mystical mumbo-jumbo, self-evident, of course you needed the wind to fly, that was how wings worked.

Raz took her hand. She invited the wind.

She'd tried last night, three times, and three times fallen, plummeting ten stories until Aev swept down to catch her. No room for failure now. Wings wide.

Two beats buffeted the deck. The Suit did what she asked, when she asked, but she felt like a climber with a finger grip on a narrow ledge: the wind was there, but she could not pull herself atop it.

The demons reached the port-facing rooftops, gaining altitude.

You can't muscle yourself up from this position. Change the angle. Use your body, not your arms. Swing.

She bent her legs, gathered Raz to her, and leapt.

He squawked, undignified. The deck receded below, the ship rocking from the force of her departure.

She began to fall.

Come on, wind, she thought. I need you.

Her wings filled. She saw deep currents rising from the city, colored red below red: heat, a path she could use. Beneath her—beneath her!—lay Alt Coulumb, port streets she'd patrolled, the warehouse where she cornered the gargoyles the year before, Pleasure Quarter alleys down which the younger woman she had been staggered sickly and strung out hunting for an easy fix, and there, ahead, the tower of Kos Everburning. A moon shone on her spread wings, and another on the skyline, atop a tower in the Ash, where Seril held court.

Raz laughed, his arms around her, his grip tight with monkeyfear of falling.

She laughed, too, fiercely. To fly was glorious.

The demons sped north and east. Cat hunted them.

Thus Jones, in the light of an unfamiliar goddess:

"Would you consider yourself a refugee?"

"A survivor. It took me forty years to reach home, and then only in a reduced condition."

Jones stood in silver light. The world shifted as she shifted angles, like a hologram postcard. One blink, one turn of the head, and she stood before a woman whose face she almost recognized, not quite Mother, not quite her, not quite Grandma. Another blink, another turn, and the roof was gone and the sky too and the woman, replaced by a frothing silver sea.

But Jones still held her notebook.

"Your gargoyles attacked Alt Coulumb after you died."

"I was not dead. I was dismembered. Parts of me were stolen. But I lived, reduced, with and through my children. Fallen, I went mad. So did they. It took us a long time to learn to think again."

"Why did you come back?"

"I belong here," she said. "My love is here, as are my people.

Justice fails many. She follows rules without question. The night must have a compassionate face."

The crucial question: "How do you operate with Justice, then?"

"She was built from stolen pieces of my corpse. Now that I have returned, we are one and two. Her children are freer than they were, thanks to me. The system is more flexible. In her old, rigid form, Justice was vulnerable. We are better now."

Gabby's pen trailed shorthand scrapmarks on paper. She'd expected visions, mind-racking battles on a symbolic plain, gnomic pronouncements issuing from a vent in the earth. This was good copy.

"How do you respond," she asked, "to allegations—"

Then the goddess screamed.

34

Shale flew toward the tower, water cask in hand, above the tracks of a southbound train. He hadn't exactly rushed to find the reporter a drink. Honor guards were well and good, but why not linger on the return trip, to stop a mugging and right an overturned carriage?

Far away he heard his brothers and sisters sing, though the humans below did not. When he wore flesh he accepted its limits; few of Seril's children knew how tinny and limited were the sounds Alt Coulumb's softer citizens heard. (And how strange human words for what they could not hear—subsonic, as if there was no sound below the narrow band those odd small ears could catch.)

He hummed along, and beat time with his wings.

The demons struck him in midair.

He felt the impact first, three blows against his legs, and on his back between his wings—then piercing pain. He roared in shock and rage and dropped, in that second, the cask. It tumbled, he tumbled, while his mind worked out (thought came slowly, as if someone had turned down the metronome that beat the world) the truth of the situation: he'd been attacked. Illogical, impossible to be struck in flight in his Lady's city, but—

He furled his wings and fell past blurring windows and shocked human silhouettes, then stretched his wings to brake. The burrowing thorns in his back tore free, and a crystal thing shimmered under him, falling, shard edged with four broad thin wings and a sharp proboscis.

Burning eyes, multifaceted.

Demon.

He'd fought them before. Most had no opacity or smell, no internal organs, because these were irrelevant to the purpose for which they were summoned. They had claws and teeth, because these were not.

Crystal wings buzzed as the demon darted toward him. He dodged up and back and caught the creature as it passed through the space he had occupied a second before. It was fast, almost as fast as Shale. Hooked legs jabbed toward his face, but he brushed them aside, wrapped them beneath his arm. Claws raked his stomach. He blocked one; the other burrowed into him. They fell onto an elevated train track, crashed apart.

Shale leapt from the track as a train charged past. The demon blurred up from the ground. He folded his wings and dove to meet it.

He struck the demon with his full weight—and then the demon struck pavement with Shale on top, and shattered.

He crouched in the street, wreathed in demonsmoke. Horses reared. Carriage wheels clattered on cobblestones. Human shapes approached from the sidewalk. A girl held out her arm. She recoiled when he turned to her. Out here, in the light, he felt exposed.

He flew.

When he crested the skyscrapers, two more demons hit him at once.

Abelard felt glass knives carve his city's sky. He saw them through the eyes of a frightened boy on a fire escape, of an old man watching the few visible stars through a telescope, of a girl singing on a rooftop in the Paupers' Quarter.

God's knowledge washed against his own like waves at an island's shore, leaving traces of itself. Demons in the city but not of it—demons marked as Seril's people.

They flew toward the gargoyles' tower. Through an accountant working late Abelard saw two catch Shale in midair, whiplike limbs seizing his arms, proboscises jabbing. They drank from him.

On the northeastern tower, the moon began to set.

Then, a silver streak—

Cat saw Shale tumbling, held aloft by two sets of demon wings. She heard his cry through the Suit; without the Suit she would have only felt it in her bones. *We need to help him,* she said.

"You can't fight them and carry me," Raz said.

I'll set you down—

"Throw me."

Are you crazy?

Shale's roar weakened as they drained him.

"Do it."

She gathered him in her arms, let the Suit judge trajectory, and threw. He was a missile of cloth and muscle and teeth.

He landed on a demon's back, and as she closed the gap she saw him wrap his legs around its abdomen, grab its bulbous head and pull, back and up. A proboscis sprang free of Shale's back, spun around, split into snapping jaws, but too late. Raz snapped the head free of the body.

And fell, as the demon disintegrated beneath him.

Godsdammit she didn't have *time*—the fall, the Suit offered, would take thirty seconds—she tore two legs off Shale's remaining demon. Claws caught at her but Shale'd regained enough strength to help. She speared the demon through the heart with its own leg. Its carapace cracked, and twenty seconds, she planted her legs on Shale's body and dove down from him, fifteen, ten, flare—

She caught Raz thirty feet from the pavement, turned his plummet to a sideways swoop, then soared.

He was, she noticed, still grinning.

They met Shale in the air. Silver light leaked from cracks in his skin. He pressed one hand to his side, and more light trickled through his fingers.

Can you fly?

"I must."

He pointed to the tower in the Ash atop which Cat had seen the second moon.

It was setting now, and glass bugs buzzed around it.

Panic of order time breaks the.

Tara, in some sequence:

—hutched under skittering claws as a spear mouth jabbed at her face—

—threw herself to rough stone and raised her hands and a shield of Craft—

—turned from the goddess's throne to see crystal rainbows and claws approaching and—

—saw gargoyles tense and throne light flicker, Seril lose coherence as Jones dropped to one knee—

To the nine hells with order anyway. Fight.

She stabbed through her shield into demon-skin. The crystal reflected her knife, but the demon recoiled anyway, allowing Tara space to rise, cloaked in shadow.

Demons swarmed Seril's children. Gar went down beneath the weight of two; he clutched one to his chest, shattering it, but the other stabbed him with its mouth and drank. Aev fought three at once, battered a fourth with her wings. Their chorus had broken into roars and rage. Tara closed her eyes, saw their Craft.

She shuddered.

Demons (Professor Halcyon had said, pacing before class with pointer tapping against her palm) hail from continuity neighboring our own, and as a result when brought into our realm possess whatever properties they have been assigned by negotiation. Unbound, they're undefined—conscious singularities that warp the world until the pressure of paradox grows too great and they collapse, destroying territory they've tainted in the process. And that, class, is why we triple-check our summoning contracts.

The contract at these demons' core was dreadfully simple. A few provisions listed the steps by which they might be slain: basic stuff, pressure tolerances, resistances, immunities. They could absorb others' soulstuff. And they were bound to obey the holder of an indenture canceled by . . . Tara herself.

Oh, gods.

Somehow these demons were tied to the indentures Seril voided. If She fell, they'd be free—to go home, or to wreck the city, or worse.

In Tara's voyage on foot through the Badlands, she'd crossed miles of desert that bore unbound demons' taint: geometries that shifted to her desires as she passed, showed her palaces with tooth-lined doors. Hummingbirds hung frozen in the air, not yet dead. They would pass an age of the world in their dying.

That would happen here, if the demons ate Seril.

She called down starlight. The demon she had stabbed scuttled toward her again. She redefined the atmosphere around it. Individual particles of air were tiny, but considered as a class rather than as individuals, as a blanket shrouding the planet, air weighed a great deal. (This trick wouldn't work against normal matter, which understood its own rules too well, but demonstuff was a stranger here.) The demon spasmed as it sawed the edges of her—admittedly specious—argument. Given time it would recover. So she stepped forward dancerlike and drove her knife through the top of its head.

The creature exploded to steaming dust.

She stumbled into the space where it had been, weak from conjuring. Not enough starlight here for proper magic, and the moon was spoken for.

The roof boiled with battle. Demons fed from gargoyles and grew stronger. Seril's children fought, bleeding but fierce. The struggle's score was bass and treble with no midrange—torn stone and broken glass. Blood ran down Tara's cheek. She did not know when she had been cut.

In the center of the roof Seril spun, dim and demon torn.

The demons attacked Her children. Seril sustained the gargoyles as they fought, and She fought on their behalf: moonlight trapped one demon-bug in silvery crystal, and time slowed for another. But there were so many, and as the gargoyles fell, the demons drank, and Seril weakened. This was how you fought a goddess: tore her between obligations until She spent herself in Her people's service. You built unwinnable scenarios and forced her into zero-sum games.

The gargoyles fell.

Tara wasn't kitted for war, lacked glyphs and weapons. But the demons were focusing on Seril and Her children. They'd ignored Jones for the most part, even as she attacked them with a collapsible club she'd produced from within her coat. If they ignored Tara, too, there were bindings she could work, procedures for demon outbreak. If she could talk fast enough.

She raised her hands and began to chant.

A sharp weight struck her. She spun in glass and blood and torn shadow, ripped herself free. She bled.

Demons flanked her.

Of course. They didn't care about Jones. But Tara, may all gods burn and bleed, was a priestess now.

She bared her teeth and made her blade long to fight.

By the time Cat and Raz and Shale reached the broken tower in the Ash, the moon was almost dead. Demonic waves washed the tower top. Claws of drowning gargoyles rose from the glass, tearing wings, breaking arms, but the demons were stronger than before.

They took strength from the goddess as they ate her.

Tara fought shadow-clad. Aev's great arms seemed sluggish. Seril's light showed dim through demonglass.

Cat felt her pain through Justice.

"We can't help," Raz said. "Not against that many."

The other Blacksuits said: we're coming, but we won't be there in time.

The Goddess said: *I need you.*

Shale dove, trailing silver from his wounds and wind from his wings. He disappeared into the flood and froth.

We can't help, she said. *But we can fight. I'll set you down. Bring the other Blacksuits—*

"No," he said. "We go together."

They flew into the sea of knives.

Abelard watched Seril lose her war.

It was a small war as such things went, but even the smallest wars were vicious. Demons broke. Gargoyles fought, impaled. Tara slashed, cut and slowed but lightning-wreathed. Cat and Raz joined battle, tearing demons off Aev's back so she could help her brothers and sisters—and the Blacksuits neared—but they would be too late. Seril was falling apart.

He felt the wheel of her thoughts twist on its axle.

God burned, watching.

—Why don't you help? Abelard asked.

You asked me not to.

—They'll die.

You were right. Are right. If I help them, it will hurt us all. (Each word formed from a hundred voices molded by a potter's hand from the turning clay of the city's minds.) If I help, I risk my people, who do not know Her as I do, and do not love Her as I do.

—We can teach them.

Can we? Can they learn to love her in time?

Abelard did not know. Yes, he prayed.

You feared, before, that I did not trust you. Here we are. You asked me to let Her stand alone. Ask me again, and I will.

—You don't play fair.

I don't play at all, He replied. None of Us do. Ink has been spilled on the subject. Did you fear I mistrusted you, or did you fear what my trust in you would mean? I offer you a choice. No tricks. I will save them, or not, as you ask.

Abelard's soul strained beneath those words, which were more than words, as if he were trapped between the bolt and hole of an enormous lock.

Bede had asked him to talk Kos out of doing exactly this. The Evangelist was not a bad man. He knew much Abelard did not, and his faith was deep. But so was Abelard's.

And his friends, and His, were in danger.

—Help them, he prayed.

There came a sound so enormous Abelard mistook it for thunder.

Later, thinking back, he would realize how much it resembled knuckles cracking.

Tara was not, probably, about to die—appearances (demon beset and bleeding, one arm limp at her side, suit mostly shredded) to the contrary.

She owed the Hidden Schools ten souls of tuition, which made it just the low end of worthwhile to keep her—*alive* might be a stretch, but at least roughly *compos mortis*. There were, of course, consequences to being bound to unlife by a single obligation. It distorted the psyche, discarded bits of consciousness irrelevant to the bond. Craftsmen who kept their bodies into old age had stolen—or borrowed—enough from the universe that the universe wanted a return on its investment. Reinforce those obligations with extensive personal leveraging, premortem prep, and the creation of phylacteric trusts, and an individual could endure the flesh-bone transition mentally intact, depending of course on one's philosophy of consciousness.

Die in overwhelming debt to a single provider, though, and less freedom remained to you. A Tara resurrected to repay her student loans would not remain interested in Alt Coulumb. There were stories of dead indebted Craftswomen processing contracts in beehive crypts beneath the Badlands, reviewing foundational wards in sleepless monotony. She'd never heard anyone confirm these rumors. Nor had anyone denied them.

So, while these demons might not exactly kill her, her likely fate was not pleasant.

Her senses filled the rooftop, spread through the shadows her Craft cast. She fought through pain. Cat flailed beneath a pile of demons. Raz ran to help her, ignoring the pieces of himself he left behind on claws. Tara caught a demon in an ontological twist—watched it trip and thrash to reassert its own existence, though the twist refused to accept the testimony of a nonexistent being. Before she could kill it, another tackled her from behind. Claws pierced her shadow guard, down and in, and she roared with the pain and so did Seril—

Then, on the rooftop, there was light.

More than light.

Fire.

She smiled as the demons burned.

35

"You might want to watch this," Daphne said, and passed the binoculars.

Ms. Ramp raised them, squinted, adjusted focus, and scanned the horizon until she found the tower. "Well, that's one way to resolve our—"

Daphne was looking at her boss, not the tower, so she only saw the firelight upon the woman's face. By the time she turned, the fire had faded to cinders upon stone.

Ramp lowered the glasses and blinked. "Godsdamn." She screwed her eyes shut, and tears leaked from their corners. "Never mind." She waved at the balloon's burner. The flame there shriveled, and they sank. "Shame."

Above, the moon shone brighter than before.

"I really do like this city," Ramp said. "Good theater. Better Old World restaurants than you'll find anywhere else in the New. And there's a special feeling to the light. I don't know if you've ever sat in a sidewalk cafe on a spring morning with a view of the sanctum— nice cup of coffee after full meal, nothing to do but sip and digest. Then the sun hits the sanctum's peak, around nine or ten depending on the date and which cafe you choose—and there are only really four anyone should choose in this city. The tower reflects a pure spark of sunlight in the center of the sky, the union of a star that existed millions of years before the gods, and a city only humans would be mad enough to build. Hold that cooling coffee in your mouth, black and thick, and watch the reflection. It looks like it will last forever." She sighed. Daphne had never heard her sigh before. "It doesn't. But we always hope, don't we? Still, the place will recover once we're done with it. And the theater might not even suffer. Actors are good as roaches for survival. You know, during the Camlaan Blitz, they performed a musical about the life of Ursus in the subway tunnels?"

"I didn't know," Daphne said.

"Good reviews. Shame I missed it. But, you know, a city doesn't bomb itself."

Matt waited in the hospital. Corbin Rafferty slept curled around himself, covers crinkled by his body. Matt felt uncomfortable watching him. He hadn't often seen another man sleep. Rafferty's position reminded him of Claire's on the couch.

The hospital room had two chairs. Claire sat in one, Matt in the other. The light was off. Matt didn't think he had slept, but there was no way to mark time here, with the curtains drawn. He read a few magazine stories about places that did not exist as far as he was concerned, about people whose problems might as well have been made up. He went to the bathroom. Wandering the halls, he found a pot of weak tea and cups made of a pale foamlike substance that sat badly against his skin and tasted like aerated bone. He returned.

Claire watched her father.

Corbin woke.

Just a snaking beneath the sheets at first, a protrusion of knee from covers. He thrashed against synthetic pillows. Claire's sudden tension made Matt look. Rafferty's eyes were open, staring straight up as if a sword hung over his bed. No sword, though, only a pitted moonscape of drop ceiling.

"Father," Claire said.

Matt thought he answered "Daughter," but the word was really "Water."

She poured him a cup, brought it to the bedside, and set it on the table, just in reach. Rafferty did not look at the cup, or at Claire.

Matt thought he should not be here. He almost excused himself, then realized his movement would draw more attention, and kept still.

"I took care of the deliveries today," she said. "The girls are well."

"I saw something last night," he said. "It was last night."

"Yes."

"I wasn't in my body."

"You were."

"I was and wasn't. I remember. I hit Matt. And Sandy."

"You almost hit Ellen."

"I scared her."

"Us."

"I was angry."

"Yes."

"I've been angry. Angry or drunk. For a long time."

"Yes."

"I can do this. I can hold it together."

"Sleep, Father," Claire said, and he did.

Matt and Claire did not speak on the ride back.

The gargoyles were not gone by the time the Blacksuits arrived. The toll of battle was too great. The demons had carved deep grooves in the gargoyles' stone, and dried moonlight coated their limbs. Cat stood among the fallen. The Suit kept her standing. It pressed her wounds together and filled her mind with song to drown out the background wash of pain.

Raz slumped on the dais. Tara leaned against a wall, shadows trembling around her, bleeding and exhausted but whole. The reporter, Jones, was trying to help Aev stand. Shale lay still; stone around him decayed to dust as his wounds knit. Nor was he the only Stone Man— she corrected herself—the only gargoyle in need of healing.

The demonglass steamed away. Large pieces endured longest, like gutter snowdrifts in new spring.

She felt her fellow officers climb the tower, gray beetles swarming around obstacles, leaping from windowsill to windowsill. They crested the tower and joined her, a chorus of which she was but one voice.

—see to the wounded—
—stone for the gargoyles—
—bandages—

Ten blocks away a train of ambulances wailed through the night, a Blacksuit crouched atop each.

As the Blacksuits arrived, Jones rose to stand between them and

Aev. "These people are hurt. They need help." A note of defiance on "people." She thought the gargoyles and Blacksuits were enemies.

Justice considered possible responses, settled on the truth, and settled on Cat to deliver it.

We understand, she said. *We will protect them. They are part of us, after all.*

Jake opened the door before Matt could drive home the key. Donna's voice issued from Peter's bedroom, which was the girls'—"Is that your dad?"—and Jake stood aside. Hannah sat on the couch, strangling a pillow. Simon brought her a glass of water from the kitchen. Her fingers unclenched slowly. No one had cleared the dinner table yet. Tomato sauce streaked the flatware red.

Ellen lay on the bed in Peter's room. Donna sopped sweat from her face and forehead with a rag. "She went stiff at the table. Cried out. They're eating her—that's what she said." Ellen mumbled a word Matt could not catch. Donna pressed the cloth to Ellen's cheek. "Scared the boys to all hells." Her, too, though she didn't say as much.

Claire walked to Ellen's side and offered Donna her hand. Donna passed her the rag before Claire remembered to say "Please." She got "Thank you" out okay.

Matt went to the kitchen for water and brought a glass back. By the time he returned, Claire had pulled Ellen upright in bed. Ellen shivered despite the heat. Donna found her a shawl, a black cable-knit thing her mother made that smelled of the cedar chest where they stored it. The girls spoke in a low voice. "Do you need us?" he asked Claire, and after a hitch of hesitation she said, "No."

Donna wanted to stay, he could tell, but she left. "We'll be in the next room." They cleared the table together. He spooned pasta into a tin lunch box for tomorrow, made another box for Donna, and left the rest in the covered casserole dish. He washed and she dried. "How was the hospital?" Donna asked.

"Corbin spoke." He ducked the sponge in soapy water, scoured the steel pan clean, and passed the pan to her. "But he's in a bad way."

"We're helping the girls, at least." She dried with a coffee-colored dish towel.

"You should have seen Claire this morning. She can run the whole business by herself."

"How old is she?"

"Seventeen."

"How old were you when you ran the stand alone?"

"About that age."

"There you are." The dish rack's silverware basket was full. She emptied it to make room for the spatula. "I know it's no business of ours, but they're under our roof now, for however long."

"I should have asked you before I brought them home."

"We're fine for a few days, though it's tight quarters. Had to sit Jake on an end table at dinner. But the girls keep to themselves." Silverware rattled as she hipped the drawer shut. "I think it was harder for them to come here than for us to take them." A cry issued from the next room. He turned from the sink with sudsy hands.

In the living room, Jake was chasing Hannah around the couch with a toy thunder lizard; she was running, and laughing, and turned to hit him in the face with her pillow.

By the time Cat finished her interview, Raz was gone.

The explanation took longer than she expected; Jones asked the right questions. Justice supplied memories and words Cat lacked. The other Suits cleaned up: drove Tara, protesting, to a hospital, and the gargoyles to nearby buildings where they could safely drain the stone to heal themselves. The tower roof was crumbling, and most of the gargoyles too hurt to fly. The Suits carried them.

But Raz—when Jones broke off their interview, Raz had disappeared.

You're hurt, the Suit whispered to her. Get to a hospital. You've done enough for the evening.

Where did he go?

Justice integrated and sifted the Suits' perceptions. Memories not hers melted as she clutched for them.

She remembered climbing crumbling walls, the vertigo of seeing herself in conference with Jones, tending the wounded and the dead. And there, Raz rose and shambled down the dark stairs. As far as the Suits guarding the tower's base could tell, he never came out.

I have to find him.

No, Justice said. You need a medic. Now.

Hells with this. Cat was off duty. She let the Suit go.

Pain hit her from nine directions at once. The sky dimmed, and the air chilled-warmed-chilled again, her skin unsure what to feel after so long inside the Suit.

Cat walked to the dark stairs because she could not run and lurched down winding steps shafted with moon- and streetlight through fresh cracks in the walls.

Raz lay in a nest of rubble at the tower's base. His clothes were torn, and his skin intact. He was very still.

She'd seen him gutted at least twice on the tower, and hamstrung once, healing almost as fast as demons could hurt him.

She limped over concrete and broken rock to sit by his side. "Raz?"

No answer.

A millipede scuttled up his pant leg. She brushed it away. The wound in her side pulled beneath her hand. She needed a hospital. Dust rained down. "Got to get you out of here. Place isn't safe. This isn't how you bite it."

His chest spasmed. "Bad—" Coughing. He raised his hand but could not quite reach his mouth to cover it. "Bad choice of words."

"Scared me for a second there."

Another shiver in his chest. They didn't need to breathe—he didn't need to breathe—but the voice box still worked the same. "Me, too."

"We should—" The ruined tower spun a sundial's revolution over her. "We should get out of here. Building's breaking down. Can you walk?"

"Don't think so." His lips moved so slowly they must have weighed as much as continents, and fangs tipped between them. "Glad you found me."

"Here, I can—" She reached for the chain around her neck, for Justice.

He grabbed her hand before it could close. "Not her," he said. "We need to talk."

"This isn't the time."

"It's never the time."

"I can't carry you out alone." His neck was cool as a marble column. "You took a claw meant for me."

"It didn't hurt."

"Let me say thank you, dammit." She felt his chest swell and contract against her side. "You're breathing."

"Old habits," he said. "Hindbrain knows you're hurt, tells you you need air. Instinct. Doesn't help."

"Story of my life," Cat said. "Old instincts that don't help." She slid her arm around his shoulders and tried to pull him up. They made it halfway together, then slipped and hit the rock hard. Raz laughed.

"I'll put on the damn Suit," she said. If she pressed her back against this big rock, bunched her legs under her, and pushed up with them as she leaned—

Before she could try, Raz caught her arm. She cursed. "Fuck did you do that for?"

Red unblinking eyes fixed hers. His way of moving reminded her of cellar insects, so still when seen, but look away for half a moment and they're gone.

He was hungry and hurt and so was she.

Points showed between his lips.

She nodded, then said, "Do it," to make her meaning clear.

He drew close to her. Her veins sang for the sharp pain and the spreading joy. She wanted to become a candle, a bonfire in the dark.

His tongue flicked her cheek, rough and dry, more like a cat's than a man's. It lapped blood from the cut on her forehead, the slenderest of tastes. He swallowed, and that swallow rippled through his body. She felt her self drawn into him—no desperate, fiery whirlpool but a tide receding to leave a slant of sparkling saturated sand.

He drew back. She thought she should say something but couldn't think of words to match the moment. Too many were questions, and could wait. The roof creaked. She grabbed his shoulder. The firmness of her grip surprised her. "Let's go," she said.

They lifted each other to their feet and, leaning, limped from the tower.

By the time Ellen emerged from Peter's room, Hannah had beaten Jake three times at checkers—their détente involved Jake not minding when Hannah won, and Hannah not minding when Jake marched his toy thunder lizard through the victorious checkers, devouring errant disks in a frenzy of dagger-toothed revenge. Matt hadn't expected his youngest to get on with the Rafferty girl, but perhaps he wasn't threatening—or maybe Hannah just liked lizards.

The apartment settled as they all prepared for sleep. Through the wall his bedroom shared with Peter's, Matt heard Hannah and Ellen talking in low voices like the bubbling of a fountain. Donna held him, and he held her back.

"You're right," he said.

She pressed her face into the side of his head and hummed satisfaction. "Call for a mason. Set this occasion down in stone."

"I say that a lot."

"Not out loud."

"The girls need space. Seeing Corbin in the hospital like that— he's sick, has been the last three years, since June left."

"Sleep, Matt. There will still be problems in the morning."

"That's what I'm afraid of," he said, but kissed her, said he loved her, and heard her say she loved him back. He waited on his back. His wife's breathing slowed. The ceiling was an unmapped territory.

Soft ghostlight glowed in the crack beneath the bedroom door: Claire, reading, in the living room.

"Claire, go to sleep!"

Ellen's voice.

The light shut off with a click, and they slept.

36

The next morning's dawn found Matt and Claire returning from their rounds. Their golem cart plodded up the long low ridge, beyond which Alt Coulumb's towers peaked. A flash of color cut across the road from tree to tree, and somewhere, something sang a sweet song.

"Beautiful bird," Claire said.

"The singer or the flier?"

"Both."

"The singer's not a bird. It's a gracklet."

She turned to Matt. "What?"

"Spider-lizard kind of thing. Mimics birdsong. You can tell because of the hiss before it sings."

"Do I want to know why it mimics birdsong?"

"Guess."

"Gross."

"Circle of life," he said, and hummed a few bars of a mystery play song. "Gracklets are good for the forest. They keep the bird-mind from eating people."

"Now you're just making fun of me."

"It's in the history books. The first Old World settlers came to Alt Coulumb after a plague hit the city, around the fall of the Empire in Telomere. Before the plague, locals used rallybirds to talk with people a long way off, because the birds' minds tie together. In plague years, the birds escaped, bred uncontrolled—and the more there were, smarter they got. Millions of them lived in the forests at the height. They'd eat crops ripe for harvest, pick a man's flesh from his bones if they wanted."

"And the gracklet?"

"A trader went to Southern Kath and found that even though the coastal jungle near Ajaia's land was full of wild rallybirds, they didn't get so smart. She asked around and learned that gracklet kept the birds in check. Their song breaks up the bird-mind, and then they eat the birds. The trader, she went into the heart of the forest and came back with a chest full of gracklet eggs. Planted them in the Geistwood, and here we are today."

"Where did you learn all this?"

"I read a book. Besides, it's part of the language."

"What do you mean?"

"Well—the larval stage of your gracklet, called a vurm, looks like a centipede yea long." He held his hands a foot apart. "They make cocoons in the trees. The rallybirds didn't realize what was going on until it was too late. But the more they lost, the dumber they all became, and grackle can eat a lot of rallybirds. More food makes 'em breed faster."

"Okay," she said, warily.

"Why do you think, when we talk about the virtues of industry and clean living, we say, 'The rallybird gets the vurm'?"

Golem feet trod down the road with unbroken stride, and wagon wheels rolled.

She hit him in the shoulder, hard.

"Ow."

She hit him again, then pushed him so he almost toppled over.

"Careful. You'll spill my coffee."

"Do you know what a dad joke is?"

"Nothing wrong with a good shaggy-gracklet story."

"You are a horrible person." But she had to say it through laughter. He rubbed his shoulder where she'd punched him. "I thought Corbin's jokes were bad. Do you get them from the same guy? I could tell the Blacksuits and get him locked up, for a nice reasonable time like let's say forever."

"Your dad tells jokes?"

"Not as much as he used to."

He remembered that, dimly—Corbin Rafferty never precisely pleasant, but at least wry, vicious in a way that put all the room but him to chuckling. Recently, though, just mean. "How is he, at home?" Felt dirty to be talking about this after a good laugh, but for once, and maybe because of the laugh, Claire seemed in a mood to talk.

"Drunk a lot. You've seen him angry. He gets sad too, when he doesn't think anyone else sees. Keeping life together is hard for him."

"Is he—is he hard to you and your sisters?"

"That in the square, that's as mean as I've seen him. He shouts. Shoves. Screams. Breaks things. Sometimes we shout back. Hannah especially. We're all cats drowning in a bag at home." Claire flicked the reins, though the golem did not change stride. "After Mom, he tried to keep it together. He drank to take the edge off, I guess. Only Corbin has a lot of edges. You can take off one after another until only a little nub in the middle's left, and once you've gone that far maybe you keep going."

"So you take care of the girls."

Her arms clenched, drawing back the reins, and the golem slowed. Matt watched her force herself loose. The tension didn't leave her shoulders, back, or arms, but she faked relaxation well enough. "I pick up what he drops. I maintain."

"What that gargoyle did to him won't last forever. He comes back, he'll walk the same trail as before. And that's bad for him, and dangerous for you."

"I know, Mr. Adorne."

Which was a door closing.

"I'm sorry," he said.

"If there was a way to force him to rest, I'd take it. The girls need the space. So do I."

A bump shifted crates in the truck bed. Matt turned to right a few squash which further jostling might have rolled onto his eggs. "I might have an idea," he said when he settled back beside her.

"What?"

"Rather not say much until I've talked to people. Don't want to promise anything."

They crested the ridge and descended from the forest to the city below, its road-veined circle quartered by the bite of the bay. "Matt."

"Yes?"

"The story. Gracklet?"

"They're real. I made up the bit at the end about the vurms, and there's a name for rallybird that sounds better in Eld. But gracklet are about as common as mountain lions in the Geistwood, maybe a quarter the size, solitary for the most part. They claim territory like spiders do. Friendly, though. Human soulstuff's too tight-wound for them to drink, and they'll only go for you with their fangs if they're hurt or you threaten their eggs. I saw one once when my dad took me camping. Scales aren't as bright as they get down south, but still brighter than you tend to find up here in winter country. You see one, you offer a bright feather to Kos and a silver coin to Seril."

"If this is another setup for a joke, I will hurt you."

"Honest. Old Coulumbite tradition there. Mom's side of the family, and her people go back to this soil. It's a strange world we live in."

She nodded, though that might have been a bump in the downhill road.

Tara woke beneath a too-familiar ceiling. Pale yellow metal beams supported white panels overhead; a metronome ticked her heartbeat and a needle pen scraped the sound's shape onto a palimpsest. She sat up and swore at the pain in her skull, then swore again when she saw the man reading a magazine in the chair across from her bed.

The metronome popped prestissimo as she forced herself to her feet, arm still fabric-cuffed to the heart monitor. Her hospital gown billowed, and stitches pulled in her side. She drew her knife by reflex; the speed of its departure grayed her vision.

Not that there was anything objectionable, on first glance, about the man in the chair, reading a copy of this month's *De Moda*. He was lean and strong, a pleasant topology of muscles evident beneath white shirt and charcoal slacks. Good chin. Very green eyes. Emerald, almost.

"What?" Shale said, half-risen. "What's wrong?"

She caught her breath and guided her nightmares of claws and teeth and chains back to the prisons where they lived in daylight. Her knife faded into the glyphs that ringed her hands and webbed her arm. "Nothing," she said. "I haven't seen you looking human in a long time."

He glanced down at himself, confused. "Did I get it wrong?" The features looked different draped over his skull.

"No. I mean, the wardrobe's a bit missionary."

"That's the point."

"The last time we talked like this was after I cut off your face and stapled it to a mannequin."

"I remember," he said without humor.

"So, we survived."

"Nobody's more surprised than I am."

"I did what I could," she said. "There were too many."

"Is this how Craftswomen say thank you?"

"We don't, as a rule. But, thank you. I remember the ambulance. Before that it's blurry, except for . . . the fire. Damn. So he did it."

"Kos aided us."

"He shouldn't have. I need to get to the sanctum. Where in the nine hells are my clothes?"

"Shredded. Unless you want to pass for a cover model on a planetary romance, I think they're a lost cause. Try these." He pointed with the rolled-up magazine to a garment bag on the chair beside him, which bore the crossed-keys logo of Adelaide & Stears. "I guessed your size. Hope I wasn't too far off."

She snatched the bag and closed the curtains around her bed with a wave. As she untied the back of her gown, she heard him say, "You're welcome."

The nurses had a fit when Tara tried to check out. Fortunately, the hospital knew how to handle fits. Tara ignored the usual arguments: that she should spend the day in bed at least; that her injuries, though superficial, merited observation given the slow infections that could spread from demonglass. Not a risk to her. Probably. Under normal circumstances. Regardless, she couldn't afford the time.

"That was an unorthodox exit," Shale said when they were safely a block away from the hospital. "They probably aren't used to patients who turn into eight-foot-tall shadow monsters and jump out a window."

She removed her jacket and clipped off stray tags with her work knife. "They'll be happy to have their bed back. Why shops put so many pins in button-front shirts I'll never know." She drew one from her collar, the third she'd missed in her hurry to dress. "Blood for the cotton gods?"

"It's so you can wear them fresh without ironing. You'll see it most often with golem-loom shirts, though a few tailors use them, too."

She donned the jacket and flexed her arms to test its fit. The fabric was the color of churned cream, and lush to the touch. "Fashion's an odd interest for someone who wears clothes once every never."

He crossed his legs. "I was made to be a scout, a spy." His voice sounded strange denuded of its rumbling bass undertones and the susurrus of gravel.

"I remember." Another pin in her side. That one at least had to be part of some weird ritual, or else a joke. Not that there was much difference between the two, in her experience.

"Infiltration is more than speed, and stealth is more than shadows. This flesh mask helps me walk through a city unnoticed, but skin is only part of the problem. People notice clothes that don't fit. Before the God Wars it wasn't hard. Clothes changed slowly. I once knew the traditional attire of all walks of life from the old Quechal kingdoms, from Iskar and Telomere and the Ebon Sea and Schwarzwald, Dhisthra and the Gleblands, Zur and Trälheim and the Shining Empire. I could pass for Telomeri street scum, a Zurish horse-lord, a midrank Imperial scholar with a gambling dependency. My knowledge staled slowly, since few were so pampered as to change their attire for a season's fashion. After the God Wars, though"—he shook his head in wonder and confusion—"golem mills and Craftwork-enhanced manufacture made clothes cheap, and as gods' holds relaxed, fashion churn spread from fops to the normal world. Though recent Iskari scholarship has challenged that narrative." He shrugged, which gesture too seemed strange in his human guise—less threatening without wings.

"You read fashion magazines to be a better spy."

"In Dresediel Lex four years ago, young men wore spats to nightclubs. Spats. Three decades back, young New World urbanites developed an affection for flare-hemmed trousers and suits the color of stained wood. Imagine trying to enter an office wearing such dress today. I would be memorable, and memorable is bad for a spy. And, having made a study of the discipline, it's fascinating to see the ways you people—mean humans—repeat old themes, coding religious iconography into fabric. Last year a hemstitch developed in the gowns of priestesses of the Vasquan man-gods made a forceful appearance at the Tehan Fashion Show."

"It's a good suit," she said, removing what she hoped was a final pin, and with some reluctance added, "How much do I owe you?"

"Nothing."

A larger part of her than she was comfortable with wanted to take him at his word. She had enough soulstuff saved at First of Alt Coulumb to cover rent and loans, but doubted her tiny surplus could absorb a shopping trip by a fashion-bug gargoyle. Still—"I can buy my own clothes."

"Yesterday you fought for our Lady and were hurt in her defense. So were my brothers and sisters. Scree will take a long sleep in stone before she wakes, and Aev bears new scars. We are built for war. We were made to endure such wounds. You're human."

"Only a bit," she said. "I'm glad to hear the rest are safe." And. "I'm sorry I didn't ask about them before. I woke up and ran to the rescue. I didn't think. Would you like to go to them?"

"They need rest. In flesh, I can ignore my injuries. If helping you aids my Lady, I will help."

"And if it doesn't?"

"Then I remain strong enough to hurt you."

The cab halted before the temple doors. "Good enough," she said. "Come on. Let's bust some heads."

37

Abelard sweated before the Grand Tribunal.

"Let the record further state that in conference with God last night," said Cardinal Evangelist Bede as he paced the flame mosaic floor between the benches upon which other prelates sat, their faces lined and drawn and, where male, bearded, "as part of your vigil you did beseech Him to let Seril and her children stand alone." What exactly, Abelard wondered on the Bench of Question as he took a nervous drag on his cigarette and held the smoke inside for a rosary bead's pause—what exactly did all these Cardinals do when not called to intimidate Technicians? He could name most of the elders in attendance, but he'd worked with less than half. Sister Justiciar's seat was empty, since this was technically an informal hearing. For an informal hearing, though, Bede had summoned a lot of people, most of them angry. At least Sister Miriel looked sympathetic. He exhaled. "At which point, you say, Our Lord Kos drew your attention to an attack on Seril and her children, and asked you if he should intervene."

An inch of ash quivered at the tip of Abelard's cigarette. He tapped it into one of the two braziers that flanked him. Their heat made him sweat, and incense fumes clogged his skull. The Lord's Flame purifies half-truth and illuminates falsehood, ran certain texts which were at best embarrassing to the modern faith, relics of violent younger days. He wished he'd worn lighter robes. "Yes, Your Grace." He should have lied. God would understand his reluctance to oppose Cardinal Bede, his need to preserve the church in time of trial. But when the Cardinal Evangelist had run into the sanctum last night, anguished, furious, Abelard told the truth.

He didn't know why. No doubt Cardinal Librarian Aldis could offer three or four bookcases on the ethical underpinnings of his decision. But given the grumpy owl's glower she directed at him from the benches, he doubted she was inclined to help. Her downward-curving mouth suggested the texts topmost in her mind were those at best embarrassing volumes—especially the bits with detailed diagrams indicating where one should apply the clamps, and at what speed the pincers should be spread.

At least this was better than the last time he'd been dragged before the tribunal. God wasn't dead at the moment.

As *it could be worse*s went, even Abelard had to admit this was less than compelling.

"You have been privy to many discussions concerning our church's, and our Lord's, vulnerability where Seril is concerned."

"That is correct, Your Grace."

Abelard took a shallower pull on the cigarette this time. Back during God's death, or near-death, he'd felt himself sicken with every drag. The Lord's blessing prevented cancer and heart disease and other problems. Abelard took small comfort in His presence now.

"You know the dangers we face."

"Some of them, Your Grace."

He heard an argument outside the hall—raised angry voices punctuated by a heavy blow that threw the double doors wide to admit Tara Abernathy and a man Abelard did not recognize. A protesting cloud of novitiate flunkies followed, trying without success to impede their progress. Cardinal Librarian Aldis stood; the city priests on the right wing squawked at the interruption. Tara looked furious. For a second Abelard allowed himself to hope the room would dissolve in, well, not violence, but at least a good old-fashioned shouting match that would distract the tribunal from him.

Cardinal Evangelist Bede thought fast on his feet.

"Brothers and Sisters," he said, arms raised, "be calm." He had the pulpit trick of voice that let his words silence a crowd. "Ms. Abernathy, welcome."

She sometimes smiled when she was angry—not so much a display of joy as a baring of teeth. "You won't try to throw me out?" With emphasis on the word "try."

"Were this a formal proceeding, I would ask you to respect our rites, which limit the chamber to priests. But since this is not a formal proceeding, and you are a trusted advisor, you're welcome to remain. As for your companion . . ."

"I vouch for him. As a trusted advisor."

Bede spread his hands beneficently. Wide sleeves draped from his arms to form a fabric wall. Abelard risked a wave and a smile, neither of which Tara acknowledged. "I was just asking Brother Technician Abelard why, though he knew the danger God's aid to Seril would pose to our city, church, and Lord, he nevertheless advised Him to help Her." Bede revolved, slow as a planet, to face Abelard, and the room's focus followed him.

Dear God. Abelard had joined the Technical Novitiate because he never liked preaching, always felt naked on the stage. Silent seconds spiraled to centuries. But through all the centuries, a fire burned.

He stood.

"Because my Lord trusted me," he said. Bede opened his mouth, but Abelard pressed on, like running: falling forward to catch himself word by word. "My Lord showed Himself to me, though I did not see Him at first." Tara stopped moving. He didn't know how to read what he saw in her. "Last night, by asking my advice, by giving me a chance to choose, He led me to understand Himself: Lord Kos loves, and He must fight to defend those He loves. He would not be Himself if He let Seril fall, any more than I would be myself if I abandoned my friends, or my church. To turn from that truth is to turn from Him, as did Cardinal Gustave—to deny our living God and satisfy ourselves with the worship of His dead image, of a picture on a wall that does not change or ask us to change. We must accept that He needs Her, that He was less in Her absence. In Her return, we come to know a face of Him hidden for fifty years. You say I have endangered our God. I say I have grown to know Him, and the greater danger that lies in deafening ourselves to His purpose, in abandoning His truth for a version of Him that may seem comfortable. Faith is a state of constant examination and openness. In faith we must be vulnerable. Only in this seeming weakness do we live with God."

No one spoke. Bede's mouth closed.

Abelard breathed out a long thin sigh of smoke. "If I am wrong, I submit myself for guidance. But I do not think I am."

Tara despaired of understanding the religious mind, but she knew how to read a room. When she entered that strange almost-court (no Craft circles to be seen, no judge, not even a bowl to catch shed blood), she'd pegged Abelard for dead.

Then he spoke, and many in the audience made the three-fingered triangle sign of the Flame and lowered their heads in an attitude that looked like prayer.

His argument didn't even hold, unless the words had different meanings than she thought. Faith, for example: How could one's fiduciary duty to church and God compel one to act against the interests of both? Yes, God and priests had goals beyond their own survival, but survival had to be prior certainly?

Her mind groped around the edge of a question she did not know how to ask. She wasn't alone: Cardinal Evangelist Bede stood stunned. "Thank you, Brother," he said. "Cardinals. I have no further questions, and must consider the Technician's words."

He bowed stiffly and swept out.

Tara cut through the crowd (not literally—these were her clients, after all) to Abelard. He still stood and stood still, cigarette in hand, head pendant on his long thin neck. "You saved my life," she said.

"I'm sorry I made things harder for you."

"Thank you."

She held his gaze though hindbrain reflexes demanded she look away. Much swam in there she couldn't read, but she found no blame.

Abelard smiled. "I should be thanking you. I don't often have a chance to save the day."

"That was a hell and a half of a speech."

"I didn't mean to go on so long." He stuffed his free hand deep in the pocket of his robe. "I thought a lot of things when I saw you in danger. Not all of it fits into words. I'm glad you're safe."

"I wouldn't go so far as to say safe," she said, "but I'm alive, so thanks."

She did look away, then. Shale stood behind her, accompanied by a nervous-looking junior monk. "Ms. Abernathy?" The monk bore a white business card in both hands, as if it were very heavy. "You have a visitor. As do the Cardinals." Other monks sought red-robed senior priests and priestesses in the crowd.

Tara didn't read the card. She knew the name printed there. Ramp. "Duty calls."

Abelard glanced at his fellow clergy. "I'll be fine."

He winced when she squeezed his shoulder. "Catch you later. Stay strong."

She left, and the tide of monks closed in.

38

The Evangelists, thank any and all gods, had coffee: grim, nasty stuff, notes of hydrofluoric acid, undertones of charcoal, ground glass mouthfeel, aftertaste of squid. The sheen across the top reminded Tara of oil slicks she'd seen. But at least it was coffee, by someone's definition. "I don't understand," Shale said. "Why do you drink the stuff if so much of it is foul?"

"Addiction," she replied, "or hope. Inclusive or."

"Some people add milk."

"If I wanted milk, I'd drink milk."

Through the meeting room's glass window Tara saw Ramp chatting with the Cardinals—Bede at the head of the table, fingers laced over his broad belly. Tara tensed. As Cardinal Evangelist, Bede's word on how to deal with Ramp was final. Had he understood Abelard? Or had he left the tribunal angry?

Daphne waited, one arm propped on a cubicle wall, examining crayon drawings tacked to the gray felt. She wore a fresh suit, but her skin looked slept-in.

"Morning, Daphne. Long night?"

She nodded cloudily. "A bit. Your assistant?" Raising her travel mug to Shale.

"Basically." She felt him bristle, but didn't care.

"Glad you made it. I dropped by your office earlier, but the doorman said you were already at the sanctum. This won't take long."

"That's what worries me."

Daphne's forefinger brushed a drawing of a house that looked the way houses looked in Edgemont, correcting for a five-year-old's tenuous grasp of architecture and perspective: peaked roof, two stories, front door, square window. "Priests have children?"

"Contractor."

"Wonder if the kid has ever seen a house that looks like that."

"Did you even ask Ramp to reconsider?"

"She's the boss. Our clients have millions of souls invested in your God. This isn't a game where you let your kid sister win because she'll feel bad about losing."

"Six million people live here." She did not raise her voice, she thought.

"And billions live on this planet. A cascade failure if Kos collapses—"

"He won't."

"If, I said." She turned a quick circle to see if anyone else had heard them. Elevator doors dinged open; the Cardinal Librarian swept past in a whisper of robes. "You always told me to run the odds. Our analysts say there's a real chance of cascade. Altars deserted. Continents failing into collection. Swarms of ravening undead. Demonic repossession. Lords alone know what would come out of Zur or the Golden Horde. And King Clock squats in the Northern Gleb—the Deathless Kings can't fight two wars at once and strangle one another at the same time."

"Fearmongering is no substitute for argument."

"Do you want our clients to pretend the world's a place where nothing bad ever happens?"

"I can fix this. Give me time."

Daphne counted bodies through the meeting room's glass. "That's the last of the Cardinals. I'm sorry, Tara. They can't start without you."

Chin high, shoulders back, she marched. Shale remained outside, arms crossed, inhumanly still.

Bede had saved her a chair. She settled and tried to look calm. Daphne sat near Ramp, who finished her scone, pocketed her gloved hands, and reviewed the room with mild, pleasant surprise, like a host receiving friends. "Your Excellencies, I'll keep this brief." She smiled at her own bad joke. "Yesterday you said Kos's aid to the goddess Seril represented onetime largesse. Last night we observed a significant transfer of power from Kos to Seril in a time of need, suggesting the goddess is in fact an off-books liability." From her briefcase she produced a white envelope that must have been made out of stellar core to judge from how it drew the Cardinals forward in their seats. Even Tara felt the document's pull. "In light of this new information, my clients feel compelled to action. They are exposed to any undisclosed risk connected with Kos, and the risk Seril presents is functionally limitless. My clients believe your church defrauded them by failing to disclose that risk, and they are filing suit against you. They intend to seek a Court-mandated restructuring of Kos and Seril, to protect themselves and the world."

"That's insane," the Cardinal Librarian said.

Ramp shrugged. "My clients have fiduciary duties to their investors."

"You can't do this."

"Aldis, please." Bede set one hand on the table. The Cardinal Librarian's teeth clicked shut. If she'd held a sword, Tara would have feared for Bede's safety. "They can claim whatever they're willing to fight for in the courts. And we'll fight back."

"Of course you will," Ramp said. "I've tried to talk my clients down, but they can't wait long—three days at the most. You'll find notice of our suit here." She tapped the envelope. "But there is another option."

Ramp produced a second envelope, thicker and red and sealed in wax, from the inside pocket of her jacket. "Less bloodshed and mystic battle, more compromise. This"—laying the envelope beside its bone-white sister—"is a binding version of the agreement we discussed yesterday. Sign this, and your church affirms its separation from Seril Undying. The language here formalizes an open market relationship between the two deities. Your gods' personal affairs remain their own business, far be it from me to assert otherwise, but this will stop any off-book shenanigans, unmediated by contract. If Seril needs help, she's free to offer market-rate payment, or seek outside investment. If Kos wants to work with her, he'll have a range of options, including formal merger. It's a good deal. I fought hard to convince my clients to offer it. Sign this, and save us both a lot of trouble." She lifted her hand from the envelope. "But I can't hold off my filing while you consider. If you want to take the deal, I'll need blood on paper by end of day."

Hard sharp silence followed. The red envelope and the white

glowed on the table. Classic hustle, Tara thought, scornful and admiring at once: hard road and easy and little time to choose. So classic she doubted the red envelope held any poison beyond the deal. Deception was beside the point. Formalized separation left Kos protected, and Seril exposed.

Everything Bede wanted was in the red envelope: an out that would save his God and church from Seril, regardless of that God's own will. The Cardinal Evangelist had hauled Abelard before a tribunal for making the same choice the wrong way. Tara might not be able to change his mind, but she needed time to try.

Bede didn't give it to her.

His robes brushed the ground as he stood. Knuckles planted on the table, he leaned forward. "We need no time to discuss." Hells. None of her options looked good: preempt Bede in front of the Cardinals? Suicidal. Slip inside his mind, force different words out of his mouth? Ramp would notice, and Daphne—they knew better than anyone what tools she had at her disposal. Besides, such an approach was unambiguously evil. Give the man a brief heart attack?

Bede licked his lips. Sweat beaded on his brow.

Only in this seeming weakness do we live with God.

Tara prepared the heart attack.

Before she could act, Bede spoke. "Our Lord and His Lady have endured a thousand years. For us to sign that document would be to fail in our faith."

Tara kept her jaw from dropping.

"Very well," Ramp said. The red envelope burned. The stink of hot wire filled the conference room. In seconds only ash remained on the undamaged tabletop, beside the bone-white envelope. "A pleasure as always, Your Excellencies. We'll see you in court."

39

Cat lay in bed, head gummed and teeth filmed and most of her hurting. Sun and shadow from slatted blinds striped her slantwise. Healing wounds pulled when she stretched, and she yowled. Her hand explored her ribs, all gauze and tape, ridged stitches and regrown flesh. She sat up. You never realized how well your skin fit your body until it didn't anymore.

Swing legs over the bed's edge, lean forward, stand. Dirty clothes crumpled underfoot. She picked up a stained shirt with her toes, transferred it to her hand, and tossed it to the hamper, where it rolled down the heap of dirty laundry already there and wedged against the wall. Cat felt more satisfied than she should have. The shirt's disposal left a gap in the layer of clothes that otherwise carpeted her floor.

Always felt strange to sleep late on a workday. Justice—Seril—brooked no argument on the subject. *Go home. Sleep until you wake up. Heal.* She hoped she'd get paid for the downtime. Last night was easily a double shift.

Of course, that assumed there was anything left to pay her.

Barefoot in bra and pajama pants, she padded into the living room. Dark here, too, blackout curtains drawn. How long had she slept, anyway? Seventy-seven demons from seven hells did the can-can on the right side of her head. Fuck. Cursing felt good—relieved the something or other. The cat-shaped clock hanging over her sink ticked its tail back and forth and showed a time she did not want to believe.

She opened the blackout curtains, pulled up the slat blinds, and leaned her forehead against the window. Eight floors down, a woman pushed a baby carriage along the broken sidewalk. A train passing two blocks over rattled the window, and Cat felt-heard the rattle in her skull. It didn't hurt. And she smelled—burning?

Behind her, someone screamed.

She turned just in time to see a reddish blur streak from her couch to bedroom. By the time the bedroom door slammed, the rest of the night had caught up with her: the trip to the hospital, the pain of healing, endless tests, after-action report, the order to go home, staggering back as dawn blued and pinked the east between skyscrapers. And with her that whole time—

She opened the window to let out the smell of burning skin, and tugged the blackout curtains shut. "Raz?" She ran to the bedroom door. "Shit, Raz, are you okay? I'm so sorry, I didn't—I forgot you were here. Say something!"

The door opened a crack, and a red-brown eye peered out. Above that eye stretched a charcoaled forehead, regrown skin wet and tender beneath the blackening and cracks. "Your room is a mess," he said.

She reached for the burn and he pulled back. "You can come out."

The crack between door and jamb widened to admit Raz's whole face. "How can you sleep in here?"

"When I'm tired. I keep the public space clean."

"I clean the place I sleep."

"You're a sailor, and you sleep in a coffin. You don't have much choice in living arrangements."

"Or not, as the case may be." He slid out the door. With one fingernail he peeled back an edge of blackened skin.

She made a face her mom wouldn't have liked, but to hells with Mom. "Does that hurt?"

"Yeah. Garbage?"

"Under the sink."

He leaned the can against his leg and deposited charred bits of self inside.

She watched, intrigued at first. "You want coffee?" She caught herself too late. "Habit, sorry."

"Don't worry about it."

"No coffee." She squeezed past him to the sink and poured water in the kettle. "I never put that one together."

"Coffee's one of the few I miss." Flakes of burned skin made a sound like light rain as they struck the trash bag. "I didn't notice the first few days of headache. I had a lot of getting used to do, after." His wave included fangs and all. "Later, withdrawal symptoms were worse.

Stabbing muscle cramps in my legs and back. I thought the transformation went wrong. Turns out that's just the drug leaving your system. Not fair, if you ask me. If a dreamdust addict turns, most of the time she finds someone to share the high. By the time I wake up, most of you have metabolized your caffeine." His skin was clear, mostly. He returned the garbage can to its cabinet, bent over the sink, splashed hot water on his face, and scrubbed. She'd ground her coffee with a hand mill and dumped the grounds into the press. "Sorry I gave you a hard time about your room. Where I live, you have to tie stuff down."

The kettle whistled. She plucked it off the burner, waited half a minute, flooded the grounds, and stirred. "I've been busy at the office, and getting my act together. Some things slip through the cracks. Plus, I don't have many guests. Mom and Dad live out in the Fell, and we haven't spoken in years."

"No gentlemen callers."

"No callers, gentlemen or otherwise."

"Thank you for inviting me to your secret lair." He leaned against the counter and watched her press the coffee. Flared nostrils invited the aroma, and he exhaled. "I could have found a hotel."

Light tessellated the coffee's surface as she poured. "My memory of last night's hazy."

"Mine, too," he said too quickly. "We can just—"

"You drank my blood."

"A taste, to regain enough strength to move."

"It felt different."

"It would."

"Why?"

"It's complicated."

"I want to know."

He touched his chest. "I need what you have, the way you need air. For most suckers that settles the question. Blood's a resource, like water or oil, and like water or oil, the people who need it do whatever they need to get it. That attitude ignores the *why* of the condition."

"Okay," she said, meaning, *go on.*

He did, with arms crossed. "I only know so much theory, but here it is. When you take the curse, it seals your soul and self. The curse stops change. That's why my hair grows back if it's burned off, why my muscles don't tire. But the seal makes it hard to take soulstuff in. Humans, you get paid or eat a good meal or meditate and you draw the world into yourself. We don't. This is how we refill." He pointed to his mouth. "The curse is thousands of years older than Craftwork, but the idea's the same. Imagine if the only way you could connect with the world was to steal it from someone else."

"But you don't."

"I use tricks. The *Bounty* has its own soul, and we share. There are other ways, which boil down to knowing the other person well, so you can accept and trade, rather than just taking. That's why it felt different." He stopped. "Feeding makes a connection between us. The curse wants it to be one-way. I can force it back. At Andrej's, when you—surprised me, it felt so good, and I wasn't ready. The curse took over. I freaked out."

"Then you blamed me for it."

"That was an asshole move on my part."

"Yeah," she said. "Why fight what you are?"

"Because the curse isn't me. I'm what I was before, only the curse tries to make me something else. It's old, and it's had a lot of time to learn how to make people see other people as food. Most suckers don't last fifty years. They go mad, or get killed, or sleep their lives away. Or they walk out into the ocean and never come back."

"I haven't heard that one before."

"We don't talk about it much," he said. "I don't like any of those options. I've walked the line for decades, but I still slip."

"And last night."

"Last night, you'd saved my life three times, and I'd saved yours at least once. I trusted you. I was ready."

"Are you still?"

They were closer than before. She'd pushed herself off the counter and approached him, step by tender step. His mouth was open.

There was a knock on the door.

"Yes," he said. "But I don't know if it's right for you."

Again, the knock, followed by a voice like a knife scraped over a guitar string. *Ms. Elle?*

"Just a sec."

She marched toward the door and realized halfway there she still wasn't wearing a shirt. Dammit. A bathrobe hung on a hook in her bedroom; she grabbed it, tied the belt around her waist.

A Blacksuit stood in the hallway, female of figure, glistening.

"What's up?"

You are summoned.

"It's my day off."

There is to be a council of war.

40

"We're in trouble," Tara told those gathered in the cramped black stone room. The Cardinals listened, along with Shale, and Abelard who'd arrived escorted by a few eager monks who in any other setting Tara would have described as groupies, and a few officers of Justice, and Cat. They were all here: clerics, gargoyles, Blacksuits, and the gods they served, whose attention she could detect, when she blinked, as ripples in Craftwork spiderwebs. "Much as I support Cardinal Bede's decision to decline Ms. Ramp's deal, he's left us in a hard spot. In three days, Ramp will bring the weight of the world down on our shoulders. We can't fight that alone."

"Can we fight it at all?" Bede rubbed his pipestem as he smoked. He'd put on a brave show before, but he was worried. Good.

"Let's review the plan: your creditors will claim the church misrepresented the risks to which Kosite was exposed. They'll use that to bleed Him dry."

Madeline Ramp stood feet wide-spread on roiling chaos amid nightmare clouds, hands clasped behind her back, shoulders broad and square as a general's. Daphne watched, taking notes.

Lightning licked from cloud to cloud as immense shapes swelled and sharpened into faces: skulls with eye sockets in which strange fires danced, ruined visages of women, cracked marble countenances that might have stared from ruined temples onto trackless wastes, beings bird headed or goat bearded, the world's secret chiefs swelled to the size of mountain ranges. Some were gods. Some were Deathless Kings. Some were not quite either—she recognized a Southern Throne-Lord by her pitted face and dried tight skin.

Call them clients. Easier that way.

"It is a pleasure to see you all again," Madeline Ramp said. "And thank you for coming on such short notice. Alt Coulumb has taken up our gauntlet. Soon, we begin the war."

The thunder laughed.

"Fortunately," Tara said, "Kos can fight back. He has a broad worshipper base and a diverse portfolio. We can make a strong case Seril has had little impact on his operations, or his creditworthiness, so far. Seril just isn't big enough—her balance sheet disappears into his operating budget. That's your first line of defense: cleric up and bluster through. The 'come at me' option."

"Which leaves the Lady vulnerable," Shale said. The Cardinals, particularly Nestor, squirmed in their chairs.

"Right. Alt Coulumb's people back Kos, but they won't support Seril yet." She took a sip of bad coffee and grimaced. A scribe arrived at the door, bearing copied documents; she passed them out, though they were short one copy, so Cat had to share with the Blacksuit rep. "Ramp's opinion of our side isn't high. She sees a junior Craftswoman and priests she's quick to dismiss. Since she thinks we're weak, she'll press Kos first—like inviting an idiot's mate in chess. She'll try to win quickly. If we don't crumble, she'll turn to Seril for the endgame."

Ramp regarded each of her thunderhead clients in turn.

"Kos's clergy's faith is shaken. First we will strike their core operations, with accusations of mismanagement and undisclosed risk. If we succeed, we sweep the field: if found malfeasant, the priests will have to surrender control over Kos."

A man who wore a mask of flesh showed green-flashed teeth. "Your chance of success seems low."

"We don't hope to win this round, just to force Kos's clergy to retrench theologically. They'll proclaim faith, affirm core principles, rouse the masses. Which, in turn, will undermine the moon goddess's attempts to establish herself among the populace."

"So we should let Kos take care of Himself, and focus on defending Seril."

"No," Tara said. "We use her feint as an opportunity."

The skin around Nestor's eyes crinkled like an apricot's. "Because it gives us more time?" He was a man of gears and fans and belts, not thaumaturgy. Tara had to slow down, or lose him.

"Because chess is a bad analogy for an argument. We don't start with an array of forces and remove them from the board one after another. We start with a blank board and build our position in the context of theirs. They'll expect us to defend Kos so fiercely we'll ignore Seril."

"What do you mean?"

"How would you shore up faith in Kos, ordinarily?"

"Preach," Abelard said. "Encourage prayer and reflection."

"Using your current theology?"

"Of course."

"Which sees Kos as the center of your faith, and Seril as an afterthought, or a rival."

"Ah," Abelard said.

"That's her goal: her attack will push you into fundamentalism, exposing your flank. Then she'll strike."

The chaos beneath Ramp's feet whirlpooled down and out to form a miniature of Alt Coulumb. Claws of light surrounded the model city, curved down, and pierced.

"That," Ramp said, "leaves Seril to us. The moon goddess is not strong enough to defeat a direct attack, and we are not bound to respect her as we are Kos. Since she signed no treaties after the Wars, she is technically a combatant still. If we break her, we resolve the main issue and obtain a captive goddess, not without value. But if Kos comes to her defense, we have him."

The raven-faced creature croaked a thunderclap. "How can we be sure of defeating Seril?"

"She is doubly weak: directly and through her creatures." A mock gargoyle crouched upon Ramp's open palm, fangs gnashing as it beat its broad wings. She closed her fingers, and stone dust rained onto the miniature city. "When they break, so will she."

"Justice might also be a target," Tara admitted, turning to page three, "but Ramp will probably ignore her. The parts of Seril connected with Justice don't have enough slack to support the Goddess's mind. If all Seril has left is Justice, she'll be as good as dead."

"How do we protect Seril, then?" Abelard asked. "Evangelism?"

"Seril draws faith from her new following in the Paupers' Quarter. Jones's interview will help, but it's not enough. The church has to come clean." Cardinals shifted uncertainly around the room. "Tell the truth about everything that happened last year, about Cardinal Gustave's death, even." She challenged each Cardinal with her gaze. "Support her."

"What if the church pivots to support Seril?" asked a voice made from the screams of children.

"Doctrine," Ramp said, "does not corner well. Which brings us to the church's second, more profound weakness."

"Which is?"

"Ms. Abernathy."

"We have heard good report of her," the crimson elephant said.

"She is a good Craftswoman, but she's young. The church will retain other help for the battle itself—Kelethres Albrecht, most likely—but Ms. Abernathy's decisions today will determine much, and she's an optimist. She'll believe the church can woo a city to supporting Seril—which will not happen in time."

"You're basing a great deal on your estimation of her character."

"My assistant"—she pointed to Daphne, who waved—"knows her well. And I have inside knowledge. Besides, Abernathy will remain our principal adversary in the Seril matter. Craft firms can't defend Seril, since she has made no formal peace with them. Which brings us to the best part."

"You expect us to undo forty years of religious education in three days."

"Of course not," Tara said. "Hope springs eternal, but the spring constant's not infinite." Blank stares. "This is the part you won't like."

Bede crossed his arms.

"I have a plan to save Seril."

Silence.

"When She died in the God Wars, Her killers carved her to pieces. Denovo remade what was left into Justice, but Seril's butchers took large sections of her portfolio for themselves. If I get those back, or compensation for their theft, Seril will be able to defend herself against Ramp. She can rise in glory through the night, rule from her high tower, all that good stuff."

"Why would we not like that?" Bede asked.

"There's a big catch. I have to leave the city, today, for Dresediel Lex."

"You can't." Abelard rose halfway from his chair. "We need you."

"You need a team to defend Kos. I'll build one. But no Craft firm will touch Seril with a lightning rod, and if we don't find her missing portfolio, she dies. If I go, we have a chance. If I stay, it's to fight a losing battle." She spread her hands. "If anyone at the table has a better idea, feel free to speak up."

"Tara Abernathy can't defend Seril. She faces a long grinding battle with defeat at the end. And nothing is more alien to Tara Abernathy. She is brilliant, talented, and fierce. She came from a podunk farm town near the Badlands and worked caravans studying with hedge witches for seven years before she reached the Hidden Schools. The schools kicked her out a thousand feet in the air above the Crack in the World, and she crawled home across a desert surviving on cactus flesh and vulture blood. This is not a woman who knows her limits. Back her into a corner, and she will seek a long-shot solution—or invent one. It's a big world. Plenty of long-shot solutions out there. Deals with old slumbering powers. Pacts with the Golden Horde. Demon mortgages. Lost grails and hidden powers in all their forms. Brilliance can't bear the prospect of futile struggle. So she'll go for an edge play."

"And fail," the thunder said.

"Quests take time she doesn't have. And when she fails, Alt Coulumb will be ours." She clasped her hands and shook them as if preparing to cast a die. "Either way, gentlemen, I look forward to the next few days."

The storm tolled satisfaction, and high dark clouds laughed, grim and vicious and proud, though not so grim nor so vicious nor so proud as Madeline Ramp.

"Okay," Tara said. "Let's get to work."

41

"Thanks for coming," Tara told Abelard as they rode north to the Alt Coulumb offices of Kelethres, Albrecht, and Ao.

"You really think this will work?"

"Maybe." A pothole jarred them. "If the Cardinals hadn't played so close to the vest since Seril came back, we wouldn't be scrambling now."

"Churches don't change overnight," he said.

"We've had a year."

"A year is overnight for a church." He leaned back into velvet cushions and crossed his arms, smiling around his cigarette.

"Why so smug?"

"You said 'we.' "

The carriage let them off at the base of a forty-story glass thorn unmarked by gargoyle prayers and veined with elevator shafts. The building had no door, but one opened anyway when Tara approached.

Black marble and chrome walled the lobby. There were no security guards visible, visible being the operative word. Tara noticed, while they waited for the elevator, that striations in the marble moved when she wasn't looking.

"That one looks like a mouth," Abelard said. "So does that one."

She said nothing. The elevator dinged.

On the ride up, she said, "The next few days will be hard for you."

He lit a second cigarette with the ember of the first. "I'll do what I can. Trust in the Lord and His work. I wish I could go with you."

There was something swollen in her throat. Lousy time to come down with a cold. "I'll be fine. We both will. This will work." He didn't ask how she knew, for which she was grateful.

With a ding, the doors rolled back, and they emerged into a glass maze.

Anywhere else, Kelethres, Albrecht, and Ao's local office would reside in a skyspire floating over the city. Craftsmen drew strength from starlight and needed buildings that could rise above cloud cover and clinging smog. Alt Coulumb's flight interdict made such crystal palaces impossible, so the firm's interior designers adopted an aesthetic echoing the heavens they were denied.

Glass walled the foyer, and glass hallways led to glass conference rooms and offices. Some panes were smoked translucent, others matte black; employees could adjust opacity as needed. The receptionist (a suited man with thin dark hair and the thick frame of an athlete who had abandoned his sport) sat at a translucent glass desk; his lower body was a textured black blur.

Tara's skin felt so tight she feared it might split. What was she afraid of? This was just an immensely powerful firm she'd snubbed by quitting.

"Tara Abernathy," she said to the receptionist, "and Technician Abelard of the Church of Kos Everburning, for Elayne Kevarian."

The receptionist rifled through a book whose writing tangled and rearranged as the pages turned. "She's not in the office. And she's dreaming."

"It's urgent. Any way you could slot us in?"

"Your name, again?"

"Abernathy."

He flipped to the rear of the book, consulted an index, changed back, frowned, scribbled a note on a slip of paper, and slid it into a pneumatic tube.

Far beneath the wooden floor, in a chamber walled with concrete, silver, polycarbonate steel, and sound-deadening foam, rows of dreamers lay chained to tables, gagged and blindfolded. The gags muffled their screams and kept them from gnawing off their tongues. An attendant took the receptionist's note from the pneumatic tube, bent beside a dreamer, removed the muff from her ear, and whispered the message there. The woman went rigid, twitched, and with the quill pen bound to her free hand scribbled a response on a roll of paper that spooled beneath her pen nib. The attendant razored the response free, returned to the vacuum tube, and—

Tara knew the process—she'd never been much of a nightmare

jockey, but one did familiarize oneself with the basic tools of one's profession—but she was glad she didn't have to watch. Blood and piss didn't mesh with professional attire. But that, as the Iskari said, was war. No arguing with efficiency: in under a minute, the pneumatic tube vomited her answer. "A technician will join you shortly." A complex Craftwork sigil occupied the center of his desk, all correspondence runes and irreproducible angles. He traced a glyph-line sequence, and green fire trailed his fingertip. "Have a seat."

"Maybe we could leave a message?" Abelard whispered.

"We can still talk to her. We have to jump a few hurdles first, is all."

"What kind of hurdles?"

"Don't worry," she said. "We'll be fine."

The tech escorted them down a smoked-glass hall to a chamber of tables with tops molded to fit the usual human extremities. "Lie here," she said, with a slight Camlaander lilt, "side by side, if you please."

Tara kicked off her shoes and lay back. The table adjusted to her body's contours. Abelard drilled his finger into the tabletop, then watched the wood flow to fill the pit he'd made. "Come on," Tara said. "We don't want to keep her waiting."

Abelard reclined.

"Do you sleepwalk?" the tech asked.

"I don't think so."

Tara shook her head.

"Good." She adjusted a few levers and turned a few wheels beneath the bed. "Any preexisting medical conditions? No smoking, please."

Abelard set the cigarette, still burning, on the table.

"Thank you." From a drawer in the wall the tech produced two paper-wrapped wreaths and slit the paper with a knife. "Completely sterile. Hold still." The circlets were stainless steel and hinged. Sharp prongs jutted inward.

Abelard squirmed as the needles settled against his skin. "Is this necessary?"

"Yes," said Tara and the tech at once.

She'd done this before, but still she drew her breath when the tech bent over her. The circlet crimped her hair as it closed. Stupid design—probably built by balding Technicians to balding spec. The circlet's spikes needled her skin.

"Very good," the tech said. Had they chosen her for her accent? It should have soothed, but nothing set Tara so on edge as the sense she was being soothed. The tech's fingers pressed firm, soft, and cool against her wrist. The woman was paid to touch people, and did so with as much routine disregard as one would expect. Tara wondered—not a prurient interest, just abstract curiosity—whether the tech had to set all that aside when she lay with a lover, the way Craftswomen learned to discard habits of boardroom argument at home. Were this woman's hands always her instruments?

Abelard laughed when she took his pulse.

"Hold still," the tech said. "You'll feel a tickling sensation."

Then the needles went in, and the pain started.

Fangmouthswallowinggroundingoutgearsanddigestedtopulpbyathicketofthorncurledshapes

to wake from the dark dream of herself in a well-appointed office where, told to sit, she sat

Walkforwardtosomethingyouthinkisfreedomdownahalllinedwithrazorsangledin

and with every step the razors near, halfway down the hall and they press against your skin, dimpling flesh, and you can't turn back because the light beyond the door at the end of the hall is so beautiful you could fall into it forever, at last, happy—there's a monster behind you but you're not afraid of monsters, even ones like this sculpted from childhood centipede fears, hooked legs too large for that enormous body and moving fast, a primal terror that barely makes sense because when save in the farthest mouse-shadows of history did your ancestors have to fear spiders? No, monsters do not scare you. But to face them, to defend yourself, would be to turn from the light at the end of the razor hall, which you cannot do. Your life waits there for you. Light washes you like water, like the tears you weep, like—*Mom*—rare as a father's approving smile, it's there and only your own skin is stopping you so you

step

into
the
razors
and
the
razors
bite
and you scream, you bleed, they're inside you, cold lines rasping bone, but you've done this to yourself and having come so far what's another
step
or
scream?

As Tara struck the deep and primal unifying terror, unseen machines channeled her through that fear, tore her to a gurgle of white noise like grinding glass and seashore rush and trills on a sharped violin.

And she was through.

Panting. Crouched. Naked.

She made herself clothes: the cream-colored suit Shale bought her. Arranged her hair. Looked down through glass into a city.

She crouched under Rampart Boulevard in Alt Coulumb's Central Business District. Skyscrapers plummeted to a vanishing point beneath her. Men and women and golems and snakelings and skeletons strolled below, their feet inches from hers, separated by a translucent pane of crystal perfectly flat on Tara's side. They did not realize they walked upside down. Robes, slacks, and dresses draped in the usual way. Braids did not fall up. A carriage rolled past. She heard nothing.

Stomach and world turned somersaults together. She looked up in hope of relief.

Bad idea.

She stood on what seemed a crystal plane, beneath which Alt Coulumb jutted down into blue sky. But the plane was in fact a shallow bowl rising in slow swell on all sides, here slashed with ocean froth, there scraped with green, the crystal curve at vision's edge so tall it would shame the tallest mountain Tara had ever seen—no, not the bottom of a bowl at all. She craned her neck back and back, and far above the walls arched and joined to a domed roof, and up there she saw stars that were streetlights and stars that were also stars.

She stood in the empty inside of the globe.

She felt the architecture of this dream. She could scream into the void. She could pound the glass with enough force to crack planets and burn stars. It would never break. The world's hollow heart was her empire and her tomb.

But she was not alone.

Abelard lay beside her, moaning. He flickered in and out, by turns old and young, corpse shriveled, rotten, infant, empty robe, man-shaped inferno.

The dream's third occupant stood with her back toward them—a slender woman in a dark suit, with short storm-white hair. This was a strange angle from which to see Elayne Kevarian. With her back turned, she might be anyone.

She was not.

Ms. Kevarian took a silver watch from her pocket. She snapped it open, consulted its face, closed it again.

Tara gripped Abelard's shifting shoulder. "Pull yourself together."

The shivers slowed, and his form congealed. She helped him to his feet. "Thank you," he said. In the crystal globe's silent center, even a whisper carried. "Does everything you do hurt this much?"

"Are you both decent?" Ms. Kevarian asked. "I have a tight schedule."

"Yes," Tara said.

Her old boss's footsteps were loud as drumbeats as she turned. The face was much as Tara remembered: sharp, marked with thin lines cut by decades of Craftwork. Black eyes flicked over Tara, right to Abelard, and back to Tara for a second review. The mouth, efficient as a lizard's, turned up at one corner. "It is good to see you, Ms. Abernathy. I've heard much about your work with the Church of Kos. The community is palpably relieved Kos's church finally has a competent full-time advisor—even if their gain was my loss."

She felt a thrill. Once she would have done anything to please this woman. Once? "It's good to see you, too," she said. "You remember Abelard?"

"Of course. You have come up in the world, Technician. Congratulations."

He bowed his head, too nervous for the formality to take. "Thank you."

"You're on a case?" Tara said.

"As ever. The Shining Empire this time. A member of their Divine Guard has died. I'm charged to resurrect her without disturbing the giant monster whose consort she is. An interesting problem. What can I do for you?"

"I don't suppose you can tag out of your current case for a few days? We have a situation here."

"Kos is in trouble," Abelard said. "And Seril."

"In three days," Tara explained, "our creditors and shareholders will challenge Kos's by attacking Seril. I have to focus on a long shot that might save us, and I need—we need," she corrected with a glance to Abelard, "to stall the enemies at the gates." She produced a folded document: a copy of Ramp's challenge.

"Who's the opposing counsel?"

"Madeline Ramp, with Daphne Mains assisting."

"Ramp. Interesting."

"You've worked with her?"

"A practicing theorist—the most dangerous kind." Ms. Kevarian flipped through the document. She nodded at various points. "Ramp was involved—you're aware of the Alt Selene outbreak, in the eighties?"

"I know she lives in Alt Selene. I didn't realize—"

"She waded into the singularity and killed it before the city died. She wrestled omnipotence into submission. I'm sure she has a raft of interesting stories." Ms. Kevarian shrugged. "Also a prominent contributor to the *Forum on the Will and Its Transformations*, the misguided knitting circle Alexander passed off as a journal. She's competent. I wish I could help."

"You can't?"

"The Shining Empire case is consuming the overenthusiastic

murderball coach's proverbial one hundred ten percent of my time. In a week, I could assist. But you do not have that week."

"This is a formal request from the Church of Kos," Tara said. "There's budget behind it. We're not asking for a favor."

Abelard stepped forward. "Technical Cardinal Nestor and Cardinal Evangelist Bede sent me to retain your services." He seemed proud he'd said the whole line without stumbling. Strange he should be so daunted by a pro forma request, yet able to deliver that speech in front of the tribunal. Tara always found heart-baring stuff harder. "Ma'am."

"I wish I could abandon this project," Ms. Kevarian said. "But several hundred miles of coastline and a hundred million people are in danger of attack by, I swear, giant moths, if I abandon my work. However." She slid the folded paper into her pocket; Tara felt the information slip from dream to dream, like playing cards sliding past each other. "Thankfully, my firm has other partners." A black notebook appeared in her hand; she paged to the end, frowned. "Young Wakefield should be through in Regis by now, and has experience with this sort of thing. Wakefield's no friend to gods, but the challenge won't require empathy to defeat. If that's all . . ."

"It's not," Tara said, "actually."

"Is this the part where you ask for your old job back?" But from Ms. Kevarian the jab felt easy. "I'm afraid you may be too expensive for us at the moment."

"Nothing like that," Tara said. "This long shot I have in mind. I need to talk to people who might not take a meeting from me otherwise."

"I can make introductions. With whom do you wish to speak?"

"I need to see the King in Red."

"We have not spoken in a while," Ms. Kevarian said. A deep pit lay beneath those words. Tara felt that if she stepped wrong she might tumble through them and fall forever. "We are not so close as once we were."

"We need Seril's lost portfolio. The custody chain stops with him. There's no time to bring formal action against the King in Red—I doubt we could win in court. His pockets are deep. But I need to try, and the Deathless King of Dresediel Lex won't take my card." Ms. Kevarian darkened in the dream. Don't press her, a wise inner voice counseled Tara, but Tara never had much truck with wise inner voices. "I'm sorry. I didn't realize there was bad blood between you."

"I'll contact him," Ms. Kevarian said. "I cannot guarantee it will help your cause."

"I'll take the chance."

"I should go. The Imperial guard needs its monsters. It has been pleasant to see you both. I must visit Alt Coulumb soon, in peacetime."

"I'd like that," Tara said.

Ms. Kevarian turned to leave.

"Um," Tara said, which stopped her. Stupid syllable, but she'd spent the entire conversation curious. "When we worked together, I called you Boss. I'm not sure what I should call you now."

She blinked owl-slow. "Elayne, Ms. Abernathy."

"Tara."

"Tara." She seemed to find that amusing. "Good luck."

And as Elayne smiled, the glass world shattered into day.

42

Black cuts lined the lips of the man in the hospital bed. When he spoke, his skin pulled against fresh scabs. "Water." His Kathic bore an accent Cat didn't know.

She nodded to Lee, who poured him a cup and passed it over.

"You're in Alt Coulumb," she said. "In Blacksuit care." She rested one hand on the rail at the foot of the bed. "We recovered you from an exploitative indenture two nights ago. I'm Officer Elle. This is Officer Zhang. You can call me Cat, if you like. What's your name?"

The *h* in "Ko'hasim" had a rough edge Cat didn't look forward to failing to imitate. "Call me Hasim."

The name structure at least she could place. "Talbeg?"

"I am a Doctor of Divinity from Agdel Lex." He finished the water. Lee poured him more. "Alt Coulumb. Are the others here?"

"A few went to intensive care. Most are unconscious. The girl, Ala"—she pointed to where the child lay asleep—"told us we should talk to you, or to the woman with the braids, who's passed out. She's fine," she said when he opened his mouth, "just sleeping. You all had a long night."

"What happened?"

"We hoped you could tell us," Lee said.

"We found you in the hold of a smuggler ship called *Demon's Dream*, captained by Maura Varg. That sound familiar?"

"I do not know either name." Hasim seized the rails at the side of his bed. Muscle in his thin arms corded as he pulled himself upright. "If this is Alt Coulumb, we seek asylum."

"We'll get there," she said. "But we need to know more about you. How you got into that hold, for example. You're responsible for some confusion."

"Last night," Lee said, "when Officer Elle tried to wake you up, demons crawled out from inside you. Caused a lot of trouble before we stopped them."

Hasim's fingers trembled as they traced the scabs around his mouth. "What my partner's trying to say"—Cat frowned at Lee, who crossed his massive arms, unconcerned—"is that we're wondering how you got in that ship. I know this is hard, but if you think back—"

"There is war in the Gleb."

"I heard." She wished she'd heard more, or paid attention when she had. Even Criers mangled the names. "Didn't realize it had reached Agdel Lex."

"Refugees have," he said. "I run a clinic for small gods. In the backcountry, desert spirits devour the bodies of gods fallen in the Wars. They claim one town at a time. They come to the villages to eat their gods, or bind them to service. Some survive. Some run, and many to our city. I take them in, if I find them."

"When did you start using dreamdust?"

Cat made a mental note to talk with Lee about interviewing witnesses. Lee spent most of his shifts Suited.

"I have never taken dreamdust," Hasim said. "It is a distraction."

"How did a smuggler end up with your indenture, then?"

"I do not know." Hasim peered around Lee's shoulders to examine the rest of the room. Eight beds, each occupied. He relaxed— recognizing the others, Cat thought.

"The rest are nearby," Cat said. "I have names of the ones who've woken up so far. I'll give you that once we're done here, but I need the whole story. You ran, what, a hostel?"

"A sanctuary. We took in those we found. Such an endeavor requires protection. To afford that protection I, ah, borrowed. The demand grew. One day, it struck me all at once. The children collapsed first. I tried to save them, but I was not strong enough. I remember nothing until I woke here." He shook his head. "I have never dealt with demons."

"Thank you, Doctor. The nurses will bring you the list. Could I have the name of the bank you worked with in Agdel Lex? The one that issued the loan?"

"Grimwald Savings."

Cat kept her poker face, barely. The Grimwald Concerns dotted the world, shadowy presences with massive holding networks and questionable morality. She'd never heard of a Grimwald convicted of anything, but they hovered in the background when you read about Craftsmen going down in flames. Legitimate businessmen, people called them, with an emphasis on the first word that no one ever used when talking about, say, a bakery. "Thank you. As for asylum—you're in Alt Coulumb under the protection of Seril Undying." For whatever good that does you. "She'll accept any thanks you offer." And she needs it, Cat did not say.

"Seril," Hasim said. "I thought her epithet ironic."

"Nope." It felt good to tell the truth to someone who wasn't already part of the conspiracy. "She's alive. The doctors say most of you will be good to go after a physical. We'll reach out to the Talbeg immigrant community in Alt Coulumb. The Church of Kos has guest houses for new arrivals, too. Your choice. If you need anything, go to the Temple of Justice and ask for me—Catherine Elle."

As they descended the hospital front steps, Lee gripped the back of his own neck in one hand and squeezed. His biceps were a sharp-cornered prism under his uniform shirt. "Refugees, Cat. I don't know."

"Don't know what?"

"They're a foreign problem, from a foreign war. Don't we have enough of those?"

"They're here," she said. "You want to send them home?"

He grunted.

"Just you wait. If the next few days go poorly, we won't have to help them after all."

"Why not?"

"Because we'll be in the same boat. Come on." The Suit covered her like liquid bliss, and its strength made the world seem simple.

The moon rose in Cat's mind as she ran across midday rooftops toward the temple. She leapt in a silvery arc over a rushing train and lost herself in the logic wash of Justice, her mind a riverbank down which a clear stream of dispatch orders and deductions ran—flash of gutted corpse in Hot Town back alley, calculated vectors for an arrow's flight, analysis of last night's criminal activity patterns, comparisons of faces and fingerprints, the thrum of arriving and departing ships, a chorus of half sentences. Then she jumped again, and the river stilled into the silver silence of a smile.

You want to talk with me? the Goddess asked.

She did, though she hadn't realized it yet. You need help, Cat said.

Yes.

Cat landed with a skid on a tar paper roof, cornered hard, and scaled the building next door, fingers spidering into cracks. It felt good to run. If you broke Justice, ended the Blacksuits, you might be strong enough to fight Ramp.

An interval of surf-rushed quiet followed. Cat swung from a flagpole to the next roof.

The last time I rode to war, I trusted my city to my children. When I died, they went mad, and their madness left scars. If I broke Justice, I could use its power, but then Justice would be no more. And She has Her cold uses. She protects my city, even against me.

You might die.

This reply too was a long time coming. *I was born to protect Alt Coulumb. I failed it in my death. These people once feared me as the rabbit fears the hunter, though the hunter comes not for the rabbit but for the fox. Now they fear me as children fear those who strike them. I will not be that Lady again.*

If you don't win, we all lose.

But Justice will remain.

There has to be some way the Blacksuits can help.

Against what? What laws have our enemies broken?

I'll think of something, Cat said. And: If I offered myself to you— as, you know, a priest—would that change anything?

Are you?

Cat unframed her mind from prayer, and ran alone over rooftops, threaded through with crime and ice.

43

Matt, half-dead on his feet by noon, back sore from long hours standing and selling, almost missed the Craftswoman when she passed
his stand. Generally the sixth hour after opening was when his
shoulders sagged and thoughts of cold beer filled his mind with the
self-sustaining fixedness of a fetish. Claire was likewise drained,
and Hannah. Even Ellen had come to the Rafferty booth today,
cheerful if quiet as she tended the shrine.

So he almost missed the Craftswoman. When he said, "Ms. Abernathy," though, she stopped and turned.

"Mr. Adorne." She shook her head as if to clear cobwebs from it.
"No eggs today. I have to pack for a trip."

"I have a business question I hope you can answer."

"I need to go. I'm so sorry." But she did not. "What's your question?"

"It's not for me," he said. "Could you meet us on Cadfael's rooftop in half an hour? Just a small issue. Won't take a few minutes of
your time. I can pay."

"Are you in trouble, Matt?"

"I'm not," he said. "They might be." He nodded to the girls—to
Hannah taking inventory, to Claire frowning at the ledger, to Ellen.

"I have to leave at one," the Craftswoman said.

"Plenty of time."

Matt did not remember the last time he closed his stall early. Claire
had left the Rafferty booth in Hannah's and Ellen's care—Rafferty
and Adorne both closing early might have caused the sky to fall, the
seas run red with blood, or locusts boil from the earth. Far as he could
tell from his corner seat on the empty roof of Cadfael's, the sky hadn't
cracked yet. Shame: a crack might have let the heat escape. Conden-
sation collected on his glass. He hadn't yet drunk.

"She won't come," Claire said.

"She will."

"Even if she does, what can she do?"

"Give answers," he said.

Tara arrived on the thirtieth minute by his watch. She stepped blinking into sunlight, escorted by a waiter who indicated with outstretched hand a path through empty tables to Matt and Claire. Tara limped. As she lowered herself to her seat, she kept one hand pressed against her side.

"You're hurt."

"Rough night."

"I know the feeling," Matt said.

"I doubt it." But she looked more amused than offended, and ordered a beer. "Busy day, too," she said by way of justification, though he'd asked for none. When the waiter disappeared: "What do you want?"

"You know Claire Rafferty."

"Not by name." She held out her hand. Claire hesitated, then clasped it.

The waiter brought beer. Matt ordered a sandwich, Claire a sandwich, and Tara nothing. "I'm just passing through." When the waiter left: "What's the problem, Matt?"

When Matt tried to speak, he found his throat dry and his words all twisted. Tara's expression wasn't fearsome, exactly, but behind it ground the gears of a great machine.

"Matt wants you to help me take the business from my father," Claire said.

"Tell me more," Tara said.

"You know about the argument in the market a few days back. The gargoyles. That was us. My sister dealt with them before, and my father wanted her to show people for—some reason. He got violent." She held her water glass in both hands. "I do most of the work in the stand already. And he needs help, which he won't get on his own so long as he works."

Tara drew a dry circle on the tabletop with her middle finger. "And he leads the family Concern."

"Yes."

"If he really has been negligent, you can press him out." Tara set her beer down on top of the circle she'd been drawing. "One afternoon at the Court of Craft and you'd be done. But the Craft is serious." She laid her hand on the table, fingers softly curled. The sun dimmed and knelt. A chill wind blew from nowhere. A flame leapt from Tara's palm to her fingers and danced from tip to tip—but flame was not the right word. Matt didn't know a word for it, or the not quite glow it cast. "A bond through the Craft is as like, and unlike, a real relationship as this light is like a fire. This burns, but there's no heat, and it has edges that cut, which a real fire does not. If I do what you ask, it will burn your relationship with your father and replace it with a Craftwork bond. It's an option." She closed her fist around the flame. Almost-light ran in rivulets up her arm along tracks like tattoos Matt hadn't seen before. "But there are others."

"Like what?"

"Mediation," she said. "Which requires talking to him—with a Craftswoman present, to ensure your bargains take. It's hard, but offers more chance of healing. If you care. Either way, the choice is yours."

Neither Claire nor Tara had looked at Matt. He folded his hands. Sunlight kneaded warmth into his skin.

"I'll be out of town for a few days. When I'm back, if you still want to go to court, I'll help." She looked as if she wanted to say something other than what she said next: "Think it over. Either way, I won't charge."

"Thank you," Claire said.

"For what? I only offered you a hard choice."

"At least I have one."

Tara pondered her remaining beer. "I have to go. Flying out of Alt Coulumb this evening. Lots to do before then."

"You seem worried," Matt said.

"I am." She stood. "But I can't talk about it now. Take care of yourselves in the next few days, okay?"

"We will."

"Good luck."

After she left, the waiter brought the sandwiches.

44

Tara caught a cab at sundown and settled in to read and ponder fate.

The near crash shocked her awake. The horse reared, hooves pawing. The carriage rocked and landed hard on bad shocks.

Tara dove out the door, blade drawn, shadow-clad, expecting cutpurses, demons, treachery, some machination of Madeline Ramp's. She found Shale in the center of the road dodging hooves, hands raised. A black leather valise rested at his feet.

Tara released her knife and banished her shadows. "What the hells are you doing here?"

Shale snatched his bag and darted past hooves toward her. "Coming with you."

"No." She touched the beast's flank, and it steadied, though its ears slicked back.

"You needed me to translate. You might need me again."

"Aev put you up to this."

"She would be angry if she knew I was here," he said. "I already bought a ticket." A white hologram-stamped card protruded from a side pocket of his valise. "I will follow you."

"I could stop you."

"You are fighting for my people. I endangered us all two nights ago. Let me help."

The horse snorted and scraped a spark off the cobblestones.

"Fine," she said. "Get in before I change my mind."

He carried the valise as if it weighed very little—not that Tara's luggage was much larger—but a blink told Tara the bag lacked any magical capabilities, folded space, or hidden compartments. "That's all you brought?"

"Books," he said. He pulled the door shut, and they rolled west into the night.

"No toothbrush? Clothes?"

"This flesh doesn't work the same as yours. Close enough for imitation only. I do not need to eat in this form. My sweat's pure water unless I wish it otherwise. Conserves salts."

Tara pushed back the velvet curtain. They rode past a broad dark space walled with brick: a park or a graveyard. Shale would know which. Wind shifted leaves like clouds above the wall. If there were graves, she could not see them.

Leaving a city was like peeling off a sticky bandage: no matter how fast you tried to go, a few grimy traces still lingered on your skin. Even after buildings gave way to open fields, Tara still didn't feel as though they'd left Alt Coulumb. The skeleton of a burned house stood watch over swaying wheat.

"The moon roads would be faster," Shale said. "All places are one where Seril's moon shines."

"The red-eye will get us to DL by sunrise, and I don't want to take any more of Seril's power than I have to. If we need her roads later, we'll use them."

They crested the western ridge and took a right turn through a spur of the Geistwood. Stars shone clear in the dark. Tara tasted their light. In Alt Coulumb, where human fires blunted the stars, wielding Craft felt like doing surgery wearing wool mittens. Out here, the mittens fell away, and her scalpel was sharp as ever.

"Was that really why you refused?" Shale asked.

"What, you think I'm unnerved by the thought of Seril carrying me through the god-realm? Conventional air travel's safer, more comfortable, and almost as fast."

The trees failed and the cab descended a long shallow slope to the airfield. Crystal fangs surrounded a blacktop paved with some distant volcano's ash.

A dragon crouched on the runway.

Even at this distance, its scale beggared thought. The road passing beneath the dragon's left wing to the embarkation hall seemed no thicker than a hair at this distance. Word problems: Based on that proportion, estimate the size of the creature on the tarmac. Determine the width of those black shining scales, the curvature of those teeth.

Trick question. No number could match the beast. Math did not follow the mind down such dark roads.

The dragon faced west. The tail gave an earthquake twitch. Broad chains crisscrossed its back, supporting the gondola. The observation deck across its shoulders perched on hydraulics to keep level as the wings beat. Vast slitted eyes cast spotlight circles on the ground.

"Safer," Shale said, doubtful.

A bus rattled past them, bound cityward and uphill, carrying only an old woman in dark glasses, her hands crossed over a carpetbag.

Gavriel Jones ducked under the police line and entered the topless tower in the Ash where she had almost died the night before.

She picked her way across ground-floor rubble. At the entrance to the long, dark, winding stair she hesitated, though she would never have admitted any reason for the pause beyond a wish to finish her last cigarette.

The climb was easier than she remembered. Moonlight leaked through chinks in the tower's mortar, but did not relieve the darkness.

A long time later she emerged onto the tower roof.

Last night she'd found a troop of gargoyles waiting here. Troop probably wasn't the correct noun. An intimidation of gargoyles? And a throne, and a Lady atop the throne. The interview of a lifetime, half-finished.

The troop was gone. The throne lay broken, one great horn snapped off at the base. Demonglass had melted like dew, leaving scores on stone to mark last night's battle.

"You shouldn't be here."

She did not, to her credit, jump. Her Hot Town alley savior emerged from behind the broken throne: broad-shouldered and tiger-faced Aev. Curled beneath her wings, she'd blended with the rubble. Clawscratch mapped her skin.

Gabby remembered Aev wrestling with demons last night, remembered the moonlight that wept from her wounds.

"The rooftop is not safe." Aev rounded the dais. Dust shivered at her footsteps. "We drained this stone too much for you to trust it."

"You're still here."

"We have spent much of our faith here," she said. "We made this space holy, thin and timeless. Someone must guard it, though the stone here is no longer strong enough to heal us." She touched the scars across her chest. "I remain. The others sought holes in the soil, deep shadows in the water, abandoned warehouses where they can recover."

"Will they?"

"One has passed," Aev said. "Karst. You did not know him."

"I'm sorry."

"We will carve another in his honor," she said. "If we live so long."

"You don't—die—often."

"We do not age in your manner. Few accidents harm us. We fall in battle, or never. But that is not so rare as you may think."

"This is my fault," she said.

"Did you let demons into Alt Coulumb?"

"If I hadn't reported on you, none of this would have happened."

"Or it would have happened later." Aev sat on the dais and laid one hand on a fallen horn of stone. "You might as well call this my fault for saving you, when you entered the Hot Town. My child rebuked me for that. We are both creatures of obligation, Ms. Jones: I was built to serve. You haven't walked the path of a cause until you molded yourself to its form."

"Why did you save me? You knew what I was."

"They were hurting you."

Gabby kept quiet for a while. "Seril isn't here."

"She is everywhere. But She is not here as She was last night."

"I wanted to finish our interview." The words sounded foolish even to her. She brandished her notebook.

"The time for interviews and revelations has passed. We live under threat of attack. Soon Alt Coulumb will face a fire fiercer than its god."

Beyond the tower's rim, the city burned.

"I heard," Gabby said. "That's my job. And that's why you need this interview. People don't know who you are, why you're here. I can tell Seril's story. Or yours."

"Mine?"

"Why not? You're at least as scary, in most people's minds, as your goddess."

"We are imposing by nature."

"It's not helping you." Gabby approached the dais, leaving footprints in dust, and sat beside Aev. She flipped to a blank page in her notebook, took pencil and knife from her pocket, and cut the pencil sharp. "Just say what comes naturally."

"Where should I begin?"

She looked out, and down. "Start with the city."

"You should leave," Cat told Raz that night by the *Bounty*'s wheel, while skeletons and snakelings and the rest of his shadowy nighttime crew busied themselves on deck.

"Leave?"

"Leave Alt Coulumb. Get to sea. There's bad stuff coming."

She'd found him working through a ledger on a low table by starlight. No lanterns. He didn't need them. The book creaked as he closed its spine. "Tough day?"

"You have no idea." She leaned against the wheel. "You know how long Justice's regulations are?"

"Few hundred pages?"

"Try a few thousand, all dense Craftspeak, little shades from act to act. Ninety different kinds of fraud. Seven classes of assault, each with seven subclasses. Why seven, don't ask me."

"You're not the type to spend her off hours reading rules."

"No. But we'll be under attack in a few days, so I figured it might help."

"Attack."

"Craftsmen coming for Seril, or Kos, or both of them. Kos can handle himself; Seril can't—the part of Her that's Herself, I mean, the conscious bit. She doesn't have enough power. I wanted to make the Blacksuits help. It's not easy. Turns out Justice wasn't built to interfere with Craftwork. This will get bad. You should go."

He capped his pen. "To save myself."

"Fighting these bastards is my job. I don't want you doing hero stuff on my part. Leave. Get safe." It hurt to say. "Come back when it's over."

"I can take care of myself."

"You couldn't fight the demons last night," she said. "And you can't fight what's coming, either."

"Worse than demons?"

"Bigger," she said. "Craftsmen riding engines of war."

"I'll help."

"You can't swashbuckle this problem away. Unless you have some crazy secret vampire pirate god you haven't told me about."

He ran his nails over the leather cover of his book. "Tell me the problem."

"Seril needs allies. No one will stick their neck out to help her. What's it to you, anyway? You don't care for gods or Craftsmen. Look out for yourself and keep clear of land, isn't that the way you play it?"

"Usually."

The deck between her feet had gone through more cycles of scuff and swab and polish and scuff than she cared to guess. "So what's stopping you from leaving?"

"You," he said.

She couldn't answer that. Her face felt hot.

"If Seril dies," he said, "and Justice remains, she'll go back to the way she was before. You'll lose yourself in the Suit. It'll get you high again."

"What's your point?"

"Seril's been good for this city. And for you." He stared out over the water. "I know people who might help. I don't like talking to them, but they'll listen to me. And there will be a price."

The ship's sinews hung limp in the still night. "If you get hurt on my account, I'll kill you."

"Someone beat you to it."

Airfield security was the usual pain: prick of the finger to draw blood, and a winding passage through three layers of wards all of which could be subverted in minutes by any half-blind idiot with a shred of determination. After security, at least the decor improved. Crystal chandeliers hung from high arches, and clockwork songbirds flitted from perch to perch while chrome raptors circled. Brass orchids grew amid hedges of real plants. Restaurants and coffee shops dotted the concourse, mostly caged shut; the ten fifteen to Dresediel Lex was the evening's last flight and boarding now, as indicated by the glowworm sign upon which three of the fake songbirds perched. Tara led Shale up the marble stair to the gantry level.

Birdsong broke into squawking panic. She glanced back: two birds had flown from the sign, their resting place usurped by a raptor. Of the third clockwork songbird there was no trace.

Shale frowned at the metal birds. The raptor preened and puffed the razor feathers of her breast. An organ tritone down the hall signaled preboarding. "Come on," she said. "We're late."

They ran past janitors mopping floors; the dragon eclipsed the sky outside the window. A deep rhythm pulsed through the floor tiles. At first she mistook it for the thrum of ventilation or of escalator machinery, but they'd passed no escalator, and ventilation would be softer.

Heartbeat, she thought.

Passengers waited in long lines by the gantries: beings human and once human in robes and suits. A three-meter-tall statue of silver thorns in the economy line held this week's *Thaumaturgist* open with two hands and turned the pages with his third. The fourth fingered his ticket sleeve nervously.

She reached the business-class gantry and fell into line behind a woman with long golden braids and a man wearing a mask of tanned skin. The ticket taker's smile was riveted in place, literally. The tritone sang again.

"Tara!"

She turned, and saw Abelard sprinting toward them.

The ticket taker extended her hand to the braided woman. Tara waved Shale on. "Get to the cabin. I'll follow."

Abelard tripped over the thorn statue's valise. His robes flared at the hem, and he hopped one-footed three steps until Tara caught him by the wrist.

"I worked all afternoon," he said, breathless. "When I looked at the clock I realized it was nine, and I'd last seen you in that nightmare."

"How did you get in here?"

"I kind of shouted my way past the guards. Said I was on a mission from God."

"I really have to go." Shale had vanished down the gantry. At the third tritone, economy passengers filed over their bridge. "Shale will get in trouble if I'm not around."

"When I looked at that clock," he said, "I realized: she could just leave. Nothing ties her here. She could go to Dresediel Lex and let us deal with this ourselves."

"I wouldn't."

"I know," he said. "You could, but you wouldn't." The coach line was almost gone. Tara felt faintly ridiculous, as if underdressed— exposed in the high-ceilinged hall.

"I'll be gone a couple days," she said. "Hold the city together while I'm out, okay?"

He hugged her. His arms were tight and narrow, and the body beneath the robes might have been made of thin pipe. His close-cut tonsure prickled against her temple.

She patted him on the back. Her hand made a hollow sound against his ribs. She squeezed and tried to remember the last time she'd touched someone or been touched, not for instrumental purpose, but for the sake of touching. She had been too busy to notice the lack. "Thanks," felt lame by comparison.

"Come back to us," he said when he stepped away.

"I will," she said. "Make sure there's something for me to come back to, okay?"

"I promise."

The thorn statue glanced over its spiny shoulder; Tara thought she heard it clear its throat.

"Take care," she said, and saluted him, and retreated to the business-class gantry. The ticket taker met her with a smile full of knives. At the foot of the gantry, Tara looked back. Abelard waited, watching.

She waved, and so did he, before she entered the crystal tunnel.

45

What grim beast lay on Alt Coulumb's back that night?

Ellen cross-legged on her rooftop watched a filling moon, and hummed, and rocked to her heart's beat.

In a hospital room, Dr. Hasim rose from rough, overstarched sheets. His long fingers explored the cables and straps at his wrists and arms, unbinding each in turn. A puzzled smile pulled the wounds on his lips; his tongue traced stinging sores inside his mouth where demon legs had cut. He framed his mind in prayer. Hospital bonds fell from him. He walked between beds, consulting charts and confirming diagnoses. (Divinity grows from mortal souls; a doctor of gods need not be a doctor of the flesh as well, but it doesn't hurt.) All asleep: young Tariq in deep dreams, wrapped around and through the Lady he bore with him from the sands. Large-bellied and fierce Akhil held his waymaking master/mistress to his heart. A goddess fragment walked the labyrinth of the girl Aiya's dreaming face.

When the door opened behind him, Dr. Hasim turned to the orderly. "Please take me to the roof, and fetch me paper, pen, and ink." Bare-assed in a hospital gown, Dr. Hasim commanded, and the orderly obeyed.

Elsewhere in the same building, Corbin Rafferty curled like a pill bug in his delirium. In the once empty bed beside him another man lay, massive and still, and there were no scars on his mouth.

Atop a tower in the Ash, beneath the jagged remnant arches of a never-quite orrery, Gavriel Jones sharpened a pencil with her pocketknife. Aev watched her work. "How do you see yourself?" the gargoyle asked.

"I don't know what you mean."

"My brothers and sisters are protectors, scouts, warriors. My youngest, who has gone with Ms. Abernathy to her war, thinks he is a rebel. What are you?"

"I find stories that are true," Jones said. "And I tell them."

"A poet, then."

She did not know how to answer that, but a laugh did not seem wrong.

By ghostlight, Cat consulted her blank gray bedroom carpet. The twenty-four-hour laundry on the corner of Bleak and Lattice had taken the sackful of clothes from her hamper without comment. She'd refilled the hamper with clothes from the floor. Clean, her room seemed both smaller and larger.

She touched the statue at her neck.

Cat had fought for Seril, and saved her, and argued with her, and would fight again. She'd risked her body. But she had never risked her soul. *To fly, we must invite the wind.*

She had never, quite, prayed.

She took the statue on its chain from around her neck and opened her blinds so the moon could peer through.

Abelard knelt once again before his altar. Priests at late-night services across the city preached to full congregations.

Dr. Hasim, seated with pen and paper on the hospital roof, examined the moon and wrote. Behind him the orderly stood with arms crossed, wary and wondering, primed to lunge should the patient turn suicidal.

Ellen rocked. A door opened behind her, and she recognized Claire's footsteps. "I'm fine," Ellen said. "They tried to kill the moon last night. That's why I collapsed. She's better now, but they'll try again soon."

Claire lowered herself to the roof. Ellen read loneliness and exhaustion on the planes of her face—emotions that would one day frame themselves into lines. "I don't know what to do," Claire said.

"Sit with me."

She did. And because Claire was not used to sitting, she spoke. "We could kick him out. Cut him off. But he'd stay Dad, somewhere. I went to the hospital. I wanted to confront him, but I couldn't. I've spent so much time trying to keep our life together, I'm not brave enough to break it. So what good am I?"

"You're my sister."

"I haven't been here for you in the last few days, or for Hannah. I'm sorry." She hadn't said more words to Ellen at once in months. Years, maybe.

"I need your help," Ellen said.

"With what?"

"The moon."

"Ellen—"

"She's in trouble. She needs strength. I've prayed to her, but I can do only so much alone. She's helped so many in the last year. I could bring them together. But I don't know how to start. I need help."

"Okay," Claire said.

Even the moon casts shadows, when bright enough.

A brass band marched through the Pleasure Quarter, and revelers wound behind it, a gyrating snake of hips and arms and naked backs. Hairy, big-bellied men and sweaty women pounded feet against cobblestones. A gymnast in gemmed pink cartwheeled alongside; two acrobats tossed a spinning third into the air in place of a marshal's baton.

In many rooms and on some balconies, people made love.

So whither the beast, and whence its roughness? Insects keep their skeletons on the outside; human beings only display their structure under force. The doom that neared Alt Coulumb, the twilight of the gods sung by street-corner Criers, pressed down with grand weight. But not all that's wounded breaks.

Not, at least, at first.

Dragon-borne, westward bound, Tara woke in need of a walk.

Shale slept like a stone, which she supposed was reasonable. He did not even lie down: he sat on his bench-bed in their cabin, hands on knees. The creases of his slacks fell like plumb lines to his shined shoes, swayed by the wingbeats that rocked the gondola.

"You awake?"

No response.

"If you're ignoring me, I'll do something horrible to you."

Nothing.

"With chisels."

Hollow circles in crimson and cloth-of-gold patterned the ceiling, and these stared down at her, judging. She stood in her pajamas, slid into her slippers, and walked the empty, dim hall, hair clouded around and above her head. False flames glimmered behind smoked glass along the dark baseboards, illuminating the maze-patterned rug. A light blinked green over the door to the observation deck, indicating the platform was mostly safe.

She emerged into the chill of great height. She shivered from the breeze, but she soon adjusted. It was not so cold as it should have been. Craftwork managed wind and pressure, and oven warmth radiated from the dragon's scales. Broken clouds scudded below, and beneath those lay puzzle piece fields. They were east, yet, of Edgemont, but the country looked similar from so far up. She'd crossed these fields a year before in the opposite direction, with a job offer and an uncertain destiny.

Wings claimed the sky in huge slow sweeps. Her stomach lurched when she watched those spreading bones and the taut scaled skin between. Raz had told her about a time when a hurricane caught him at sea, and walls of water rose higher than the *Bounty*'s topmast. We're plains apes at root, he explained. Loping strides and a regular horizon, that's what we like. Our body thinks nothing large enough to be landscape should move.

Tara needed stars. She gripped the observation deck's railing and vaulted over.

Glyph-lines woke on her skin and whispered moonlit arguments. Old deals the first Craftsmen struck with the sky arrested her fall. She stood on a platform of air and walked uphill beneath and around the wide neck.

The double drumbeat of the dragon's heart faded as Tara walked. Another sound replaced it as she climbed past the shoulders' shelf and along the four-story neck: a deep mellow drone on the low edge of hearing, accompanied by creeping dread in her gut. The sound she heard was only an overtone. The dread was the note the dragon hummed.

The dragon's head was twice the *Bounty*'s size, its crest taller than the ship's mainmast.

She reached the slope of its brow, high and arched like an eagle's, and continued forward, contemplating the ground. Breath steamed the air. It smelled more of ozone than of the sulfur she expected.

The gut dread stopped.

She stood beside the dragon's eye. It was taller than she was, and not completely closed. A curve of hunter's moonlight showed beneath the lid.

The eye opened.

It glistened, wet, immense, slit-pupiled like a cat's. The dark beyond the pupil seemed sharp, as if there were facets inside.

"I didn't mean to interrupt," she said. Dragons did not eat people often, certainly not ones they'd agreed to carry.

The dragon watched her as they flew west.

She looked up, because down was too far and so was out, and back and to either side only confronted her with more dragon. The space between the stars comforted her, thick and rich as good chocolate. She'd spent too long in cities. Even the stars above a Craft-ruled metropolis could not match a country midnight. Her eyes adjusted, and the universe emerged. Meeker stars assembled into constellations for which she knew a hundred names, and at last the galactic bow curved above, milky and mottled with indistinct millions. "Nice night."

—Yes.

Sound below sound composed the voice. She did not fall, nor did she yelp, though she almost did both. Even a Craftswoman could fake only so much composure set beside, well.

"I'm sorry if I disturbed you."

—There was song before, and there will be song after.

"I see."

—I play no role in cabin service. If you have trouble, please direct your concerns to the crew.

"I don't," she said. "Or at least I don't have any trouble they can fix. I needed a walk. Were you singing?"

—Meditating.

"Dragons meditate?"

—You do not carry all your soul within yourself.

"I'd go mad. The more you have, the faster your mind spins. It comes apart. That's what banks are for."

—Imagine how it feels to have a hoard.

"Oh," she said. "So you meditate to handle it?"

—Some lose themselves in riddle games or chess or weiqi. Some tell tales or explore. Some dream new worlds. I still the spinning.

"I could use some of that myself."

—Yes.

"And you carry people from place to place."

—Yes.

"Why?" After she spoke, she felt a stab of fear that drawing the dragon's attention to the ludicrous fact of its employment might cause the creature to shrug free of chains, cabins, and gondola alike.

—Are you interested in the particulars of my case, or in general philosophy?

She did not know how to answer, so she said nothing.

—You wonder at power yoked to service. You wonder because you have come into power young and are learning that power comes through the acceptance of a bond. But if to have power is to be bound, then what is power?

"I wouldn't have put it that way," she said.

—I bear these people because Craftsmen, broadly speaking, do not love what they cannot use, and destroy what they do not love. So I make myself useful in some minimal way, as do others of my kind.

"Because you're afraid of us?"

—No. Because I enjoy flying far and fast, and I find this work more pleasant.

"Than what?"

—War.

"I'm glad to hear it," she said. "But don't you find it sad that you have to live like this? That you can't just hum in a cave somewhere?"

—No.

She waited.

—I find it funny.

"What?"

—We are what we ever were: huge, strong, and ancient beyond your reckoning. We have crossed vast gulfs of time and space. And you think (the subsonic dread returned in sharp pulses rather than the earlier sustained note, and her mind named the dread pattern *laughter*) you think because looking at us you can say that one draws a salary, this one bears us from place to place, that your limited comprehension gives you any measure of safety or control.

Far ahead, lightning flashed green between towered clouds.

"I'd like to stay out here for a while," Tara said. "If it's all right with you. I won't talk. I just want to watch."

The great eye closed.

Soon the hum returned.

46

"I hate this place," Shale said as they fought through the plaster labyrinth of Dresediel Lex Metropolitan Airport alongside three thousand other people and their luggage. Most of the crowd were business travelers, but a fraction trailed bellhops and brass luggage carts driven by rat brains—and, like pebbles in an hourglass, that fraction was more than enough to stem traffic's flow. "Why would anyone live here?"

"The weather's nice."

"They have to import water"—with audible scorn—"from outside the city. How good can the weather be?"

"It doesn't rain, for one thing." She danced sideways to avoid tripping over the rolling suitcase of a scale-skinned Craftsman who'd turned an unexpected left. "Except once or twice a year. Then it floods."

"Every fall like clockwork the whole country catches fire. The earth shakes!"

Recovering her footing, Tara almost bowled over two women arguing in a language she didn't know. "What do you expect? They have enormous lava serpents underground."

"Before the wars, the gods kept the rain coming here. But with the gods dead, what's left? The city survives only because it steals water from others. These people are an affront to the world."

"Now you're being dramatic. The world doesn't mind."

"Fires. Earthquakes."

"Lava serpents, like I said." Signboard arrows suggested that three different hallways all led to GROUND TRANSPORT. Tara chose right, saw a construction bottleneck, and reversed course. Shale, turning, upended a golem, who sprang to his feet, raised scissorfingers, gnashed fangs, and chattered a clockwork challenge. Shale didn't speak demonic, but he understood the body language and responded in kind: chin up, shoulders back, pecs tense under his shirt. Tara grabbed Shale's bones with a slip of Craft meant to animate skeletons and jerked him after her, ignoring his glare as he recovered his footing. "The city's bigger than what it costs."

He frowned. "I don't understand."

"Dresediel Lex is a symbol to the Craftwork world." The long hall narrowed and grew brutalist, without windows or even ads to relieve the pale plaster. Glass doors opened at the hallway's end, and past those doors she saw another pair, and after those, sun. "The God Wars lasted a hundred years give or take. Imagine fighting your own people for a century."

"I don't have to imagine," Shale said.

"Fair enough." Almost outside. Free air melted on the tongue like spun sugar. "Gods owned the earth and hated us, so we built our nations in the sky. By the time the wars crossed from the Old World to the New, both sides were exhausted, desperate, mean. Dresediel Lex was our great victory. Once these gods fell, Liberation cascaded through the continent. For the first time in history, there was a city where the dead walked, and we could fly."

They swept through, past sign-bearing chauffeurs and waiting family. Two dark men embraced. The second layer of doors rolled back, and they emerged into Dresediel Lex.

Tara felt the city's hot breath on her skin and its sun on her face.

She was done walking for a while.

She'd visited Dresediel Lex in her caravan days to hock wares in dusty markets and fill warded wagons with goods for sale to the farm towns of the central plains—and she visited again on spring break with friends from the Hidden Schools. So it was not surprise that made her stop.

It may have been awe.

Overhead, the sky was dry and enormous, the color of paintings on Shining Empire pottery. It did not hang or arc or curve. It rose forever.

Crystal towers hung upside down in air above the free city, breaking sunlight to a billion-prismed rainbow. To the west, juniper and manzanita matted the Drakspine hills dusk green, but at street level palm trees and clawfoot azalea grew emerald leaves that boasted of piped water in defiance of all drought.

Pyramid peaks crested above the hills.

The heat was an oven's, and a magnifying-glass sun beat down. Her skin, long accustomed to weak Alt Coulumb light, felt its use again.

A buzzing came across the sky.

Shale, beside her, recoiled. Of course: he did not know this city, or its odd ways of moving people. Dark forms speared from the high blue to earth, and as they fell became four-foot-long dragonflies with broad wings. They landed upon the men and women outside the airport, gripped them with long legs, touched feathery proboscises to the backs of necks, and bore them skyward.

"What are those?" Shale asked.

Tara grinned. "Our ride."

As families reunited and drivers swept businesswomen toward carriages, as food carts hawked bottled water and candied nuts, as an old man played a Quechal tune on a three-string fiddle, the newcomer to Dresediel Lex took flight. Their wings laid rainbows on the earth.

"Gods," Tara said. "I missed this."

Gods, Abelard prayed as the meeting entered its fourth hour. *Deliver me.*

"And if you require further information on our foreign bond positions, Brother Amortizer Stefan has prepared detailed archives of relevant scripture. Our record-keeping procedures are normalized according to the Interfaith Standards Council 19001, so they should be fully interoperable with your systems. Now, if you'll turn to page eighteen—"

Deliverance was not forthcoming. The team from Kelethres, Albrecht, and Ao turned to page eighteen.

The five Craftsmen and Craftswomen sat interspersed with Cardinals and the clerical team. Abelard had assumed Tara and Ms. Kevarian were typical Craftswomen, but these didn't match his expectations. At least the partner, Wakefield, seemed right: distant and elegant in white suit and vest, thin lips carved to convey the air of a person who's just told a joke no one in attendance gets. Aside from

Wakefield, the team consisted of one woman—Saqqaf, with a ruby fixed in place of her left eye—and three men whose names Abelard hadn't yet got straight. Skane was the tall one, no, Cao was the tall one and Skane had the deep belly and the slumped shoulders and the diagonal scars on either cheek, no, that was Hedge, which made Skane the man with the thin mustache. But then Wakefield referred to *him* as "Mr. Cao," interrupting Bede's review of page eighteen. "Mr. Cao is our team's document management expert. He'll bridge the field team with the courtroom, which I'll hold."

But the tall one—Skane?—almost opened his mouth before the man Wakefield addressed—Cao, evidently—spoke. "I'll coordinate document intake and review. For this contest, we need deep knowledge, not just thematics. We need instant access to moment-by-moment data. Brother Amortizer Stefan—"

"Cannot help you there," said Cardinal Librarian Aldis, stern faced beside Nestor, who looked amiable and lost as ever. "The archives are mine. Anything you need within them, I or my subordinates may grant. Use no open flames or corrosives. The sub-basement archives hold documents several centuries old. We're happy," though neither her expression nor her tone of voice supported that claim, "to work with you to determine reasonable substitute processes."

Wakefield nodded once. After four hours, that white suit still looked fresh from the cleaners.

There was a city beyond the conference room and far below. *What gods think near is distant for man.* Here they sat, air-conditioned, discussing the logistics of response, containment, and interdepartmental coordination. This was an important meeting, Abelard told himself. Poorly informed Craftsmen were worse than no Craftsmen at all, and without Craftsmen they would lose their case against Ramp, and the gods would die. This work was necessary.

But not for Abelard. He had little skill in thaumaturgy; he was here due to his relationship with Lord Kos. Out there on Alt Coulumb's streets, Prelate Evangelist Hildegard led teams of brothers and sisters through to preach the new moon gospel. Abelard should be with them. The Cardinals knew this. So did God Himself.

So why was he here?

"—Ms. Saqqaf will be responsible for shareholder outreach,"

Wakefield was saying. No trace of—*what?*—touched that pale gray eye. "Interest" was the wrong word for what was missing, since there was interest there, the interest of snakes in mice. "Emotion" was no better fit, because scorn was an emotion. Maybe "humanity"—but that was a bit chauvinist.

"Thank you," Saqqaf said. "After we were retained, I reached out to the core shareholders on Cardinal Bede's list, reaffirming our fundamental thaumaturgical stability. Large-scale clients, while understandably anxious, are for the most part willing to honor their agreements, though the cold-blooded squids at the Iskari Defense Ministry"—and Abelard had an intimation Saqqaf was being precise in her description—"request further guarantees to compensate for the risk they face in dealing with us." Grumbles around the table. Bede champed his pipestem between his teeth. "It's a small stake, with an option for buyback in a year's time. I say we give it to them, since our negotiating position is, let's say, constrained." Translated: We don't have time to fight this battle. Why not pay to make it disappear?

Bede took hold of his pipe and leaned against the table. Abelard did not listen to his response. Maybe God had brought him here to correct the Cardinals if they went astray? But he barely understood the issues under discussion. He could hold his own against anyone in matters of engineering, but when the conversation veered to evangelism and archive work, he was lost.

But God wasn't.

Oh.

Snarled gears unmeshed in his mind to mate again.

Abelard prayed, for real this time, and conference voices blurred into a polyphonous drone.

He greeted the Lord of Flame with a still heart. He surrendered his worldly mind to the spark. Fire curled an autumn leaf into a fist of ash.

He listened—not for words, splinters of the Lord's thought, but for the rhythm beyond words.

Kos had been betrayed by Cardinals before, and if traitors were to strike again, now was the time. But gods made poor detectives, their perspectives unmoored from time. Who better to be Kos's spy than

Abelard? So He whispered to the Cardinals and folded the young Technician in their confidence.

Because He was afraid.

But He was wrong.

Bede was more loyal to Kos than to Seril. Nestor was a busybody. Aldis had her territorial insecurities. No person, no church, was perfect. But the Cardinals were faithful. Bede could have taken Ramp's deal and left Seril to die.

Kos did not trust His Cardinals, so He inspired them to include Abelard in their work. And the Cardinals were smart. They knew the score.

You're micromanaging, Abelard prayed, *because you're scared.*

Only crackling fire answered.

These people love You. They joined the church to serve You, and they do so now, though service scares them. Let them serve.

The fire in Abelard popped and pitted, and sparks burned his skin.

We're wasted in here, You and I. We could be out in the city, spreading miracles. The work your Cardinals do is important, which is why You called priests to do it for You. Trust them.

Presumption? Temerity? Pride?

Of course.

But what was a saint for, if not to talk with God?

Sun warmth spread through his limbs. That was Abelard's answer.

When they broke for coffee and tobacco—sorcerers' hunger for caffeine surpassed only by priests' need for a smoke—he sought Cardinal Nestor and Cardinal Bede. "Your Excellencies. Thank you for including me in this meeting, but I'm no use here. I can best serve Our Lord by working with Prelate Evangelist Hildegard."

"Thank you, my son," Nestor said, and Abelard felt embarrassed by the relief he read in the old man at the news God trusted him. Even Bede's shoulders rose.

"Do what you can," the Cardinal said. "Go with God."

"And you as well," Abelard replied.

47

"Whatever happens," Tara cautioned Shale as they flew west between skyspires and over the mansions of the Drakspine ridge, "do not try to kill the King in Red."

"Okay." Shale sounded unconvinced.

"This is important." She fed their optera from her expense account—far from bottomless, but she could afford the ride. Travel by dragonfly felt strange at first. She'd been surprised when Shale accepted one rather than flying under his own power.

"He's a monster."

Tara shook her head. "He's a respectable citizen. This city wouldn't exist without him."

"A man can be both citizen and monster. Especially here."

"In which case he's a monster *and* a respectable citizen, whom we're about to ask for a big favor. Besides, if you try to kill him, you'll probably just piss him off."

"We almost broke him in the Wars."

"Almost only counts with horseshoes and elder gods. He's grown since you fought. And, honestly, I know you've had a rough few decades, but I wish things like *don't attack the immensely powerful necromancer we've come to ask for help* could go unsaid."

Streets crazed the irrigated ground like cracks on the scab of an infected wound. Elevated carriageways laced between pyramids— the largest, at 667 Sansilva, eighty stories tall and obsidian sheathed. Black glass grooves cast an illusion of writhing serpents on the pyramid's steps.

As far as Tara could see, the city bore little damage from the eclipse fiasco a few years back; she'd been at Contracts with her friend Kayla when the news came through, and waited with her in the long line of weeping students at the nightmare telegraph to call her dads. The dreams around Dresediel Lex were so tangled Kayla couldn't get through for two days, which Tara spent on the couch in Kayla's dorm, sleeping poorly; she'd told Kayla to wake her if she needed anything, and the girl took her at her word. Kayla's dads both lived—one broke his leg in the riots and the other spent three days stuck in a collapsed mall—but the waiting, not knowing, hurt.

Rebuilding, the city had turned a quarter mile of Sansilva Boulevard into a memorial walk. Tara decided she would visit if there was time.

For now, they had business at the Grisenbrandt Club.

North of Monicola Pier the beachside shops grew more expensive and elegant until they reached an expense and elegance singularity: the Grisenbrandt, a red-roofed, white-walled palace on the continent's edge. A ward misted the air above its courtyards and rooftop baths, to keep even the most inquisitive journalist from observing the club's clientele. The ward might have been opaque, but that wouldn't have allowed spies and onlookers to envy the rainforest green inside.

Tara and Shale landed on a riverrock path between two lawns that beggared any adjective but "verdant." The doorman (a Quechal fellow in sunglasses and a funereal suit, whose posture suggested experience as valet, bouncer, and special forces commando) frowned as their optera flew away. People who belonged in the club arrived under their own power. Rentals were for those not rich enough to own.

"Hi," Tara said with the cheer she always felt when about to ruin a snob's day, and produced the invitation the porter had delivered to her cabin this morning. "We have an appointment."

The doorman took the invitation, skepticism evident even through his dark glasses. Tara savored his surprise as he read the document twice, turned it over to check for a watermark, then read it again.

"Of course," the doorman said joylessly. The doors opened at his gesture. A young woman in a white blouse, an uncomfortable black skirt, and heels that forced her *en pointe* emerged. "Antonia will guide you." Antonia's smile slipped when she read the invitation. "Enjoy your visit."

And to the nine hells with you too, Tara thought as she led Shale into the club.

They followed Antonia down a pillared arcade between two

courtyards shaded with plant life stolen from around the world. Antonia's absurd heels left bloodred footprints on the white marble tiles. Ripples of color spread from those footprints as they faded, interlacing with the ripples Tara's and Shale's footsteps cast.

In a courtyard, a jazz quartet played soft music while clubgoers, skeletal or amorphous or many-limbed, broke their fast at an enormous buffet: glistening piles of fresh-cut exotic fruits and bewitching pastries, an omelet station, an elegant silver bowl of wriggling insects that laughed when eaten. In a salon to the left, a Shining Empire magistrate sipped tea with a Zurish mask-lord in the shade of a broad-leaved Dhisthran tree, all equally far from home.

The part of Tara that would always hail from a farming village on the edge of a desert pondered the expense of the shifting marble, the plants, the wards, the water, the band, the silver, the price of Antonia and the front-door jerkface and their comrades, carried the three to the ten million's place—then abandoned the exercise. In a way, this kind of wealth was easier to accept than the ease with which Daphne picked up their check at lunch. Even if Tara made partner at Kelethres, Albrecht, and Ao, she wouldn't have lived in this world. You earned this power by stealing continents and breaking nations; this was wealth you tore from dying gods.

She frowned at the thought. What kind of radical was Alt Coulumb making her, anyway? Focus on the mission, Tara. Follow Antonia in the absurd heels.

The club doors opened onto a marble stair that led down to a white sand beach. Tara blinked brilliant ghosts from her vision.

The beach was empty save for a man who was not a man anymore.

Antonia extended her hand. Tara thanked her and descended.

The King in Red lay in swim trunks on a lounge chair, his pale anklebones crossed atop bamboo slats. The red gold crown set into his skull glinted dull and bloody in the sun.

White sand pillowed Tara's footsteps. Waves rushed and rolled. Bodies thronged the beach a hundred meters to her left and right: college kids tossed Frisbees, musician circles played guitars and drums and fiddles, surfers charged the breakers. Children kicked ullamal and cackled as they fell. Tara did not hear them. Their voices died on the crystal air.

The King in Red kept still as she approached. She gave his chair wide berth, rounding to the side. His ribs jutted from the chair like tree trunks a fire had stripped of bark and left to die.

One skeletal hand held a round glass three-quarters full (or one-quarter empty) of a weapons-grade pink cocktail shaded by four paper umbrellas and sporting a spear of tiny melon cubes interspaced with jadeite giraffes. Ice shifted in the glass.

He wore sunglasses, which made no sense. Golden tabs affixed the glasses to the holes where his ears would have been.

She stood, hands clasped behind her, watching and waiting. There were greater powers than the King in Red. It was just hard to think of any at this precise moment.

He raised the glass to where his lips once were, and drank. She watched the liquid disappear.

"Your Majesty," she began, to be on the safe side.

"I know who you are, Ms. Abernathy. I know why you've come." His voice was almost human. The difference mattered.

"That will save time, Your Majesty."

"Drop the Majesty. I have enough. I told Elayne I'd see you, and I have. You can go now."

"I want to present my argument."

"It's good to want things." He drank again, and again the fluid disappeared—reduced to chaos, all useful properties stripped to feed the Craftwork that kept the King in Red whatever he was. "Alive" was the wrong word. "I want to hear from an old friend once in a while for some reason other than business. You want me to hand you a fortune for no reason. Your stone companion wants to murder me, though he's displaying admirable self-control."

"Would you like me to stop?" Shale asked. Jewel facets glinted beneath his imitation human eyes.

"Try me." The skeleton sounded bored. "Get this over with. I've killed so many of you before, in very many ways." His voice went singsong for that last bit, then lost all humor. "I tore your goddess open and ripped her heart and lungs from the ruin of her chest. Break yourself on me, if you like. You're not the hundredth or even the thousandth to try. And when I'm done with you, I'll go back to my drink."

He took another sip. Translucent giraffes danced with sun.

"Shale!"

There was no Craft in Tara's cry, but Shale stopped anyway, halfway to the King in Red. He'd begun to change. His skin was veined with gray and hatched with gleaming gaps, his back a wreckage of wings. The human seeming reasserted itself; the jaw cracked to fit shrinking teeth together. He knelt, gasping, on the sand. His shirt hung tattered from his shoulders. Scars crossed his back where the wounds had been.

The King in Red sat up and turned to face them both, elbows on knee bones, ridged spine rising between his shoulder blades. Cocktail sweat darkened his fingers. Of their own accord, the sunglasses slipped down to reveal the dead-star sparks in his eye sockets. "Interesting. It listens to you."

"*He*," Tara said, "is an envoy of my client, Seril Undying of Alt Coulumb. Who is still alive."

"As I learned yesterday."

"News travels fast."

"Fast as fear."

"Ramp approached you."

He shrugged. "I own a good deal of Kosite debt in my own name. Red King Consolidated holds more. She's approached everyone with a substantial stake. Some of us have better things to do at the moment than fight a war, even a limited one." He waved toward the waves. "As you see. So you needn't worry about me participating in her coup."

"I wasn't."

"Why did you listen to her?" he asked Shale. The gargoyle had recovered, mostly. Sweat slipped down curves of muscle. "Here I am. You've hated me for decades. I killed your lady, or close to it, and I liked it. I'll even give you first crack. No shields, or wards, or tricks."

Shale stood. Tara prepared to bind him, in case her voice would not suffice this time. Given how hurt he'd seemed in that momentary shift, her restraint might break him. He wasn't in shape for a fight.

He might still try.

"Tara asked me not to fight you."

"And you listened," the skeleton said.

"Yes."

Crimson sparks turned on her. "You've inspired a divine monster's loyalty. Nice trick. It earns you my time." He glanced at the sky. "In five minutes the sun will turn the waves to gold and mark a path straight out over the bay to my favorite island. The air and sea are perfect, and the world sings. You'll be gone by then, one way or another. Speak quickly."

"When you killed Seril in the God Wars, you stole Alt Coulumb's skies from her."

"They were spoils of war."

"Alt Coulumb's liturgy holds that Kos owns Alt Coulumb's skies in the event of Seril's death."

"Which is why I've never been able to use the rights I won, outside of as collateral." He finished his cocktail, ate the fruit, removed umbrellas and straw and jadeite giraffes and arranged them on the sand. "I claim ownership, Kos resists. I almost got my way when he died, but it turns out he was faking."

"Neither of you rightfully owns that sky. It belongs to Seril."

"Who we both thought was dead. When you hurt someone like I hurt her, she tends to die, goddess or not." He tightened his grip. The glass cracked, grimed and gritted, and slid as sand from his fingers to the beach.

"You pledged Seril's sky as collateral for loans to develop Red King Consolidated."

"I pledged everything to support the Concern. My soul. Others'. If not for that, this city would be a desert now." He raised his hand. Another drink floated over from the clubhouse.

"Do you think your partners would be happy to learn you used stolen property as collateral?"

"I paid off those loans long ago—not that I accept your characterization of the property as stolen. If you want to argue that point in court, send my people a date, and I'll schedule my countersuit of libel for the same day so we can get all this over with at once. Is this the best you can do, Ms. Abernathy?"

She felt the same anger she'd seen in Shale, and squelched it. "A fight wouldn't be good for either of us. I have a thousand years of documentary evidence on my side. And you're—you."

"Then why are you here?"

"Where does it end? You've killed my client, and your own gods, and your own people. You just tried to goad Shale into suicide by Craftsman. How long can you keep this up?"

The glass settled in his hand. "I'm a Deathless King. I can keep this up forever. Sort of in the job description."

"Why don't your old friends visit you anymore?"

The sky cracked and blackened and split with lightning. The earth opened, and fangs of fire jutted up. Black thorn-vines curled around Tara's limbs, growing as they pierced clothes and skin and meat. Far away, everyone screamed.

Then she stood unharmed on the white beach beneath the blue sky as the sun crept to apex. Waves rolled. The world endured.

She remembered it ending. It had, a second ago.

The King in Red swirled his drink. Pink alcoholic slush churned beneath paper umbrellas. His laugh sounded like the rasp of sandpaper over fingernails. "You do speak your mind, Ms. Abernathy."

She did not trust herself to move, but she could speak. "You're long in Coulumbite bonds. If Kos falls, you lose millions of souls. Give Seril back the sky, and your stake's safe."

"Or I could swallow the loss and watch your self-righteous mistress die, because it amuses me to do so."

"My client," she corrected. "Not mistress. And with all due respect, if you wanted to do that, you'd have joined Ramp."

He sipped his cocktail, and damn him if he didn't make her hold her breath.

"I'm afraid," he said, "you're speaking with the wrong guy. I donated my aerial rights to Alt Coulumb when Kos returned from the dead."

"Donated?" The word felt strange in her mouth.

"Gave them away. Like a sacrifice, only no gods involved. We're supporting a spinoff Concern of, I guess you'd call them paladins— heal the broken world, protect the innocent, all that crunchy granola stuff. The sky rights don't move the needle for RKC anymore, but they're a key asset for the Two Serpents Group's portfolio." He snapped his fingers. A white business card appeared and floated to her hand. "Their team's up north, dealing with a mining disaster in Centervale. My office has the details. Have fun telling the do-gooders they should stop feeding orphans to save your goddess. I'd watch, but your five minutes are up, and I want you out of my nonexistent hair."

"Thank you," she said.

He grinned, not that he had a choice. "Tell Elayne to drop by when she's ready to talk. We're neither of us going anywhere."

"Come on," she said to Shale. "We have work."

The King in Red waved to them, then settled back into his chair to watch a view that seemed no more or less perfect to Tara than it had five minutes before.

48

Stone walls narrowed the sky over Claire's head to a slit. "You're sure the woman we want lives down here?"

" 'Sure' is a funny word," Ellen mused from farther down the alley. Scratches and graffiti marred the stone higher than human hooligans could reach. "It's not spelled like it sounds, and in plays when someone says they're sure of something, you know they're wrong."

Claire slipped in something she hoped was mud and caught herself against balloony painted letters that read BEWARE LEOPARD. That morning before dawn she'd sat beside Matt for a grim ride through the fog during which they'd both failed to think of things to say. He'd gone silent after their chat with Ms. Abernathy the day before. He didn't know what to tell Claire to do.

As if she needed telling.

Which didn't mean she was eager to do it. Last night, on the moonlit roof, offering Ellen help seemed a way to make a difference without returning to that cold hospital room where her father lay. This afternoon, rubbed raw by coffee and hoarse by shouting after customers in the market, she felt less sure. "You can't trust folks in the Ash."

"That's Dad talking."

She caught her retort between clenched teeth. Ungrateful—
Sister.

"Sorry," Claire said.

Ellen stopped, surprised. She'd leaned toward Claire as she did to resist the wind, or their dad when he was shouting. "Thank you," Ellen said. "Hold on." She closed her eyes, and when she opened them again Claire thought she saw light inside, like when a priest offered blessing. The light passed, though. Maybe it was only a reflection. But Ellen's smile, too, seemed like a younger girl's—the smile Claire'd received as payment when she let her five-year-old sister win at tag. "This way."

Carriages rolled down Summer past the alley's mouth. Ellen stopped on a dirty stoop, straightened her blouse, and knocked.

No answer came, nor any sound of footsteps.

Overhead, a crow called.

"Nobody's home," Claire said. "We shouldn't wait around."

Ellen tried the knob. The door creaked open onto a narrow winding stair. "Come on!" And before Claire could react, Ellen ran inside and up, jumping three steps at a time. Her skirt flared as she disappeared around a corner.

Claire caught up with her on the third-floor landing. Ellen had already knocked on the door of apartment 3A, and stood, hands behind her back, face fixed in an expression Claire also knew: nervous, and trying not to show.

Hard rhythmic taps approached behind the door. A cat cried. Claire wanted to leave, but not so much as she wanted to look strong for Ellen.

You think you know a city, she thought. You've lived here all your life, and then you follow your sister down a side street you'd never walk alone, and you remember there are people in this town we don't know, and things that aren't people but wear their skin, and maybe we're about to die because you just knocked on some monster's door.

The footsteps stopped. A cracked voice said, "Who's there?"

Hells, Claire thought. I'm as crazy as I think she is.

"Ma'am, I'm Ellen Rafferty. We share a friend. She's helped us both, and now she needs our help back."

Chains unchained. Locks unlocked. The door cracked.

The woman within—dark skin and white eyes and a narrow white cane with a rubber tip on the end—wore a housecoat and fray-hemmed trousers, and did not look like a monster at all. "Come in," she said. "Tell me more."

A large and scared and ugly crowd gathered to hear the evening news.

Abelard on tiptoe craned his neck to see over the mounded shoulder of a bald, jean-jacketed man who stank of fish and salt. Past him and a sea of surging heads and shoulders and clapboard signs, the bare stage rose before the Crier's Guild doors. Fisherfolk and dockhands, secretaries, line cooks, stevedores and factory women, Craftsmen and priests and bartenders off-shift had come hungry to hear what truth there was to the rumors of a Goddess's return.

The sun declined.

Abelard ached from a day sprinting around the city preaching to preachers. The dawn song had conveyed Ramp's challenge, and fear of the coming struggle burned through the city. Abelard went where Hildegard sent him, spreading grace to parish priests and local deacons. The Lord, he repeated, is pleased by the Goddess's return. He asks for our faith as He fights on her behalf.

Even among priests, reactions ranged: acceptance, rage, glory, denial. One man, bent-backed and broken-voiced and old enough to remember Seril leaving for the wars, wept. Abelard held his hand.

Tonight Lord Kos would have many long talks with His chosen shepherds.

But their flocks took the news harder.

So Abelard had come to the Guild for evensong, in case of need.

"We can't deal with this many." Sister Evangelist Hildegard pressed beside him in the throng: crimson robed, dark skinned, hair bound in a kerchief. "The Suits rerouted traffic down through Providence, but any trouble and we'll be crushed." Bodies filled the square and the blocked street. "Those guys make matters worse." She pointed up to the rooftops, where a ring of silvered Blacksuits stood.

"Justice can keep the peace."

"You don't stop a riot by punching people."

"If you punch enough of them, maybe."

"That would just make things worse."

"Stun nets?"

"Can kill. Let's hope the Criers give a good show. If they don't—" She clapped Abelard on the shoulder. "Good thing we have a saint handy."

The doors of the Crier's Guild opened, and the crowd hushed.

Zurish tribesmen don't have 120 words for snow. It rains every day in the jungles of Southern Kath, but folk who live there lack the 70

names for water falling from the sky that armchair wits on six continents commonly ascribe to them. Grow up in the Northern Gleb and
you'll see a lot of sand, but it's all sand in the end.

Gabby Jones knew this. But the myths had roots: live with anything long enough and you'll learn its grades. Girls from Northern
Zur, where the sun takes three months of vacation every year, know
the differences between snow that falls like a rock and snow that floats
like a feather and snow that burns.

In the same way, performers learn varietals of silence. There's the
cut-rate hush of the obligatory concert on a too-hot summer afternoon,
and the sweet tense calm before a loved but rarely seen performer steps
onstage. The sad quiet with which a crowd awaits a casualty report
sticks and clings. The silence of a barroom when a sweating Crier calls
"Extra"—the pause before an enormity's announced—that silence cuts
surer than glass.

But such silences take their form only when the performer steps
onstage. Behind the Crier's Guild front door, at the head of her choristers, Gabby heard the crowd's rumble: angry, expectant, exited, confused. Robes swayed as her singers shifted.

She opened the door, and the silence fell.

The crowd filled the square, filled Providence, filled Flame beyond.
She stepped, helpless and proud as a bowsprit carving, onstage.

She'd done this before.

Admittedly, not in front of so many people. Each member of the
Crier's Guild had her own specialty. Gabby wrote music and reported
stories to match that music. She sang to keep her voice in trim. And,
rarely, for pieces she could not bear handing off to Madison or Stern-
bridge or Yao, she directed the choir.

But this was bigger than the Ash Riots or the dreamglass crisis.
These people were angry and scared. They needed security, which
her interview with Aev and Cat and Seril did not offer. She would
challenge their faith at a time when they yearned for its comfort.

She was about to set this crowd on fire.

She turned her back on the audience. The choir stood in mixed
formation. Cross, the deepest bass, had vomited for several minutes
in the bathroom before warm-ups. Thank gods and demons alike for

mouthwash and toothbrushes. But a choir was a corps. They had discipline. Even faced with such a crowd, they held together.

She raised her hands, and they sang.

Seril Moon-mother did not die in the wars.

Abelard listened.

He knew this story. He'd lived the tale's unraveling. But knowing did not prepare him to listen while the Crier's Guild recounted his life in counterpoint and fugue. In the goddess's own words, no less. And Aev's.

We returned to see our Lady carved into a mockery of self.

I was diminished, a lost voice among the trees.

Seril's voice twined soprano and bass; Aev, alto and tenor.

The music was masterful, but mastery could go only so far.

The crowd rumbled. "Bullshit" was the word the man before him whispered.

The first cry of "Blasphemy!" came from back on Prospect, but others took it up fast. The crowd chanted against the choir.

They should have done this earlier. They should have trusted the people earlier. There was no time to convince them now.

They needed a miracle.

"Pray with me," he told Sister Hildegard.

Onstage, her back to the audience, Gabby heard the anger. Her shoulders tensed, and the beat her hands carved in the air slipped. The singers looked scared.

Should she stop? They'd almost reached the restatement of the theme; the piece's harmonics weren't yet resolved, the story half-done—she had to explain Seril's return. Failure to finish might make the situation worse.

Curses filled a brief fermata; she invited the choir to sing louder, wrecking the dynamic effect. Soon they'd throw things at the stage. She hoped for rotten fruit. It was soft.

Stop, a wise voice inside her urged. Or change the story. Give these people what they want to hear.

Fuck what they wanted to hear.

This was news.

Faith on the corner of Providence and Flame was a tangled net, a self-propagating snarl at Kos Everburning's core. Lord Kos was born from His people, and grew with them. He changed them, and they changed Him, through time.

So if the crowd was confused, and angry, so too was the God—and hurt, and scared. A small core within Him revolted against Himself.

Abelard prayed through chaos and uncertainty. The many voices clashed and cackled, senseless.

—Cannot believe what she's selling—
—they think they are, that's not how God—
—can't be, impossible—
—tear them off that stage and show them fire—

They need to hear this song, Abelard prayed, and felt Hildegard and other priests throughout the crowd join him. *They must know its truth.*

*—wish **that** I could hear the part—*
     *—**we** should just rush the fucking stage—*
*—how **can** I get out of here—*
*—just have to **do**—*

And the fire sang.

When the crowd hushed, Gabby heard new voices.

The guild recruited evensingers from the best choirs in the New World. They could memorize a piece faster than a scribe could copy it. Even Gabby, who knew how to listen, could not identify an individual breath in two hours of performance. They shaped notes to perfection, matched sound to sound with crystal purity.

No human choir could match them.

The new voices were not human. Nor were they, exactly, new.

Streetlight gas lamp flames unfolded above the crowd, and within each stood Gabby's choristers—their voices grown within the fire.

Some in the crowd looked at the lamps. Others stared farther up. Into the clouds.

Which the sunset stained red, and which shaped themselves as she watched—*oh God*—into her, and her choir, miles tall, singing with flame-touched tongues.

Singing her story. Seril's story.

Some in the crowd fell to their knees. Gnarled fingers framed the sign of the Lord.

Gabby wanted to kneel as well. But when her beat faltered, so did the song in the sky.

An unfamiliar warmth filled her.

She was not the target of this miracle. She was its vessel.

Gabby set aside shock and glory, and focused instead on sound, speed, rhythm. The amplified voices screwed with her blend. Cacophony loomed, discord overlapping chord, dynamics squelched as delays crushed rests. And the mix had to slip a little: amplification goosed the tenors and shrilled the soprano line.

Yes, she prayed, *like that, but softer on the high end, and if you can do something about the delay—*

She coaxed the singers with her fingertips, shaped their sound, invoked the basses, and ushered sky-borne echoes back into the blend.

Skein voices spun into song.

(Which should have been impossible. Sound had a finite speed, like light. The words her choir sang on earth ought to take a fraction of a second to reach the sky, and seconds more to return. But gods were outside time. And *that* thought, in turn, had implications she resolutely ignored for fear of going mad.)

She directed her choir, and her gods. Alex in the alto section wept, but her voice kept steady.

They sang truth, and the city listened.

49

The Godmountain had many names. Failfire, some Badlands tribes called it, and told its story. At time's dawn, a tide of flame burned the green world to ash from sea to sea, burned the ash to bare stone, and would have burned the stone itself had not the Lady of the Plains challenged it. Proud, the fire came, and when it came the Lady wrapped it three times round: first in a cage of her hair, second in a lake of her blood, and third in a mountain of her bone. The fire, more fierce than clever, scorched her hair, and simmered her blood, and blackened her bone—but the hair, scorched, melted to wire, and the blood, simmered, thickened to lava, and the bone, blackened, fused to stone, and the more the fire burned, the worse it trapped itself.

Still, the Lady of the Plains knew one day the fire would burn free. So she wrapped it in a fourth and final maze made from her own mind: mirrors reflecting mirrors within, so the fire could burn and burn but only burn itself. Beneath Failfire, the Lady plays time's game, deceiving, outracing a pursuing flame. Some holy men and women enter the Godmountain's caves to chant old chants and eat certain mushrooms and hear her laughter and her cries.

Homesick, Drakspine fisherfolk called the mountain, for soil taken from its slopes pulls always toward the spot from which it came. The fisherfolk made necklaces from its stone in ancient days when their boats roamed the Kathic coast and crossed the ocean Old Worlders call the Pax, to Xivai and the archipelagic West. (Their descendants, who live in Kovak, claim their fathers and mothers even reached the Shining Empire, that those wandering weathered explorers were the Ocean Sages of Imperial legend—but tell that to an anthropologist and they'll offer you a good deal on mousefeathers or the Camlaander Channel.) But this much is true: Homesick stone does always point toward home, and each piece of the mountain let off its chain will swim oceans and worm across earth until it returns to the face from which it was hewn.

Site A-313, the Kovak Central Mining Concern called it. "Which," Tara said, turning a page and squinting to read by lantern light, "tells you everything you need to know about the Kovak Central Mining Concern." Site A-313, rich in copper and rare elements essential for high-energy Craftwork, rail-convenient to Kovak, Regis, and Dresediel Lex, ripe for exploitation. "You need these elements for industrial-scale necromancy, and there aren't many places in Northern Kath you can get them without pissing locals off, since the mining process leaks."

"Leaks?"

She compared her travel guide's map to the flyspeck printing on the sheet the Two Serpents Group offices gave her. "Mining runoff enters the groundwater, people who drink it have higher mortality rates, and one or two sigmas greater than average chance of doing the wandering brain-chomping undead thing after death. No big deal."

"It sounds like a big deal." Outside the carriage window, over the tops of trees, the mountain grew. Its vicious black stone peak jutted toward the stars.

"Long as the Concern uses proper containment, there's no outbreak. Problem is, containment isn't working."

"So there's a zombie horde out there?"

"I mean," she said, and trailed off.

Shale looked at her from across the carriage.

"Horde is pejorative. So's zombie, for that matter, if you're not referring to the Archipelagese religious practice."

He did not speak then, either.

"Fine. Yes."

"That explains why we had such a hard time getting a taxi to the camp."

"Basically." They'd had to pay the horse double, with a promised tip that would gouge away most of her expense account.

"And you wonder why the God Wars happened."

"That's not fair. The containment system should have worked. This is an isolated event—one site with one problem. Without the resources we pull out of the ground here, no one could do large-scale revenant agriculture. Price of food goes up, people starve. Do you want children to starve?"

"It's just one problem at one site."

"Yes."

"So's a stab wound."

"I'm not having this conversation with you anymore."

A high-pitched howl split the night, and others joined it. "Let me guess. Undead wolves?"

"Shambling wildlife," Tara said, "isn't the real problem with a leak."

"You didn't answer the question."

"Yes, fine, undead wolves. But the issue, believe it or not, is weeds."

"Weeds."

"The seepage spread south into the water supply for industrial farms in Centervale. Have you ever farmed?"

"Not as such."

"Trust me, it's hard enough when you kill weeds and they stay dead. Imagine what happens when they come back." She pointed to the newspaper headlines reproduced on the back of the Two Serpents brochure. "Northern farms were the first hit. Crop strangled under rotting vegetable matter. The unblight spreads slowly, but it does spread, and it started soon after KCMC began their core extraction op. KCMC stopped digging two weeks ago and called in the Two Serpents Group, who have sent their executive staff to address the problem."

"Is that normal?"

"Small organization. Not much redundancy. Like playing small-stack poker—you fold or go all in when the odds are right. On the plus side, that means all their execs are in the same place. We go in, convince them to give up their sky rights, cab back to the airport, and make Alt Coulumb by dawn. A whole day to spare, even with this detour." They crested a low ridge. The many-named mountain's stone rose in sheer barren cliffs. Eyewateringly brilliant ghostlights blasted through the trees. "That's them." The howls rose again, prolonged, gurgling, and punctuated by bowstrings' twang. The carriage horse reared and shied.

They emerged from the tree line into a broad field of clear-cut earth that swarmed with—well, "wildlife" was no longer an accurate term.

There were wolves after all—or anyway the rotting half skeletons of wolves caught in death spasms of hunger, fear, and rage. Mound-shouldered bears stalked the clearing, hides hedgehogged with arrows that seemed to have inflicted at best cosmetic damage. Weasels and stoats and mice swarmed the barricade at the field's edge. The smaller creatures could not pass in the silvered razorwire with which some perspicacious soul had draped the barrier, but the wire wouldn't stop bears.

A blink told her the creatures weren't bound to any Craftswoman, and that the camp's territorial ward remained intact, if dormant. The blind and ravenous fought the blind and desperate.

"Those wolves are looking our way," Shale said.

"Not a problem."

"They're running now."

"On it." She opened the carriage door. Cool night air rolled in. Pine and putrescine fumes burned her throat. She tossed the travel guide to Shale. "Hold this." She clutched the door with one hand and the empty driver's bench with the other and pulled herself up, ignoring the approaching wolves and the pain in her side.

The horse reared as she reached the driver's seat. She offered it more soul, and it mastered itself again. Hooves dug into dirt and pushed. Bowstrings thrummed to her left, wolves fell, bears shambled—but one wolf dodged the arrows and sprinted toward the barricade. Meanwhile, a rodent tide scurried toward Tara, smelling meat.

No problem.

The mining camp's spotlights were an issue, so she killed them. No time for elegance: glass shattered in a puff of expanding gas and freed spirits. Night reclaimed the mountain, and stars bathed the field in glory.

She gobbled stellar light, funneling power and pattern through glyphs that woke on her skin. She seized the mining camp's ward. She had been sent by the King in Red (technically correct), and the King in Red was a Kovak Central Mining investor, along with Alphan Securities, Grimwald Holdings, and a half-dozen other firms. On the King in Red's behalf she could invoke the wards and extend their protection to the private access road leading to the camp. The rat-revenants were in essence tiny, unprofitable Concerns, simple consumption-action loops trespassing on KCMC territory.

Shadow charged with blue fire rolled out from her carriage. The fire caught at the access road's edges, and undead rodents screamed. Their tide broke into a burning wave as warded soil repelled them. Across the field, the wolf leapt—only to slam against an invisible barrier and fall. A streak of blood and grime sizzled in midair. The wolf twitched to rest.

After days of boardroom wrangling and terse, tense arguments with recalcitrant deities, Tara had to admit she enjoyed entering a besieged camp to cheers and applause. From the carriage driver's seat she surveyed the people she had saved: miners and aid workers in vests embroidered with the Two Serpents logo. She bowed, though she felt their celebration premature, since the creatures outside were not so much gone as temporarily repulsed. She didn't say as much.

A Quechal woman in slacks and sweat-stained blouse approached her from the barricade. "Thanks for the help. Took you long enough to get here."

"Glad to provide," Tara said, "but I think you may have me confused with someone else." She produced a business card. "Tara Abernathy, Church of Kos and Seril. I didn't come because you called for me. I'm here to speak with Mr. Altemoc." Judging from the Quechal woman's flinch, she'd mispronounced the name.

"Weird," the woman said. "I sent a nightmare SOS yesterday; the King in Red's offices responded this afternoon with your name and description."

Far away, beyond the undead howls, Tara thought she heard a skeleton laugh. Why spend your own resources when another will volunteer for cat's-paw? "Here I am, either way. Can I speak with Mr. Altemoc?"

Her interlocutor drew breath through her teeth. "He's indisposed at the moment."

"Where?"

The woman pointed, and Tara looked—past her, past tents and supply depots, to a gaping hole in the mountainside. The shadows within were the shadows of an open mouth.

"Wonderful," Tara said.

50

"I never thought I could have so little fun after dark with ropes, knots, and a partner," Cat said as they sailed into the bay.

Raz adjusted his grip on the lines. "You don't like this? Sea spray in your face, good moon overhead?" The wind changed. "Duck, please."

She did; the boom swung quarterstaff-swift overhead. Wind bellied the sail and swept them east. "I'm barely happy on a ship that doesn't try to kill me whenever the breeze changes."

"A small boat's more personal," he said. "Don't get me wrong, I love *Bounty*. You can't haul cargo in a dinghy like this, or fight, and a tall ship has its own soul. But sailing a small boat's like juggling knives. Your every action's magnified, and so are its consequences."

"Did you just say, in this thing's defense, that it reminds you of knife juggling?"

Moonlight glinted off his teeth.

Cat leaned back. "What's this big secret, anyway? Or do you plan to kidnap me and save me from the battle?"

"Why not both?"

"My duty's back on shore. And I'm pretty sure I can beat you up."

"Who would sail you home?"

"I'd fly. Or use your breastbone for a paddle."

"I'll scratch kidnapping off the agenda." The sail's lower edge flapped like a flag in a breeze. He let out line, and it filled again.

She turned back to the glow ashore. City towers shrank to needles of light.

"Looks beautiful, doesn't it?"

"A bit," she said. She trailed one hand in the waves. The V's that trailed her fingers caught moonlight. She thought about time and water.

"We'll soon pass the continental shelf."

"I shouldn't be out here," she said.

"That makes two of us."

She flicked salt water toward his face. "I should be on patrol. That song at sunset—Justice needs everyone on the streets."

"Fair."

"You said two of us, though. Why shouldn't you be here? Isn't the ocean your thing?"

The sounding weight made a small splash. They watched each other as the line unspooled. She touched the back of his hand. It felt as cool as the water.

The reel clicked.

"I'm about to tell you something we don't talk about much," he said. "Did you ever study history?"

"What, you mean in high school?"

"Do you remember what happened to High Telomere, to the Empire?"

Those schoolbook words sounded silly out here at night. She stifled a laugh with her knuckle against her lips.

He was not laughing.

"Cult, or something," she said at last. History was a stuffy schoolroom a decade gone—more than that, gods—with big Mrs. Askel pacing through pillars of sunlit dust. "Took over the Empire. Expanded. Fought Schwarzwald tribes. They allied, invaded back, broke Telomere to pieces."

"Burned the topless towers," Raz said, "tore temples stone from stone and sank the stones into the Midgard Sea. You can still find them, if you dive."

"We're two thousand miles from the Midgard. I don't think there were any Telomeri temples here to sink."

"Do you remember anything else about the cult?" he asked.

"If we're playing Questions, I think your turn's over."

"Humor me."

Chalk screeched blackboard in memory; the back of her hand stung with a ruler's impact. She'd drifted off, forehead on crossed arms, pigtails against her ears (didn't cut her hair short 'til tenth grade, and she dropped out soon after), tired from fighting with Mom the night before. Mrs. Askel wore heavy powder on her face. Miss Elle, recite the next section of the text. "Usual sort of accusations people level against folk they don't like. Eating flesh. Drinking blood. Raising the dead." She blinked. "No."

"The sucker's deal," Raz said, "shows up on its own every few centuries. Elayne says it's baked into our species, though that sounds like what Crafty folk say when they don't want to admit they don't know the answer. The point is, you don't see as many, ah, people like me around, not anywhere near as many as you'd expect given how easily kid leeches lose control."

"We kill them when they slip up." *Them*, not *you*. She wasn't sure how she felt about making that distinction.

"You don't kill everyone," he replied. "And the Iskari and Schwarzwaldens and the angels of Alikand didn't kill the Imperials—not all of them. What's good for the temple's good for the cultist. You remember back in your apartment, when I mentioned walking into the ocean?"

The night grew brighter as her eyes widened.

"It's a good life down there, if you don't need this one. Dark and cool, with like-minded company. And there's plenty in the sea that bleeds. I stay clear; to them I'm the one that got away. I should have been a fresh father for a new line. The way they tell it, I should join their congregation, settle down, start a colony of my own. Stop rambling. A life for which, as you can imagine, I have little taste." He unbuttoned his shirt. Age-paled scars hatched skin the color of rosewood. "But you need help, Seril needs allies, and desperation makes strange bedfellows. They want me. If I can use that to help you, I will."

"I was joking," she said, "about vampire gods."

"I wasn't." He pointed down into the depths. "Good thing you sink in the Suit. We'd have had to bring weights otherwise."

"We can run," Dr. Hasim said when they were safe behind a locked door. "Or we can stay and help these people fight. We must choose."

The refugee council gathered in an empty on-call room Hasim had persuaded the orderlies to lend them: Aedi who'd worked with him in the Refuge for a decade; Akhil who collapsed on their doorstep five years back, having wandered half-blind out of the Wastes shrunken as a dried fig; Zola who handled the shrines' day-to-day management; quiet Mohem to whom the Refuge's younger guests looked in their troubles.

Mohem, to his surprise, was the first to speak, her voice velvety with rare use: "We are all here, and gods too. Seventy-one awake, and twenty-eight still sleep. Of those, twenty-four dream shallow enough for me to taste. Four are too far gone for me to hear their voices."

Zola had found herself a clipboard and everyone proper clothes, though the fabrics were coarse and the styles ill-fit and ill-fitting: Hasim wore twill slacks three sizes too large, a belt in which he'd awled an extra hole, and a cotton shirt with ill-considered checks. Zola had not said how, in a building where people died regularly, she acquired the clothes.

She consulted her clipboard. "Our debts appear to have been canceled." Murmurs around the circle. Akhil looked up from his stitching. "We have a soul apiece, offered by the Goddess Seril. I applied for credit at HBSE and First Camlaander, without success. By freeing us, the Goddess has placed us in thaumaturgical limbo: we are members of Her community, under Her protection—but the broader Craftwork world does not acknowledge Her existence."

Akhil had been, among other things, a tailor before his town fell, and was adjusting his Zola-found shirt to fit. He pulled his thread taut, pursing a long seam's lips. "Then there's the chorus in the sky."

"What do you make of that?" Hasim said.

Akhil tied off the thread and cut it with a scalpel liberated from a nursing station. "The city is in danger. These aren't the days, and this was never the land, for a God so leveraged to Craftsmen to address His people directly. He's afraid."

Zola turned pages on her clipboard. "The locals love Kos, but few remember Seril as anything but a threat. Their faith is structured for a diad, but they don't have the praxis."

Akhil cocked his head to one side. "How do you know what the people think? We've scarcely had a chance to leave this building."

"A hospital—" She frowned, set a hand to her mouth, shook her head. Hasim recognized that expression. The word had pulled at the cuts on her lips. "A hospital tangles many lines. Nurses have one background, doctors another, and everyone falls sick sometime. People talk, especially when they do not think one speaks good Kathic. I have limited my vocabulary in public spaces."

Mohem rubbed her upper arms. "We could run to the ghost cults in Alt Selene. A train leaves tomorrow."

Akhil pinched, and pierced, and drew the needle. "Would that not violate the terms of our redemption?"

"There are no terms." Zola flipped back to the first page. "Seril refused to recognize our indenture. Her soul-gift is simple grace. We owe her nothing."

"If she falls, the indenture may seize us again."

"We can be safe under a new guardian before that happens. I know it sounds ungrateful, but this is not our fight. Someone—presumably Grimwald Holdings—attacked us, and we woke here. Seril stands against our enemies, but she will fall. We have"—Zola checked the wall clock—"thirty-two hours to find a better bulwark. Alt Selene's ghost cults offer generous asylum terms. Alternatively, we could sue for Kosite asylum in the Court of Craft, claiming Seril is subsidiary to Kos, and he inherits her obligations."

"Which would aid the Craftsmen who attack Her," Hasim said. "I dislike that idea."

"We have to protect ourselves, Doctor. And our Partners."

"And so the choice remains," he said. "Run or fight."

Zola leaned back in the chair and caged her long fingers. "I say run."

"As do I."

Zola turned in surprise to Akhil, who shrugged as if their agreement were not a momentous occasion.

Mohem pressed her lips into a line as she thought, and when she decided, they unfolded and filled with color again. "The Refuge took me in, back in Agdel Lex. I helped it in return. Seril took us in. I think we should help her. We fight."

"I agree," Hasim said. "She needs us as much as any broken deity who ever stumbled to our doorstep. What are we for, if we desert her now? Fight."

One by one they turned to Aedi. Aedi spoke seldom when she was not praying, and when she spoke she did not use her own words, drawing instead from scriptures the source of which mystified even Hasim. In the Refuge, as each new destitute arrived, Aedi sat reading beside them, working the prayer beads woven into her hair between knuckle and thumb. She was older than Hasim, and wiser. He did not know how great was the gulf between them in either category, but since they first met, he had grown to suspect it was considerable.

Aedi's braids snaked over her shoulders when she nodded, twisted left and right when she shook her head. They snaked today. "There will be war," she said, "even in the dry places of the earth."

51

"Boardrooms," Shale said as they entered the mountain. Circles of light from their hand torches played over blast-hewn tunnel walls. "We should expect boardrooms and arguments, you said on the flight. You didn't mention mines, or undead beasts."

Tara led the way, thankful for her borrowed boots, which were large but at least had traction. In the flats she brought, she'd have broken three bones by now. Water dripped from a wall seam to the tunnel floor. "If I expected this, I would have packed for it."

"If I expected this, I would have—"

"Stayed home? Let me do my job?"

"No."

"I didn't think so," she said, and checked her watch, as she had three times since arriving in camp. If it took them more than an hour to find Altemoc, they'd miss the evening flight back to Alt Coulumb. Another flight left the next morning, and after that nothing until sunset. Miss both of those, and she'd not make the court date, with or without the deal. She snapped her watch shut. "Shouldn't you be happy? This seems like your kind of place."

"Unfinished stone?" His face twisted in disgust. "I was born in Alt Coulumb. My block was quarried from a moonlit pit and weather-shaped on rooftops. Descending into living Rock—it doesn't feel right."

"You're made of stone."

"You're made of meat. Maybe after this we can find a nice tight wet dark meat tunnel for you to squeeze down."

"Point taken." Her stomach unclenched slowly.

They reached a three-way fork in the tunnel. Each path led down, and all were smaller than the main concourse they'd followed so far.

Tara folded and unfolded the map until she found the relevant square. Altemoc's route continued straight.

She set one hand on the stone and closed her eyes. Lightning spun spiderwebs around her and down into the bones of the world. "Ms. Batan said her team went for the mine offices while Altemoc led his into the depths. Batan heard the scream, went to find him, but ran into a 'wall of shadow.' She pushed at the wall; it tried to pull her in, but she escaped." She frowned. "Huh."

"Problem?"

"The Craftwork in these tunnels is weaker than it should be. Something draining it would explain the slurry leaks, the revenants. But I don't see any trace of shadow walls or the other stuff Ms. Batan describes." The mountain pressed around them, blacker than black, squeezing tiny lines of human Craft, which *quivered* like seaweed as a leviathan moved through—"Shit." She grabbed Shale's wrist. "Run!"

He did, as the tunnel walls began to glow. Ore veins shone brilliant red, and Tara smelled ozone. Red light chased them down the tunnel, casting crimson shadows. Behind her, a roar issued from no throat. Tara glanced back and saw blinding fire. Her boot struck a jutting rock. Her ankle turned. She stumbled, swore. Shale had pulled ahead of her. She skipped three steps, tried the ankle again—sound, though gods and demons did it hurt.

The roar was nearer. She heard a lightning crack. She could not outrun the coming fire.

She tried, though, dammit, even as the hairs on the back of her neck stood up and her skin charged with the memory of fire.

A stone hand pulled her into a side tunnel. The thunder ate her squawk of protest. She brought her knife around, brilliant in the shadows, before she recognized Shale in stone form—though not the healthy sculpture she remembered. Moonlight bled from deep wounds, from the missing corner of an ear and a hole in his right wing.

Red lightning carved grotesque shadows from the dark. Tara woke her glyphs, more for reassurance than out of faith they'd save her if whatever-it-was in the tunnel struck them.

Lightning jumped between crystal veins in the tunnel wall.

Another bolt followed, and a third, and then they came too fast to count, arc after arc crisscrossing fractal dense. Her brain constructed figures from their dance: bison-headed men and goat-legged somersaulting acrobats, artifacts of spark and flame, the roar their laughter.

She did not know until the lightning passed how bright it had been, or loud. Her ears rang. For a long time all she saw was the red that endures when the eye is overwhelmed.

She returned to herself through the silver of Shale's wounds.

Light seeped from him. His stone felt cool as ever, but the light, when it dripped onto her fingers, was warm. He pulled back from her touch, bared his teeth, snarled; her ears had not recovered yet, but she felt the sound in her bones.

"Thank you," she said.

She heard his voice as if through a pillow: "One second." His stone twisted, inverted, melted to skin again. "There." His voice was not so loud as before, but her hearing had recovered to match.

"I didn't know it was that bad," she said.

His grin would have had a different effect were his teeth still long and curved and sharp. "They don't hurt as much when I'm like this."

"You should have stayed home. Taken care of yourself."

"Aev and the others are resting before the battle. I can work in flesh, for a while."

"How long?"

"Long enough."

"No macho jerk answers, please. Be honest with me."

"This stone, unworked as it is, helps a little. I can handle another day. Which is all we need, one way or another."

She tried her ankle. "Fuck."

"Lean on me."

"I'll use the wall." If she couldn't quite walk, at least she could hop. "Slower than I'd like. Let's move."

"Down?" As if he hoped she would give up. Not tonight. Not with gods and goddesses and friends counting on her two thousand miles away. Not with so few hours remaining. Her watch lay heavy in her pocket.

"Down," she said.

52

Silverclad Cat splashed through the ocean's skin, plummeting toward a darkness that paled all color: moonlight shafts ended in the shadows below, embedded in the flesh of a beast too large and cold to care.

Cat sank. Bubbles clung to the Suit, and as she kicked they slipped free, tickled up her flanks to form a whirling trail. Justice's song buzzed beneath her conscious thought. She was far from the community of cops. Seril's light followed her, warm inside her mind, a caress she couldn't call a mother's—not her mother's, anyway.

She did not have to breathe while wearing the Suit. Blood rushed in her ears, and the water's pulse twinned her own.

She heard a splash as Raz dove into his element. The speed of his descent slicked back his hair. Naked from the waist up, he joined her as she fell. He swam with beautiful efficiency.

Westward rose the continental shelf, steeper than any cliff could be in air. When Cat was a kid, old Father Clemson at the Quarter parish who owed gambling debts to half his congregation told myths during weekend services. Cat would have beaten up any kid who suspected how much she loved those stories. She had no time for sermons, which were one more way folk told you to sit down and listen, but she liked the strange tales and weird poems, and one line returned to her thoughts as she looked down into the black: something about spirits *brooding on the abyss.*

She pointed down and shot Raz a questioning glance. He gave her the thumbs-up. Pointed down. Thumbs-up again.

Great.

She brooded on the abyss like a champ.

Water pressed her in an embrace tighter than the Suit's used to be before Seril came back, and the Suit stiffened to match.

Cat's heart beat faster. Raz kicked into the deep, somersaulted, and waved up at her with a smile.

Pressure at this depth could warp a body from within. The City Aquarium displayed the corpses of dead things divers dredged from the deeps, spiny and toothed, many-clawed, tentacular. Special care had to be taken, the exhibit's brass placards read, in recovering such specimens, due to the pressure difference between ocean floor and surface. If she removed her Suit down here, she'd die.

Her eyes adjusted. No human eyes could have, there wasn't enough light, but human limits did not bind the Suit. Raz's white pants flashed when he kicked.

They passed few fish at this depth, and no vampires she could see. They'd almost reached the bottom. Sharp grim coral towers jutted from the murk below. White flakes of sea snow flitted between the peaks. Could Raz have been mistaken? He'd sounded so sure.

The coral towers moved.

Earthquake was her first thought, though there were no quakes in Alt Coulumb. The movement's scale was too great for anything else. It could not be a living thing—nothing so large could live, on land.

But they weren't on land anymore.

The towers swelled and reddened as they approached, sharp pitted texture filling out with roseate skin. Blue sparks crackled beneath a translucent surface. High-pitched cries filled the deep. Arms the length of Alt Coulumb's coastline coiled, wreathed by clouds of dust. Currents tossed her as the thing beneath bloomed, the coral forest transformed into a city-sized mantle. The Suit fed liquid beauty through Cat's vein, but chemical confidence was little help. As she grasped and failed and grasped again at the sheer inconceivable *scale* of the thing coming oh gods *toward her,* its displacement current pulled her down, tossing Raz head over heels—

And what she'd taken for wrinkles on the creature's skin were blade-sharp ridges—

She caught Raz and pulled him close as the star kraken crashed into them.

Blade-flesh drew sparks as it scraped her Suit; she tumbled into a canyon-sized wrinkle, bounced off a rubbery wall, pushed herself away—Raz tugged her out of the groove before it snapped closed, mouthlike. She kicked off and down again, and realized they were not alone.

Nearly human creatures slipped through the water around her. She'd taken them for snow at first, decayed dead things fallen to the benthic plane. They swam, long limbed and webbed, skin every color she had seen, jaws distended with curved teeth. Darting about the kraken, they pierced its flesh with spears and carved broad wounds with knives. She saw a slick naked girl unhinge her jaw and sink fangs into punctured kraken flesh. Blue blood leaked from the seal her lips made. The girl swallowed convulsively, released the monster, and howled.

Not all the shapes were human, or humanlike: Cat saw sleek bottle-nosed bodies, fangs curving from their open beaks. Hundreds streaked through the night—tiny beside the kraken, but pale corruption spread where their spears bit, and their teeth, and the kraken shriveled as it rose.

The kraken hit her again. She sprawled on its mantle as a translucent sack of flesh inflated overhead. That bloodred mass held many eyes, their pupils figure eights within which Cat could have stood upright.

Then the mantle collapsed and they fell, propelled down by the kraken's jet. Cat stared up into a beak that could crush mountains, ringed with lightning, and within that gnashing mouth a furnace. The speed of the kraken's retreat slapped its arms and tentacles together, and Cat and Raz and all the hunters tumbled down, down—

To land dust-clouded on a stony plain.

Raz recovered first, which pissed her off. He offered her a hand. She ignored it and stood on her own.

Around them the dust curtain settled, unveiling an ancient city.

What she'd taken for a stone flat was in fact a plaza ringed with column-fronted, wedge-topped buildings. She remembered the style from textbook woodcuts, though those ruins had never been crusted with coral and seashells. Towers rose beyond the temples.

Vampires surrounded them.

They hung in water, red eyed and alien, half-visible at this depth even to her. Were they living, she could have seen their heat. They were not. Coins glistened in wide red watching eyes. She looked up and saw no surface overhead. The hunters returned, blood-wreathed, spears and teeth sharp. Dolphins swam alongside. Sonar clicks played over Cat's skin.

Raz swam into the center of the crowd. His hands moved, not just for swimming. Sign.

A woman emerged from the crowd. She might have been thirty or three thousand. Seaweed trailed her limbs. The signs she addressed to Raz were crisper and more elegant than those he offered in reply. Whatever their language, he spoke it only haltingly.

The conversation continued for tense and quiet minutes. Raz frowned after the woman—the priestess—responded to his third statement with a hook of her finger as if inviting. Their exchanges grew sharp. The priestess bared her teeth. Cat doubted this indicated progress.

Excuse me, Cat said.

A ripple passed through the crowd. Heads turned toward her.

I'm sorry if we interrupted you, she said. *I'm—we're—from the surface. My name's Cat; Raz brought me here because he thought you could help.*

Silence, full of clicks and curiosity.

My Goddess, she said, *is in danger. Her enemies want to kill Her. She needs strength to fight them off. Raz hoped you could help us.*

The priestess swam toward Cat like a snake would swim. Long braids trailed her. She stopped just beyond Cat's reach. Her feet did not touch the seafloor. The priestess's head cocked to one side, as if she'd been presented with a joke and was deciding whether to laugh.

Do you understand me?

The priestess nodded.

They pushed you down here centuries ago. They're trying to push my lady out now.

The priestess opened her arms and twirled a circle, taking in the city and those who swam around her.

Cat was about to ask what she meant, when she heard the singing.

Water might garble ordinary speech, but song carried.

—*What God*
—*Shall we seek*
—*Save the Blood?*

They laughed.

—*Let us see*
—*Your need*

The priestess held out her hand and raised her thin lips to reveal fangs more beautiful than any Cat had ever seen.

Cat reached—

The glamour broke. Raz interposed himself between them in a blur. Through the weight of water, she heard him hiss.

Cat touched him on the shoulder.

Raz. It's fine.

The priestess nodded, once.

Raz looked back at her, scared.

I can do this.

She did not know what to call his expression as he swam aside. Despair, maybe, or hope.

She offered her wrist to the priestess, who accepted, and bent her head.

Her teeth dipped through Suit and skin with equal ease.

A line of incandescent pleasure shot through Cat's heart, spread out and up and so much more dangerously down, to her crotch, through arms and legs, fingertips, toes. Joy rattled the cave of her skull. Her thoughts came to pieces in a single pulse.

Her taste of Raz in the ruined tower had been strange, surreal, exciting, but Cat had felt like this before. She knew to ride the feeling. She did not collapse or go mad. She'd felt weaker versions of this rush in Paupers' Quarter backstreets or on the Business District's rain-slick rooftops.

The priestess was not drawing her, thank gods. Cat felt enormous hunger behind the woman, old and overwhelming, deeper than the ocean. The priestess tasted Cat's soul, that was all, savoring her need, and through her the Suit's, and Seril's.

Cat followed that taste back and in, to a network of which the priestess was but a piece—the blood of all assembled here in the sea's night ran through her, and hers through them, joined to a throbbing heartbeat greater than any one alone and wiser, a mind that shook her to ecstasy with its faintest touch. She could offer herself to that hunger, fall into its perfection, let herself be hollowed out and worn as a glove by God—

No, she told the hunger.

The priestess lifted her fangs from Cat's wrist, and the connection broke.

Cat fell. She tried to gasp, by reflex, and choked when the Suit did not let her.

After timeless time, she calmed.

The priestess's head declined and rose again, in a slow, gentle nod.

The priestess drew a line across her own wrist with her thumbnail. A stream of blood snaked through the water and curled into a cloud rather than dispersing. The priestess took the cloud in her palm, and squeezed. When she opened her hand, she held a smooth oval of red jade that caught the not-light strangely. She offered it to Raz. He drew back at first, as if the sun lay in her palm. Then he looked at Cat, and sagged, and accepted.

It was done.

Cat had wondered how they would return to the surface—Raz could swim on his own, but even the Suit might tire with the strain of bearing its own weight back. Two from the congregation—the girl who drank the star kraken, and a slender man who had been Dhisthran before he became this—bore her skyward.

Rising, she heard the music again: a choir of superhuman voices howling praise in the abyss, their meld an imperfect reflection of the living web she tasted through the priestess. It echoed undersea. No, she realized as they rose, those were not echoes but other songs, the ocean chanting glory and blood through eternal night.

By the time Cat pulled herself back onto the dinghy and let the Suit slip away, the sky was purple with the threat of dawn. Open air felt weak, easy. The sunrise seemed obscene. Raz flopped to the deck.

They lay alone on the water.

When she could bear to move again, she reached for him. Her hand fell heavy on his leg, and squeezed. His did the same a second later, on hers.

"That," he said when he found words to speak, "was a brave dumb thing you did."

"At least we were dumb together. And brave."

He laughed, then coughed—and coughed and laughed harder, until he had to bend over the boat's edge and hack water out of his lungs.

She slapped him on the back. "Let's get to shore before you burn."

53

"It's dangerous for you and your sister to be out alone," Matt told Claire as they opened the stands. He'd chosen his words in the silence of their morning rounds, which had not been silent at all but full of rocking wagon wheels, plodding golem feet, the leafy shiver of lettuce loose in crates. For the second day in a row, they had not talked on the road. Dark circles undermined Claire's eyes, and she stared over the golem's surging shoulders. She napped when he drove, which she had never done before.

While he waited for her answer he unlocked his stand's cupboard, removed the carved wood signs and stepladder, and climbed the one to hang the others from brass hooks. The paint caught dawn's blush. He hung EGGS, and ADORNE, and FRESH between them. "I was worried for you."

"Worried" was too neat a word. He'd stayed up an hour past bedtime at the kitchen table with Donna, drinking mint tea brewed with leaves from their window garden. Hannah and Jake had abandoned their game of checkers and thunder lizards long before that; Hannah was sweet with the kid. Then again, neither Donna nor Matt was so free as Hannah to pin Jake down until he said sorry.

Waiting, Matt and Donna counted sirens through the open window, and fistfights, and curses, and mating cats' cries. Matt wanted to go look for them, but Donna counseled him to stay. After an hour they switched roles, and after that again.

He slept, expecting to wake and find them still gone. But when he emerged robed after his morning shower, Claire was back, with a pot of coffee strong enough to double as industrial solvent.

He'd asked her a wordless question, which she hadn't answered and still wasn't answering.

"Your sister needs looking after," he said, "and the city's full of crazy confused people." He arranged cartons of eggs, and a loose pyramidal pile in their center. Claire hauled a crate of eggplant onto the Rafferty stand's counter and pulled plump dark plants out two by two. She set them down hard enough to bruise the flesh, but he didn't say anything about that because she certainly knew. "What if your sister had another episode?"

"Stop," was the first word she'd said to him all morning other than "hello." "Matt." She leaned against the counter, lowered her head so her blond hair fell across her face, then turned to him. He held one egg in each hand, and felt faintly ridiculous. "You think I don't know?"

"I'm worried," he repeated, and put down the eggs.

"Yesterday we met a blind old woman who fell, alone, in her house—her son who lives with her was stuck on a double shift dockside—she hurt herself and no one came to her but—" She pointed up, and she was not pointing to the sun. "A five-year-old girl's cat escaped through a window cracked open at night and she chased it out of doors only to lose herself until Seril's children found her. A university student was being"—she shook her head, to clear it—"raped. Until. A single mother lost her job and would have lost her home if not for. Ellen talks to them all. People I couldn't see. You don't let others' pain inside, you know? Not if you have enough already, and everyone always has enough."

"I don't want you to get hurt."

"Everything's dangerous in this city, Matt. Especially for women. I'm not a religious person, but Ellen is. Seril's good for her, and for us. You've seen that."

"Gargoyles can't solve the world's problems."

"But they can help. They have helped. And Seril needs help now. Ellen wants to get everyone together, everyone who's prayed to the goddess."

"You can't fight Craftsmen."

"We can try. This will be over in a day or two, one way or another. For now, my sister needs me." Lettuce shook as she dropped heads onto the counter. "You saw what happened to Ellen when they hurt Her. I won't let that happen again."

He finished his pyramid of eggs. Then he built a second.

"Hey," he said after a while. "I'm sorry."

Ray Capistano's knife blade struck his butcher's block.

"Donna and I care about you. If we can help, let us."

When he looked at her, she was looking back.

"As a matter of fact," she said.

The red lightning struck more often as Tara and Shale descended into the mountain.

Not without warning—always the growl behind them or ahead. When crystal veins in the rock took fire, they ran or hid. Once, they could not run. Tara knelt in the tunnel's center, Crafted a ward, and held Shale close as the fire buckled her shield. If the mind that moved this mountain wanted to crush them, it would.

"Are you certain there's a mind?" Shale asked.

"I hope there isn't, so I'll assume there is."

They descended for hours. Back on the mythical surface, the Alt Coulumb express winged east. Tunnels turned back on themselves, confounding Tara's stubbornly two-dimensional map. She could see Craftwork woven through the stone, which would help her retrace her steps; finding a way down was harder.

She thought she recognized a triple junction through which they passed. Were they lost? She carved a glyph into the stone above the center passage. When they reached the triple junction again, the glyph was gone. Either she'd been wrong, or the something erased the glyph.

Cave air tasted close and dank.

She had to sleep, after a while. "That or collapse." One side chamber, hewn to store drill bits and spare equipment, had walls free of crystal, which she hoped meant they'd be safe from the lightning here.

Shale kept first watch. Tara unfolded a sleeping pad from her pack. She hung her jacket on a lantern hook, made a pillow of her knapsack, and slept in a cave silence broken only by Shale's breathing.

Nightmares struck, as hoped: a message from Wakefield, reporting the Alt Coulumb team was ready to defend Kos. Next she saw Abelard, praying alone in an enormous chapel; the altar grew, and the chapel's flames melted his flesh from his bones. She did not know if Abelard sent her that dream, or if she built it for herself. After that, the bad dreams were real.

A hand on her shoulder woke Tara to the tunnel's black. She recoiled from the touch, scraped her knuckles against the wall, cursed, and summoned a light. Shale crouched beside her. "We should go."

"You kept watch without lights?"

"I thought we should save the hand torches," he said. "I hear well."

She smoothed the wrinkles in her suit and adjusted her slept-on hair. A small rodent had crawled into her mouth, died, and rotted. She swished canteen water in her mouth, gargled, and spit in the corner. Checked her watch again—the dawn flight had left already. "Any more lightning?"

"Five clusters passed."

They returned to the tunnels and the blunt smell of undisturbed stone.

"Do you think the lightning-balls are guards?" Shale asked.

"Bad ones, if so. We're not dead yet."

"They'd have killed us already if not for you."

"And the first would have got me if not for you. Good thing we keep each other around."

"Glad to hear I'm a useful asset."

"Not an asset," she said, remembering the dragon's voice.

"What, then?"

"A friend," she said. "If you like."

He chuffed, and she thought she saw him smile. "What are they, if not guards?"

"A goddess, maybe. Or god."

"A goddess is doing all this?"

"She might *be* all this. Remember the myths about this place: the lady and the fire."

"Myths," Shale said. "Fingers pointing at the moon."

"That's an interesting point for you to make, knowing someone who *is* the moon."

"Our Lady is not 'someone,'" he said. "And the goddess in the guidebook story lacks even a name. Who believes in her? What life could she possess?"

"Human minds are a good divine substrate," she said. "But they're not the only one. Goddesses can be trapped with bone thorns and blood-cooled silver and other tools. The traps keep the goddess from fading when her faith is broken. Maybe something similar's at work."

"Sometimes I forget how evil you can sound."

"The Craft," she said, "is not inherently good or bad."

"Its best efforts notwithstanding."

"The point is, to trap a goddess, you might build a system much like this: a conductive lattice webbed through a rich deposit of necromantic earths."

"You're suggesting the mountain is artificial, and alive. And nobody discovered this during the mining operation."

"Miners bind local spirits before major excavation, but this place is too big, too rooted, for it to even notice normal bindings. All this"— she tapped a crystal vein—"anchors the goddess, puts her on a clock so slow mortals don't register. Excavation must have woken her, made her mad."

"Hence the zombies."

"It's a theory."

They walked for some time in silence.

She folded the map, refolded it, frowned. "We should have found Altemoc's team already. The chart shows a huge chamber that isn't here. And we're running out of time."

Shale hummed. "You say we're inside a goddess."

"Maybe. Or something like one."

"And it is hurt."

"Wouldn't you be pissed if someone bored holes into you?"

"Not angry," he said. "Hurt. A person who's hurt guards her wound. The mountain curls around the place where the blade went in. It would explain why we can't find Altemoc—he sought the injury, made it worse, and she's enclosed him."

Tara stuffed the map into her jacket pocket and turned to Shale in the gloom. "I can't fight something this big."

"You don't have to fight," Shale said.

"How else do we make her let us in?"

"Ask," he said.

"I just did."

"No. Ask her."

"You are making no sense."

He laid his palm against the wall. "You Craftsmen have odd ways of being. You force the world to your will, and you force your wills on one another. Your power's built from bonds and obligations. There are other ways."

"The world doesn't just . . . do things because you ask."

"Have you tried?"

She raised her arms to the ceiling. "Hi! We're here to help. Take us where we need to go!"

Nothing happened.

She fixed Shale with a stare she'd used to curdle milk.

"You could use a less sarcastic tone of voice. And say 'please.' "

She did not let up the stare for a few seconds.

She closed her eyes. That made it easier.

"Hi," she tried. "You don't know me, and you don't have reason to trust me. But if you show me where it hurts, I think I can help."

Silence.

Oh, what the hells. "Please," she said.

Rock ground rock. A thunderstorm smell stained the air. Strong wind struck her in the chest. She tried to steady herself on the wall—

And failed, because there was no wall beside her anymore.

A tunnel gaped to her right, its black walls covered with enormous painted figures that glowed the same red as the mine's crystal veins.

"Not one word," she told Shale.

He offered none.

They descended together.

54

Cat waited in line for the sunset service at the Church of Sacred Ashes in Slaughter's Fell. The locals had come out in force, heavyset men in pit-stained work shirts and women with worn fingers. A mom in denim slacks caught her youngest by the arm and yanked her back from the street. Cat stuffed her hands in her coat pockets, hurting for a smoke, a drink, a fang, avoiding the blank stares of black windows in whitewashed houses. She watched the houses so she didn't have to watch the people. A scar-cheeked young man beside her offered her a cigarette, which she declined though she wanted to say yes.

It had been a long day after a long night.

Church doors opened and they filed in.

Parishioners packed the pews. As many stood in the back as found a seat. Cat scored one of the last pews, though the benches were so tightly packed she might have rather stood, or popped wings to give the locals a taste of real divine intervention. She squeezed between a bearded man in a golem mechanic's shirt—CAPISTANO SERVICE & REPAIR, grease stains included—and a dark-skinned girl with bushy hair, thin wrists, and thick glasses, who, after her mother hipped her into the pew beside Cat, slid the prayer book from the wooden pocket, and buried herself in the order of solstice ceremonies, high rite, second version, summer colophon. The evening congregation was a brew of hushed voices, pressure, and too-close bodies' heat. Cat smelled shoe leather and popcorn, oil and engine grease, aftershave, deodorant, perfume, and the bodies all that aftershave, deodorant, and perfume were meant to cover.

The people filled the church floor, but they did not fill the church. Arches made the roof seem taller than the sky.

On tiptoe she could just glimpse the cage-throne for the god's fire on the altar.

"Huh," she said.

It wasn't burning.

"The altar?" That was the man beside her, the mechanic, Capistano. "They don't keep it lit in Deliquescence. Guess you don't come often."

"It shows?"

"Safe guess. You think church's this busy any given day? Lot of people scared tonight."

"I haven't done much churching since I was a kid," she said.

Moon-whisper, soft and still: *You worship through your work.*

"It's easy." Not the mechanic—the girl to her right, her eyes large and liquid behind glass. She raised the book. "They'll tell you what page to read. You say what it says in italics, like here. If you don't know how to say it, I can help." Because in this part of the city it wasn't fair to assume everyone who came to church could read. And Cat was wearing Feller drag, jeans and jacket and worn boots, top two buttons of her shirt undone, a tear at her knee and a fray at her cuff. This was how she dressed growing up, how the kids she collared on patrol still dressed. Not much changed in Slaughter's Fell, though what change would look like here she didn't know. Suited uptown kids like those pricing out the locals up near the PQ market wouldn't fix anything, for sure.

"Thanks," she said, which carried farther than she meant. A hush fell over the assembly.

She followed the girl's gaze to the altar, and the priests.

Old Carmichael stood in the center. Cat recognized none of the acolytes who followed her, and wondered if she'd come to no purpose. But the old woman spread her hands and intoned, "Behold His fire," and from stage left (did priests call it stage left? altar left?) Abelard emerged, bearing in his cupped hands a burning coal. He set the coal inside the altar's cage-throne. The flame danced. The choir sang. He took his place.

The girl guided Cat through the services so well Cat lost her way only once—her own fault, when she flipped two pages instead of one and landed in an exorcism rite. Carmichael's sermon focused on duty, faith, and hope. Cat was too tired to follow most of it, but the congregation drank her words like thirsty earth drank rain. They needed.

Seril laughed moonlight when Cat joined the long alterward line to receive the ashes from Abelard. She moved slowly, like a tourist in a fabled city, weighing each street sign, intersection, tree, and graffiti mural, while locals sprinted past to work.

Her line evaporated and left her exposed to her friend, who held the dish of fire. She stepped toward him, set one arm across her chest as the service book indicated for those who wished a blessing but not the ash. He did not recognize her until he'd already dipped his hand into the fire. His eyebrows rose, and his body hitched in its performance of the rite. He caught himself before he spilled the flame.

His fingers, when they touched her scalp, were harder than she expected. Calluses, like those that glazed her knuckles.

The girl and the mechanic waited for her in the pew. The girl glowed with faith and sweat.

After service, Cat lingered outside the sacristy door, leaning against a tree trunk. Acolytes emerged two by two, and at last came Abelard, wearing rust-colored everyday robes, cigarette smoldering. "You did well," she said from the shadows, and grinned when he started and turned.

"Half gave me a heart attack."

"God will provide." She hugged him. "Nice service. Why didn't you give the sermon?"

"It's Carmichael's congregation. I wouldn't presume."

"Not even now that you're a saint?"

"I'm no more a saint than you are."

"Low blow."

"Technical branch doesn't sermonize. If I tried, I'd scare these people half to death with stress tolerance analogies."

"Gustave preached. And Tara said you made a good speech at the church hearing."

"I had to," he said. "I'm surprised you're here. Usually couldn't drag you into church with a team of horses. Or back to the Fell, for that matter."

"I tried to find you at the temple, but they said you'd gone to hold evening service. I figured you'd come here."

"What do you want?"

"I need a reason to see a friend?"

He ashed his cigarette onto the sidewalk, crushed out embers with his shoe. "Walk with me?"

They did, down Wilson and north on Candlemarch. "Been a long time since I was back here," she said when they passed gated Alowith Park. Puddles broke streetlights to rainbows. "Out of uniform, I mean. You remember Nick Masters? Offered me a smoke in line for the service tonight. Didn't recognize me, or if he did, he didn't say."

"You broke his big sister's nose."

"It was a fair fight. I was six, she was eight, and she had it coming."

"You're limping."

"Turns out," she said as they passed the park, "not everyone reacts to apocalyptic news as well as the good people of Slaughter's Fell. There was a riot dockside. I got run over by a wagon, if you can imagine. In the Suit, but I'll still have a nice bruise when this is over."

"Sounds bad."

She threw a pebble at a squirrel. The squirrel leapt to another branch, and then to a different tree. "It was, a bit. How do you think we'll do tomorrow?"

"The people have faith, though it's a stretch to get them supporting Seril. Bede's confident Wakefield can defend Kos. The question is, what will happen when Ramp turns to Seril. We can't help Her without exposing ourselves. So we'll see." He lit another cigarette, offered her one.

"Not my poison."

"I'm headed to Mom and Dad's before I go back," he said. "Come with me. They'd be happy to see you."

"I have work," she said.

"Tara will get back in time."

"I'm not worried."

"You've heard nothing from her."

"A nightmare came through last night, but it wasn't clear."

"Give me an old-fashioned letter any day."

"I know the feeling," he said. "Now, Cat, will you please tell me why you're here?"

She grew interested in the sidewalk between her boots. He waited. She'd learned to wait when she became a Blacksuit, but she hadn't expected Abelard to have the knack as well. All that kneeling must add up. "I have a plan to help Seril. You said it yourself—there's only so much the church can do."

"Cat—"

"Kos listens to you. If you ask Him to keep me safe, I think He will. And in a fight, everything you want to do that isn't win is a weakness. If He tries to shield me, He'll be helping Seril, which won't do us any favors."

"You think He'd look after you just because I asked?"

"Yes," she said, and stepped in front of him, turned so they could see each other. "I think you've asked Him already."

He looked away.

"Let me do my job, Abelard."

"It will be a hell up there," he said. "The things these people do. You know how scary Tara gets, and she's friendly by their standards."

"You want me scared?" Something behind her eyes felt hot. "Okay, I'm scared. But I can help, and if I can help I have to, and I'm asking you not to stop me."

They reached his family's door: black wood in a red brick building three stories high. A candle quivered in the third-floor window. A long time ago she'd drawn chalk heroes on the sidewalk where they stood, saviors in pastel.

"Okay," he said. "Just."

"What?"

"Come up for tea. The folks would like to see you. So would I."

"Okay," she said, and they climbed the steps together.

55

Night claimed Alt Coulumb. Dockside, Blacksuits swept up remnants of the riot. Churches and chapels and street-corner confession booths crowded with the living and the dead in search of counsel. In the Pleasure Quarter revelers danced and spun in frenzy. Long braids described black circles as fire-eaters breathed light into the dark. "Tomorrow" was a word few tongues dared whisper. Criers sang the coming doom. There was faith: the city remembered the choir in the sky. But fear flourished in faith's shadow.

So lovers loved, drunks drank, preachers preached, fathers fathered, mothers mothered, daughters daughtered, sons sonned, and reporters—

Gavriel Jones remembered the Paupers' Quarter market as an angry crowd and a swinging cane and stone wings beneath an impossible moon. The crowd tonight was softer and less dense. Rugs and carpets and chairs lay around the Crier's dais, and people, mostly women, busied about assembling camp. A girl with short spiked hair dyed pink and half her face tattooed in the pattern of a skull lifted a rug from a cart.

"Expecting more people?" Jones asked the girl.

"Yeah." She unrolled the rug with a snap of her strong arms. "Claire says. Grab those, put them down here, and here, in an arc." Then she saw Jones for the first time and saw, more to the point, her orange waistcoat. "Shit." The girl flowed up from her crouch, folded her arms, cocked her head up and back, a picture of the kind of punk Jones had been herself years ago, though she never let the needles near her face. "You aren't here to help."

"I might be," Jones said.

"You're a Crier. You want a story."

"Doesn't everyone?" she said. "What's yours? Don't often see a Hot Town kid setting up a sit-in."

"What do you know about it?"

"More than you think. We could compare scars sometime."

"Yeah?" Her curled lip and bared teeth skewed the skull-tat weird. "Maybe we could. Anyway, I'm not talking to you."

"Current evidence to the contrary."

"Fuck," she said. "Lady's got my back. I got hers. You forget that when you put on your fancy coat?"

"That why you're here? Manners?"

"I'm here to unload carts. You want to help, then let's go." She pointed with her head, a lioness's move, languid and slow. "Otherwise you talk to them."

Jones recognized the three to whom she turned: the big man moving stiffly, and the girls. "Adorne?"

"Ellen," she said. "Or Claire."

"Thanks. I think we got off on the wrong foot. I'm Gabby Jones."

"I know," she said, then: "Kim," and turned back to the cart and the rugs and the work of unloading.

Claire—blonder of the two, hollow cheeks, sharp controlled movements—met Jones halfway, leaving Ellen to resolve a question of supplies. Gabby almost hadn't recognized either girl: when she last saw them they'd stood hostage to their father. They'd grown in two days, or she had. "Ms. Jones," Claire said. "What are you doing here?"

"I keep my ears open, and I hear things. What about you?"

"The Lady needs help."

"You shouldn't be here, kid. I've seen people side with gods against Craftsmen. That doesn't end well."

"Seril helped us," Claire said. "We'll help Her tomorrow."

"You read much history, Claire?"

"Enough."

"You don't want to be out here when they bring the big guns."

"If you won't help us," Claire said, "at least don't get in our way. We have work to do."

Damn kids, damn idealists. But to sit here and pray as the sky burned overhead—there was a stupid courage to that, even if Gabby knew how that sort of courage ended. Tomorrow Aev would fight in the skies. And Gabby would watch from the sidelines. That was her job. She'd told Tara as much in this very square, days ago.

"Ms. Jones." Gabby jumped. Ellen's approach had been soundless. She carried a sleeping bag under one arm. "Our Lady doesn't stand much chance alone."

She remembered Aev in the alleyway: moonlit talons and jewel-like glittering eyes. And she remembered fire falling in Dresediel Lex, a long time gone. "No."

"You came because you want to help, but don't think you can. Stay. Tell our story."

Jones had a beat to cover, leads to follow and ledes to write.

But she had started all this, in the small way a teller starts a tale. And if they died and she didn't, she could forge of their story a weapon to throw against the wizards in their glass towers. To fight back, as she hadn't fought twenty years ago.

"I can't join you. It's not . . ." Professional ethics made a hollow sound when struck.

"You could help us build camp," Claire said. "If that won't strain your morals."

"No," she said. "I can do that much."

56

The nurse led Dr. Hasim to the room where Umar lay. A pale man slept there too, in a long white bed separated from Umar's by a blue curtain. "I'm sorry," the nurse said as they entered. "There weren't enough beds; we had to fit him somewhere. We'll move him soon, now most of your group's awake. But he hasn't responded since he arrived."

"Thank you," Hasim said. "Leave us, please?"

The man left.

Hasim placed a chair by the bed, so soft it made no sound. Umar did not twitch. Even so light a movement would have broken his normal featherweight sleep. Sunrise could wake Umar through blackout curtains. A cat's padding across the carpet made the big man twist and grumble. Falling temperatures, or rising, or a gust of wind, or the moon in the acacias, snapped him awake and philosophical. Hasim himself slept deeply, and shared these moments only in the half consciousness that ensued when Umar shoved him awake to talk. Fear haunted Umar at night: fear they would be attacked, the city would fall, the Refuge would fail. Many predators preyed on small gods. But he also jostled Hasim awake to debate the reality of shadows, the meaning of prayer, the logic of resurrection, the lives of gods.

Mention these matters to Umar in daylight, and he would laugh. Umar's god, like him, preferred the strength and speed and blood of living things to scholarship. Hasim enjoyed Umar's game of anxiety and denial. It was one of many games they played together.

In Alt Coulumb, now, Umar's hand lay on scratchy sheets, far from the delicate cottons of their bed. Hasim took his hand, felt hard callus ridges. Umar's palm was heavy with muscle. He squeezed. Umar did not respond.

"We'll fight," Hasim said, leaning close to Umar's cheek. "Aedi cast the deciding vote. If you can believe that."

He watched for a twitch in the broad chest, a flare of a several-times-broken nose. None came.

"I wish you were here to help us." His voice caught, and he forced himself to laugh. "I'll fight, Umar. Me. Life's road takes strange turns." No answer. "I thought you would find that funny. I won't shame you."

That was how they talked to each other, building trust falls into conversation. You could never shame me, that was Umar's line. But Umar said nothing.

"I won't shame you," he repeated, louder, so wherever he was he could hear.

He kissed him once. His beard was dense and pillowy against Hasim's cheek.

Hasim left the chair by the bedside. If the nurses did not move the chair back, and Umar woke while he was out, Umar would see Hasim had come to sit with him. Just in case, Hasim left a note. *We are well. I love you.* Superstition tugged at Hasim as he signed his name, but the hexes he feared were all an ocean away. He doubted many here could even read Talbeg.

He wrote Umar's public name on the envelope, and added a seal so the letter would burn if opened by anyone but him. He set this on the bedside table before he left.

As the door closed, Umar shifted beneath the sheets.

Late late late, and more than a little drunk, Cat wove toward the *Bounty.* They'd drawn up the gangplank, but with a running leap she cleared the few yards between dock and ship, caught a net slung over the side to dry, and face-planted against wood that smelled of tar and salt. She climbed the side, caught the railing, vaulted over, and was promptly tackled by a skeleton.

The tackle didn't go well for the skeleton, since skeletons by and large don't have enough mass for tackling. Cat tossed the skelly across her shoulder to the deck. Poorly linked bones jarred loose as it fell. Two blades glinted in firelight to her left. She grabbed the skeleton's fallen sword, slipped, and tumbled into a front roll that she hoped looked planned. Upright more or less, she spun sternward to face the blades: a shiny woman—with gills?—and a man whose left arm was some sort of golemetric construct. She raised one hand, palm out, lowered the sword. "Hey. Hey. No trouble. I just want to see your boss."

"Should have climbed higher," Raz said from the foredeck. She turned and waved with the sword. Lantern flames added orange to the scab-red of his eyes.

"I was just looking for you!"

"I know." He landed in front of her, strong enough his weight didn't cause his legs to bend.

"Show-off."

"You're drunk."

She laughed. "You're funny." She set the sword on the deck. Well, maybe dropped would be more accurate. No worries. Swords were tough.

"Come inside. Let's get you something that isn't poison."

He led her into his cabin and poured her a tall glass of water. She sat on the couch-bed, dimpling the velvet with her fingers. The cabin was silver and gold and crimson everywhere, neat and dusted and polished—Raz couldn't have space, so he compensated with luxury. "Went to see Abelard's family. You know. End of the world stuff. We drank to solve problems." She touched the badge at her neck and invited Justice to burn the alcohol from her blood. "See? All better."

"Drink water anyway. I know what you're like hung over."

"Friends drink with you," she said when the glass was half-done. "Good friends make you hydrate." She set the empty glass on the end table.

"Why are you here, Cat?"

"Can I see the token she gave you?"

He produced it like a street conjurer summoning a coin. Up close it seemed clouded and deep. Strange shapes shifted within. Her head swam as she watched them. She passed the stone back. "What does it do?"

"It's their blood," he said. "Their family. Two thousand years and more of not-quite-life, feeding off the great monsters of the deep. Two thousand years of recruiting sucker refugees kicked out of their homes by torchbearing lifers, two millennia of converts and dark miracles. All that power, all that hunger in a single package."

"It's a drug."

"It's a religion. It's more than a religion."

"You take it, and they own you. Like the dreamdust."

"They don't own me," he said. "When I take this, I can use their power. All the family's hunger is mine, as I need it. And when I'm done, when the power recedes, the dregs of my soul drain out into the ocean with theirs. I'll have to go there to fill myself. And what I get back won't be *me*. It'll be one drop of my blood to a million of theirs. I'll be a faint flavor. Most of what's left will be them."

"You'll die."

"You need help, and so does Seril, and so do Abelard and Tara. I've lived a long time already." He sat on a chair before his writing desk. "You're going to tell me to let it go."

"No."

"What, then?"

This was the part she'd had to get drunk for, and she wasn't drunk anymore. But then, if being sober made some things hard to say, maybe the things said were better for it. "You're not doing this because of some half-assed sense of civic duty to a place you don't live. You like Tara, and Abelard, and the others, but you're not doing it for them. You're doing it for me. Because Seril helped me get unfucked in the head, and you're afraid if she goes, I'll slide back to the way I was before."

"And this is the part where you curse me out for presuming to live your life for you, where you say you can handle yourself—"

"Listen to me."

He stopped.

"We keep second-guessing each other. I don't think we've been on the right foot two days running since this thing started."

"Maybe if you hadn't broken my neck that one time."

"Shut up," she said softly. "Please."

Water slapped the ship's side. A dockside drunk sang a warbling Talbeg song.

"Tomorrow I'll do something dumb for my goddess, and I might die. Tomorrow you'll do something just as dumb for me, and you might die. Tonight we deserve each other's honesty. This isn't my habit talking. I want to be with you now. Do you want to be with me?"

He said the word she was afraid to hear.

He could move faster than the human eye could follow. Now, though, he moved slow as a statue would be if it decided to walk. He joined her on the couch. His fingers were cool against her cheek, and she let out a breath as they traced the line of her jaw to her neck, and the line of her neck to her shirt.

She ripped his getting it off him, and tangled his pants in his boots; they had to stop and tug, laughing, together. The couch velvet was hot and soft against her skin, and he poised above her, one hand firm against her side. "Oh," he said, and cursed, rolled off the bed and returned a second later with a sheet. "Sorry. In case."

"It's fine," she said, and stood naked in the cabin; he was, too. Moonlight lit old scars on his skin and hers, but for now the scars were not the point.

They reclined again. She held him like a vise, and then, and then—

Mechanically, it wasn't altogether different from her other trysts. There were mouths and two tense bodies. He was strong, and so was she, which he knew when they were dressed but it took him a few minutes to understand it was still true when they were naked. She wouldn't break. Neither would he. There were teeth, too, and there was some blood, which the sheet caught, and there was sweat and meat and bones and spit and slickness.

There were no strange-godded cities beneath the waves; there were no necromancers lurking in the shadows. There were no contracts, no gargoyles, no moon, no water, no Justice.

Just us, she thought, and laughed.

It was enough.

Well. Once wasn't. So after a rest they tried again.

57

"I hate dungeons," Tara said when they reached the third lightning-lit gallery. Far above, leathery wings fluttered, too large and loud to belong to normal bats. A grim red glow lit their path, and as they walked Tara tried not to think about the writhing shapes in the shadowed halls to her left and right, or the stone's tremor underfoot like the quivering of a wounded animal's skin.

"It is a neat effect," Shale said.

"Neat is how a room looks when it's clean. This place could crush us." Crystal veins grew thicker on these walls, and their light left her shadowless and red. She switched off her hand torch. The tunnel narrowed; walls warmed her fingertips. She did not touch the crystal. "You know why we use anesthetic in surgery?"

"To spare the subject pain?"

"That's a nice side effect, but the real benefit's for the surgeon. Patients thrash when you cut them open. The body fights intrusion. Muscles clench and skew the scalpel." Another peristaltic tremor passed underfoot. False sunset lit the curving tunnel wall ahead. She smelled ozone and salt and bone. Something creaked. She hoped it was not the wall. "If your theory's right, we're performing surgery on a mountain. How do you sedate a rock?"

"I don't know."

"Exactly," she said, and then: "How long do you think we've been following this tunnel?"

"I—" He stopped. "I don't know."

"Neither do I." She showed him her watch. "Either we've lived through the last hour three times over, or she's adjusting time for reasons of her own."

"Are we still on schedule?"

"I have no idea." She stuffed the watch back in her pocket, not bothering to conceal her frustration. "What's fast here might be slow out there, or the other way round. The mountain's reflexes are fiercer near the wound. Which is why it's good and bad we're getting close."

"You expect trouble?"

Which was when they turned the corner and saw the bone-thing. "You could say that."

Their goal lay at the tunnel's end: the largest gallery yet, daylit almost with crystal and flame. Tara ignored that for the moment.

The bone-thing filled the tunnel mouth. Creaking, chattering, tangling and unwinding, it was no one shape entirely: an enormous bat's skeleton propped with smaller bones, needle-sharp tail links of cave mice and translucent ribs from dead blind fish, a surface monster's horned skull bleached by centuries. Wings tipped with curved claws flexed. Crimson lightning arced within the cage of its chest. Claw toes screeched chalk-white lines against the tunnel floor. Its jaw opened to roar, but no sound came.

Shale stepped forward, but she held out her arm to block him. "Surgery. No anesthetic. The more we fight down here, the worse it goes for us."

He growled. She knew how he felt.

The bone-thing pounced. Claw wings filled the tunnel.

Tara closed her eyes.

Fractal silver schema rushed toward her, the bone-thing a story told by the mountain's need. Tara's first aesthetic reaction was contempt. If she had submitted such sloppy work at the Schools, she'd have spent a week helping golems dig up corpses to remind her the costs of brute force.

Her second aesthetic reaction, though, was pleasure. Such baroque profusion of power! The bone-thing was so dense she could barely see its individual strands. Crufty dynamism at its best. No calculating mind would make something so excessive. But the bone-thing *was* made, for a purpose, which you could see if you knew where to look—

Help me it hurts it hurts it HURTS—

So all she had to do (though quickly, because the clawed critter's crossed half the distance between us already and only a fool trusts the arrow-flight paradox to keep her safe) was seize and redirect that purpose. I can ease the pain, if you help us.

She offered a simple contract to the bone-thing.

It fell in a clattering cascade. Wing tips drew sparks from stone walls as it tumbled. It landed in a crouch, so close it could tear out her throat before she blinked.

It did not.

It knelt.

She set her hand on the skull between its horns. Her fingers traced the bone's grain. "Think I'll call him Oss," she said. Glancing over her shoulder, she caught Shale staring. "Come on. Let's finish this before more show up."

Oss drew its wings aside to let them pass, and followed.

Tara had hoped the next gallery might be the last, and for once reality conformed to her wishes without sorcerous encouragement. The chamber into which Shale and Oss followed her was the largest they'd yet seen, cathedral tall, thicketed with arches and outcroppings of red crystal. Ghostly fire danced on its walls and floor. She was no geologist, but even ignoring the rest of their excursion so far she would have suspected there was something unnatural about the cave.

Aside, that is, from the man impaled by lightning in its center.

He hung like a fly in an enormous spiderweb, or a specimen mounted on pins of light: three feet off the ground in the center of a lightning column, limbs splayed rigid, eyes shut. More lightning shafts danced from his body to the crystal in the walls and back, lancing him only to fade and lance again. She remembered Hidden Schools' descriptions of brains, and the way a god looked splayed out in operant space beneath the knife.

Glyphs burned crimson on the man's skin, sharper and cruder and more extensive than she'd ever seen. His entire body was a single system designed by some twisted thaumaturge—no patterns, no machine tooling, just pictograms carved into his flesh by hand. She tried to imagine the pain of such work, the distortion of the mind, the risk of soul-rot from so much Craft. Who would dare?

"Is that him?" Shale asked.

"Altemoc," she said. "I think so. Matches the pictures. And those around him on the floor"—prone bodies covered by ghostflame—"must be his crew. Let's go."

She entered the lake of fire, and its flames shied from her feet. Beneath, where she expected rock, was a pane of what looked like diamond. Beneath the diamond coiled immense ropes of demonglass.

Tara blinked, and the nested thorns of light below nearly blinded her. Demon coils battered and scraped the floor. "Don't look down," she said, and knew from Shale's drawn breath that he had.

Green flame dripped from the walls. It bubbled and convulsed as she approached the floating man, and assumed huge apelike forms.

Oss's teeth clattered.

Shale regarded the fire-apes skeptically. "Can you fix them like you did our friend here?"

"The closer I come to Altemoc, the more damage my Craft does," she said, voice level. If she didn't stay calm, who would? "Oss should buy us some time."

"I'll see what I can do," Shale said. Displaced wind battered her. He suddenly occupied more space than he had moments before.

She neared the lightning nexus. Fire shapes closed in. One lunged at Tara, but several hundred pounds of gargoyle bowled it to the diamond floor. Oss charged two more elementals, and its bone talons tore through fire.

Tara set down her backpack, smoothed the lapels of her jacket, and stepped toward the lightning.

Uniformed figures splayed prone on the diamond floor, breathing deep. A cane lay at Altemoc's feet. She was close enough to see the man himself, thirty-two or -three, nice cheekbones, jawline a bit too narrow. The glyphs that shone through his suit were not glyphs at all, but scars.

She cleared her throat. Behind her, Shale roared and punched through an elemental's face. "Good morning," she said. It was morning somewhere. "I'm Tara Abernathy. The Two Serpents Group sent me to negotiate for your prisoners' release. To whom am I speaking?"

Altemoc's head jerked down to face her, a poorly managed marionette's movement. His eyes opened, and the space between his lids was flat and blinding red. Not a good sign. He opened his mouth. Bloodlight lit his teeth from within.

She was almost ready for the voice when it came: a man's wrapped around and through a woman's, if that woman were a thousand meters tall and made of fire.

What/have/you/done/

"Let's start with a name. You have me at a disadvantage."

Two elementals seized Shale's arms and tried to pull him apart. Moonlight from his wounds spilled on the diamond floor. His wings beat, the elementals lost their footing, and he pulled free—to rip one's leg from its body and swing it clublike into the other's face.

Firekeeper/call/me/or/Deathwarden/Thunderspeaker/Shewhoburns/

"Ms. Keeper," she said. "I think I understand most of your situation, but let's see if I have it right."

Speak/

"Down there, under our feet, you've trapped a raw demon, one that entered this world through a crack, unsummoned, without limits on its power. I didn't know that was possible in the pre-Craft era, but if you made me guess I'd say it came through during a war between gods, a few thousand years ago. About right?"

Gods/serpents/thosebeyond/outspiders/skazzerai/

"I don't need particulars. Most of the time, unbound demons pop into singularity and take a few cubic miles of planet along, but this one's big. It might have chewed up the whole world before it burst. So you caged it." Keep her talking. Don't think about what the thing beneath your feet might do if you screw up. "You tricked it into a part of your mind you clocked slow—a subjective second every million years, say. Must have used half the necromantic earths in Northern Kath to build this place. Impressive systems redundancy: any elements taken from the mountain will return in time. So millennia passed, until Kovak Central Mining started drilling."

An elemental tore Oss's wing free, only for the wing to transform to a bony claw that strangled the fire.

Ignore the battle. Focus on the—what was she at this point? Deponent? Witness? If so, Tara should be asking more questions.

Torment/tear/efficiency/reduced/lose/seconds-on-century/

"The mine damaged containment. You patched the wound by draining a convenient power source, which turned out to belong to the miners' filtration system. Necromantic slurry seeped into the water table, and zombies rose throughout Centervale. You didn't know what was happening—without human worshippers, your mind operates on a geologic time scale. So when Mr. Altemoc came to rescue his people, and used his scars to engage with you, well, you found a well-prepared mind to work through. He's fighting back, though. You can't think fast without him, but you can't digest him any more than you can digest a knife."

He/feels/no/pain/visions-dreams-past-paradise/offer/

"Let me be straight with you. You face a damages claim from Centervale Conglomerated Agriculture, another from KCMC, reckless endangerment and grievous harm from my employer, maybe tortious interference, a violation of the rule against perpetuities depending on whether you're technically alive, and that's before we address any personal claims brought by Mr. Altemoc, or by these folks on the ground." The Keeper was older than the Craft. How to translate? "The kind of power about to descend on you, it eats gods for breakfast. Neither of us wants to go down that road." Especially since your hole card's terrifying. "But we can make a deal."

Explain/

"Your containment system is, let's say." She licked her lips. Oss tried to bite through an elemental's face but only blackened its own jaw. "Inefficient. We've developed better. We know more about demons now than they did in your day—we might be able to put the devourer-of-worlds down there back where she came from. Even if that's impossible, the redundant ore you can spare by improving your efficiency will fetch a lot of soulstuff on the right market, and we could use that power to automate containment. You could walk the world again. Find believers. Or at least live without a demon gnawing your entrails."

No answer. Battle raged behind Tara, and below, demon coils grated against the diamond floor. Elementals piled on Shale, dragging him down. He ripped at their arms with his fangs and claws, but they were too many. He knelt. They pressed his face into the flame.

How/

"Let Mr. Altemoc and his people go. Then we broker a settlement with the mining Concern and CenConAg. If you play your cards right, there's freedom at the end of the tunnel. You've missed a lot in the last few thousand years."

Without/mouth/how/speak/

"There are ways. We could make you a golem. Mr. Altemoc might even volunteer for the task. But I need him now."

He/leaves/we/feel/no/time/why/trust/you/

Because I need you to. "Because we're going to make a deal," she said.

Performance/clear/what/consideration/you/offer/

She licked her lips.

What would the Keeper accept? Tara didn't have the time or resources to build a vessel for the mountain-mind. No promises of future payment would satisfy, since without Altemoc's mind the Keeper had no sense of time.

She needed a body.

Terror welled from a pit within Tara, filling her stomach, heart, lungs. Blood rushed in her ears. Doors long locked inside her mind swung open, memories of shadowed days, the feeling of herself bent by another's hands. But she could do this. Her glyphs would offer the goddess purchase on her mind, and keep her intact—for a while, at least.

Shale could make their case for Altemoc. If he faltered, the goddess could speak through him. It was a long shot, but what other chance did they have, outfought in the mountain's depths, surrounded by flame? Without Altemoc, they had nothing. Without Tara, they had a chance.

Nothing was worth losing herself again, feeling another wear her. Nothing?

Moonrise over Alt Coulumb seen from the ruined orrery. From the air, gargoyle-borne, the city's rampant streets made sense the way some abstract paintings did, the ones mad drunks made by throwing cans of paint onto canvas. Dancers twirled at the Club Xiltanda. These were beautiful and broad, too large to hold in the mind. But she remembered Cat, and Abelard that night in the tower: *I don't trust God anymore.* And, later, in the airport, an awkward embrace.

Nothing, no thing, was worth what she was about to do.

Maybe some people were.

She opened her mouth. "I—"

"I'll do it."

She turned, too shocked to speak.

Shale stood beside her, bleeding silver through his cracks. Carbon scores crisscrossed his chest. One arm had burned black to the elbow. Fire dripped from him. The elementals were gone. He must have beaten them back while she wasn't looking.

Acceptable/vessel/

"No," she said. "No, dammit."

"It's the right choice," he said.

"It's not any kind of choice. We are not doing this. I won't let you."

"We need you to finish the negotiation. To get back to the city."

"If Seril loses you, She'll—"

His laugh was shallow and sad. "Without me," he said, "She may weaken. Without you, She will fall."

"There has to be another way."

"You were about to give yourself up. If there was another option, you would have taken it."

She said nothing.

"I will stand in his place," Shale said. "You will return, and save me."

"If we win."

"If we lose, I would have been dead anyway. And you will not lose."

"It could take years to get you out. You'll be in pain the whole time. You'll barely even be you."

He shrugged. His right arm hung at a wrong angle. "I have endured worse. My wounds will help: if the Keeper forces too much of herself through me, I will shatter and she will return to timelessness."

"That is a stupid definition of 'help.' You'll be in pain down here until—"

"Until you rescue me," he said, and to the goddess: "What do you say, Lady?"

Yes/

"It's the right choice, Tara."

It was. That was the worst part.

You can't outsmart everything.

There was a heat in her eyes she did not want to name. She looked from the goddess to the gargoyle, and back. "Shale," she said, "is my," and there was only the slightest pause before she said "friend. If you hurt him in any way, I will carve your bones into his monument. You have slept too long to know that you should fear me, but I am a Craftswoman of the Hidden Schools, and my people have slain the hosts of heaven and bound continents in iron chains. I will snap your spine and drink ichor from your skull, I will break you and the demon downstairs alike and send you wailing together to the stars as a feast for the beings that lurk there, if you give me cause. Do not fuck with me."

Lightning quivered. Tara did not breathe. Neither did Shale, which was to be expected. He took her hand.

Understood/

Shale touched her shoulder. "Finish this," he said.

"I will."

He approached the lightning, and with a wingbeat rose level with Altemoc in the air. He leaned into the red and brought his muzzle to the other man's lips.

He screamed. A tower fell.

The lightning took him by pieces, darting forks tonguing stone skin before they approved the taste and pierced. His head rocked, his wings draped, his teeth flashed. A hundred ropes or spears of light bound him to the chamber walls. The brilliant central column vibrated like a plucked string, a thunderous cascade that went on and on.

When the world stilled, Shale hung in the light, and Altemoc lay crumpled on the ground.

Tara ran to the man; he groaned. She slapped him on the cheek. No response. Twice, three times, leaving sharp white finger tracks on ocher skin. His eyes opened, neither fixed nor focused. She heard a deep groaning, cracking sound. The ground beneath them shook. So did the walls.

"Who—"

She slapped him again for good measure.

"Hey! Who the hells—where—"

"Introductions later. We need to get out of here."

He groped for the fallen cane and struggled with its aid to his feet. His shoulders bent into a U. "My people."

They were waking up, slowly. She scanned the chamber for a tool, and saw, shattered to pieces but still clattering for someone to fight, Oss. Still hers.

Assembling him would take too long—gaps opened in the floor, and the walls were closer together than they had been. The cave system was reconfiguring to fit Shale. But Oss's bones still moved, and they would serve.

Oss's pieces scuttled to lift the fallen crew. A wing separated into centipede spines, wrapped limbs and lifted; a claw propped up another. Arm bones prepared themselves to roll. Multiplicitous phalanges supported a fallen woman. They skittered toward the door as the cave collapsed. "Come on," she said. "My friend back there made a bad deal with a mad goddess to save you. And I may have threatened her, just a bit."

He blinked. "You're crazy."

"You always question the sanity of women who've just saved your ass?"

He smiled, too broad, and almost fainted. She grabbed him by the lapels. "No time for that. We need to move."

Shale stared down on them through the lightning. Hells burned to ash in his eyes.

Run! she said through him.

They did.

58

Abelard kept dawn vigil on the morning of the war. Bede and Nestor and Aldis and the rest of the Council of Cardinals gathered in the sanctum to kneel, knees permitting, before the flame. Their chant swelled. Stars pinpricked the gray-blue sky. Eastward past the docks, a pale pink glow heralded the sun.

Crystal palaces flew south through the Business District, wreathed in sparks and rainbows. Their edges bled starlight. They should not be here, not in Alt Coulumb, free city of gods and men. Even the Hidden Schools had breached the city's airspace only once, while his Lord was dead.

These skyspires were not scavengers or opportunists. They came to kill.

No. That wasn't quite true.

The spires were weapons built to break cities, but even the fiercest weapons were only tools. About the spires, before them—so small they should have been invisible at this distance but were not, were instead singular points radiating darkness—hovered Craftsmen. Their fingers rested on rune-marked triggers.

Abelard blinked. He lacked training in the Craft, but God let him see its traces. He was glad he lacked training. Were his sorcerous vision more acute, he would have been blinded by the burn.

Hellfire webbed the black. Bonds of power tied the invaders—the opposing counsel—together. And two shapes hovered at the center of that infernal rose: a spider of crystal and thorn, and something else, a roil of worms and teeth.

Daphne Mains and Madeline Ramp, vanguard of the opposition.

"Impressive, aren't they?" Cardinal Evangelist Bede stood by his side. He squeezed his hands as if working dough. "Each member of

Ramp's commission has sent observers to watch us fall. All this because I did not sign their deal."

The Cardinal, Abelard realized, was scared. Abelard had no reassurance to offer.

So he was surprised when he found himself saying, "They'll be disappointed."

"Do you think so?"

He hadn't before he spoke, but he remembered Slaughter's Fell, the depth of faith in that young girl as he marked her forehead with ash above her glasses. Even the church's smell seemed golden. "I believe in this city. I believe in Tara. I believe in our Lord, and His Lady."

Bede's head declined, and rose again. "Thank you." He squeezed Abelard's shoulder and went to kneel with the other Cardinals.

And thank you, Abelard prayed. The words had been his, and the urge to speak—but a greater power calmed his fear to let them pass his lips.

He felt the fire beneath Alt Coulumb and within its people.

He turned to the altar. Craftsmen would fight the external battle. Theirs was the inner war.

Nestor stood before them. For once the old man did not clear his throat before he spoke. "Let us pray."

Kneeling, Abelard joined himself to God.

Madeline Ramp and Daphne Mains stood on air. A city lay at their feet and a host at their backs.

"Pleasant morning," Ramp said.

Beautiful, in fact. The air sweet with coming triumph. Pleasure climbed Daphne's backbone and nestled behind her heart. "Yes, ma'am."

"Are you ready?"

"I am." She hadn't realized it until asked.

A silver circle surrounded them, and beyond it stood the Judge, clothed in the shadows of her office. She burned too black to bear.

Daphne squinted and turned away; Ms. Ramp's second eyelids closed.

"I call these proceedings to order," the Judge said in a voice that should have broken the ground and let devils spew forth. "We consider the matter of Associated Creditors and Shareholders against Kos Everburning of Alt Coulumb, and Seril Undying of the same."

"For which our thanks," Ms. Ramp replied. "We are prepared, once opposing counsel show themselves."

"Oh," said a new voice, scalpel cold and similarly curved, from across the circle, "we're here."

The voice's owner wore a white three-piece suit, immaculate. A silver mask covered half a face Telomeri artists would have given their tongues to paint. The eye beneath that mask was red; its mate, still human, the blue Daphne had seen in glacial fissures. One skeletal hand closed around a cane.

Two associates in charcoal gray flanked Ashleigh Wakefield. They might have been Wakefield's shadows, or afterimages.

"A pleasure as always," Ramp said with a sharp slight smile. "Your clients have willfully misrepresented their God in market filings. Kos Everburning is a greater investment risk than his priesthood claims. In specific we allege that the God and His church are exposed through their off-books relationship with the renegade Goddess known as Seril Undying."

Wakefield's head edged to one side, like a cat considering a mouse that, rather than cowering, had performed a backflip. "Unfounded accusations. Kos's filings were correct, his exposure is managed, and his relationship with Seril Undying founded on mutual collaboration rather than strict liability as you claim. The nature of Kos's bond with Seril does not subject investors and creditors to undisclosed risk."

"You'll forgive us if we don't take your word for it."

"Why else would we be here?" Wakefield said. "Surely you would not waste Her Honor's time."

"You're dangerously close," the Judge said. "Present arms, Counsel, or get out of my sky."

Ramp raised her hands, a staged surrender. "Of course, Your Honor. By all means, let us reach the point. We begin with the portion of our complaint directly addressing Kos's personal vulnerability, and that of his church. Permit me to introduce to the court my associate, Ms. Mains."

With those words, the cold behind Daphne's heart turned. She thrilled to the sensation of herself unlocking, of long-dormant glyphs drawing light from the sky and power from the army arrayed behind her. The tight-wound trap of her mind sprung.

Somewhere in the unfolding, a girl screamed with her voice.

She ignored the scream.

Wakefield's human eye widened slightly, but the being who was still, basically, Daphne noticed.

She smiled with sharp teeth and moved to the circle's center. "Thank you, Ms. Ramp. Now, let us begin."

She raised her hands, long fingered and strange, and made the world go mad.

Tara and Altemoc and the bone-borne bodies landed on the dry ground of the miners' camp as the tunnel collapsed behind them. Dust choked the sky, but sharp morning sunlight shafted through. Tara stared into the sky's bright face as the dust settled, and knew despair.

They'd spent too long wandering in the Keeper's twisted time. Human shapes approached through dust, shambling over unsteady ground; they seized her arms and bore her from the tumbling rock. She choked on polluted air. She had not realized how tired she'd become, how little soul remained to her.

The sky blued as they carried her from the dust. Altemoc ran to the Quechal woman who had met Tara on her arrival at camp. His rhythm was off, or Tara's was, the clock of her heart erratic. The woman hugged him, fierce, stepped back and shouted words Tara couldn't sort from one another. Altemoc pointed at the mountain in stutter-step motion, slow and too fast at once.

Gray chewed the edges of her vision, and her colors bled. The ground was not where she expected it to be, the force vector into her ankle a crucial few degrees off just. She fell hard on her knee, felt trousers, stocking, and skin tear.

Human speech was wind through a flapping aperture of meat. Altemoc ran three-legged toward her, mouth producing more dumb meat-sounds. The fields back home looked like this in the hours before dawn, hueless and achromatic. But the home wind tasted of earth and dew and waking things. Where was that taste now? Had she lost it?

He caught her, and his scars burned green.

The sun rose.

59

Corbin Rafferty heard a thunderclap of silence.

That was new.

The screams weren't. There were always screams inside his head these days.

But he had never heard (or not-heard) silence like this. It fell like a ten-ton sandbag and broke as suddenly. The cries and hospital noise, metronome ticks and cart wheels and doctors' footsteps, returned as if never interrupted, until the silence struck again.

The silent bell peals were hands that squeezed his heart, lungs, stomach.

Am I dying? Is this how death feels?

His arms did not tingle; he felt no pain in his head. He *heard,* but there was nothing to hear.

The moon had dragged him through so many nightmare memories, his life seen from outside as if a stranger lived it. He did not like this stranger. But this silence was not of the moon: always in those dreams he heard the crash of surf on the beach where he'd wept when she left.

He opened his eyes. He could not do that in the dreams, which was part of their torture: he felt his body as an inmate felt prison walls. But he opened his eyes, and closed them at the brilliance of the day. No, not of day: of fire in the sky, of fire that was the sky.

He howled in panic and the sky *clenched.* Silence pealed through him, broke his cry in half. When he could hear again, he closed his mouth.

He was awake. Some cataclysm had struck the city, and in the chaos he'd wormed free of the moon's grip.

He sat up in the narrow bed. A tile floor lay cool beneath his bare feet. He looked down at himself. Twiggy limbs jutted from the hospital gown. How long had he been out? Days. His stomach turned when he remembered the Paupers' Quarter market, remembered his fury at the world, at his daughters, remembered his hand raising the cane, remembered blood on Sandy's face and Matt's—

He doubled over, choking stiff, wet sobs the waves of silence made staccato. He clawed his sheets.

Anger filled him. Fury. At Matt for his betrayal. At Sandy Sforza. And above all towered his rage at the Stone Men and their wicked moon, the laughing white face, the cruel gentle hands that made him watch his own life mad and broken in a dark mirror.

He wanted to vomit, but there was nothing in his stomach to cast out.

He had to leave this place, these scraping sheets, this disinfectant stink.

Corbin stood, fell, stood again with his hand on the mattress for balance. His knees wiggled. A curtain hung beside his bed. If he clung to that, he could reach the wall, and then the door.

He gripped the curtain, trusted it with his weight—

And fell. Curtain rings tore free of the frame and he stumbled into the neighboring bed, occupied by a mountainous man, dark, bearded, with close-cropped hair.

A chair rested beside the bed, and a folded and sealed letter lay on the nightstand, addressed to Umar.

"Sorry, Umar," Rafferty mumbled. Nurses must have heard him fall. If they found him, they wouldn't let him go. Matt would have pressed charges, or Sandy. Or the girls. He couldn't bear another minute here. The silence came again, and went. Lightning cracked the sky, without thunder to match.

Umar's eyes were open.

Rafferty cried and lurched back. Blue wheels spun within Umar's brown irises.

Umar sat up. His movements were inhumanly precise. His neck moved independent of his torso. Shoulders and jaw popped, but he did not seem to notice. He stared at Rafferty.

Corbin raised his hands, but Umar moved faster. One hand caught Corbin's throat and squeezed. Corbin went kitten limp, but Umar kept squeezing, as if he didn't plan to stop until his fingers reached bone.

Then the hand loosened—barely.

"She's touched you." If Umar's movements were wrong, his voice was worse, deep and resonant with bass, with another voice underneath or inside, a woman's if glass spoke like a woman. Transparent tendrils writhed between the man's teeth. "I can taste her."

Corbin could almost breathe. There was no doubt which *she* he meant. "Yes," he said. "Seril." The name stung his lips. Damn her moon that burned in his mind, damn her sea that rose to drown him, damn her stone that cased his arms and legs. "Cursed me. Turned my own against me."

"Aid me," Umar said. "I will give you vengeance. You will help slay her."

Was vengeance even possible? "She's a goddess. We can't." Babbling, humbled, terrified, Corbin felt strangely unashamed. Umar's wrist was as thick as Corbin's neck. Bantamweight Corbin Rafferty had fought men three times his size to prove he could, got the shit kicked out of him and laughed. It was—comfortable?—to face a man he could not fight.

Umar's grip tightened again. Corbin pried at the man's fingers without success.

Corbin might die here. Die here, at the hands of this man who had offered him revenge. "Yes," he croaked. "Yes, dammit."

Steel-clamp fingers released Corbin's throat. He fell to his knees, panting, rubbing his neck. He'd have a bruise for a collar. Umar reviewed the room's contents. He did not seem to notice the letter on the bedside table. "Let us go."

"We can't just go. We need—"

"I need nothing."

"You need pants."

"Follow." Umar walked toward the door. Rafferty looked away from the open back of the man's gown. Somehow he found his feet and balance and followed. Revenge. Was it possible, to kill a goddess? To break her hold on him, and on his girls? To cast off his own humiliation, to reclaim his life from the lies the moon-dreams spun?

Orderlies wheeled a convulsing patient down the hall. Umar turned in the opposite direction, toward the stairs. A gray-uniformed guard emerged from the stairwell door, saw Umar and Rafferty. "Get back in your rooms. There's an emergency. We need—"

Umar did not let the guard finish. Corbin didn't see what Umar did, but the guard fell and lay still; Umar knelt, pulled off the man's shoes, and removed his pants. Then he shed his gown, pulled on the guard's slacks, and buttoned them. "Pants," Umar said.

"You just—" The guard groaned. "Hey!"

Umar turned back to Corbin; another guard ran out from the stair behind him. That guard's mouth opened when he saw his fallen comrade; he reached for the truncheon at his belt, but Umar caught him by the neck and slammed him into the wall. A peal of silence ate the thud of the guard's skull against plaster. The guard fell, and plaster flakes drifted down onto him. Umar knelt, placed his fingers precisely to either side of the guard's jugular, and pressed. The man squirmed like a caught snake, kicked twice, then rag-dolled. Umar pointed to the body—still breathing—stood, and walked away.

Corbin pried off the guard's shoes, pulled down his pants, and started to unbutton the shirt. Umar had already vanished through the stairwell door. Corbin tore the rest of the buttons from the guard's shirt and followed, hopping into pant legs. "How are we going to do it?" he shouted to Umar. "How can we hurt her?"

The ground floor was a mob of running orderlies, shouted commands, cries of pain and need. Ghostlights flickered. Periodic silences shattered the noise to nonsense. Umar broke the crowd like a tugboat's prow broke waves—poorly, with a lot of froth and commotion. When they reached the fire exit, Corbin tensed, ready to run, but Umar touched the alarm box, said words another silence ate, and opened the door.

The alarm did not protest their exit into the alley.

They were free.

Corbin looked up.

He was a simple man. He bought vegetables from farmers, and sold them. He worked with simple men who prayed for blessings on their crop, who plowed with oxen and fertilized with cow shit and sweat. Not for him the death-tainted fields of Central Kath, zombie workers and demon-haunted scythe machines and alchemical poisons. Corbin

Rafferty, and his girls, avoided all that. They kept the soulstuff they earned in the same altar his great-grandfather carved from the heartwood of a tree he felled. Corbin drank—who didn't?—but he never touched dreamdust. The last few days were easily the strangest of his life.

So he had no words for what he saw overhead.

A silver wheel burned in the center of the sky—its exact center, no matter where he looked, as if the city he inhabited was only a reflection of some deeper city to which the wheel belonged. A seamless curtain of fire stretched from the wheel, burning in all the colors fire really was but people never said: purple and green and black as a week-old wound. Needles of light pierced the fire. But the needles were also enormous worms, *eating* the fire with mouths of crystal teeth. And in the center of the wheel he saw another wheel, in which a star of black and a star of white danced, moving so fast they left tracks in air. When the tracks met, the world turned, and the silent thunder pealed—and in that emptiness he heard words that made no sense yet were more real than the air he breathed.

—as maintained in the quarterly report, which if Your Honor will be so kind as to—

Somewhere a hammer struck a wooden table and made no sound because the sound it made was silence.

He knelt. He could not look at that sky. And worst of all was the chattering inside him, that if he just looked up long enough he could understand everything, why June left and why he hurt and what he should have said—

A hand caught his shoulder. There was no tenderness in the touch. "Follow," Umar said.

Corbin wept. "I can't." He gestured openhanded at the sky. "Look at that. It's so big."

Umar did not look. "I do not need you," he said. "But you can aid me. And in return I will let you hurt her. No god is so great that small weapons cannot bring her low. I will make you mistletoe. Without me, you will rail for eons outside her temple and end trapped in nightmares. Be of use to me, or surrender yourself to her."

Needs warred in him: safety, revenge, control.

Corbin would have done anything to turn from that bleeding, burning sky. If Umar, or the thing that rode him, told Corbin to tear his eyes from their sockets, he would have hooked his thumbs and gouged.

But this was better. This way, the moon would die, and he would own himself again.

Corbin followed Umar through empty streets. Concrete tore his bare soles.

60

Tara woke in an army-green fog. Two blinks, three, focused the world, added edges and depth and form to color. Words came next: tent, cot, sun. Shale. Once she worked past monosyllables: mission.

She sat up fast, blinking blood-motes away.

"Here," someone said. She reached for the voice, found a glass of water, and drank until the water froze to ice and clicked against her teeth. Frost feathered from her grip on the glass.

She heard a man laugh, and swung round on the cot to face him. She was clothed—shirt untucked, slacks torn and wrinkled, and unshod, but dressed enough for modesty if not for armor. She set down the glass and glared across the tent at Altemoc. "What's so funny?"

He sat in a folding chair, ankle crossed over knee, cane propped against his hip. His fingers trailed over the frog crouched on a silver globe that served for his cane's handle. "You reminded me of someone," he said. "How's your head?"

"Outside of the tap-dancing elephants, I'm fine." Exploring, her fingers found a scabbed cut beneath her hair. She asked the question she'd been dreading: "What day is it?"

"You've been asleep two hours."

"I grayed out. I shouldn't be up for days. If ever."

"I gave you soulstuff. You're fine."

"What was the contract? What did you offer? What did you ask me for?"

"Nothing." He raised his hand. Green fire danced down his scars and faded. "That's not how we work."

"You offer services free of charge."

"Not exactly," he said, and spun the cane. "Our beneficiaries aren't the ones who pay. A Deathless Queen on a throne of melted swords asks us to heal a War-made plague in a border village. The plague poses her no threat, but she doesn't want the people of that village dead."

"Out of the goodness of her heart?"

"I used to think that," he said, "but that's a village of potential customers. Hard to rule if your instrument of rule breaks the land it touches. Craftwork destroys the world, so it must learn to heal."

She did not rise to the bait.

Only three hours lost. Somewhere in Alt Coulumb, the case began. There had to be some way to salvage this. For Shale, locked under a mountain in a goddess's mind. For Seril. For Alt Coulumb, besieged. "How much do you remember?" she asked.

"Most of it. I was alive, inside her. Her will was mine, but not. Like I was part of something bigger."

Tara knew the feeling. She did not shiver. "You know my name. You know why I've come."

"You're Tara Abernathy. And you need something from me. I have little enough to give."

The ice in her glass melted. She tried to stand, and swayed, and settled back onto the cot. "Last year, the King in Red gave you some unreal estate—specifically, Alt Coulumb's sky."

"He did."

"Do you know why he was so generous?"

Altemoc trapped the spinning frog between his fingers and spun it again. The movement was tight, practiced, obsessive. She remembered a friend from the Hidden Schools, Daphne's ex, a sometime gambler; he kept a stack of poker chips on his desk to rifle as he read. "He likes our work."

"He gave them up because they weren't his to give. He took them from the corpse of Seril Undying, Lady of the Moon—he thought. Deathless Kings accept the right of salvage; the King in Red used his rights to Alt Coulumb airspace as collateral, even if he couldn't exploit them directly due to Kos Everburning's competing claim. Back in the Wars, when people thought all gods would be dead by the century's end, those rights were worth millions of souls."

Altemoc whistled.

"With those funds, the King in Red rebuilt Dresediel Lex and made himself a peer of the world. Without them he would have had to accept more outside investment in RKC, which would have reduced his control over your city. Ancient history. The King's salvage rights depend on Seril's death, but she wasn't really dead. She returned last year. Her survival negates the King in Red's claim. Theft is more optically uncomfortable than salvage. Modern banks do a lot of business with Old World sovereign churches, which don't like reminders of the bad old days."

Spin. Trap. Spin. Trap. "He gave us the sky."

"I imagine he wrote it off as a tithe on his foreign income filings, since your Concern looks a lot like a clerical aid bureau."

"He's a donor," Altemoc said, as if that explained everything.

Here's the critical part, Ms. Abernathy. Take care. "Seril sent me to ask you to return Her sky."

He stopped spinning the cane. Bad tell, that. "You're offering a trade?"

"No. Seril is under attack. She's too weak to defend Herself, let alone pay market value for something so enormous."

"You're talking about two years of operating budget. We could rebuild cities with that power. Heal people."

"If the Goddess had anything to offer in trade, I wouldn't be here."

"I wish I could help you," he said.

That was it. The flat no.

She heard gods die a long way off, and did not like the sound.

"Mr. Altemoc."

"Caleb." His voice was flat and a little sad, as if his first name were the greatest concession he could offer.

"Caleb. I studied your Concern on our trip here from Dresediel Lex. A bridge between gods and men, that's your slogan."

"Yes."

"That's Alt Coulumb. The city's not perfect, but its gods are trying, and so's the church. For forty years Kos ruled alone, complacent. With Seril back, He's worked more to help His city. If She goes, He'll collapse."

"I have to care for my people." She heard the thorn twisting in his voice. "What would I tell the board?"

"Tell them you spent their donations to save a city. To heal a wound made long ago, in the Wars." She shifted forward on the bed and laced her fingers. "I'm not a hired gun. I have friends in Alt Coulumb. I left them to fight a losing battle on the chance you could help us. Shale, who took your place, he's under that mountain wrestling a demon-goddess from the dawn of time so we can have this conversation. I am breaking every rule of negotiation: I have no leverage to exploit, and no alternative. You don't know me well enough to know how hard that is. But here I am. What would you do, if these were your friends?"

He had an even, unreadable expression.

Gambler, for certain—and knowing that, she knew illegibility was a mask he wore to hide.

His eyes were darker than hers, but a gold halo surrounded the pupils, like a false-colored picture of a collapsing star.

"Save them," he said.

She waited.

"The board will kill me."

She wouldn't fault them if they did, but she didn't say that. Nor could she say any of the other preprogrammed words: you've made the right decision, or, pleasure doing businesses, or let's talk details. She managed "thank you," and hoped it was enough.

He touched a bruise on his cheek. "Now I know why you hit me so hard."

"You have a punchable face."

"That explains a lot." He held out his hand. The scars there took fire. "Good luck, Ms. Abernathy."

"Tara," she said. Small concession for a small concession.

"Tara."

They shook, as did the world.

61

Corbin followed Umar down empty Ember Street. He did not look up at the impossible sky, but could not escape it by looking down. Weird lights cast weird shadows. Twisting reflections shimmered from shop windows, from parked carriages, from skyscrapers, from the muscles of Umar's back.

Corbin rarely ventured this far into the Business District, domain of witches and madmen in jackets that should have been straight. But he knew it was not supposed to be like this: streets and sidewalks bare, workers huddled in offices or homes. Several blocks away a Blacksuit shouted *Remain calm. The danger will pass.*

The danger did not look like it would pass to Corbin. He could not tell how much time had elapsed since he left the hospital. There was no sun, or else the sun was everywhere.

Umar did not seem bothered by the sky, by the emptiness, or by his bare feet. Corbin's soles were dirt crusted now, his steps ginger. "Where are we going?"

"Here." Umar pointed as they turned left. Corbin felt a chill that had nothing to do with the atmosphere.

A white marble colonnade supported a peaked roof. White steps descended from double doors to the street. A robed statue of a blind-folded woman stood atop the steps, one arm raised, holding scales.

"There should be paint," Umar said. "Many colors. The white is a mistake."

"Why are we going to the Temple of Justice? Will it help us against"—he still could not think of the moon without cringing—"her?"

"I need a weapon," he said.

"You can't break into a temple."

Umar pointed to the sky. Corbin did not look. "Justice is busy."

"There are three Blacksuits on those stairs."

"We will not use the front door," Umar said. "Follow me. Or not."

He did.

Umar led him down an alley to an office building stitched by skyways to the temple and surrounded by a tall fence. Umar vaulted the fence and somehow severed the barbed wire at its top. Corbin climbed after him, landed harder than he'd hoped on the other side, and hopped after Umar, brushing gravel from the pads of his feet. He knew better than to speak, though he also should have known better than to follow.

Still. Revenge.

Umar broke the chain off a loading dock door with the heel of his hand. Behind the door, steps led into a darkness made deeper by dim light. Umar climbed down.

Corbin looked up out of habit, to search the sky for guidance. At that moment, the world's colors inverted, reddened, and failed; everything became matte black with edges suggested by thin lines like those a razor left through paint. The illusion, if illusion it was, could not have lasted a second, but when it ended he had a sense it had endured much longer—that something had gone out of the reasserted world, some note stilled he'd been hearing so long he no longer knew how silence sounded.

He ran into the basement and pulled the doors shut to close away that sky.

The basement was not built to reassure. Bare pipes dripped onto bare concrete floors. Piled boxes closed him in, their cardboard stamped with serial numbers and bar-code glyphs. No Umar. A door in the far wall stood open.

He slid through the door into a hallway broad enough for four men abreast. Voices carried around a corner. "Freeze!" He heard bare feet, running.

A crossbow bolt tore down the crosswise hall, leaving a crackle of spent lightning. Corbin peered around the corner in time to see Umar vault a desk at the hallway's end and punch the guard in his throat. They fell together. Umar's hand tightened into a fist, then descended with the sound Ray Capistano's cleaver made when he cut steak.

Umar stood, holding keys. He tried one key in the lock of the door behind the watchman's desk, and when it didn't work he tried another.

"They'll hunt you down."

"They are busy."

"They'll come for you when it's done."

"If they find me." Corbin had grown used to Umar's doubled voice, but that laugh still twisted in his chest.

The fifth key worked.

They walked between two wire cages, behind which rested neat arrays of shelves: a library of danger. Corbin did not recognize most of the contents of those shelves, and when he did, he wished he didn't. A diamond-bladed sword bloomed with purple light, and a paper tag marked its gold hilt. Beside it lay a pipe with a rusty stain at one end, likewise tagged. Bags of powder in many colors. A single six-sided die. A spike-knuckled glove slicked with greenish oil. A deck of playing cards. A pair of red slippers. A sheaf of blasting rods. Tagged, tagged, tagged, tagged, tagged. That was the first floor.

On the next level down, each shelf held a single object surrounded by a blue Craft circle. Nothing here struck him as unusual in form: a book bound in pale tan leather. A corduroy blazer. A bow tie. A silvery mechanical wand with a green gem at one end. An unadorned ring. A knife with a wooden handle. A clay cup.

The knife whispered like a woman, not like any woman but like June in bed when they were young together, before everything. The wand sang. The blazer pulsed when he looked at it too long.

He drew closer to Umar.

On the third floor each cage held a single item, and he did not look at these.

The fourth floor held no cages, only doors: three on either side. Ghostlights glowed green above the lintels. Umar walked to the last door on the left, stood in front of it, and placed one hand above the latch.

Corbin felt cold. Sweat drops studded Umar's face. His lips curled open, a skeleton's grin. Shadows deepened in the hollows of his cheeks. Flared nostrils expelled steam. Corbin had seen Umar move through men like wheat, but turning his hand a few degrees clockwise seemed to break him.

The latch clicked open. The light above the door went red.

Umar sagged.

Frost covered the doors and walls. Corbin shivered, not just from the cold. "Open," Umar told him.

He should not. Whatever was inside this room, it was bigger than Corbin Rafferty. But he'd come this far when he should have turned back at every step. And he knew no other way to hurt Her.

He opened the door.

Inside was more a closet than a room. A single table occupied most of the space, surrounded by a glowing silver circle on the concrete floor. A folded jacket and slacks lay on the table, and worn brown leather shoes. Red suspenders coiled like snakes atop the clothes. Beside them stood a steel box.

Corbin pointed, mutely, to the circle.

"It will not hurt you," Umar said.

Corbin stepped across, as if diving into the ocean on a winter day. He did not die. He felt nothing, in fact.

"Bring me the box."

"What's inside?"

"Bring it to me."

Corbin touched the box, found it cool. Lifted the latch. Packing immaterial swathed the inside, viscous and opaque. He reached into the immaterial and felt a pitted surface like dried, bleached wood. His fingertips traced a dome larger than two big fists pressed together, and ridged at the front, with two large holes and a third triangular gap beneath them. Many-voiced incoherent whispers filled his ears.

Wind whistled through bare grass on a stony moor. Sirens wailed.

He lifted the skull from the box.

Silver lines crossed and recrossed the bone, and cut his eyes like knives. They moved as he watched. Turned. Danced.

The skull weighed nothing in his hand. It grew, filling the closet cell though somehow it still fit in Corbin's hand. Bone bowed out the concrete walls. Corbin stared into the gulf of its eye socket. At that bottomless pit's bottom, he saw a glint of fire. He could fall into the skull, burning like priests said rocks burned as they fell from space, to become the fire there himself.

"Return the skull to the box," Umar said. "And close the box. Bring both to me."

Given the choice between nameless dread and simple obedience, Corbin's body chose the latter.

He dropped the skull, or tried. It stuck to his hand. He must have been too afraid to let it go. That had to be the reason. But at last the skull slipped from his palm into the packing shadows, and the box snapped shut. Corbin must have closed it. The evidence locker sub-basement felt too still, too quiet.

He cradled the box to his chest, carried it back across the circle, and offered it to Umar. "Take the thing." Cold spread from the metal into his arms.

"Not now," Umar said. "Follow."

He ran. So did Corbin.

The sub-basement blurred around them, lockers and cages and unconscious guard, bare-piped basement and concrete steps. Then they were out in the yard, running under a coal-black sky tangled with ropes of green-purple light like sailors said they saw far north. But those were supposed to be soft lights, while these were hard like thorns, and rainbow blood flowed where they stuck. Umar climbed the fence first, held out his hands. Corbin tossed the box to him and followed. Chain links rattled beneath his weight like they hadn't under Umar's.

As he crested the fence, he heard a nightmare voice.

Stop.

Shit.

He fell hard. His ankle twisted. He felt no pain, from his ankle or from his torn soles—he was too scared for pain. Umar sprinted for the alley. Corbin's legs wouldn't do as he asked. A Blacksuit chased them. Only one, the rest on patrol or doing gods knew what, but one was enough.

Corbin ran into the alley, into Umar. Who had stopped.

"We cannot outrun it," Umar said, and set the box down.

Light quaked monochrome again, leaving serrated patches of light and dark. Umar's face looked like saws fucking.

Corbin tried to speak but made no sound.

Experience broke to key frames robbed of movement, like woodcuts in a children's book. Umar looking up. Corbin turning. The Blacksuit frozen in midleap (it was a woman, under the Suit). Umar, dodging to strike the Suit's face with his fist. The Suit fell, recovered. Hit Umar in the gut. Knocked him into the wall. Umar hit the Suit in the jaw with the heel of his hand. No effect. Suited fingers reached for his neck. Umar's mouth snapped open. Glass wires flicked from between his teeth and caught the Suit, and pierced and peeled. The Suit staggered. She fell beside the box, silver pooling reflective from her skin to leave her human.

Motion returned, and color, the loud bark of those silent seconds' sound released at once. Umar panted. Cuts around his mouth bled black. Corbin stared at the fallen Blacksuit. She lay still, but breathing.

Umar lifted the box. "Come." His voice sounded less human now.

Corbin hobbled after him. With every turn and every block he expected Blacksuits to descend. Maybe Justice was distracted? Maybe whatever Umar did, or whatever the thing *inside* Umar did, broke the Suit's tie to its Lady? But to think such a thing—to attack Justice herself, to fight her messengers and win—was to frame a world gone mad.

Madder still: to find, after a long run through twisting alleys, an open post office. To follow Umar in, watch him empty the steel chest's contents into a cardboard box, tape the box shut, and write an address Corbin could not read. A clerk waited behind the desk, cheek puddled around his knuckles, bored, as if the day were sunless due to rain. The clerk looked twice at Umar's bare chest, but only twice. "Anything fragile, liquid, perishable, or hazardous?"

"No," Umar said, and paid what he was asked.

"What the hells did we just do?" Corbin shouted at him when they were safe in the empty street again, if anywhere beneath that sky could be called safe.

"We sent the package," Umar said. "Now, you will lead us."

"I don't understand."

"Seril has touched you." Umar touched Corbin's forehead. "We have seen to the weapon. Now we must strike. Some within this city pray to her. She hides herself from me, but you can follow her. Lead me to them, and she will suffer."

The words opened Corbin's mind. He had been lost in the dream of Umar, carried in the big man's wake. But Corbin heard the prayers Umar meant, the moonlit surf that washed through his nightmares. He heard his girls' voices in that song. The world was mad. Great powers broke his family apart. Umar would help him stop all that.

He staggered west, following a distant song.

62

Tara climbed the mountain to meet her Goddess.

She walked steep trails until she found an iron ladder riveted to living stone. The ladder's rungs chafed her hands. Fortunately she kept her nails short, and wore sensible shoes.

By three rungs she'd climbed past the treetops. Pines grew tall in these western woods. She'd never been northwest to Regis or the Maw, but people said the trees there were taller than mountains, older than the Imperium, older than most gods: broad, deep, ancient, and invulnerable.

The higher you climbed, the smaller you felt. The mining camp below might have been a toy for an older child—no one would trust a toddler with parts so tiny.

She tore her jacket as she pulled herself onto a ledge. If she made it home, she'd look a sight before the court: wrinkled and ripped and bruised, sweat-caked, hadn't showered in days; one advantage of slacks over skirts was that it wouldn't be obvious she had not shaved either. Appearance mattered in court. Everything mattered—everything you did, everything you were, told a story to the Judge, to the opposing counsel, to the world.

She wished there was time to climb back down, make ablutions in camp, fix her suit. But while appearances mattered, court dates mattered more. There was no way for her to fly to Alt Coulumb in time, which left one option she did not like.

Her briefcase floated up and settled beside her. Its weight crushed chalky gravel to powder. The deal lay within, a few printed pages bearing her signature and Altemoc's.

She removed her shoes. Crossed her legs. Tried to still her mind, and failed.

Back on the east coast, the team of Kelethres, Albrecht, and Ao must have spent the day wrestling with Daphne, and with Ramp, defending Kos. Abelard and the church would marshal faith, liturgy, and song in their support. Blacksuits patrolled in case of riots or opportunistic crime. They held. She hoped.

She would know if Seril was dead.

She breathed out.

She'd worked for the goddess since last year. But that was a clear relationship, services rendered for a salary. What she was about to do transcended contract.

She remembered sprinting, ten years old, through cornfields in a rainstorm as deadly winds spun overhead, her arms outstretched, her body thrown so far forward she was less running than catching her falling self with every step—flying, only with feet between her and the ground. She chased the joy of power, the glory of taking without asking, of forcing the world to dance. She knit her will into the world. There was no drug sweeter than control. Few orgasms compared.

You do not love what you cannot use.

And while she hated Alexander Denovo, while she had dreamed of killing him only to make him wake and die again, sometimes in dark nights she wondered what had been the greater horror: to have her will subverted, or her dream of control turned against her?

Not that it mattered.

She was not trained for prayer, but prayer was needed now.

Wind swayed trees. The writer Gefjon spent summers in a mountain retreat watching forests for fires. Gefjon's woods might have looked like this from a height. She was in the right country, more or less.

Tara's mind spun. Power let the mental loop close too soon: desire collapsed into reality and freed itself to seek further satisfaction. She had chased the freedom power offered from Edgemont cornfields to the Hidden Schools and Alt Coulumb. She'd freed herself from everything but her need.

She had asked Altemoc—Caleb—to help. She had no leverage over him, no carrot to offer, no stick to force compliance. She asked, and he gave it to her.

She focused on the forest, but it was too big to see all at once. On the trees. On one tree. On a branch of the tallest trunk, waving in a stiff breeze.

Shale lay entombed beneath her. She sat atop him, as when they flew through Alt Coulumb's skies.

When she touched the stone, it felt like his skin.

All stone was stone, a doorway for the Goddess.

She asked for Her by name, and felt the answer through her flesh. *Took you long enough.*

The situation here was more complicated than I thought. Shale—

We will come back for him.

If any of us live that long. I have the contract, but I can't get to Alt Coulumb in time.

Tara, the Goddess said, and touched her cheek from the inside.

You could take me by the moon roads.

The moon is one everywhere.

When there's a moon.

When it rises, we'll bring you through.

There's three hours' time difference between the west coast and Alt Coulumb. Ramp will attack at moonrise on your end. Can you last that long?

A pause ensued, of wind in high places. *I think so.*

Then Tara truly began to pray.

The crowd in Market Square had grown.

Jones assembled tables, Jones unrolled carpets, Jones heated water for tea, Jones ran to a corner chemist's for medicine, but most of all Jones took notes. She moved among the faithful and spoke with those willing to speak. An Aokane Holdings desk clerk had come because her daughter told her about the gathering. Two men who kept shop in Hot Town visited around noon to crowd-watch and stayed to tend fires and distribute food. A woman in a wheelchair, wearing Iskari medals and a service jacket and old enough—just—to be a God Wars vet, rolled herself into the market, to the front of the crowd by the Crier's Dais.

No one watched the sky.

Jones had seen all this before, back in Dresediel Lex, as the gods woke in the Skittersill Rising. She'd walked among the crowd before the riots started; later, she watched from afar as the fire fell. She wanted to run. She stayed.

"These people aren't safe," she told Ellen, when she caught the girl carrying a jug of water to people huddled on blankets at the crowd's rear. "Do you see what's up there?"

"Of course," she said.

"They could kill us all without breaking a sweat."

Water sloshed over the jug's lip and wet Ellen's hand. Her arms were thin, but they did not shake from the work. She looked very young to Jones. "She needs everything we can give."

"I'm here to report," she said. "To write your story and sing it later."

"You've met Her children."

"The gargoyles." She remembered Aev's rumbling voice, the certainty with which she spoke before her Goddess's wrecked throne. "Yes."

"You talked with them—and with Her. You've heard Her voice, written songs to praise Her, and worked miracles in Her aid. You're part of us. It's okay to be afraid."

The girl's face was very pale.

Jones remembered the smell of burning flesh and singed hair in a square much larger than this one, a long time ago. She looked away.

"I have to go," Ellen said, and lifted the jug.

63

The sun set over Alt Coulumb.

Though the sky was burned, though Craft imposed its own schedules on the world, the sun still set and unveiled the stars. Craftworkers welcomed stars, after all. From these they took their food.

The court hung in midair, ringed by crystal towers, overseen by the Judge, above a layer-cake world: the physical city, and beneath it the argument-city of planes and burning wires where plaintiff's and defendant's Craft mixed, and beneath even that the raw noumenal Truth. Probes and accusations peeled back layers and stitched shut wounds. Fire wreathed Alt Coulumb, but the city was not consumed.

Of course not. This was war in a purely spiritual sense, war against gods as the God Wars should have been, no mucking about with civilian casualties. Clean. Fierce. Contained.

Not war at all.

This was surgery, with stars the operating theater lights.

Daphne watched moonrise—or, a piece of Daphne did. She was built of shells within shells, like the city. The moon rose fat and sweet as a ripe apple. She could taste the apple's juice on her tongue. Saliva wet her mouth, and she swallowed acid.

Innermost observer-Daphne, walled off from body and endocrine emotion, wondered how this trial would appear from the ground. The shell surrounding that innermost watcher was not Daphne Mains at all, but a substitute made of tense strong worm-flesh and gnawing teeth. One layer closer to the surface, there was another piece of Daphne again, screaming.

She had been screaming for a long time.

She was built of shells, and shells, and shells, and around all these a final sheath of skin containing a thing that was and was not Daphne Mains. Her teeth were sharp. Soot smeared her face, and blood. Her jacket was torn, her skin burned and cracked. Worms wriggled through her flesh, around bones that were not bones. She extended many arms, and breathed, though she did not need to.

Wakefield stood on empty air across the circle, wearing an expression mixed from smirk and smile and dead skull's grin. The immaculate suit was maculate now. Wakefield's discarded mask rested upon the unfloor. Blood dripped from many wounds and dried under manicured nails.

"At this point," Madeline Ramp said, "we believe Kos Everburning's weaknesses have been adequately explored. It is time to turn our attention to the moon goddess, Seril Undying."

"The court recognizes this request."

Wakefield's dead smile lost some of its mortal character. "In which case, I must cede the floor to Seril's own representatives."

"An irregular approach, Counselor."

"The two entities are separate, Your Honor. Opposing counsel would like nothing better than to establish that Kos can be relied upon to defend Seril. If I, retained by the Church of Kos, stood for Seril as well, would that not prove Ms. Ramp's and Ms. Mains's points for them?"

"We certainly would not complain," Ms. Ramp said.

The Judge removed her glasses and polished them on her robe. "Every case this court tries, it asks itself whether it is too much to hope that for once counsel would rely on the strength of their arguments, and leave grandstanding for somewhere that still has grandstands. It seems we are to be disappointed once more."

"Apologies, Your Honor," Wakefield said.

"Who will replace you, Counsel?"

"Tara Abernathy represents Seril Undying in this matter."

"Ah," the Judge said, as if this explained everything. "The woman expelled from the Hidden Schools."

"Graduated," Wakefield said. "Technically. She is a Craftswoman in good standing."

The Judge raised her hand. "Then let her appear."

The sun's last splinter passed beneath the horizon. The moon hung full.

In the ensuing pause, Daphne beneath her shells noticed how still the city seemed. They were not far up: there should have been noise, rumbles of traffic and murmurs of distant conversation. Instead she heard only a cathedral silence.

Cat and Raz crouched on a Business District rooftop, looking up. The court's wheel hung naked in the sky. No lightning lanced from it, no shadow spread to devour the newly risen stars.

"You're okay?" He touched a bruise on her arm.

"It's fine," she said, but did not draw her arm back. "Dockside trouble this afternoon. Big fight among the foreign sailors."

"Rioting?"

"Not as much as you'd expect. Small disasters kept us busy. Fires. A bit of looting down by the university, kids being kids."

"Looks like it's time," he said, with a nod to the sky. "That was Tara's cue."

"I know."

"No word from her?"

"Not since the last nightmare two days back." She ran her fingers through rooftop gravel. "Seril says she'll be here, if we can hold the line."

"How long?"

This was the part she didn't like. No, strike that. Made it sound like there was only one part she didn't like. "Three hours."

"Gods."

She didn't give the obvious reply.

"You see why I try to have as little to do with the mainland as possible."

"If you wanted me to believe the ocean was any better, you never should have shown me what goes on beneath."

"I have a whole thing," he said, "a speech, really, about how the ocean doesn't lie to you."

"That's nice."

"What if Tara doesn't show?"

She touched the goddess statue on its chain around her neck. "Then we'll fight."

Shadows globed the circle. The Judge frowned. "Ms. Abernathy is not in evidence, Counselor."

Wakefield nodded. "I apologize. I was not informed of her delay."

"Will you stand for Seril, then?"

"Beyond my remit, I'm afraid."

"In which case we'll have to continue without counsel for the defense."

Ramp's smile might have been a toothpaste ad. "Our pleasure. Ms. Mains?"

Daphne opened her claws, called upon her power—and stopped.

Spotlights burned her, blinding, so many colors they blended into white. Stone wingbeats filled the sky. The night moved—not with Craft, but with gargoyles.

She'd seen them before, though never all at once, never so near, never with wings spread and gem eyes burning. From a distance they were admirable weapons. Up close—

Some part of Daphne Mains was always screaming. But her innermost core, which felt nothing at all, still wondered at their form and strength.

A gargoyle hovered outside the circle, wings spread, fangs bare. A silver circlet shone from her brow. Enormous meathooks and machines of Craft pierced the Judge and grafted power to her. Authority radiated from the gargoyle, because of who she was.

The world held powers older than the Craft, Daphne thought.

None greater, though.

"I am Aev," the gargoyle said. "Leader of Seril's children. We have come to defend our Mother."

Wakefield looked nonplussed. Even the Judge shifted uncertainly on her throne.

Daphne smiled razors, raised her hands, and called upon dark powers.

And then the night was claws and teeth and wings.

64

The square fell silent when Ellen climbed the Crier's dais.

Gabby watched her from the blanket she shared with Mandy the university janitor and Xiaofan who worked in data entry for an uptown Craft firm and a Hot Town beggar girl who didn't tell Gabby her name when she asked. The rest of the crowd watched, too.

Ellen was not used to public speaking. No matter how you prepared there was no way to know how you would feel the first time you spoke and a few hundred people listened. Mercenaries talked the same way about battle: there are those who grow accustomed, those trained to it, and those born. No one learned they were the last until they shed blood.

Ellen had worked a miracle the last two days, by assembling so many people, and performed actual miracles as well, but she had a small voice and swayed under the crowd's attention.

"Seril needs us," Ellen said. "The battle takes all Her strength. Aid will come, but She has to build a bridge to bring it here."

She pressed her hands together.

"We're different people," she said. "We all have different visions of Her, but She is the same. Help us, if you can. If She's meant anything to you, let Her draw upon you now. Please."

I'm just going to watch, Jones told herself.

That's all. Watch, and listen.

Like last time, before the fire.

But the sky broke, and burned, and froze. Craftsmen fought gods for the city's future. In Dresediel Lex, she'd watched, and after the slaughter she left—crossed a continent to flee the memory of crisped skin and seared flesh and the chemical stink of gripfire. In twenty years she'd made this city her own, fought for its people with the only weapons she knew, with voice and pen and conductor's baton.

If Seril lost, the city would break. The voices would stop—the God-sent dreams, the brief intimations of a city striving toward justice. Chains would bite the gods' flesh, and bind.

Gabby was afraid.

She would have struck anyone else who suggested it, but she could not strike herself. She was afraid. These girls fought—easy for them. They did not know what loss might mean. By staying quiet, staying small, staying on the sidelines, you could outlast even that madness in the sky. People who did not fight, survived.

And Aev was in the sky, dying. Aev, who saved Gabby from danger she'd taken on herself.

She prayed.

There must have been words for this back before the Wars, but Gabby didn't know them. She directed her mind to moments her life touched the Lady's, silences in which she felt a presence, an intimation, a still voice from still water, a whisper from stone. Not Kos's all-embracing, all-consuming love, not the voice that left you ashes, but something cool and deep and lonely. She was asked, and she gave.

The silence lived with stories. Jones felt them: a square of people offering themselves. Trade was a pale echo of this feeling, of raw self offered up to Someone who knit it to a whole.

There were so many tales.

Hundreds clashed and recombined in the market, bitter with suffering, gingered with joy. They drew sparks when they struck. Every person here knew the Goddess in a different way. They lacked tongues to name Her, myths and prayers to fit Her. They offered themselves with love or humility or fear or pain, and if the Goddess accepted them all, She would break herself to shards.

Joining those shards was a priestess's task, and Ellen was not ready.

She shook with strain. Scoured by private terrors, the girl could not shoulder her congregation's burden, could not filter their pain through herself.

What had Gabby expected? For Ellen to knit a people from scattered threads beneath a demon-haunted sky?

She felt the first stirrings of despair.

Then she heard footsteps.

"Excuse me," a man said behind her.

Gabby turned.

A group of people wearing mismatched clothes had entered the market from the south. Their leader, a tall, thin man with a graying beard, approached the dais beside Ellen, working his way through the congregation while his fellows spread out to ring the crowd. He held out his hand, and Ellen accepted.

"Hello," he said. "You may call me Dr. Hasim. I am a Doctor of Divinity, which means I heal gods. Your Lady saved me, and she saved my friends. We offered Her our help in turn. She asked us to come here, to tell you Her stories, and pray Her prayers with you. She is a Lady of great age, with as many stories as She has faces."

"Tell us, then," Ellen said, and Jones heard her relief, her desperation.

"No." Hasim did not turn from Ellen, and though he did not shout, his voice filled the market. "Gods do not know how best to help themselves, any more than human patients do. I know old stories, written for a different time. You must tell Her tales yourself."

"I can't," she said. "All our stories are different."

"All people are different," Hasim said. "They are also more or less the same. In your tale, they will hear their own."

Ellen let his hand slip. She looked out over the crowd.

Gabby held her breath. Claire stood rigid beside the stage.

"My father," Ellen said, "roars."

65

War is a hard problem. Even simple physical conflicts have so many moving interlocking systems, physical and moral and technological, meteorological and geographical and historical, that attempt to name their edges far out into the borders of complexity theory. Craftwork battles leap over those borders and swim in the chaos beyond. Courtly wards and rules contain that chaos like rolled-up towels on a bathroom floor contain gushing sewage.

Good thing Daphne Mains was built for battle.

Part of her was, anyway. Somewhere within the shell game of her soul, she observed the seams of her construction: her hands drew glyphs in air precisely as a machine tooling metal, and words in a dozen dead tongues spilled from her lips without trace of affect. Back in the Hidden Schools she'd had no talent for languages, progressing slowly from rote memorization through info-gap exercises with classmates to actual contact with contorted other-dimensional horrors. Each syllable had cut her throat from the inside, as if the words themselves were demonglass.

Tonight they flowed from her like water from a faucet.

She had not always been this way.

But she could not remember how she had changed. Other systems forbid her such speculation.

Knives peeled back the night, and the cuts laughed. Gargoyles seethed through the sky. Thorns of lightning lanced them, finding mostly emptiness but sometimes stone. Chips and dust fell. When Daphne's Craft pierced rock skin, she drank moonlight.

The goddess went down sweet and sour, like buttermilk.

The gargoyles could not cross the circle; the court would shelter Daphne so long as she worked to prove the bond between Kos and Seril, and would help her test the Goddess. It would be inelegant to kill Her in the process, but since in the court's view Seril was already dead, Daphne would be guilty of deicide in only the most vague and theoretical sense.

The gargoyles, denied Daphne, struck her weapons. They caught the spears of her will and tore her mind. But Daphne drew strength from their injuries. By the time they freed one comrade from her clutches, the gargoyle she'd struck was already tainted with gray ash.

She trapped them in redoubled space, she spread time, she played elaborate games to spoof their theory of mind. Some they avoided, some resisted. One small Stone Man fell into an airless infinity and emerged howling and mad.

The old tricks were the best.

The Goddess fought, too. Seril changed the world with a fluency even Daphne could not match. The goddess broke Daphne's thorns, slid past her swords, battered her with awe. But Daphne did not fight Seril directly. She could break her through her children.

Good times.

Daphne abandoned temporospatial shenanigans to address the gargoyles' stone. Stone, she argued, cannot move; stone cannot feel. They slowed.

Lightning flew from her fingers and lit eyes that were and were not hers.

The goddess convulsed.

The Sanctum of Kos smelled of incense and priestly sweat. Abelard and the Cardinals chanted. That no longer amazed him—to be here, surrounded by Cardinals, praying.

Glory to Your Flame
Everburning, All-transforming—

Nestor's voice led their prayer from the front altar, the docent's role having shifted around the circle back to him twice so far. Each time, Abelard refused to lead. Vestments flowed like lava from the old man's shoulders.

Priests throughout Alt Coulumb chanted these words, in this time. They entered God's presence. They gave themselves to Kos, felt His pain as the Craftsmen struck and tested Him.

And they felt a different sort of pain as He watched the battle in the air, and did nothing.

The altar fire burned hot, and they knelt and prayed.

My father roars.

He didn't always. There was our mother once. She's gone. (Murmurs, some, throughout the crowd. They knew the story.)

Imagine living with a lion. It prowls great-maned and strong through the house. But when you live with a lion, you see its teeth, and know its voice.

Many days its voice is the only voice you hear, because when a lion speaks, it deafens. You shout back even to hear yourself. There may be girls who can shout louder than a lion. I am not one of them. I was afraid. To shout louder than a lion, you have to scream, and things that scream are food.

Lions work. Lions prowl. Lions thirst, especially when they're sad, and when they thirst they drink, and when they drink they roar louder.

I never felt his teeth. I was, we were, lucky that way. The lion was never hungry when we were near. But you don't have to feel a lion's teeth to fear them. His muzzle was often bloody when he came home. Sometimes the blood was not his; often it was. Tend a lion's wounds as it breathes. Tend wounds around its mouth, in reach of its paws, and smell the kill blood on its breath.

(The sky's war painted Ellen many shades of fire.)

Each of my sisters dealt with the lion in her own way. Hannah was sweet and charming and often gone. She laughed and danced, and did not talk at home. Claire went with the lion in the mornings, and worked with him, sometimes in his place. She grew strong and hard and brave.

I'm none of those things.

One night the lion did not come home. He often stayed out late hunting. But the hours passed. I watched the sand in the glass and knew the later he came back the louder he would roar, the more he would be hurt, the more he would need.

He did not come home that night, or the next morning. That night I waited, too.

I was afraid. So was Hannah. Claire wasn't, but when we went to find him, she came.

We lost ourselves in the Pleasure Quarter. Not even Claire knew the way. I prayed. The Lady sent Her child to me. He led us home.

The lion wept when we returned. I never saw that happen before, though I heard it some nights through the wall. He embraced us. He was bloody, and he was hurt, but more than that he was afraid.

My sisters think that was the first time I prayed to the Lady. But I called to Her then because I knew Her from before.

There was no room for my voice in a house of roaring. I could not talk with my sisters, because when there's a lion in the house all you can talk about is the lion, and who wants to talk about a lion all the time?

I spoke to the night instead.

The night does not fear lions. It knows them. It makes their voices small. The night gives birth to day, and when the sun rises the night waits behind the star. It is big, and it listens. The night's smile turns shadow to velvet and blood to silver.

I prayed to the Lady before She returned. When the dreams came, I honored them. I spoke to Her, because the night hears whispers louder than a roar.

Some people here found Her in terror, in torture. I found Her in the undoing of a knot into which a lion's roar tied me.

She saved me, and transformed me. She was my door to faith.

My father lives. He will roar again. But now I have the night.

Ellen's voice carried through the crowd in defiance of all acoustic principle. The faithful souls were jigsaw puzzle pieces turning in the god-realm's airless dark, and Ellen's words guided them to one. Or they were filings and she the magnet, or they particles in suspension and she the crystal seed, or, or—

Dr. Hasim stood by the stage, haloed with a flickering light as if he stood before a bonfire. Green rivulets overflowed his form and his face, illuminating the head of a long-billed bird around or beneath his own. His companions had other shapes, and bonfires of their own, some dim, some fierce. Their hands, or the hands of the gods who shared their bodies, or both, combed story into story, faith into faith, folded the crowd into Ellen and her into them.

"Pray with me," Ellen said, and Gavriel Jones did.

Praying, she felt the goddess's pain.

66

Sunset veiled the forest beneath the Keeper's mountain. Below, the Two Serpents Group lit lanterns and manned barricades. Its people knew what was coming, because Tara had told them.

From her height, Tara saw the forest move.

Shadows detached from the trees—wolves and bears and hawks. Groundwater contamination hit hardest at the food chain's highest links; squirrels and field mice limped while the wolves ran smooth, faster in death than life. Birds arrowed through the purple sky.

Dead things flowed up the mountain slopes. The Keeper called them home, as she called to ancient sailors' compass needles—the earth stolen from her had seeped into these beasts, and now they returned to rest.

They left trails of rotted flesh, and when they found a niche that fit, they curled there and slept. A wolf pillowed its chin on its paws like a dog beside a fire and wept metal tears that soaked into cracked stone.

A fingernail of shadow took flight from the Drakspine and approached.

No. Tara must have had the distance wrong. It couldn't be that big. There were dragons in the world, of course, but not here.

She caught her breath when she recognized the sweeping wings.

The condor landed above her, settling onto a rocky throne. The bird was twice her size, with pinions long and black and red. Worms turned beneath its crest.

It was beautiful.

The condor looked down, and Tara looked up. The Keeper had called her children home. How much of the goddess lived in each of them? Could Shale hear her through this bird?

"I'll come back for you," she said.

The condor nodded, or bobbed its head. The sun's last light caught its eyes.

Okay, Tara prayed. Sun's down. Moon's up. Whenever you're ready.

I'm sorry, the goddess replied. *We're experiencing technical difficulties at the moment.*

The gargoyles lasted longer than Daphne expected. Stone did not tire as did flesh. Lacking any well-mannered metabolism, their muscles could not be poisoned by the by-products of their use. Good thing Daphne did not tire, either.

At last a gargoyle slipped—she caught it in a shell of infinite space, held it still, and pierced. The goddess scrambled to free Daphne's prisoner, too late—Daphne snared two more, and then a fourth. The goddess tried to burn Daphne from the world, but the circle blunted that attack. Needles of red light pierced gargoyle throats, and the power she tore from them was sweet.

The fight against Wakefield had been a Craftswoman's struggle: structures of proof and argument falling before Daphne's knife only to re-form in answer to each cut. That work was elegant; this, routine. All she had to do was repeat, again and again, the simple, incontrovertible fact that gargoyles could die.

As could their goddess.

It would not do to yawn before the Judge. So when the machine Daphne had become finally snared the gargoyle queen, when the Stone Men and Women weakened, she pinched her earlobe between thumb and forefinger—a stopgap remedy an herbalist once suggested she try to keep alert.

That cleared things up nicely.

Blood dripped from her earlobe onto her suit. One more bill for dry cleaning.

Fire flared on the sanctum altar. Nestor fell. Bede knelt by his side and cradled the old man's head.

Rage swelled in Abelard. He smelled blood, and Craft, and blasphemy.

He'd spent a day opening his mind to God, and now felt His fury.

Cardinal Aldis groaned. Veins stood out on the backs of her hands, and at her temples. She fought—they all did—to contain God's wrath.

Lord Kos could burn the Craftsmen from the sky—exposing Himself as He protected Seril. To survive, He'd have to kill them all, to press the battle to the world's corners, to fight and win a God War on his own. Impossible.

He might try anyway.

Moans of pain, grinding teeth, shattered prayers, Father forgive, blessed by flame, transfigured into sacred ash—their voices burned with the Godhead, their twiglike fingers clutched to stay a charging boar.

Bede had caught Nestor when the old man fell. No one had yet stepped up to lead the prayer. Cardinals babbled, drunk on vintages of rage grown rich through years of cultivation.

But Abelard was no Lord of the Church. He was younger, and less confirmed in anger.

His knees shook as he stood. Hands reached for him, voices rose to reproach his temerity. He climbed to the altar and turned to face the Cardinals. Their stares fixed him like a butterfly to a board.

Surely it was harder to die and rise again than to lead the Cardinals in prayer.

Surely.

He held out his hands and spoke the words.

Glory to Your Flame—

The machine that was Daphne Mains advanced to the circle's edge. The gargoyle queen strained against her razor web.

"Your Honor," Daphne said. "Kos's off-books relationship with Seril is doubly insidious. Kos's exposure to her undermines his own operations and poses a serious threat to global thaumaturgy. Even when limited by contract, such off-books dependencies are dangerous. This bond, however, depends not on obligation or performance but on a reasonable facsimile of *sentiment.* Of love."

She gestured, and Aev floated toward her in the air. The gargoyle reared against her bonds. A crack opened in her left bicep, so deep that moonlight flowed through.

"The Craft recognizes noncontractual relationships between competitors only. As Justice Iron Hand affirmed in the Antitrust Cases, thaumaturgical dynamism requires the existence of free entities in competition. There is no direct competition between Kos and Seril. The equipoise of opposites leads to stagnation. Nor does this theological juxtaposition even qualify as equipoise, for the positions of these opposites are not equal. Kos shelters this moon goddess, this memory of a dead age, in her weakness. He has embroiled his creditors and shareholders in a risk with no demonstrated reward—a risk that might well be infinite, for no matter how Seril is attacked, he will always come to her rescue. And rescue will be required, because she is weak."

Aev roared.

"Objection," Wakefield said, "on relevance."

The Judge frowned. "Counsel. Please decide. Do you stand for Seril, or not?"

"I do not. But as Ms. Mains's argument touches on my client, I believe I am entitled to speak." With one hand Wakefield indicated the gargoyles, the crystal towers, the broken sky and cringing city. "We hardly seem to have stood on courtroom procedure thus far."

"Proceed."

"Ms. Mains has introduced evidence documenting Kos's previous onetime infusions of soul into the moon goddess Seril. But two instances do not establish a pattern." Wakefield pointed to the snared gargoyles. "These theatrics might have been saved for a juried case. Despite the torment Ms. Mains is inflicting on Seril at the moment, my client has not intervened. I for one would appreciate it if Ms. Mains either arrived at a point, or stopped wasting our time with procedural pretense and cut to the villainous guffaws. If she wishes a mustache to twirl, I imagine the city below contains a costume shop willing to provide one."

"Counsel has a point, Ms. Mains," the Judge said. "What do you plan to accomplish by tossing these war machines around my courtroom?"

The moonlight that dripped from the gargoyle queen's wounds smelled like honey and would taste so sweet. Daphne ached to cross the circle and tongue the broken stone. "I am sorry for the delay, Your Honor. My argument requires one further step."

"Take it."

"I will show you how vulnerable this off-books relationship makes Kos," she said. "Now."

She held her hand palm down and curled her fingers into a small, tight fist. Her knuckles cracked.

Glass-blue tendrils dug into the gargoyles' limbs. They roared with voices of stone.

And the machine beneath whose shell Daphne, weeping, lay—it sipped Goddess, and shivered.

Cardinal Librarian Aldis turned her gaze on Abelard and for once he did not flinch. Her voice joined his. The others followed. Bede, kneeling, cheeks wet, beside the dais, cradling Nestor as Abelard had cradled another imperfect servant in another dark time, also prayed. Their voices were one voice from many throats.

And out from the ashes of deep time
Did answer to our still greater need—

Abelard knelt. The city was their army, and he sprinted at the vanguard toward a great Known, a fire bigger and deeper than time.

He was the city. A church group gathered in the basement of the Slaughter's Fell chapel where he held service the night before, and he was their cooling coffee and their prayers. Three sooty children in crates dockside whispered prayers to candle flame, and he was with them.

So was He.

And He was furious.

There is no drug in all the worlds like a goddess's taste: an all-body high, a skin-crawling vein-throbbing rush richer for its transgression. Soulstuff not drawn from the natural world, not borrowed or traded from human minds, but raw meaning, ontological satisfaction heated 'til it bubbles in a spoon and shot into the arm with a needle lathed from a child's fingerbone. Even Daphne-beneath-shells, Daphne-observer, felt that, lapped at it even as she hated the hunger each taste instilled in her.

Daphne-outside, though, the fighter, the monster built to win— she loved this. Power surged through the engines that comprised her.

Maestre Gerhardt had written: gods are beings with which human communities exist in relationship.

Fine. One relationship was that of diner to meal.

Seril flagged. Soon Kos would come, and she would have him too.

The God raged. A day of stings, tests, and violation, of questions posed by gnats to His own person, all reached a head in this pustule of indignity. He had ignored the Craftsmen as they broke the world, for there were crimes on all sides of the Wars. He had not joined Seril in battle, for She endangered Their people by fighting. When She died, He wept. He would not lose Her again. Not here, in His own city, when all He had do was *close* his *hand* and *crush*—

No, Abelard prayed. No, my Lord.

There was a timeless pause through the city.

The Goddess screamed, and Abelard knew Her voice. Cat was in that scream, and Aev, and his mother, and Tara, and they were dying, they were being pulled to the edge, they would break—

Wait, he prayed.

They need us.

They do. But if we go to them, we surrender the cause they suffer for.

She hurts.

Trust Her, though. Trust Tara.

"It looks bad," Raz said. "They're about to give."

"Okay." Cat crouched on the rooftop. "Here we go."

And there was silver.

What are you doing? the Goddess roared. There was too much pain for Her to do anything but roar. Cat felt that pain through the Suit, as if she'd touched a burning kiln. *We had a deal.*

Sorry, she prayed, and flew.

And Cat, Abelard added as a silver streak rose through the distorted sky. You can definitely trust her.

Daphne did not expect the cop.

Winged, quicksilver, she was a thing of violence bent to other ends than war. She flew to the circle's edge, and her skin reflected Daphne transformed, freed from flesh.

Ms. Mains, the cop said. *You are under arrest.*

She blinked. "You have no authority within the circle."

I am not concerned with the case you have come to try. You are assaulting several citizens of Alt Coulumb, including these gargoyles and their goddess.

"Then Kos claims responsibility for Seril."

You'd like that, the cop replied, and there was an edge of smile beneath the silver. *But no. Justice is supported by both Kos and Seril, but she's a separately managed subsidiary, charged with protecting Alt Coulumb's people. Seril and her children are, technically, people of Alt Coulumb. If you attack them, you face Justice.*

Daphne turned to the Judge, who shrugged, then back to the cop. "Nonsense."

I spent a lot of time in the library piecing this together, the cop said. *And I hate libraries. But if I'm right, that circle protects you from people who want to interfere with your case. Question is, whether it will also save you from someone who wants you on criminal charges. Let's see.*

She stepped forward as if the air were a floor, and crossed the circle's edge.

The cop shifted her neck as if to crack it.

Well. That's interesting.

"Your Honor," Daphne said.

"She has a point, Ms. Mains."

"The circle isn't technically in Alt Coulumb."

"The circle isn't technically anywhere. But Alt Coulumb has longstanding mutual extradition arrangements with the Courts of Craft. You are, of course, entitled to defend yourself."

"Very well." Daphne called lightnings to her. "Arrest me, or try. Do you think that silver suit will save you? I can see its weaving. I will break you and the witless construct you serve."

Which is why I didn't come alone.

She pointed down.

The rooftops swarmed with silver. Hundreds of figures waited there, tensing to jump.

They whistled like arrows through the sky.

Then the cop hit Daphne in the face.

There we go, the Goddess said. *Back on track. Are you still—*

I'm fine, Tara prayed. Just bring the road.

The moon filled from its crescent, and the sky darkened as lesser stars failed. The mountain, too, faded, and the camp below, and the forest, and the Drakspine ridge—everything but the rock on which Tara sat cross-legged with her briefcase.

"What's happening here?" she said, out loud, to the moon. "I mean, really happening."

Does it matter?

"Yes."

We are all patterns after a fashion, though of different orders. I can usher you from your order into mine, and sustain you as you travel. Distance is one, here—the moon is the same everywhere.

"You're wrapping me inside yourself."

For a while.

"My briefcase, too?"

Do you always question miracles this much?

"Yes."

Your belongings will remain intact.

"And my soul?"

If you wish, though it's a bit bent. I could help you, long as you're up here. Ease out some of the sharp turns and snarls.

"I'd rather walk."

I care for my own.

"I am not yours," Tara said. "Let's get that clear. I crossed a continent to save you. I challenged gods and Deathless Kings and I left friends behind. I did all that for my own reasons—none of which were, because you told me to."

The Goddess laughed, but her laughter hitched in the middle, as if She was in pain.

"You have priests and priestesses, and you use them. That's not my path. I won't command you, but I won't be your servant either."

What, then?

"Your partner. If you'll have me."

I love you, she said, *strange as you are.*

"Do we have a deal?"

Partners. Now, for Spider's sake, Tara, get on the damn road. Cat won't last much longer.

"There's no road," she started to say, but there was.

She stood. She took up her briefcase, and stepped onto the moonlit path.

67

Corbin Rafferty wandered through the shadows of his mind, down empty streets beneath the bloody blasted sky. He walked the road's centerline, following moonsong.

Umar trailed him. He was shadow, presence, weight. Corbin did not need to look back anymore. He knew his role.

Near sunset he found himself home, at the apartment he shared with the girls. Lacking a key, he climbed the fire escape outside and pounded on the living room window—would have broken in, but the place was empty. The apartment looked as he left it the night he fell, the night the moon overwhelmed him. The girls had been gone for a long time.

Where?

The song bore him south to Market Square. He had expected the market to stand empty as the rest of the city, and was surprised to find a crowd. The stalls were closed, more than closed, they'd been *cleared,* pushed back to make room for an audience, hundreds of them, a thousand, even, on blankets and towels, on the filthy cobblestones Ray Capistano had wet with blood each morning for twenty years.

This was wrong. They should not be here. Something had broken his market. He knew its smells of trade and need. No one should sit rapt in this square. Who had done this? Who had stolen his place from him?

He knew. He heard. He smelled the stench of silver.

She was here.

She had convinced all these fools, seduced them with false comfort. But desperation tainted the silver stench. She needed these people to believe her lies. He could show them. This was his revenge.

He ran into the square and followed the gaze of these assembled sheep to the Crier's dais, where, haloed with moonlight, his daughter stood.

"Ellen!" he roared, and ran to her.

Raz watched the war in heaven from his rooftop.

He saw more than a human could; he sensed the forces that warped the world above. But he ignored them and watched Cat fight.

She was more than fast: she was the only Blacksuit comfortable in the air. Some of the others spread wings, but none could stay aloft for long. They leapt, instead, and bounced off shields, or caught in webs of light. Their Suits turned against them. Broad-winged skeletal bats flew from the Craftswoman's briefcase to tangle Blacksuits in thickets of bone.

Cat wrestled a creature made from broken glass. When the Craftswoman hit her, she bled silver.

Raz walked the blood jade down his fingers, and up again. There was a song inside it. He felt its hunger, bigger, older, deeper than his own.

He wanted it. He watched her.

When?

Tara walked the moon road.

Tara walked with/was the goddess/moon walking herself.

Space did not exist out here, so how could there be time? How could one being endure separate from others? In this realm stories told each other, tales tangled in tales. On the mountain there was a monastery and within the monastery was a young monk and an old, and the young monk asked the old, master tell me a story, and the master said, on the mountain—

She was is will be

moon mother tiger stone water woman wolf tooth sickle claw winter

human goddess more

falling, fallen.

The goddess tumbles to the desert floor, the goddess lies broken and bleeding in her many parts, and if she is always everywhere then she is always here, she is always dying, always the Craftsmen's hands are inside her pulling out gobs of flesh, seizing her parts to force her story to their service. Her wings are flayed and she burns and—

—*something is wrong*—

Tara, for Tara was still, is still, here, felt terror larger, older than herself.

The goddess strained. She had built a hidden redoubt, a community of faith formed into a pocket through which Tara might pass and remain intact, but that pocket was in danger—

The moon that is a mirror of itself cracked and monks and mountains and sitters and spinners scattered all askew—

Matt didn't recognize the ragged man as Corbin Rafferty until he spoke, until he shouted Ellen's name over the silent market. His hair was matted, his beard tangled, but he pointed toward her, accusing. "Ellen, get down from there, what the *hells* are you doing?" and spinning to see the crowd, "What the hells are you all doing? Don't you see what's happening up there? We have to get safe."

Ellen was afraid, and the crowd shook. Whatever was happening here, with the goddess, Matt was only on its edge, but Ellen stood at its center, and as she came apart so did the web she'd knit from these people—like a whirlpool in a sink stopped when you replaced the plug.

He ran to Rafferty. "Corbin, stop it. You don't know what's happening. Calm down."

The eyes that stared up into his were sharper than he remembered Rafferty's eyes being, and the hands that gripped his outstretched arms stronger, too. "Matt, that's my girl. Don't you step between a man and his family," with man and family spat. "Ellen! We're going home."

Matt forced Corbin against the wall.

But when Corbin's back touched the bricks, he snarled and went limp. Matt lost balance, stumbled forward. His nose struck Corbin's forehead. Bone crunched. Corbin kicked Matt in the knee. He started to fold, refused to let himself. Caught Corbin around the waist with one arm. An elbow crashed into his shoulder, and again.

"Ellen, get down from there!"

"No," she said.

"We are going home. Now." So loud, so shrill, his voice was almost breaking. "You listen to me."

"Stop it," Claire said.

The demon that rode Umar made him blend with alley shadows and observe the Market Square, the gathered congregation of this little goddess, lending her their faith so she might perform miracles.

A girl stood on a dais before them, and the Lady of the Moon was with her. Through her ran a path to the goddess's heart, to freedom. All he had to do was seize her, and drink.

The demon tensed Umar's legs to run.

Then the shadows turned jade.

A thin man stood in the alley mouth. He wore a gray goat's beard and mismatched clothes, and behind him—or in place of him, as if he cast a brilliant shadow or were himself the shadow cast by a greater form—rose an ibis head in green. The thin man's cheeks were wet.

The mind the demon rode named the figure: "Hasim."

"Do not speak my name," Hasim said, "with his tongue. You debase it."

The demon made Umar move, fast.

Hasim's light moved faster. The ibis struck. Its beak passed through Umar's chest, but did not pierce. It clutched the demon like a frog and drew it screaming from Umar's body into the strange cold world where these fleshlings lived. Exposed, about to die, the demon fled—seeping through small holes in this alien world back to its own.

Umar opened his eyes. Hasim's light stung them. They embraced, and kissed. Umar's shoulders heaved once, a sob that strangled itself.

"It hurt," Umar said.

"Not anymore."

Claire, dependable Claire, the iron prop on which Corbin leaned, advanced upon him, full of rage. He released Matt, and sought the wall for support.

"Claire," he said. "Ellen doesn't know what she's doing. We need to help her. Where's Hannah?"

"Hannah," Claire said, "is safe with Mr. Adorne's family. Ellen is where she needs to be. We are not yours to order. We aren't your kids anymore. You haven't let us be for a long time."

"Claire, the girls don't know. The moon, she's lying to you all. They need help."

"I bought your line, Father. I helped you too damn much. I held all this together for you. I shored you up and I kept my sisters weak."

"Claire!"

"You're sick," she said. "You've been sick a long time. You need help. You—you don't get to order her, or Hannah, or me, anymore. This is Ellen's place. You can't chase her from it. If you try, I'll stop you."

Corbin's mouth opened, but no sound came out.

"Matt," she said. "Watch him. We have work to do."

She left them, and walked to the stage, where Ellen stood in a ring of light. She took her hand, and the light healed, and the whirlpool turned.

The crowd prayed.

Corbin fell, and watched his daughters lead them.

—And as fast as the world skewed, it settled back. Tara sped through the goddess's net. Those were her feet walking the moon road. She found firm footing on—what was this? More than reality. Surreality. The world above.

Whatever it was, she could walk it.

And because it was everywhere, each step brought her anywhere she wished to go—anywhere the moon answered to Seril's name.

Wait. So I've been walking inside you—and you're under attack in Alt Coulumb—so if you die there, then I—

I don't know what happens in that case. You're me at the moment, and I'm you, so maybe you die also. Or you're stuck out here in god-space. Craftswomen ask too many questions about the unknowable.

It's not unknowable. Just unknown.

There came a timeless silence.

Where do I get off, Tara asked.

Wherever I want, she answered herself.

Alt Coulumb?

Coming up. But are you sure there's nothing you'd like me to fix, long as you're here? A little guilt to absolve? Anger or self-hatred to rub away?

She felt revulsion at herself for even considering, but she heard laughter, too, high and clear.

I was just fooling. But I'm here if you need me.

I know.

Tara turned to leave the moon road, but hesitated, one foot hovering over eternity.

Yes?

Now that you mention it, this suit needs some work.

68

Little was left of Daphne Mains.

The machine built inside her defended itself. Wheels and wards, enchantments and escarpments and demonic intelligences spun against the Blacksuits who swept through the sky, and against one of them in specific, the claw-fingered angel who tore Daphne and was torn in turn. The machine needed more power, more speed, and it burned through Daphne's shells, recruiting shards of her annexed soul for the war effort. Dreams, nightmares, fantasies, mirror-memories, all melted for the sake of speed.

Observer-Daphne, at the bottom of her mind's well, felt parts of her she had not known survived grind in the machine.

She thought slowly.

Slower.

Drained of color, judgment, time.

Many hands speared Blacksuits in midair. Hurt them. Trapped them. Flayed the goddess from them. One Suit dove for Madeline Ramp instead of Daphne; Ramp raised a hand. The Suit bounced off an invisible wall.

Thoughts reached Daphne under deep water's weight, when they reached her at all. The machine moved fast, though. She caught the winged cop around the throat. The cop tore free, bleeding. She caught her again, one arm, then the next. Daphne grew two more claws, and her fingers sharpened to diamond points, to pierce.

Time went strange.

A voice spoke, over and beside the din.

"Apologies to the court for my tardiness."

Daphne, inside herself, recognized that voice. *Tara.*

"Ms. Abernathy," the Judge said, "you're late."

"I was delayed." She stood outside the circle, on empty air. "I am sorry."

She wore a suit of nacreous gray, as if pearls had been spun to wool and woven. Moonlight caught in her hair and on the curve of her cheek. She held a briefcase.

"Sorry," the Judge said, "doesn't cover it, Ms. Abernathy. Ms. Ramp and Ms. Mains at least comport themselves within the standards of the court—but these creatures entering themselves as representatives, Wakefield sniping from the sidelines, local authorities trying to arrest Craftswomen in my own circle—I won't let you derail these proceedings further."

"That's fine, Your Honor," Tara said. "I don't mean to derail these proceedings at all."

Tara looked at Daphne. It was hard to do that without letting the tears come. She could see what had happened to her now the wards were engaged, the enchantments woken, the demons risen from their slumber. Metal glinted through gaps in Daphne's skin, and glyphwork Tara could barely comprehend. The parts of Daphne their old teacher hollowed out were filled with weapons and golemetric clockwork. The demons that wore Daphne's face, many-armed, sharp-toothed, and glyph-inscribed, held two of Tara's friends by the throat.

"Sorry, Daffy," she said, and opened her briefcase.

"Ms. Abernathy, you are seconds from being held in contempt."

"I'll use those seconds wisely, Your Honor. Seril stands in Her own defense. I wouldn't dream of interrupting a case in such an advanced stage of debate. I am here only to submit relevant documents to the Court of Craft."

Ramp seemed tense. Tara liked that.

"Give them to me."

The deal, calligraphed in Tara's own hand, signed in Altemoc's blood, floated past hovering gargoyles, to the bench. The Judge cleared her throat, produced reading glasses from her breast pocket, donned them, and scanned the deal.

"Speaking of irregular, Ms. Abernathy."

"I understand your hesitation, Your Honor, but I assure you the document's legitimate."

"No payment involved?"

"Altemoc's Concern has an unorthodox structure, Your Honor. They do not seek repayment from the direct beneficiaries of their dispensations."

"I don't understand."

"Neither do I, really, but the fact remains: that document represents a transfer of assets from the Two Serpents Group to the Church of Seril Undying."

"Very well," the Judge said, and a spring unwound between Tara's shoulder blades. "Ms. Abernathy, how are you supporting yourself outside the circle? You aren't strong enough to fight Alt Coulumb's interdict by yourself."

She allowed herself a smile. "That brings us the next matter I wanted to discuss. Your Honor, Ms. Mains, dear guests"—that last addressed to the skyspires arrayed around them—"I'm afraid you are all trespassing."

The fight's pause let Daphne-under-shells think again, let her reclaim her mind from the machine. She felt a sudden tension when Tara spoke, the grinding of ill-meshed gears, the music of a dying engine.

The Judge frowned. "Go on."

"Your Honor," Tara said, "those assets represent airspace rights over Alt Coulumb, which have been the subject of tangled courtroom challenges for fifty years. You see, the sky above Alt Coulumb belongs to Seril. Kos claimed it after She died, but the King in Red of Dresediel Lex registered a competing claim based on salvage rights from Seril's presumed corpse. With this transfer, that salvage claim has been formally relinquished; the King in Red's airspace rights devolve to Seril. And now"—and the grin Daphne knew Tara thought she was hiding grew wider—"now Kos has dropped his competing claim."

Lightning stripped and squared the circle. Thunder rolled.

"Your Honor, Seril Undying owns these skies, and She doesn't care for your presence here—or the spires' either." Light trailed Tara's finger as she gestured toward the crystal towers.

"Are you threatening the court, Ms. Abernathy?" The Judge's voice was the voice of ages.

"Not at all. In fact, I believe the Lady is offering these spires' owners, and the court itself, temporary tenancy agreements as we speak. Some might call the rent She's demanding extortionate, but wait until we put this space on the open market. Trust me: the Alt Coulumb real estate market is absurd, and my client now holds rights to several hundred cubic miles of fresh territory. Ms. Ramp. Ms. Mains." The moon pulsed with rage. The bonds that held the gargoyles shattered; their stone healed. Their eyes were bonfires within gems. The Blacksuits in midair unfroze, and the healed hosts of Justice assembled in arrays. The cop slipped from Daphne's claws as if she were made of light. "If you'd like to continue your assault on my client, feel free. She's feeling a bit more battle ready at the moment."

What answer could Daphne give, or the machine outside her? The court itself acknowledged Seril's rights to the sky. Easier to move the world without a lever than fight the court from within.

Tara had won.

But Daphne heard slow applause and recognized Ramp's voice.

"Neatly done, Ms. Abernathy. But would you please refrain from declaring premature victory? It's a bad habit."

The machine in Daphne moved again.

Tara was caught by surprise. So was the Judge. The monster with Daphne's face pointed, and lightning leapt from her to the paper that bore Tara's seal, and Altemoc's.

The document smoked—the bond of ownership unraveling as Daphne attacked the contract, the ownership trail of Seril's sky. After decades of Craftwork wrangling, how could Kos renounce his claim?

Tara blocked, reinforcing the deal with Kos's own testimony, with moonlit records in city stone, with the organic glyphs of Alt Coulumb's streets: the God's claim assumed His Lady's death, but She was very much alive. His certainty stood as a wall against Daphne's spears.

The spears became vines, became water, became worms that wriggled into Tara's mind. Perhaps the spirit who called herself Seril was not the same as the Goddess who died?

But Tara fought back. Seril's children testified, with their crystal teeth and their claws and their long memories. And Kos Himself offered surety in flame. One by one, with spiderlong fingers, Tara plucked up the argument-worms and burned them as they screamed.

The machine burned faster. Daphne cut through Tara's argument: the goddess who fought in the Wars has changed to the point of death. She fought Craftswomen, and now employs them. She ruled, and now she hides. Her body was remade. Her mortal worshippers are gone, or long since converted to other faiths. She was a ghost surviving in a few monsters' dreams. The being who emerges, reborn, is not the lady who fell at the King in Red's hands, her blood smoking on his claws.

Blades of Craft pierced beneath the skin of reality, speared Seril Herself, and pried apart the seconds and ages of Her life. All Daphne's might, all the court's power, wedged present Seril from Her past.

Tara slipped beneath those blades, blunted them and redirected. Seril has changed, as I have changed, as you have changed, bitwise, slantwise, like the philosopher's ship. But Her faithful call Her by the same name, and so does Her lover, and so do Her children. And so, by rights, She is.

Tara's web closed around the blades, and hardened.

But still the machine in Daphne fought.

Seril now is Seril who was before, but Seril who was before is not Seril who is now. Seril is Seril and is not Seril. Tara is Tara and is not Tara. Daphne is Daphne and is not Daphne.

Webs of Craft reflected themselves, distorted.

Tara saw the discontinuity too late.

Craftwork logic, spun against itself, made a hole in the wielder's mind.

And a demon stepped through.

Reflections bubbled in Daphne's eyes, and the eyes themselves faceted, serrated, grew polygonal and inflated round again. Daphne became a cutout superimposed on the world. Much of her skin was gone, or shredded, but the thaumaturgical implements inside her now frayed, or turned on invisible axes to become writhing glass, devouring their complexity as the world tore.

Daphne's lips peeled back, and back, and back. The corners of her mouth split to show fangs. In those fangs Tara thought she saw

Daphne's face, or her own, or both their faces melded and forever screaming. A choir sang music no human throats could make.

Tara tried to catch the demon's edges, see its bindings. There were none. Ill-defined it passed through the portal of Daphne's broken logic—limitless and hungry.

Cat leapt for it, wings spread. The demon pierced her and she fell. Demonglass caught Tara, skinned the moonlight from her, grew inward. She blunted its assault, defining the claws by their pressure on her skin and so destroying them—but space twisted as the demon overflowed itself, reshaping Daphne's body to fit its expanded being, so fast it made itself faster.

The gargoyles fought, and Justice. Unreal blades cut down.

The demon grew so fast it seemed to be exploding: glass pierced Alt Coulumb pavement into bedrock, and more glass spread from the wound. A tendril darted left, impaled a nearby skyspire and began to suck. Crystal broke, and flight Craft failed, as the demon asserted new reality. It belonged here. Here belonged to it. Flyspeck Craftsmen fell screaming toward the city. Crystal shards rained down.

Bleeding, burned, caught in thorns, Tara imposed shapes and rules on the demon, but they slipped—it moved too fast for her to trap. Her shields broke. She made new ones. Her skin ripped.

Within her she felt Seril, and with her Kos, the silver light and the deep flame, and both were afraid.

The city began to die.

Time ran slow, because there was not much left.

Many thoughts dovetailed in Tara's head at once.

The demon that came through Daphne's mind was not protected by the Court of Craft. It crushed court wards and burst the guardian circle. Kos could engage it directly, now, and Seril, but unbound demons moved faster than faith. They might last mere seconds in real time, but in those seconds they could rewrite the world from underneath the gods. As the demon grew it would kill and convert, and as their faithful died or were swallowed by the glass, Kos and Seril would falter, weaken, change to demon-things themselves.

Glass closed her around, reflected her against herself, remade.

Tara remembered the Keeper in the mountain, her fear, her triumph in torment. She could do the same. Give this demon something to eat instead of Alt Coulumb and its gods, instead of Abelard and Cat and Aev and Raz and Bede. Something still mostly human. Something that could die.

Something like her.

She'd walked within the Keeper, seen her heart. She thought she knew the trick of it.

A cage of her hair. A lake of her blood. A mountain of her bone. A maze of her mind.

Invite the demon into the terror palace of her dreams, and, before it could break free—fall.

There were wards around a Craftswoman's dreams, glyph walls to prevent intrusion, subroutines to scrub parasites away. She turned them off. She opened her gates.

The demon swelled above her, a spider taller than buildings.

A chain around your neck, a skull's imagined voice whispered in her ear. *I was right.*

No.

"Come on," Tara said, and bared her teeth, and let the demon in.

Raz saw Cat fall. Her wings caught air, slowed her, but she crashed onto a neighboring rooftop. He smelled her blood through silver.

Above him a demon blossomed. He'd seen these before, or things like them. City smashers. Undefined, indefinable. Craftsmen had used them as weapons when the Wars turned bad.

Cat lay still.

Raz put the blood jade between his teeth, bit, and drank.

It tasted sharp.

All of a sudden even the demon in the sky seemed slow.

He put his hands into his pockets. This wasn't what he'd imagined at all, but it made a kind of sense.

He walked up into the air, humming softly to himself.

Tara offered—

Demonglass scythed toward Raz, slow as an opening flower.

He ran his hand along the blade's edge. It felt rough. When he drew his fingers away, he saw the edge had dimpled his skin.

He flicked the glass, which broke.

The demon had an outer skin, which he stepped through. Inside, he found its angles mostly wrong, so he righted them.

In the demon's center hung the remnants of a woman. He walked toward her.

—herself, and the demon—

Daphne saw the man approach, humming tunelessly.

The demon tore her, demanded her, but she was its door, and consuming her it would consume itself.

So she remained.

The man approached. The demon roared.

He cocked his head to one side, listening.

"I'm no good at this sort of thing," he said. "Want an explanation, you'd be better off asking Tara, or Lady K."

He was very close to her now.

"You're dangerous because you're undefined, because the world doesn't know what limits to place on you. Now, the thing to which I just joined myself—it's very old. Older than gods. Nothing lasts this long unless it's quite simple."

He sounded sad.

"You know the joke, that there are two kinds of people in the world, the ones who think there are two kinds of people and the ones who don't? This is the former. As far as it's concerned the whole world's made of things it's eaten, and things it hasn't yet." He bared his teeth. "As far as it's concerned, you're not undefined at all. It knows just what to do with you."

His fangs went in. Glass cracked around her.

We can choke him, the demon said, and Daphne realized it was talking to her. He can eat us, but he does not know if we can die. You're the only part of us that can. Endure, and we can clog him with ourselves, we can sate even this hunger. Stay strong. Work with me, and we'll have glory you cannot imagine. And the pain will stop.

Daphne's broken memories held a man in suspenders with a pleasant smile, who cupped her cheek and said the same words to her in a voice so sweet and steady she could not help but listen.

This time, she turned away.

—Died.

Tara waited for the crack in the world she knew was coming. It didn't.

She gasped. She hovered, empty, in air. Alive. Free.

Demonglass cooled and hardened. Weaker pieces shattered—boiled off to unreality and tumbled to the pavement as drops of wet confusion. A three-legged arch remained, towering above Alt Coulumb. It caught the moon, and shone rainbows on the earth.

Gargoyles and Blacksuits flew; the Judge let her diamond shield dissolve. Ramp was gone.

At its apex, the glass arch held a single flaw. Tara could not look on it directly—the light it shed hit her eyes wrong. She thought it was a woman's silhouette.

Jones felt the change in Market Square—they all did. The world was dying, but then it wasn't, and a glass arch bloomed to the north. Jones had never seen anything like it, which in her experience meant her next step should be run to a safe distance and take notes.

She stayed.

Then they heard the cheers—from the sky, from the surrounding buildings, and at last from their own throats, cheering before they knew why, tumbling over one another, rolling and laughing and pointing at the arch and the moon at once smiling and impossibly full. Onstage, the Rafferty girls embraced. Jones saluted Aev and her people, up there in the sky. Then someone tackled her from the side and kissed her, and to her surprise (she wasn't a casual girl, ask anyone) she kissed back.

Abelard collapsed, laughing and weeping, when he felt the demon break. Cardinals and Technicians rejoiced, overcome by awe.

Then Abelard noticed the moon through the sanctum window, and felt the Everburning Flame warm against his neck, and heard—thought he heard—the clearing of an enormous throat.

"My masters and teachers," he said. "Our Lord would appreciate a bit of, um. Privacy."

In five minutes the sanctum was empty for the first time in Abelard's memory. He was the last to leave.

That's two I owe you now, the fire said to him.

Don't mention it, he replied. *What are friends for?*

Cat was mostly conscious when the vampire crashed to the roof beside her.

She lay in the ruins of her own skin—the Suit ablated to break her fall. She had some broken ribs, one leg didn't work, and she'd stuffed her fist against the hole in her side to keep the blood contained.

The vampire, fallen, made a crater in the roof. She crawled toward him, dragging her useless leg. He was very still. Then he coughed, rolled onto his side, and vomited a glassy fluid that evaporated as it left his lips.

"Sexy."

He turned to her, his face a horror mask. She caught his wrist before he could pull out of reach, and held it.

"I'll—Cat, I am so hungry. It wants to eat and eat and eat. I have to go."

"Don't." She felt as weak as he looked.

"I can't hold on, dammit. Your blood's right there, I'll—" Teeth, out, pointed, dripping. The eyes were Raz's, and not. A new emptiness at their pits made their colors turn, like ruddy whirlpools. He seemed to be drawing inward toward a point not present in any physical geometry.

"I get it." She winced. "Eternal hunger. Call of the deep. Here." She reached for her medallion.

"Your Suit won't help."

"Shut up for one minute." Took a second to work the thing out one-handed. The holy symbol swung between them: the blind woman enrobed.

One last chance.

Okay, Lady, Cat prayed. *You win.*

The blind woman looked up at Cat and smiled.

Cat was stone, was sky, was an insect beneath an enormous ento-mologist's gaze. The Seril who addressed her in the shower, and on the city's rooftops, had been smaller, conceivable almost as a kind of invisible person, who saw the world as mortals did. Not so this Being. Yet She had not changed, only grown more Herself.

That made what she was about to do better, and worse.

I offer myself to you, she prayed. *Save him.*

The light waited.

You called me priestess, before.

But Cat had denied it.

I fought for you. I saved you. I learned from you. I was pierced for you. I almost died for you. I was scared of the word, that's all. Just keep him here, before he goes away forever. Please.

Nothing changed.

She would lose him.

Raz looked different. He was lit, she realized, by trebled moon-light: from above, and from her own eyes.

She set her hand on his forehead.

"I offer you asylum," she said, not knowing how the words or ges-ture came to her, "under the protection of Seril Undying. The Lady will answer any liens against your soul. I give you back yourself."

"You can't," he croaked. "They want me. They'll take me."

"They helped us, and you fed them in turn. The Lady will pay whatever more they feel they're owed."

"They won't—" He broke off, coughing. "They won't accept that. They want me. Father of a line. They'll come for me, on land or sea. And for you."

"And when that happens, we'll be ready. Together. You can live here—at least some of the time. Seril's protection's strongest in Alt Coulumb. If you're worried about the rent, I have a nice couch. And I could get better curtains."

"I hate this city."

"But not the people in it."

"No," he said.

He was silent for what felt like a long time, and so was she.

"You said you wouldn't stop me from doing something stupid to save you."

"I did." She nodded. "But I never said I wouldn't do something stupid to save you back."

"I accept."

His teeth receded. The whirl in his eyes stilled.

Far away, something ancient screamed.

He exhaled, and some of the animal left him, and some of a man she'd not yet come to know returned. "They'll be after you, too, now."

"Worth it," she said.

Lights bloomed in the sky. Silver and red nets and circles, twining—like fireworks but not.

"Now come on." She tried to sit up, and failed. "Drag me to the hospital. I'd like to beat the rush."

Tara flew over the city. Over her city. Free.

Stone wings beat, and Aev approached her. "Shale?"

She turned from the flaw in the demonglass arch. "He's trapped," she said. "Out west. He—threw himself into a monster's mouth to save us. I'll get him back. Bring him home." She heard the weakness in her voice and didn't hate herself for it.

That's new, she thought.

Aev touched her arm. Then, before Tara could push her away, the gargoyle hugged her. Her stone was cold and warm at once.

"Thanks," Tara said when they were done.

"We are wounded," Aev said. "We are tired. We will heal, and go back for him. For now, let us celebrate like free women."

"And Abelard. We should pick him up. He needs a break."

"Do you think he can keep up?"

Tara grinned. "I'd like to watch him try."

69

The gray tower stood at a cliff's edge over a cold ocean where waves frothed amid sharp rocks. The tower's windows were blind eyes against the sea, save at the summit, where one light shone.

Madeline Ramp turned from the ocean to her chamber. She required few homely comforts, which was why she carried all she needed with her: a cauldron, a well-stocked icebox, a good bed, several bookcases. In one corner, a cello swayed through an Old World sonata.

A package rested on her oaken clawfoot coffee table. The postman dropped it off "between 2:00 and 6:00 P.M. Seconday" to one of the addresses on which her front door opened. In fact the package had not arrived 'til well past seven, but under the circumstances she would not complain. She had not yet opened the box. Best to savor anticipation, the man himself had said. Like unwrapping a peasant.

She was quite sure that had been a slip of the tongue, but she'd not asked him for clarification.

She walked to the charcuterie spread she'd prepared, rolled a straw of prosciutto, popped it in her mouth, and chewed. She tasted meat and salt, smoke and fat. A bottle of pinot noir tipped wine into a glass, which floated to her hand as she turned back to the box. Bunny slippers scuffed across the gold thread of a Skeld rug.

She settled into her armchair, and with a flick of her fingers began to unwrap. Brown string untied itself and curled into a coil on the table. Tape split.

She ran her fingertips over rough cardboard and checked for signs of tampering, finding none.

She opened the lid, plunged her hand into packing immaterial, and found—

Nothing.

Wine sloshed over her fingers. She set the goblet down and groped in the impenetrable shadows. It was here. It had to be. Shrunk, maybe, or phase-shifted by post office mishandling, she'd flay the boy who brought it to her, or better yet find him in dreams and—

"Looking for this?"

Tara Abernathy sat in the armchair opposite, legs crossed. She held a silver-glyphed skull in one hand, like a jester's puppet or a philosopher's dummy.

"Ms. Abernathy," Ramp said. "I thought you would know better than to bother me in my home."

She did not need to move. The leather of the chair in which Abernathy sat split into thin straps, lashed up and around to snare and bind—

And passed through the woman as if she did not exist.

The straps reared back and swayed like confused cobras. Abernathy slapped one, and it slithered to quiescence within the upholstery.

Ramp glanced down at the open box. To either side of the lid she saw, taped, a business card: TARA ABERNATHY, CRAFTSWOMAN. No logo.

"Projection," she said. "A shame. I can't offer you a drink."

"You would have tied me up to offer me a drink?"

"I have a strict vision of hospitality."

Abernathy smiled at that, a bit.

"Do you know who that is you're holding?"

"Yes," she said, with a touch of distaste as if she'd smelled something foul.

"One of the greatest minds since Gerhardt. If not the greatest."

"I don't know about that," Tara said, assuming a mockery of the man's voice, that old country Craftsman's tones he'd faked so well. She tilted the skull down and sideways, so it seemed to be embarrassed. "I'm just a plain simple bastard."

"Impertinence. You do not understand what Alexander Denovo was, what he did."

"I understand better than you, I think."

"I worked with him for decades."

"And I was one of the people he worked on." She considered the skull. "You know, I prefer him this way. Looks less sinister, for starters." Tara uncrossed her legs, stood, and paced the small chamber, tossing the skull from hand to hand. "Justice found what was missing from the evidence locker. The package was harder to trace. We thought we were out of leads, until a friend asked for my help with a family matter. Her father showed up in the middle of our court date in the sky, ranting, warped. Someone had messed him up with Craft I recognized. Turns out he was roommates with a Talbeg priest who also escaped the hospital during the crisis. We found the priest—who's fine, by the way, thanks for asking—and we found the post office. The whole thing involved too many last-minute heroics for my taste. We had to waylay the delivery truck this afternoon. Sorry it was late."

Ramp said nothing.

Abernathy tossed the skull into the air, caught it, and hooked her fingers through the eye sockets. "During the package chase I got talking with Cat, and Raz, and a bunch of other people, and talking leads to thinking—about Maura Varg's mystery client, who hired her to pick up indentures in the Gleb and collect a load of dreamglass in Alt Coulumb, even though dreamglass is illegal there. We asked ourselves where Raz's tip came from, and I remembered the mysterious gray-eyed girl who set Gabby Jones on the Seril story in the first place. Daphne has—had—gray eyes. Jump in whenever you're ready."

"Why? So far I've heard only conjecture and spite."

"You covered your tracks well. Idols paying idols to rent the gray-eyed girl's apartment. A different set of shell Concerns and Kavekanese mystery cults to hire Varg. But the Talbeg priest who stole this skull had a demon inside him, like the demons in the others, and he sent the skull to you. So that chain leads us at least as far back as Varg."

"Your chain has flimsy links, Counselor."

"Did you attack Kos just to cover up your theft?"

"I brought suit," Ramp said, "because Seril is a weakness at a time we can afford none. Kos and the Iskari are bad enough: gods and their servants prating on as if the Wars never happened, binding simpletons to their service. They're brake pads on the troika of history. But at least the Craft binds them. With Seril's return Kos gains new freedom, which slows progress. These gods of yours are a dead end for life on this planet: a disgusting self-centered inversion, music played

on the deck of a sinking ship when we should be saving ourselves."
She shrugged. "More to the point, I brought suit because my clients
asked me to. You do remember clients? Or has your time among god-
botherers replaced fiduciary duty with faith?"

"Is that the game we're playing? Denials and pushback?"

"You accused me of acting for an ulterior motive. I tell you I had
none. But Alexander's skull is a treasure. Whoever thought to send it
to me has my thanks, whatever their methods."

"Why waste our time? There are no Judges here."

Ramp sipped wine. "Because I've worked against people like you
before," she said.

"Like me."

"Jumped-up junior Craftswomen with a swollen sense of their su-
periority to the morally compromised elder generation. You mistake
the ability to walk without a parent's aid for competence. In your world
everything has an explanation, an ultimate motive, and all you have
to do is dissect and diagram these for a Judge, as if the court were a
nanny who could ease your pain. I wouldn't put it past you to have
witnesses on the other end of this link, though it runs against common decency."

"Decency." Her fingers tightened on the skull. "As if you have a
right to talk. Daphne—"

"Ms. Mains," she said, "was a tragic loss, but don't dare talk to
me about her as if you understand. Did you seek her out? I did, after
Alexander's death. She lay in a bed, dreaming horrors. Her family
kept her in a tower room, surrounded by the stuffed toys of her childhood, tended by a live-in nurse. Unable to care for herself in the most
basic ways, at twenty-two. And she was still inside that wasted meat,
do you understand? Suffering. Broken. A mind in pieces. I fixed her.
I offered her a path out, and I made her take it. The pieces of her that
were gone, I rebuilt. I filled her hollows with demonglass. I summoned
and bound beings into her body. In the end she was almost herself
again."

"And you talk about the man who broke her as if he was some kind
of saint."

"He was a genius, which is something other than a saint. And in
his genius he left many projects, including Ms. Mains, and I daresay

you, unfinished. I have always been more of a theorist than a Technician, but we can't afford to abandon his work."

"His evil work."

"And there you show your true colors. You, student of the Hidden Schools, child of centuries of struggle, fall back on that old pathetic word fools and idiots chanted at the first Craftswomen they bound in the stocks, while they warmed the branding irons."

"We fought the God Wars for freedom, and you throw that struggle in my face to endorse the work of a madman developing better tools of slavery."

"We fought the God Wars for power, child. That's what freedom is. No one fights for any other reason."

"You're wrong."

"Which of us do you think has the surer truth?" She spread her arms. "The one who believes continents are shattered in the name of high-minded ideals, or the one who believes contents are shattered because two people who can shatter continents want different things?"

Abernathy clutched the skull in her hands as if to crush it.

Ramp took her silence as license to continue. "The world is breaking. The Wars made cracks, and we have broken it further. Our work turns soil to ash and water to poison. Even as we push ourselves to the brink of doom, beings of a size you cannot comprehend watch us with many eyes across vast gulfs of space. The universe is larger than this petty island of rock. As if we needed an external threat: this planet will not last forever, and when it dies we must be elsewhere. We have not done the work we need. Gods slow us with compromise. Small minds see only small context: local politics and squabbles of history. It takes genius to see large enough to build the tools to break the world, not like a man breaks a mirror, but like a chick breaks an eggshell. And great minds keep their secrets close."

"Here." Abernathy traced the skull's glyphs with one finger and cocked her head as if hearing voices far away. "That's why you wanted it. Access to his networks, his students, all those unfinished projects. Me."

"And again you invite me to support your demented conspiracy theory. Alexander's intellectual property assets were professional secrets, not registered with any patent authority, and many of his resources operated on a trusted pair model—the keys reside within his body. As such, his body represents incalculable value."

"I won't sell it to you."

Ramp swished wine and watched its legs roll down the inside of the glass. "Then why not help me strip the secrets from that skull, and save the world?"

"No."

She sighed. "This, in the end, was always Alexander's flaw." She removed a piece of folded parchment from the pocket of her dressing gown. "He leapt to command. Better to ask first, and hold the power to command in reserve until it's needed." She unfolded the parchment. "Do you recognize this paper? Specifically, the signature at the bottom?"

Abernathy did not need to squint. "That's a student loan contract. Mine."

"Thank you." Ramp set the parchment on the table beside the empty box. "I expected acquiring this to be more difficult, but the Hidden Schools were surprisingly cooperative. Education is not cheap; a shame, really, you haven't made more progress paying it back. Working for gods is, alas, less lucrative than private practice. You owe me ninety-eight souls." She set power into those words; the contract bound Ms. Abernathy, for all the distance that divided them. Ninety-eight souls of debt represented a great deal of leverage, and Madeline Ramp knew how to exploit leverage. "Bring me the skull, Tara."

Her will closed around Abernathy like a hand. The woman stiffened. Her fingers tightened on the skull, until Ramp feared she might damage the bone. Her lips curved into an empty smile—

And kept curving into an expression decidedly more self-satisfied. Her eyes snapped into focus, and Ramp's grip melted. "You might want to check that contract." Ramp looked down, and as she watched, a silver-ink stamp took shape. *Paid in full.* "Work with gods isn't lucrative from a salary standpoint, no. Especially not work with goddesses in incubation phase. That's why our forebears invented contingency fees and performance bonuses." She checked her watch. "I'm late for a meeting. We'll have to skip the parting-threats phase of the conversation, which is a shame—I've never done one of those before. Still have to figure out what to do with this skull, though. Paperweight? Raz mentioned this Old World game with a ball and a flat wooden bat. The kind you hit stuff with, I mean, not the kind with wings. Anyway. Bye."

Ramp stood in her tower, angry and alone.

The delegation climbed the Godmountain: Ms. Batan from the Two Serpents Group, a few CenConAg emissaries, bodies grown through with vines, a golem bearing the King in Red's vision-gem. At the rear of the trail, escorted by a Craftsman with a gold watch and skin darker than Tara's own, strode a thing that looked human, though made from shadow. Lines of darkness trailed fingers that walked a featureless silver disk down and up.

The two-page summary bios the delegations had sent around in advance did not include a first name for this person, or a pronoun of preference, or any other information for that matter.

Tara matched the shadow's pace as she decided what to say.

"M. Grimwald," she said. "I have a few questions, if you don't mind."

The shadow's head inclined. The disk flashed. Was it silver after all?

"I don't expect you have full knowledge of your, ah, firm's operations. But I believe you recently supplied a shipment of indentured laborers for delivery to Alt Coulumb. You sourced them by early foreclosure on the credit lines of a divine refuge in Agdel Lex. The indenture's purpose was to smuggle demons into Kos's city—but the persons smuggled were instrumental in disrupting the smuggler's plans. Which is a bit neat, if you ask me. Almost as if the person Ramp approached for help meant her to fail."

The shadow's footsteps sounded exactly as heavy as a normal person's. An odd patina marred the surface of the coin.

"I'm pretty far out in my speculation," she said. "Paranoid, even. But it never hurts to say thank you." They had almost reached the summit. "So, thank you."

Grimwald turned to her. Within the nothing of its face, its teeth were pure white and sharp. It offered her the coin, and she accepted. The coin was not silver at all, but cool, and rocky, and rough. The shadows on its surface were the same as the shadows on the moon.

She passed the coin from hand to hand, and offered it back.

The moon-coin vanished up a white sleeve, and still the shadow smiled.

The Godmountain's peak was flat, as if long prepared for this purpose. A stone table and chairs grew from living rock.

They sat and waited.

Shale emerged from the mountain like a bather from a pool.

The Keeper spoke through him.

Ninety percent of Craftwork was talking, so they talked. The conversation lasted three days and three nights. Tara realized as the first day stretched on that she and Ms. Batan were the only people present who needed to eat or sleep. She ordered takeout. Delivery was expensive, so she expensed it.

Sleep, she did without. That was why the Glebland gods made coffee.

On the third day, they built the body. The King in Red forged bones of steel with tools he produced from the pockets of his robe. The Grimwalds spun a nerve lattice from gold and necromantic earth. Tara made rock clay-pliant to shape the mountain's legs and belly, back and chest and arms and head, scribed all around with glyphs and grooves. She placed a small clock spring where the heart should go, then sealed the chest and stepped back.

Shale examined the body with clinical precision and some disdain. Then the Keeper kissed the form of stone, and poured out through his lips. Red crystal grew in the grooves Tara carved.

The Keeper staggered back, and looked up for the first time in several thousand years at the stars.

Shale collapsed. Tara ran to him, professionalism be damned.

His eyes were green again.

"I came back," she said.

He held out his hand, and she helped him rise.

ACKNOWLEDGMENTS

Writing this book felt like coming home—and homecomings take work. You have to hang crepe paper, bribe the band, roll out the carpets, sneak up on the fatted calf . . . Well, anyway. Profuse thanks to my editor, Marco Palmieri, and to Irene Gallo and Chris McGrath, for a cover I can make star eyes at (though I didn't mind the Spock-riding-a-unicorn mock-up, either). Gratitude and praise also to the usual band of readers, friends, and rock stars, including but in no respects limited to Alana Abbott, Vladimir Barash, John Chu, Amy Eastment, and Stephanie Neely. And, as I brooded on the manuscript, Amal El-Mohtar swung in through a window like Robin Hood to suggest a critical last-minute fix. Totally worth the broken glass on the carpet.

Every time I think I have charted the full bestness of Steph, I find whole other unmapped continents of best. If this goes on, um, well, I'd be totally fine with that.

David Hartwell published *Three Parts Dead,* and read every one of my novels after, and offered advice on each of them—and on each publication day, I sent him a nice bottle of whiskey. This year I have one fewer friend to send whiskey. I feel the loss.